To

THE

KING'S SHILLING

All Best

Hamilton

THE
KING'S SHILLING

Hamilton Wende

First published in 2005 by Jacana Media (Pty) Ltd.
5 St Peter Road
Bellevue 2198
Johannesburg
South Africa

© Hamilton Wende, 2005

All rights reserved.

ISBN 1-77009-053-3

Cover design by Triple M
Set in Palatino 9/10.5
Printed by CTP Book Printers

See a complete list of Jacana titles at www.jacana.co.za

For most us the First World War is the Western Front – the mud and slaughter of the Flanders trenches. Hamilton Wende's engrossing tale brings the war to the largely forgotten conflicts of East Africa.

His beautifully understated prose peels back layer after layer of an Africa simmering with the tensions of racial hierarchy. This Africa is vivid, painful and powerfully evoked.

But this is also a book about what happens in the hearts of those who go to war; about what happens to the ideals that drive them to war in the first place; and about how war corrodes and corrupts the humanity they try to cling to. There are also echoes of a more powerful theme: the bleak loneliness of a world of men without women.

Wende's prose is stark, precise, pared back, robust. But at times the writing is heart-breakingly tender. This is a story of what happens to human beings in extremity – to their relationships with those they love, to their dreams, to their very sense of who they are.

Allan Little, BBC correspondent in Africa 1995 – 2001

This is historical fiction at its finest: the past recaptured intact through imagination. Meticulously researched, written with passion and compassion and an insider's eye for detail by a writer who's been under fire and survived. If you've ever wondered what it was like to face Von Lettow-Vorbeck's askaris on the hot savannahs of Africa – this book will make you live the fear and the exultation, the degradation and resignation that characterised not just this extraordinary war in Africa – but all wars always.

David Lambkin, author of The Hanging Tree

For my parents, with deepest love

Acknowledgements

This book owes its existence to so many acts of kindness. Firstly, I would like to thank all the people at the various museums and libraries who helped me with my research. In writing this book I consulted well over 200 books, original hand-written diaries, letters, memoirs, copies of military orders, photographs, newspaper and magazine articles and military manuals. I am extremely grateful to the librarians and researchers at the Johannesburg Public Library, the National Military History Museum in Saxonwold, the South African National Defence Force Archives in Pretoria, the National Archives in Nairobi and the Imperial War Museum in London.

Guy, Marius and Hamish at Bookdealers in Rosebank and Geoffrey and Jonathan at Collector's Treasury on Commissioner Street were also an invaluable help to me in searching for out-of-print books and calling me whenever a rare volume surfaced. Michael Prior of Collectable Books took the risk of lending me some very expensive books that I could not afford to buy.

Maggie Davey, Chris Cocks and Kerrin Wilkinson at Jacana have, from the very beginning, inspired me with their enthusiasm and commitment to the book.

I cannot say thank you enough to Tim and Mary Carson for their friendship and for their repeated hospitality during my many trips to Nairobi. Tim drove me to Salaita Hill in his Land Rover where we discovered the remains of the original trenches and the ancient baobab trees that had been hollowed out by Von Lettow-Vorbeck's askaris.

David Smith, Belinda Hawkins, James MacFarlane and my long-suffering family read the manuscript and made many worthwhile suggestions. Alison Lowry gave me much-needed advice. I will always be indebted to Masako Osada for her many patient readings of the early drafts and for her unwavering support over the years we have known each other.

Finally, I would like to dedicate this book to the memory of Major-General Rafiuddin Ahmed who died in 2002. We never met one another, but he responded with immense generosity to my rather vague query letter sent to his regimental headquarters in Pakistan.

'All soldiers run away; the good ones return.'
The Duke of Wellington

1

MEMORY BEGINS WITH THE strangest of stimuli. It is not images that first come to mind, but sound, emerging out of silence – a squeal of iron; a hiss of steam. Human voices and the neighing of horses drowned out by the clanking of wheels and carriages. A mournful whistle penetrating the night in front of the train. We begin to move again, gathering speed and finally dropping into the slow, grinding rhythm of our progress towards the front.

It was later that night, amidst the clatter of steel and the erratic thrum of the engine, that I would dimly hear the first enigmatic whispers of the men around me. Whispers that I knew held clues to my fate and to the fate of the men I commanded. But I did not understand their true meaning until it was too late, until the choices that would come to define my war – our war – had been made. The true story of a war is always something more than the way it ends. Our deepest secrets lie hidden in the heart of our defeats, and even a victorious army comes home to live with the memories of battles lost and men betrayed.

The night sky over the dark savanna was a sea of stars, against which the trees and kopjes on the veld showed up as black, looming shapes. Orange sparks sprayed from the smokestack of the engine and fanned out in the gloom over the African and Indian soldiers clutching onto the roof of the train. The hot, filthy soot flew in through the window; I could feel it gathering on my face and in the gap between my neck and the collar of my uniform.

The train moved slowly down the line. At times it would stop for no apparent reason and sit for long minutes, even hours, while we dozed uncomfortably. Sometimes there were voices in the night, speaking in Kikuyu, Luo, Kavirondo, Swahili. Always there was a white voice speaking in sharp, short bursts and then the black voices speaking amongst themselves in longer, coherent phrases.

In the darkness we passed a group of Masai gathered around a fire. The men stood up as the train rumbled past them. Their hair was smeared with ochre and they wore leather cloaks thrown over their shoulders. They carried long-bladed spears that glinted in the firelight. Their cattle moved restlessly in the thorn boma behind them. The women stayed by the fire, but the men stared at us, turning with the motion of the train and holding our gaze through the windows as we passed them.

Sometime during the night the motion of the train changed again. I woke from my half-waking, half-sleeping discomfort to find that we were slowing down just before a narrow bridge. The brakes creaked and squealed as the train slowed, jolting the carriages.

The bridge was a low, squat, stone structure spanning an empty riverbed with thorn trees hanging over the banks. The dry white sand of the river course gleamed in the starlight and a clump of palms on an island of dry rock stood out as a sharp silhouette against the sky. A pair of nightjars lying with their wings spread out in the cool sand fluttered up into the darkness as the train clanked to a halt. At each end of the bridge there was a blockhouse made of entrenchments, sandbags and barbed-wire entanglements fixed to stakes in the ground and the bush had been cut back from the banks for about a hundred yards around.

It was late, well after midnight. The Indian soldiers assigned to guard the bridge had been driven out of their cramped makeshift forts by the surprising cold of the East African night and now sat hunched around the fires outside. One or two of them waved lazily; the others stayed crouched near the heat, looking away from the flames so they would not be blinded by the darkness for long, precious seconds if attacked. The Germans had been launching surprise raids against the railway line almost every night. In the flickering orange light the faces of the soldiers under their khaki turbans were tired and strained.

The men began to tumble off the roof of the train and out of the carriages. Other officers were still stretched out across the hard wooden and horsehair seats. I got up and eased my way out of the compartment to stretch my legs and to see how the men were doing.

Still half-asleep, I climbed down from the carriage onto the stonework of the bridge and stood beside the train. I saw Captain Carter, my immediate superior – an officer who had come out from England – a little way in front of me. He stood aloof, a solitary figure in the glow of the watch-fires. With his hands in the pockets of his tunic, he surveyed the mass of men, black and white, moving alongside the train.

I thought of going over to speak to him, but held back. Something about the thoughtful tilt of his head told me that he wanted to be on his own. I watched him as he stood there, staring into the night. He slipped his hand inside his battledress tunic and drew out a small, thin parcel from an inside pocket. He unwrapped the folds of oilcloth in a few easy movements that reminded me of the practised, almost instinctive movements that a writer makes with his pen or that a smoker uses to roll and light a cigarette. Moving a few steps nearer the light of one of the fires, he took out a photograph and a letter, looked at the picture for a few moments and then read over the letter. I wondered who it was from; news from home, perhaps, or the last words from the woman he loved. I thought of the photograph I carried in my own breast-pocket, the one Helen had given me on our last night together. I missed her so much. I had been in the army only a few months, but already her absence from my world was an emptiness I could not quite grasp, a grey blurring at the edges of my inner life. Finding Helen had made me feel complete. Now, without her, I felt my moments of doubt and fear more sharply than ever before.

I told myself, as I had done so many times, that I had volunteered to fight. This war was the biggest thing my generation would face, and I wanted to be a part of it. So many of us had felt the same way, and now here we were – tens of thousands of men who had left the world of women behind. We were not even at the front yet, but without Helen, I found myself visited at times by a bleakness I had not expected. I could sense the same unspoken loneliness in so many others around me.

Watching Carter in that dim, flickering light, I felt an almost irresistible urge to take out the picture of Helen, but I hesitated, unwilling to weaken my memories by seeing her so faint and indistinct in the darkness. Instead, I walked away and left Carter with his photograph and his memories.

Further along the line, I found my platoon inside one of the cattle trucks. I could just make out Corporal Reynolds slumped in sleep in the corner against the wooden slatted sides, his greying hair rumpled and his mouth open almost like that of a sleeping child. On the bare iron floor nearby, Sergeant Visser and the other soldiers were curled up asleep. No doubt Visser had arranged for them to share one of the bottles of cheap brandy I had noticed for sale in the streets of Mombasa.

Satisfied that they were all right, I walked back, picking my way among the dark shapes of the weary soldiers. Already the rigours of the front line were beginning to intrude into our lives. The men's eyes were wide and red-lined. They smelled of wood smoke, sweat and soot. A few of them greeted me as I made my way through their ranks, but most were silent, staring into the darkness.

I was nearing our compartment when, in the lee of one of the carriages, I heard the voice of Major Macintyre, the company commander. I could just make out his shape and that of another man standing a dozen or so yards away from me. They were talking in lowered voices. They were talking about me.

'Someone ought to tell Fuller.'

'What do you mean?' The other man was Major Reading, an officer on the colonel's staff directly responsible for our regiment. I stopped and shrank back between the carriages where they couldn't see me.

'I like Fuller well enough. I wouldn't want to see him end up like that sergeant in Afghanistan.'

'You must be fair,' Reading said. 'It happened a long time ago. People change.'

'What Carter did was unforgivable. It ruined his career. He'll never rise higher than captain now.'

'It wasn't his *career* that he was worried about,' Major Reading observed, a hint of anger that I had never heard before in his voice.

Macintyre looked down at the ground. He kicked a pebble with the toe of his boot. 'I still don't know if I can trust him.'

'Drop it, Bill,' Reading said. 'We all left the regiment, and India, a long time ago. Everything's different now. Carter's proved himself in battle on the Afghan frontier over and over again. You've always hated him, even in the early days in India, but you're lucky to have him in your company here in Africa. He's the best front-line officer we've got. You know it, but you just can't admit it.'

Macintyre shook his head. 'Carter betrayed his men once; there's no telling if it'll happen again.'

2

FLAT-TOPPED CLOUDS HUNG in the air against the distant blue hills; beyond them lay the German frontier and the war. The vast plains stretched out, dotted with thorn trees and the occasional pile of boulders. Huge herds of zebra, wildebeest, eland and a dozen or more species of game wandered across the savanna, stopping continually to graze. Birds of prey circled endlessly, the highest ones appearing as tiny black dots against the enormous pillars of white cumulus that rose above the heat haze.

Still our troop train crawled west across the plateau, heading for Voi and the front lines beyond. The train's wood-burning engine spluttered and churned out smoke and sparks into the blue sky. White troops rode inside, crammed, red-faced and spluttering, into the cattle trucks stinking of rotting dung and stale piss. Black and Indian troops were forced to find a space on the hard steel roofs. They crouched on any available flat surface on the outside of the trucks, exposed to the blazing sun.

We had all expected the conflict to last only a few weeks, or months at most. I thought of volunteering several times, but my work as an engineer was regarded as valuable. Somehow, though, the fighting dragged on into its second year and we began to realise that it was going to last far longer than any of us had believed possible. Only then did I sign up, in the last weeks of 1915. Lord Kitchener had already started talking of conscription in Britain. For the time being, though, he still had to rely on men like me, from all across the Empire, who felt that they could no longer leave the fighting to others.

By the time I joined the army many of my friends had already been killed on the Western Front. The war, and the loss of so many childhood friends, had taught me yet again to see that the world would seldom be the way I had hoped. I had set out to become successful and rich; I was not. I had watched what I had thought was the love of my life disintegrate into snarling, unforgiving hatred. I had seen my father fight his way back from a life almost swallowed up by drink, only to die from the bacteria that had spawned in a finger cut while he was doing nothing more dangerous than pruning roses. At thirty-one, and two years into a world war, I was old enough to have transformed my youthful illusions into an acceptance of life that was something more than disappointment.

This war had come into my life as something of a surprise. I had scarcely any interest in politics, so the assassination of an archduke I had never heard of, in an obscure European city I could hardly find on a map, meant little to me until I woke up one morning to find that war had been declared.

I had no hatred for Germans; quite the opposite, in fact. I had studied German at school. In South Africa, as far as we were ever exposed to European ways, I certainly grew up feeling closer to German culture than I did to Belgian, French or Italian. I had an uncle who was part Bavarian and had been born in the German colony of South West Africa. It was only the Kalahari Desert that lay between them and us. But the Kaiser had made his choice and was leading his people down a path that threatened our way of life. Over the months that followed the outbreak of war, and with the news of the death of yet another friend, I came to see that there was no longer any choice for me but to go to war, as so many men had done before me. We had to stop the Germans; nothing for it now but to fight, and to win.

I remember saying exactly those words 'to fight, and to win' to Mr Bradley, the General Manager at the Reef Mining Company where I worked as a manager of the drawing office. That was the day I told him I had decided to join up.

He sat behind his large wooden desk, listening to me carefully. Then he got up clumsily and came around to the front.

'So, Fuller, you've decided to abandon the ample pay of a mining house and to take the King's shilling instead?'

'Yes.' I was unwilling to explain myself any further.

For a few moments, Mr. Bradley stood there. I looked back into his face with the broken veins in the whites of his eyes, the flecks of grey in his moustache that was stained yellow by his cigarettes. I could smell the stale reek of tobacco on his wheezy breath.

'Congratulations,' he said. 'That's the spirit we need.' He put out his hand to shake mine. 'It's a big thing you're going to do, Michael.' He hesitated for a moment, and I saw that his eyes had turned moist. He turned his head and glanced away. 'I just wish I were young enough to join you,' he said. 'We'll miss you, of course, but I do promise you one thing – I'll hold your place open for you until you come home.'

He laughed suddenly with a false heartiness. 'Remember, Michael, once you've taken their shilling, they own your soul.'

I smiled, trying, as I always did, to laugh at his clumsy joke, but the truth was, I was looking forward to the adventure of war and the escape it offered from the drudgery of his drawing office.

After we had been passed fit for service, they gave us a week in which to sort out our lives before our training began. There was not much for me to do. I gathered my papers together. I wrote a long letter to my older sister Camilla and her husband on their farm in the Cape. I wrote a will in which I left what little money I had to their two children.

I visited my mother. We had tea together around the ornate iron table under the rustling bluegum trees at the bottom of her garden, just as we used to do when we children were growing up. There was a mulberry tree amidst the bluegums and a thick old log that had been lying on the ground for as long as I could remember. Camilla and I had once tried to make a dugout canoe from it. I would never forget that afternoon, or how, with our fingers and the corners of our mouths stained black with mulberry juice, we brushed off the spiders and began pulling at the crumbling bark to begin our task. We had grand plans that afternoon, we two – once we had hollowed out the log, we were going to erect a mast and a sail.

Every afternoon for a week we worked at it with a rusty steel pipe and an axe we had taken from my father's workshop. We hollowed out an inch or two of wood before we gave up.

I wanted to keep going. Our own boat – the thought of it entranced me – but Camilla was adamant. 'There's no point,' she said. 'There's no water anywhere near here to it sail on.' I was too little to go on without her. We left the steel pipe on the ground next to the log, put the axe back where it belonged and never spoke of our boat again.

The log was still there, moss growing in the rough, shallow groove we had hacked out of it. The steel pipe had long since rusted away. My mother poured the tea and I handed her a sealed copy of my will, such as it was. I had been afraid of this moment. After my father's death, she had made a slow retreat from reality. She tried to ignore anything that was unpleasant, but she couldn't do it. She was too sensitive and intelligent for that. Instead, she spent her days in a state of undeclared anxiety, fluctuating between the safety of her hopes and the illusion that if she could not control something, she could ignore it.

I hated to see her this way. When my father died, I had grieved terribly, but I had seen my mother's face as she mastered her own grief and handed out a plate of sandwiches at the wake. I had marvelled at her strength that day.

'Look,' I whispered to Camilla.

'Yes,' she nodded, her eyes filled with tears, and her own child, already too heavy for her, perching awkwardly on her hip, 'I know.'

My mother gave us hope then; she made us feel that somehow there was meaning in our father's death. Watching her that day of the funeral, I trusted with the last traces of the certainty of my childhood that the pattern of our lives would grow over the empty spaces, shutting out the darkness beyond. It didn't last. My mother seemed to have used up her strength in getting through the desolate weeks immediately following his death. She didn't collapse; her breakdown came slowly. She was letting go of life little by little, as if she were forgetting a language. First, it seemed, individual words escaped her, then whole phrases, until one day, I knew, there would be nothing left but the silence of her inconsolable grief.

I did not know how to help her remember again. My sister had her own life on the farm with her husband and her own children. I was the only one left for my mother.

There were so many reasons not to go to war, but leaving my mother alone and bewildered was one of the most powerful. In the end, I made the only choice the world expected of me as a man – I chose to desert my mother instead of my country, knowing all the while inside that she would never have found any cause strong enough to abandon me for.

She cried a little when I handed her the brown envelope marked 'Michael Fuller, Last Will and Testament', but then she recovered and tried to smile. I noticed that instead of taking it to file away with the rest of the family papers, she put it in the bottom of her sewing box. I had learned enough in the past few years to assume it would stay there. If it was my fate to be killed in the war, I doubted whether she would remember where she had put it. As I watched her open the wicker lid I knew I should have given it to Helen, or to my oldest and most trustworthy ally, Camilla.

It was too late for that now. I would write to her that it was in the bottom of my mother's sewing basket. She needed to know, even if only for her children's sake.

The doves' *krrrr-krrrr* echoed through the cool emptiness of the trees above. My mother poured more tea out of the cracked Spode teapot – a wedding gift to her and my father nearly forty years before.

She broached the subject of the war somewhere in the middle of our second cup of tea. 'Queen Alexandra has always been my favourite,' she said, 'what with her hospitals and her Rose Day and everything' she added. 'But George is a good king, all things considered. So I'm sure everything will work out for the best.'

I smiled and leaned over to kiss her, awkward in my crisp new uniform.

The train was held up in the blazing sun for most of a day. There were reports of fighting further down the line. The distant patterns of war were beginning to tug at our lives like unseen tides, the power of their dangerous undertow invisible to our inexperienced eyes. Few of us besides Visser and Carter could imagine what lay ahead.

It was nearly dusk before it was judged safe to proceed and, as the train began to move again, I stood at the window watching the daylight fade. The tropical night on the savanna fell surprisingly fast – I was used to the longer twilight in the south. Here the sky turned a blaze of crimson and ochre. The last of the light bled into the darkness behind the hills on the horizon. A flurry of insects whirled in the air, their wings translucent against the fading bronze of the sky.

The evening turned cool. The first stars came up, huge and bright. They grew into constellations, the Southern Cross, Pleiades, low and wavering above the horizon. There was Orion, so vast and spread across the sky – the only constellation Helen could put a name to.

Helen. We had discovered one another by chance. The war was already more than a year old and I was still recovering from the loss of a love that had left me emotionally broken, unable to imagine that love could happen to me again. Katherine – I had to say her name to remember what it had been like and how it had gone wrong.

I first saw Helen at a summer garden party held by mutual friends on the valley road in Parktown. She was standing under a purple jacaranda tree in front of an ornamental corner filled with lavender, roses and a stone urn with silent, lichen-maned lions.

I couldn't stop staring at her across the green, trimmed lawn. Even at a distance, I was captivated by the firm slimness of her waist, by the delicious swell of her breasts filling a white cotton blouse. I could not help myself watching her fine, elegant face sheltering from the sun under a wide-brimmed hat. I could see she was about my own age, twenty-nine or thirty. The woman I was speaking to, the stately Mrs Marshall, followed my darted gaze across the lawn. I found myself suddenly babbling, embarrassed at having been discovered so easily.

I couldn't help it. Desire has a will of its own; flowing like water after rain, swelling and thrusting its irresistible course into the hidden depths of our lives. We never cross the same river again, each moment is shimmering and fresh and then gone forever, a new one sliding past almost before we can see it.

Mrs Marshall was wiser than I gave her credit for. She had seen my eyes, and she knew Helen. At the very least, she must have guessed at the hidden truths of Helen's own life.

Later that afternoon she found a way to introduce us. I slid, tumbled, from desire to love from the moment I saw Helen's smile. I saw so many possibilities unexpectedly coming to life in her eyes. I marvelled at the glistening, moist curves of her lips, at the smooth, unblemished skin of her throat as she lifted her chin, caught at the edge by a high lace collar with a garnet brooch in the centre. My fingers tingled at the soft touch of hers when we shook hands. The gold of her wedding ring was a cool shock.

She laughed at something I said. I knew she was watching me from deep inside the shaded refuge her hat gave her.

The glints of her pupils were curious, waiting to catch my own eyes. She held them for a fleeting moment as she weighed me up.

Her eyes gleamed when I made her laugh again, applauding me for the effort. She told me about the work she did at the library, 'helping out, now that they are short-handed with so many men at the war'.

We talked all afternoon together, ignoring the other people at the party. We forgot about them, or at least I did, not bothering with what I knew they must be thinking, just wanting to talk and talk and hold onto the afternoon I had with this woman. Sometime as the sun moved across the lawn it happened. That sudden, unexpected plunging into the wells of memory and hope, the dark currents tugging and tingling all over your skin – the unspoken moment when we each, alone, had to decide whether to turn back or not.

The heat of the afternoon began to cool. The lacy shade of the jacarandas stretched out further and further across the garden. She took off her hat and picked up one of the purple, fluted blossoms off the ground. She held it up in her fingers and looked at it.

'Why haven't you gone to the war?' she asked.

'I went to the recruiting office in August last year when it all started. They told me I was too valuable as an engineer, for the war economy. The fighting would be all over by Christmas, anyway, they said.'

She looked away, across the lawn, the blossom half-forgotten in her fingers.

'It's just getting worse.'

'Yes.' I felt the hot flush of blood rising in my face. 'I mean to go and see again whether they want me.'

She looked back at me from under her hat. 'I'm sorry.'

'No, you don't need to –'

'Really, I am. I have no right. I didn't mean it that way.'

'No.'

'It's just that – well, so many men have already gone. There's hardly anyone left now.'

We both said nothing. It was the same silence that fell in those days between people all over our world. It was the emptiness of loss, of finding nothing to say in the face of so much young death. The memories, the layers of faces, voices, the shared laughter, crowded in on us all.

'My husband's gone.'

I could feel the blood falling away from my head, the lawn spinning. The sudden, delicious coolness of pure joy sweeping through me.

'N-no,' she said, her face draining. 'I mean – he's gone to the war. He's still alive.'

'I'm sorry. I didn't –'

'It doesn't –' I could see sharp points of red growing in her cheeks. 'He's an officer on the staff of a general in France. He's behind the lines, safe.'

'You must be relieved.'

She crossed her arms, caressing her upper arm absent-mindedly with her hand. She looked away and then back at me. Her hair was swept up in neat layers. It was filled with a faint perfume. A few strands fell loose over the others. Her eyes were the colour of shadows in a still, brown river.

'His letters, when I get them, are filled with good news and stories of how the war is going.'

I was conscious of the servants moving among the tables, clearing the glasses and plates. It was getting late. I had come with Camilla. She was up at the main house, chatting to the hostess and the last stragglers. I knew she would want to leave by now. This was my only chance. I tried to make it sound light, but my voice was hoarse despite my best efforts.

'Would you like to go to tea sometime?'

Helen took her hand away from her arm. The jacaranda blossom was still in her fingers. She dropped it and watched it fall on the grass. She reached for her hat, and we stood up together.

'It's getting late. I must go.'

It was dangerous country we were passing through. In the morning light we saw the burned-out wreckage of at least three carriages that had hit mines laid on the tracks by the Germans only a few days ago. The heavy iron frames were twisted and blackened. White ash from the charred remains of the wooden sides streaked the red soil.

The enemy we had come to fight, the enemy who lay somewhere out there in the bush, had infiltrated deep into British East Africa from their colony of *Deutsch-Ostafrika*. The German colonial army in Africa was a formidable force, made up almost entirely of black African troops with white officers and NCOs. The black German soldiers, known as askaris, were career soldiers whom the Germans had used in their colonial wars against the local tribes. When war between Germany and Britain had begun to seem imminent, the military commander of the colony, General Von Lettow-Vorbeck, had increased his efforts to train his askaris and ready them to invade British East Africa.

Their weapons were antiquated, single-shot, black-powder rifles left over from the Franco-Prussian war, but Von Lettow had trained them well. Unlike in our army, it was not unknown in Von Lettow's colonial force, the *schutztruppe*, for black corporals and sergeants to be in command of white privates. It was this kind of thing that made the askaris a disciplined army with immense respect and personal loyalty towards Von Lettow himself. I was a newcomer to war, but I knew that these men had already proved themselves a tough enemy to beat. They had devastated a large British and Indian invasion force at Tanga, and had kept our better-armed and better-equipped troops on the run for nearly eighteen months now.

Here, because of the frequent askari attacks, the line was guarded even more heavily by pickets of our own British African troops, the KAR – the King's African Rifles – and by Indian troops. They hunkered down in blockhouses made of mud and hardwood logs cut from the surrounding bush. The train clanked slowly past each of their outposts. Each clattering turn of the wheels was taking us nearer and nearer to the front.

What I had heard the night before had a strange, unsettling effect on me. It was hard enough knowing that I was about to lead men into battle for the first time in my life. It was made much worse knowing that so much mistrust was swirling around the officers above me – the men I would take my orders from and pass on to those below me.

I wandered through the narrow, darkened carriages. I passed Major Macintyre and Major Reading in their compartment. Reading was poring over a sheaf of typed intelligence reports. Now in his mid-forties, he had been seconded to our regiment from a dead-end post in Singapore, and was one of the few officers in our regiment besides Carter who had seen active service. Reading had been shot at countless times. He had seen more than twenty of his men killed or wounded in tiny, anonymous skirmishes in the valleys and on the rocky hillsides of the North-West Frontier district despite a formal declaration of peace some twenty years before. He had been stabbed in the neck with a dagger and he carried in his chest a fragment of a stone, fired from a primitive muzzleloader, that glowered darkly just under a pale, barely healed covering of skin.

In the way of many soldiers, Reading had ended up with a deep respect for his enemies and had learned to speak their language. He enjoyed telling us junior officers of how he had sat cross-legged on kelims and shared dark green tea and listened to the elders of the hill tribes recite their poetry of hawks and snow leopards, of ancient battles and lost loves, the telling of the old stories sometimes punctuated by distant gunfire beyond the walls of their gardens, high among the peaks of the Hindu Kush.

'They never lost the power to terrify me, though,' he would say and then give a high-pitched, wheezing laugh.

Sometimes when I looked at Reading, with his thinning blonde hair and blotchy white skin, I felt sorry for him. He was a man just about to pass his physical prime, who had given his life to the British army and had reached the unhappy ceiling of his career. From everything that I had seen, he cared about his men, but the very kindness he showed to them had, at times, held him back in his career. He had been passed over one too many times now, and he was unlikely ever to go much higher in the army.

In someone else, drink might have been a refuge, but Reading's passion was soldiering and the discipline that went with it. Instead of trying to dissolve his pain, he had found a way to turn it into compassion for others – his men. Even though I had only witnessed it on the parade ground and in the training camp, and had not yet seen it tested in battle, I could not help admiring his lonely courage.

In the little time that I had known him I found I liked to spend time with him, sipping a single whisky on the rocks in his tent in the training camp and listening to his stories about India and the Afghan frontier.

I knew that the war and what he did in it might change everything for him. Men with the experience of real fighting were in short supply in this hastily assembled army of ours on its way to East Africa. The war, for him, might prove to be that rarest of gifts in life, a second chance. The right word here, a tactful denial there, his input into the hard decisions taken on the eve of battle – all of these things might add up to a promotion and a reinvigorated career.

I found myself staring at Macintyre. I knew that he was only a year or two younger than Captain Carter. I wondered what it was that lay between them, what the meaning was of the whispered exchange I had heard the night before. When had it begun, this old feud they had brought with them over the years and across the ocean from the borders of Afghanistan to their early middle-age and now to their war in Africa?

Macintyre had a copy of the latest *Illustrated London News* open on his lap. The rest of us were filthy and dishevelled, but he had somehow managed to keep up appearances. His dark hair was combed and gleamed with just the faintest sleek hint of hair oil. His moustache was neatly trimmed.

The article he was so engrossed in was entitled 'Scenes From the Front'. The headline was in bold print. I had heard Macintyre declare how much he wanted to be on the European front. 'This African business is going to be a walkover,' he would say 'and then we can go on to where the real war is.'

In the middle of the page was a photograph of a German trench and two captured snipers. They were wearing full body armour – clumsy, thick rounded plates that covered their bodies like the armour of mediaeval knights. They wore cylindrical iron helmets over their heads with tiny slits cut for their eyes. On the opposite pages there were photographs of Serbian refugees sleeping in the mud under a donkey cart on the outskirts of Sarajevo, the women wearing long, ragged dresses and the men huddled together under a battered overcoat. The largest picture was of the nose and tail of a broken-backed Zeppelin sinking into the waters of the North Sea.

Macintyre looked up, his eyes quizzical and then angry as he caught me watching him. He nodded and then went back to his reading. I walked on through the lurching corridors of the train. It was the men I was looking for anyway.

Before I got to the cattle trucks where they were travelling, I found Sergeant Visser leaning out the window smoking a cigarette. I barely knew him, but in commanding my platoon in battle, he was the man I would be relying on most in the weeks and months ahead. Like me he was a volunteer, a veteran soldier who had fought with Smuts in the Boer War, but he was also a family man, with a wife who was the centre of his existence and three children whom he talked about rarely but always with affection.

We were only a few hours away from the base camp and the front line. I knew that Visser must be missing his family, but outwardly he was the professional soldier, absorbed in what was to come and in the politics of the army's hierarchy.

'Everyone all right?' I asked.

'Yes. No problems.' He looked back at me, his eyes squinting in the morning sun. The broken wooden shutters had been half-pulled up. The rays slanted through into the lurching corridor.

Visser's cigarette was pinched between his thumb and forefinger. His hands were large and powerful, the nails stained yellow with nicotine. He inhaled and then blew the smoke out of his nose.

'It's Kirkpatrick,' he said finally. 'The boy doesn't say anything, but he's scared – too scared.'

At seventeen the youngest man in the regiment, Stephen Kirkpatrick had been a source of worry to me ever since he had been assigned to my platoon. He was a pleasant young man with blonde hair and soft, intelligent brown eyes that showed his emotions clearly. But he was a sensitive boy, young for his age, who was not suited to the army and, like Sergeant Visser, I feared he was not at all suited to be going to war.

The real problem was Kirkpatrick's father. He wanted his only son to follow in his footsteps and had pushed for him to join the army as soon as he had finished school. The father, a retired British general, was a minor Victorian hero, well known throughout the Empire for his bravery during the magnificent but pointless charge of the 21st Lancers at Omdurman in the Sudan. As the squadrons of Lancers, among whom was a young lieutenant named Winston Churchill, crashed at full gallop into the mass of Dervishes, Captain Kirkpatrick had been thrown from his horse.

Winded and badly bruised, he found himself lying on the sandy bottom of a riverbed surrounded by angry, battle-hardened Arabs dressed in indigo *jibbahs* and chain-mail doublets. They leaped at him with their swords and spears. All around him terrified English lancers and their wounded horses were screaming, bleeding and stumbling under the hacking blades, but Kirkpatrick had refused to give in. He pushed back his attackers and fought his way with sabre, boot and a crushed hand through the mass of Dervishes up onto the loose stones and dust on the bank.

Behind him a young lancer, skewered through the back of the knee by a barbed spear, was trying to claw his way up the steep slope. A warrior was about to plunge his sword into his back and two others were close behind. Kirkpatrick turned to save him. He had to kill two of the Dervishes in order to do so, and was severely wounded before he managed to get him away. Covered in the blood that was spurting from his face and arm, he dragged the wounded soldier across the plain to where a group of lancers spotted them and galloped to their aid.

The young soldier died of his wounds before they could get him to the field hospital, but Captain Kirkpatrick was decorated for his valour all the same. The story of his daring was featured on the front pages of newspapers across the Empire, from *The Times* in London to *The South China Morning Post* in Hong Kong.

He went on to serve in the Boer War as a trusted aide to Lord Roberts, during which time he fell in love with South Africa. After the war he took early retirement, returned with his wife and young son, Stephen, and bought a farm in the Cape. He was still influential in political circles. General Kirkpatrick, as he was now, was a good friend of Jan Smuts and often dined, together with his much younger wife, at the residence of Prime Minister Louis Botha in Cape Town.

The hero status of his father loomed large over Stephen Kirkpatrick, especially now that he was in the army. His father expected great things of him and so, it seemed, did the public. I had often heard the admiring murmurs that Stephen must have heard too.

'You *do* know whose son he is...' was an all too familiar refrain whenever Kirkpatrick's name was mentioned. And, of course, everyone did know. No one ever questioned the wisdom of putting him in the army so young. Instead, it was seen as evidence of his potential, proof that he was a chip off the hearty old block. His presence among us was seen as the continuation of a fine family tradition in manly bravery and keenness to get stuck in to the rough work that the army and the Empire demanded of its sons.

I remembered, though, an incident at the shooting range. Both Lieutenant Matthews' platoon and mine had been scheduled for rifle practice that day. We watched the men lying on their bellies with their legs spread out behind them, firing at the paper targets at the far end of the range. Kirkpatrick had been given a rifle by his father at an early age; as a result, he was a good shot and usually scored first or second in his platoon.

The sergeant in charge of the range shouted 'rifles down, breeches open!' and the men went forward to collect their targets. Kirkpatrick looked at his target and counted the points. He had not done as well as he had hoped, or expected. In a fit of childish petulance, he threw the paper target on the ground and stalked off.

'That man,' the sergeant in charge of the range shouted out, 'pick up your target and come here.'

'Send him to me when you're finished, sergeant,' I said.

Kirkpatrick's face was frightened as he stood in front of us.

'You can't do that kind of thing,' I told him. 'You're not a schoolboy.'

'Yes, sir,' Kirkpatrick replied, 'I'm sorry.'

'Why did you do it?' Matthews asked, more gently than I had. I felt a momentary flush of shame at hearing the understanding tone in his voice. 'Losing your self-control in front of the other men like that? It doesn't do your reputation among them any good.'

Kirkpatrick looked down at the ground.

'You can't behave like that,' I repeated.

Kirkpatrick looked up at me. 'It's my father, sir. I have to send him details of my scores. He's – he's going to be very disappointed in me for this.'

The train lurched and Sergeant Visser moved his feet heavily to keep his balance. We clanked past a water tank next to the line for filling the steam engines. It was made of shiny new galvanised iron and was perched high on a trelliswork of eucalyptus logs. Water dripped from one of the seams of the tank, glinting in the sun as it fell; slow, fast, slow, like rain coming to an end. A black woman stood beneath it, holding a battered paraffin tin up to collect the water. She was wearing a stained, cast-off dress that had once been pink. Four children stood around her, three boys and a tiny girl. The boys wore torn and dirty shorts, the baby sat in the dust with just a string of beads around her waist. The biggest boy was struggling to hold a large clay pot with both hands. The woman took the paraffin tin down and poured the water she had collected into the clay pot, and then lifted the tin back under the falling stream.

The grandfather stood a little way back, holding the tether of a laden donkey. He was dressed in ripped corduroy trousers and a black woollen coat that was frayed at the shoulders. He was barefoot and his calloused feet were splayed out in the dust. He stared at the passing train, his eyes holding each carriage, one by one, as we passed him by. His donkey was thin and mangy, its skin loose over its ribs and hipbones. Strapped to the animal's back was a large iron cooking pot, some blankets, a half-bag of maize meal, and a single pair of shoes – too valuable for walking in. The family disappeared slowly behind us as the train moved on.

'Kirkpatrick will be all right,' I said. 'They all will be.'

I felt uncomfortable under Visser's gaze.

'They gave them only a month of training.'

'Colonel Freeth and General Beves know that. They won't send us in until they're ready.'

Visser held my gaze for a moment. Then he nodded and leaned out the window. He smoked for a few moments and then turned back to face me.

'I shouldn't have said anything.'

His eyes were red-lined and watery. I could smell the staleness on his breath, the faint smell of brandy.

'No,' I told him, 'I want to hear it. I'm going to need your help.'

He tossed his cigarette stub out of the window and straightened up. 'That much I can promise you, but this war – it's going to be harder than any of us think.'

3

WE PASSED AN OUTCROP OF rock caught in the rays of the late afternoon sun. It stood out golden against a dark ridge of hills. A huge termite mound rose close to the line, its mud walls curved and deeply folded. A little boy sat on the crest of the mound, his legs holding on to the hard earth surface as if he were riding a small horse. His eyes were bright as he watched the train clank and wheeze past him, sparks flying out into the fading light.

The tracks curved to meet the horizon. I looked down the length of the train. I could see the cattle truck where my platoon was travelling. They had opened the door somehow to let the fresh air in and the heat out. I was sure that before the train left Mombasa Sergeant Visser or Corporal Reynolds had found a car with a door that worked.

Kirkpatrick and his friend, Wallis, another man in my platoon, were leaning out of the open door. Kirkpatrick waved at the boy on the anthill as they went past.

The boy waved back, standing up as the train disappeared and teetering back and forwards on the edges of the anthill as he windmilled his arms in the air.

The train rounded the bend. At last we were coming in to Voi, the campaign headquarters. Here, closer to town, there were a few makeshift stalls on either side of the railway. They were made of crooked acacia branches tied with bark and roofed with a thin covering of straw. Inside them women sold little mounds of peanuts, bananas, and the maize meal porridge known as *ugali*. Some of the women held up things to the train as it crawled past. The African soldiers on the roof shouted down at them, but the train moved on. The women were left behind holding their arms in the air, pleading and half-joking with the men, waving at them to come down and buy.

The train slowed and the huge military camp that had been established at Voi came into view. Acres of white bell tents stretching from the railway line out into the bush caught the last light of the sun. A battery of 6-inch guns and carriages were lined up ready to be wheeled into battle. Alongside them was a huge clothing depot and the hospital compound. The outskirts of the camp were protected by thousands of yards of coiled barbed wire and sandbagged machine-gun emplacements. Dust from the horses, cattle, supply trucks and marching men hung in the air. Flags and pennants rippled in the breeze. A tall radio mast stretched up into the sky above the tents, its steel guy ropes glinting pink in the long rays of the dying sun. It formed a fragile, unearthly pyramid above the camp. Beyond the tent city, on a bumpy field hacked out of the savanna, three biplanes were parked on the ground next to a collection of corrugated iron huts.

The train jolted to a stop with a shrieking of brakes, in a cloud of smoke and steam. The weary African and Indian soldiers climbed stiffly down from the roofs, their hob-nailed boots clanking on the steel of the carriages. The white soldiers poured out of the stinking, darkened cattle trucks, their uniforms stained and their faces caked with sweat and filth, their eyes blinking in the fresh air.

Shouts from the sergeants erupted out of the cursing, milling swirl of languages.

'Form up!'

'Move it along!'

'B *Commpany*!'

Not since the days of the late Victorian battles like Spion Kop and Omdurman had such tremendous columns of soldiers, vehicles and guns marched through the hills and wheeled across the plains of Africa. The lines of troops swelled and shuffled on the platform as the sergeants battled to bring them to order. Behind them the military camp was filled with the growing shadows of dusk. The men were ordered to line up in full kit standing to attention alongside the railway tracks. They were filthy and exhausted; their arms ached from holding the long Lee-Enfield .303 rifles at their sides.

The sweat dripped out from under their tropical sun helmets, which carried the maroon and white flashes of the 7th Transvaal regiment. Most of the men had only been in the army six weeks. The columns swung clumsily about and began to march unevenly into camp. I could have sworn I saw Colonel Freeth, our regimental commander, wince at least twice under his helmet.

It was exciting to be here at last. It seemed incredible that we had come this far in so short a space of time. We had arrived in Mombasa two days before, and even then I could not help feeling a sense of unreality as the coast drew near. I remembered looking out at the bright green vegetation on the hillsides and the curve of a beach. We watched in fascination from the ship as the shoreline unfolded, long white sands gleaming in the sunlight, and the ochre triangles of dhows cutting across a turquoise bay. Then there was the heat, filling the deck and the calm sea, causing the sweat to pour down my chest and stain my khaki uniform shirt.

Below the green of the forest was Mombasa, the biggest port in British East Africa. The town was a gleaming jumble of white buildings and red-tiled roofs stacked on top of one another. I could see people moving with baskets and carts in the cobbled streets. Men wearing skullcaps and veiled women in long robes sheltered in cool, shaded archways. Somewhere in the centre of town the minaret of a mosque stuck out above the patchwork of houses, standing high against a streak of cloud in an azure sky.

As the crew manoeuvred the ship into position we lined the rails, men and officers together, to see the ruins of Fort Jesus at the entrance to the old harbour. Its walls and turrets were crumbling, stained red and black with age. It loomed over the bay, its presence useless now, but a witness to nearly 500 years of war that had brought first the Portuguese and now, yet again, more white men, and more guns, to this shore. Rusting cannons lay in the clear shallows where the waves lapped. Small naked boys dived amongst them and swam and fished with long thin reeds.

A flock of pelicans skimmed over the bay ahead of the ship, gliding and dipping over the low lines of breakers on the shore. Their round bodies, long necks and long, curved beaks reminded me of a set of musical notes rising and falling as they disappeared, one by one, from our view.

The sound of the ship's horn cut through the oppressive heat. The deck juddered as the screws of the engine pushed the vessel to its anchorage in the bay. There was a loud shout from one of the sailors. The chain clanked as it ran through the hawse-pipe. The anchor splashed into the sea. There was a final blast from the horn, and a few loud shudders from the engine before it stopped.

A hubbub of excitement rose up from the men on deck. A ragged fleet of lighters set out from where the sea and the harbour walls met, the oars dipping erratically into the calm waters of the bay. The first of the motley collection of boats took only a few minutes to reach the ship and begin the long process of ferrying the men, their baggage, weapons and ammunition to shore.

As the first lighters drew up at the side of the ship, General Beves, the brigade commander, Colonel Freeth and a few staff officers gathered at the top of the sea ladders preparing to climb down on to the small rolling boats. The Swahili boatmen stood on the thwarts and looked up at the white soldiers, gesturing to them not be nervous. The colonel turned and placed the sole of his polished boot on the first rung of the rope ladder and began to climb down. The boatmen pushed forward, shoving and jostling their boats to try and be the first one to receive him.

In the harbour ahead of us, squatting low on the water, lay the monitor *Severn*. Only eight months ago she had helped trap the *Königsberg* in the brown waters of the Rufiji delta and her guns had hammered the mighty warship into a wreck of twisted, red, glowing iron and mangled German bodies. The destruction of the *Königsberg* had been the first big British victory in East Africa, coming soon after the humiliation of the failed invasion of Tanga. The news of the destruction of the German warship had been received rapturously all over the Empire.

The *Severn* seemed so small and vulnerable when I thought of the job she had done and of the near-mythic status she and her sister-ship, the *Mersey*, had attained in the newspaper accounts and in our collective imagination of 'how the war was going'. It was hard to imagine that such a small quantity of sheet iron had engendered so much frantic hope among millions of people.

I barely slept that first night of our arrival in East Africa. The oppressive coastal heat bothered me, or perhaps it was just the regular changing of the sentries that kept waking me. I lay awake staring at the slices of moonlight broken by palm fronds that came in through the tent door. A chorus of insects and frogs droned in the trees around the camp. The air smelled of horse piss, hay and salt. All around us was the murmur of the sea. The horses in the cavalry camp nearby were restless, neighing quietly and bumping against the sides of the wooden stables. Occasionally, I could hear men's voices calming them.

I finally fell asleep somewhere towards dawn. The last thing I remembered were the sentries on the edge of the camp; vague shapes, half-hidden in the shadows of the palm trees against the white sand. A curved moon hung in the warm, early-morning sky. The lanterns of the fishing dhows were strung out like stars across the dark bay.

It had taken us a night and almost a whole day on the train to travel only a hundred miles further inland. As I watched the men march in the dust past the train towards camp, I thought back beyond our arrival in Mombasa to the weeks and months that had gone before. It already seemed almost another lifetime ago that I had been one of hundreds of men who lined up that hot summer's day at the Wanderers' cricket ground in Johannesburg. We waited patiently under the Highveld sun with our records of our heights and weights, our eye test results and other medical examination forms.

Across the extent of the Empire, from the humid, gin-cooled fringes of the cricket ground on the Padang in Singapore to the frozen lake shores of Manitoba, millions of other men were doing the same thing, gathering in hope and earnestness to fight for our Civilization. It was not only white men who joined. Caught up in the spirit of the age and, for many, by the belief that the white world would finally see their true worth and equality through their loyal service to the King of England, men from every race in the Empire volunteered to fight as well. This was as true in South Africa as it was anywhere else. Many black men volunteered to fight, but they were denied the privilege of bearing arms for fear of what they might do with them once the war was over. With the exception of the Cape Coloured Corps, known as the 'Cape Boys', blacks were allowed to join us and our struggle only in the humiliating position of labourers.

It was a deep irony, then, to find that we would be fighting against black men alongside other black men from Nigeria, the

Gold Coast, the Sudan, Somalia and the thousands of men in the King's African Rifles from British East Africa itself.

That day we signed up, a surprising number of men were turned away as physically unfit. We felt sorry for the men who failed to cross even this first hurdle. No one said anything as we watched those flat-footed, short-sighted unfortunates slink away without meeting our eyes, ashamed, knowing that for the rest of their lives there would always lie a gulf between them and us. Now those of us who had been chosen were finally here, only a few miles away from the front lines, but unsure of what it really was that we were expected to do.

Carter came up to me as the last of the men marched past the darkened carriages.

'We'll spend tonight here. Tomorrow they move us closer to the front, to the camp at Maktau. Get your men settled and then join us for dinner in the mess.'

The shadows of the Africans serving us at dinner loomed large against the grass walls of the officers' hut – the *banda*, was what Carter and the others called it. The servants stood behind us at the table, dressed in immaculate white outfits with red sashes. Their hands were covered in tight, clean white gloves. The faces of the officers across the table from me were half-hidden by the flickering light of the hurricane lamps strung on fencing wire from the rough beams.

The long wooden table, of boards resting on trestles, was covered with two or three white sheets serving as tablecloths. The cutlery was scratched and mismatched, but it served for this mess in the bush. Colonel Freeth sat at the head of the table, with the rest of us in ranked order below him. I was seated at the furthest end among the junior officers, below Reading, Macintyre, and Captain Carter.

The colonel began dinner by saying grace. We bowed our heads and the servants bowed theirs. Huge, soft-winged moths spiralled in and out of the flickering light. There was a moment of hesitation as he finished and then the table erupted into excited conversation.

Macintyre was sitting nearest me. Until the night before, when I had overheard him and Major Reading talking, I had not given him much thought. He had seemed a shallow, slightly aggressive man who had made himself foolish by the pretensions that some men adopt in early middle age. Now, when I remembered his face, angry and gaunt in the flickering light of the watch fires, I found myself wondering about the inner landscape of his life.

I knew, or thought I knew, the basic facts of Macintyre's life: that he had started his career in India and then, after ten years or so of undistinguished service, retired from the army. He had come out to South Africa as a businessman a few years before, but his business had not been a success. When war broke out he immediately signed up again with the Union Defence Force. There he had come across quite a few of his old colleagues from India, which pleased him enormously. Macintyre might not have been a success at his own business, but the army and its structured lifestyle suited him perfectly. He was glad to be back. He was bright and articulate, and had read history at Cambridge. His career in the army should have been a relatively smooth, uninterrupted succession of promotions through the ranks.

But something had changed that for him. It occurred to me for the first time that his confident demeanour was really a front. It served to hide more than a touch of bitterness and resentment in him and in the way he related to people.

I had once overheard some of the staff officers, men who had known him from as far back as when he had been a young subaltern in India, talk of two women in his early life, but whose memory still lingered after all these years. 'For years, he had them both on a string. They both adored him, but he could never choose between them,' I once heard one of the senior officers saying before they noticed my presence. 'He didn't know what he really felt. He couldn't choose. The inevitable happened – each woman found out about the other, and in the end, before he could act, he found he had lost them both.'

It was difficult to know how much of this was true and how much was rumour. By all accounts for Macintyre there had been so many women. There had even been a woman standing in the shade on the platform at Potchefstroom station when we pulled out. She was pretty and her dark, wide eyes were shining with the effort of holding back tears.

In the censor's office I had seen at least one letter in his handwriting addressed to a 'Miss Susan Blake, Potchefstroom'. So perhaps at last he was learning to choose.

At first the talk at the table was of sports and the latest war news from Europe. No one said anything about what lay ahead for us. I said little. I was unsure of how to conduct myself in this new world of the army, so I preferred to listen.

Somewhere in the din of loud male conversation, I heard one of the officers further up the table remarking: 'Dangerous trip, wasn't it?'

'The line was guarded all the way,' Carter said.

'But do you know who it was on duty?' one of the senior officers, Major Van Hasselt, asked.

'It was sepoys from the 63rd Palamacottahs,' Major Reading said eagerly. 'All the way from Kamptee. I went to dinner at their mess quite a few times when I was based in India. I didn't expect to find them up here.'

Van Hasselt leaned over the table. 'You know what happened at Tanga, don't you? How they behaved?'

Reading put down his knife and fork. He dabbed at the perspiration at his temple. His thin blonde hair was slick with sweat from the heat. You could see where he had tried to cover a growing bald spot. 'Yes,' he said.

One of the white-gloved servants leaned forward and removed an empty vegetable dish. Reading was holding Van Hasselt's gaze across the table.

'They let the whole force down,' Van Hasselt said.

'I don't know about that,' Reading answered. 'It was –'

'Badly planned,' Carter interjected. 'General Aitken was overconfident from the start.'

Major Macintyre frowned. He turned and glared at Carter. 'How can you say such things? And about such a senior officer? You weren't even there.'

'Neither were you,' Carter snapped back. 'But to launch a frontal assault with green troops, after *warning* the enemy…?'

Reading turned towards Carter. 'Shut up,' he hissed. Carter fell silent, his dark brown eyes gleaming in the half-light.

Major Van Hasselt, too, had been watching the exchange between Carter and Macintyre. He looked across the table at Carter. 'What you say may be true, but I wouldn't trust those Indian troops next to my men, not now,' he said. 'The question always remains; can you rely on them, after what happened?'

'It's up to the officers,' Carter replied, more quietly now. 'Good leadership can redeem any failure. If the men trust their officers, they will follow them.'

Van Hasselt allowed himself a thin smile. 'It's not always the officers who lead. You forget I was with General Botha at Spion Kop. For three days we shot your men down as they tried to climb up to us. More than once, we watched your officers behind the advancing lines using their revolvers to drive their men forward.'

'General Botha's with *us* now,' Macintyre said.

'So am I,' Van Hasselt replied shortly, 'in case you hadn't noticed.'

Someone yelled out from further up the table. 'For God sakes, stop arguing. Whatever happened at Spion Kop doesn't matter now. It's Von Lettow we have to worry about. Those cowardly Indian fuckers ran away at Tanga. They're all the same. They don't deserve to be called by the ancient warrior name of sepoy. They're useless. Someone ought to ship the whole lot of them back to where they came from.'

I couldn't see who it was. There was another voice from somewhere just below the colonel. 'Damn right. Pass the red wine would you?'

The dark hills loomed against the starlight outside the tent. The night air was cool; the moon a pale ripple of silver against the horizon. The layered, melodic sound of crickets filled the bush around the camp.

It was Katherine herself who had told me. 'Someone did a study once,' she said to me in a wistful, thoughtful way, when we were walking together along the street, 'and worked out that for every one of us, there are only six people in the world we can truly fall in love with.'

'Not one, only one?'

She stopped and looked up at me. 'Never just one. There must be more.'

'But why more?'

'There have to be more because I have to know that I'm the best,' she said fiercely. I should have been warned. I should have known then, when she said it, that trouble lay ahead.

Well, as it turned, there were more. At least, one more. Andrew, I think his name was. I never bothered to find out anything about him. Katherine had needed more than just me, and after I found that out it was too late. She could never be the best again, not for me.

In the years that followed Katherine there were more for me too — a lot more than those original six, whoever they might have been. What was best, what was even good, that all somehow got lost.

So when I met Helen, I found myself faced with a dilemma. She was married, yes, and I knew I had no right to interfere, but I had also seen that she was unhappy. I knew, too, that she was the one for me, and I for her. I wanted her, more than I had ever wanted anyone, but I knew I had to let her choose me.

It was the war that gave me the freedom to believe that it was possible for us. The war that kept me at home for nearly two years, had sent her husband away at its beginning. With him gone, she found the space to see things that his presence would have hidden from her for years.

4

THE DAY AFTER WE HAD ARRIVED at Voi they sent us up to Maktau and from there even further forward, to the camp at Mbuyuni. The railway line had been laid only weeks before. We could see where the trees had been hacked out and burned, rocks smashed and blown up and the land flattened to make way for the line. There was something ominous, almost frightening, in the relentless progress that was taking us closer and closer to the war. If there had been no war and no Germans to catch, there would have been no railway line, but now here it was, and nothing would stop us from following where it led.

Mbuyuni was the largest camp close to the frontier. The threat of enemy attack was always present. The bush had been cleared for hundreds of yards around the camp. Trenches had been dug to defend against an assault by German askaris. The boundary was heavily wired and blockhouses had been built at the corners. On the edge of camp, between the bush and the defended perimeter, lay the growing acre of crosses and posts – the markers of those killed in enemy attacks or on patrol.

Every day on the red dust plains one could hear the cacophony of training coming from among the thorn trees. From every direction came machine-gun fire, bugle calls, whistles, and the intermittent crack of rifles. There was the constant buzz of the aeroplanes floating and spiralling in the high, cool layers of the sky. Towering above it all was the white-clouded, purple grandeur of Kibo and Mawenzi, the twin peaks of Kilimanjaro.

The beauty of the landscape was ethereal. It felt unreal at times in comparison to us lowly soldiers who sweated and nursed our swollen feet under its spell. We had no real sense yet of what it was we were supposed to do. We trained and trained again, in the blazing sun underneath the looming vastness of Kilimanjaro, driving bayonet thrust after bayonet thrust into straw-filled sacks, firing round after round into targets with our Lee-Enfields, and marching for miles into the bush where we practised orienteering with compasses and maps. We manoeuvred, company by company, through the dense thorn bush, trying to follow the patterns for an advancing regiment that had been devised in the green, open fields of Europe. Shouted orders, whistle blasts and bugle calls rang out from invisible points in the undergrowth. One or other company would peel off from the main column. They would try to force their way at the double through the thick maze of branches and sharp, grabbing thorns to form a screen or rearguard against an imaginary enemy.

There was something absurd, almost boy-scout-like, in these exercises and in the way we wheeled blindly through the bush, trying to recall the half-remembered and dimly understood troop movements we had been taught in our brief spell in the training camp.

We seldom completed our manoeuvres successfully. Major Macintyre, Captain Carter and Sergeant Visser would scream themselves hoarse in frustration at the men, but at the same time glancing over at officers like Matthews and me, to make sure we understood that it was we, too, who were at fault.

Every now and then, when we stopped to rest, we could hear the faraway thump of artillery fire. A crashing rumble absorbed by the wide emptiness of the plains, and then – an eerie quiet, the leaves of the thorn trees limp with dust and the heat shimmering off the brown, faraway hills. Sometimes I tried to imagine the screams and the small-arms fire and the killing that would follow, but the fighting and the real war remained an abstraction, something we heard about only in the rumours that were whispered at the bottom of the dusty trenches and along the edges of the shining coils of new barbed wire.

On these days, when my doubts about myself and my ability to lead men into battle were strongest, I made sure that I never lost sight of Sergeant Visser in the dense bush. In civilian life he was an engineer in Johannesburg. Here he was my only link with the reality of the war that I knew was to come. On the ship between Durban and Mombasa he had spoken of his service in the Boer War, riding the long, hungry months in one of the commandos that had come down from the Transvaal and the Orange Free State.

They harassed the British all through the Cape Colony into the dry, tussocked desert of the north-west. There they were reduced to eating mouldy biltong and weevil-infested flour. Their clothes rotted. They had to wear old grain bags with holes cut in them for their arms and heads, and rough vests of stinking, badly-cured springbok hides. Visser had seen his people starving, reduced to near-skeletons from hunger and disease. All across the country they had found pathetic family groups of women and children. The only men amongst them were those who were crippled or bewildered with age. These frightened bands of refugees drifted across the empty veld, leaving behind them the smoking, blackened ruins of their simple farm dwellings, their wagons and their looted fields. Visser and the others knew that this was being obliterated because of them, by Kitchener's policy of destroying the farms to deny the Boer commandos a source of supply.

Time and again, Visser told me how he had watched his leaders forced to choose between concrete actions that might save a single family and those that might or might not help to win a hopeless war. 'The English are just over the next ridge of kopjes,' he remembered three women begging of them, 'take us with you. Guard us, or give us guns at least so we can defend ourselves. Just outside Carnarvon two of the soldiers came back under cover of darkness. They raped Anna Mynhardt and set fire to her farmhouse. She died in the flames because she saw no reason to come out again.'

The commando had no guns to spare. They gave the women what food they could and then rode on, forced to leave Anna Mynhardt unavenged. Every day they rode deeper and deeper into the trackless veld, further and further away from the people they were supposed to be fighting for.

In the end, surrender came as a relief to Visser and many others like him. They had gone to war to save their world. Instead, they had seen it being overtaken by the reality of English power. Everything they had believed in was being destroyed. They had fought against the annihilation of their republic for nearly three years and now there was nothing more they could do to prevent it happening. In the end, their only hope was to live, to survive the empty wandering that their brave, flag-waving start had been reduced to.

But, as glad as Visser was that the suffering of his people was over, he found in the years that followed that he never settled into civilian life. As he rose in the firm, from site foreman to sitting behind a succession of waxed hardwood desks, he began to realise that he was a born soldier.

'I couldn't help it,' I remembered him saying in the bright sunlight on the deck of the ship. 'I missed the war.'

For a long time he struggled with the problem of his fascination with war. One day, when he was less than halfway through checking a large pile of dog-eared, ink-stained blueprints, he suddenly understood it. What he missed about war was the exhilarating uncertainty of every moment, of not knowing when he woke every dawn whether he would live through the day. Of course, that was theoretically true of life even on site or at the firm, but what he missed was the way war intensified that feeling. What made him feel most alive was being forced to choose from within war's impossible choices.

There was nothing comforting to him in this revelation. Someone else, on realising this, might have thrown up everything and joined the army. Soldiering, however, was not a calling for a man with a family that he loved. Army pay was nothing more than army pay. Visser could not maintain his family and the large house they lived in without the manager's salary the engineering firm paid him. So for years he existed in an undeclared state of frustration and nostalgia.

Visser was waiting for a tramcar on Eloff Street in Johannesburg when he first heard the news of the assassination of the Archduke Ferdinand in Sarajevo. For the next few days he went about his business in a fog of expectation. He tried to tell himself he was content to let fate take its course, but when Britain declared war on the Kaiser he knew what he was going to do.

The company had, in a burst of patriotism, declared that it would pay full salary and benefits to the families of volunteers who had worked with them for more than ten years. This removed any obstacle the physical maintenance of his family might have provided to his signing up. Early the next morning, Visser went straight to the army recruiting office.

'Have you forgiven the British then, for Anna Mynhardt and for the others?' his wife asked him when he told her of his plans the night before.

I remembered Visser telling me this as we sat on the deck in the heat of the tropical sun. He had stared out over the blue sea, a single runnel of sweat trickling down his unshaven jowls.

'I hadn't thought of hating the British for years,' he told me. 'Of course, there were still the memories of the war and sometimes even the nightmares – the ones that wake you in the middle of the night, when you lift your head off the pillow and listen in the darkness, waiting for the attack that will never come. But I told her. "Yes, I suppose I must have."'

He had reaching up to wipe the sweat off his forehead. 'For the first time in my life, I couldn't read her eyes. "Well," she said to me. "You should go, then, and fight for their King."'

When I thought about it afterwards, it seemed to me that Visser had hoped, over the days following the Archduke's assassination, that he had found what so very few people ever do, an honourable way to solve the dilemma of living his own life without abandoning the ones he loved. But in that moment, staring back into his wife's eyes, he had learned that such freedom was an illusion for him, and that patriotism was, as in his own case, all too often the cover for a hundred other betrayals.

One day we were far out of camp doing field exercises together with the 6th South African Infantry Regiment. Our company and one of theirs were under the command of Major Macintyre. We had been given a five-minute breather. I halted the platoon and watched Wallis share his water bottle with Kirkpatrick. They were standing with two of the men from the 6th, Fielding and Smit.

'We're lost again,' Wallis said, shaking his head, the cool water glistening on his chin.

'We've been circling the same clump of baobab trees for the last hour,' Kirkpatrick added.

'Why the hell doesn't Macintyre just admit it, and get some of the locals from the King's African Rifles to show us the way through this fucking bush?' Wallis asked angrily.

Lieutenant Miller from the 6th was listening from the shade of a thorn tree.

'Watch your tongue,' he said in a low voice. 'We know what we're doing. This is the army. We don't need any of you volunteers taking command. And we certainly don't need any kaffir soldiers to show us around.'

'No,' said Fielding. 'We don't need niggers. They'll just get in the way.' He turned to an appreciative crowd of men. 'Hell, did you see that one from the KAR trying to read a map the other day?' Fielding lifted his hands up and moved them around wildly. 'Like a bloody baboon juggling a hot potato that he's stolen off a cook fire. Funniest thing I've seen in a long time.' There was a roar of laughter from the sweating, tired crowd of men.

'I've got nothing against the black man, myself,' said Smit when the laughing had died down. 'They work all right if they are properly supervised, but they'll never make good soldiers. They don't have the discipline or the backbone for it.'

'They can't shoot straight either,' another man added. 'It comes from growing up in those round huts of theirs. Their eyesight gets affected.'

I noticed Sergeant Visser sitting in the red dust under a thorn tree, smoking a cigarette. He removed his sun helmet and wiped the sweat off his red face.

'We had blacks with us at Mafeking,' he said. 'I saw one of them pick off an English officer at 800 yards. He dropped like a stone.'

I noticed Lieutenant Miller glaring at him. Even Lieutenant Matthews looked angry. He was too young to have fought himself, but his older brother had been killed at Mafeking. The memories of the war were still raw on both sides. Visser sat there under the tree, pulling on his cigarette, holding the hostile stares at bay.

'It must have been a fluke,' the same man said. 'He was probably aiming the other way.' There was another burst of laughter. Then a bugle call rang out and we began to form up to continue the march.

That night, when the manoeuvres were over, I found myself talking to Captain Carter. We were sitting on a rough bench near the wireless section. The tall radio aerials that reached up into the sky bent and wavered in the evening breeze above us. The last of the sunset was streaked across the sky, and its fading light framed the dark silhouette of Kilimanjaro in the distance.

The best we've got, Major Reading had said of him to Macintyre that first night on the train to Voi. But I didn't know what I really thought of Carter. Some of the officers, and many of the men, too, hated him. But there was no denying that he was an effective, dedicated officer who, at thirty-three, was also one of the most experienced men in our newly formed, largely volunteer regiment.

I was surprised at his coming over to talk to me. In the training camp at Potchefstroom and on the troopship I had come to know the others relatively well: Van Hasselt, Reading, Matthews, and of course Macintyre. Our relationship remained untested in battle, of course, but we had come to know at least something of each other's strengths and weaknesses in the forced marches through the veld and by the nature of the outbursts of exhausted rage or misery in the grey light of repeated pre-dawn drills.

But Carter had remained aloof from us all. He kept to himself, reading in his tent when we were not drilling the troops or attending training exercises ourselves. When he did find occasion to speak to me, what he said was always brief and to the point, wasting neither words or time. Perhaps, I thought, he felt he had done enough of that already. Despite his hard exterior, I knew now that he was hiding something, carrying some old pain within him.

I had picked up some of his story in bits and pieces from gossip in the training camp. As far as I could make out, he had started his military career serving in Ireland. He had then been stationed in India and so had missed the Boer War, but, like Major Reading, he had seen plenty of action on the Afghan frontier.

The only real rumour I had heard in the officer's mess concerned Carter and a woman in India. The core of the scandal was not so much the sexual indiscretion, but the fact that the woman in question was not white. No one appeared to know the details, but it seemed that there was enough truth in the rumours to have damaged his prospects in the army.

Some of the English officers in the regiment affected to despise Carter because of his background. His origins were humble; his father was a poor schoolteacher from Manchester, who had somehow, on the strength of his savings combined with a modest legacy from his wife's family, managed to send his son to a minor public school. It occurred to me, though, that the real motives behind the resentment the other officers in our regiment felt was engendered by the simple fact that Carter, unlike most of the volunteer officers and men, had already fought in a number of battles, had wounded and killed men, and seemed to have no compunction about the fact that he was soon to do so again.

Carter and I sat for a few moments on the bench. He was leaning forward, his hands clenched together in front of him. His wrists were slender but the muscles showed the physical strength contained in the smooth lines in the tendons and the hands. His fingers were surprisingly thin and white for a professional soldier's hands. I would have expected to see such hands on a banker or perhaps a musician. The nails were neatly trimmed. His hands spoke of power and immense self-control.

Carter was the first to speak. 'Ever since I was a child, I've always been fascinated by Africa,' he said, taking a deep breath of the evening air. 'It feels so good to be here.'

'Don't you want to be in France, where the real action is?'

Carter turned and looked at me in the fading light. 'There'll be enough action here. I can promise you that.' The knuckles on his hands turned white. He looked at me carefully. 'I hope you're not one of those officers who thinks this campaign is going to be a walkover against a bunch of unruly natives. I've heard too many men, and officers, speaking like that. It's a mistake, and it'll cost lives. I've fought against native troops before, in Afghanistan. They're as good as any white soldier, often better, because they know the territory and how to survive in it. And the German askaris are well trained, they'll be damned hard to get the better of.'

I was surprised at the fury of his outburst. I guessed it had something to do with what Macintyre and Reading had been talking about.

'I'm sure you're right,' I stammered. 'But it does seem that this campaign is a sideshow. The newspapers are filled with reports from the Western Front. The French preparing for an offensive; our own boys struggling to hold the line. All the talk of the need for our armies to launch a big counter-attack come spring. I know we're doing our bit, here in Africa, but it seems such a small thing we've come to do. And you've got such a lot of experience, I thought that you might somehow want to be over there, where it's all happening.'

Carter looked at me. 'What we're doing is crucial to the war effort.' He sat back and slipped his hands into the pockets of his tunic. 'Yes, it's true that the fighting in Europe is what really matters. But the war over there is going badly – a victory against the Germans here in Africa, even a minor one, is vital to the morale of the Empire, and for the morale of our allies too. We have to win our battles here. Whether we succeed or fail will be in all the newspapers. What happens to us here in Africa, even in the smallest ways, will have reverberations through every single trench in Europe.'

The last of the twilight was dying. In the camp, lights were beginning to wink on in the darkness between the triangular shapes of the tents. A section of Indian cavalry rode past. The hooves of the horses beat against the hardened earth and the steel bits jingled softly. They had just come in from patrol. Their turbans and knee-length khaki coats were filthy from days in the bush. They sat erect on their horses, staring straight ahead as they rode, their carbines and tall iron-tipped lances held high.

'You do know you're one of the most popular officers among the men,' Carter said.

'No,' I replied, embarrassed. 'Not me. I –'

'You are, though,' he said, cutting me short. 'The men like you, and they trust you.'

'Even if that's true it doesn't mean much – I mean, when it comes to the real thing. I've never been in a battle. I don't know how I'm going to be when the shooting starts.'

It was out now. I didn't feel any better for having said it.

'No,' Carter said slowly. 'You don't know. None of us does, not until the time comes.'

A light came on near one of the radio masts above us. Its yellow glow spilled out onto the dark ground.

'There's no point in thinking about it,' Carter went on, an unexpected kindness in his tone. 'It just makes it worse.'

'Yes,' I said. 'That's always the way.'

Carter's face was eerie in the pale light. 'You never know how a man will react to bullets. Some men are often brave for the first time because they can't imagine what to expect from battle. They have no idea what's to happen next, so they don't fear it. It's only after the second or third time that you and your men face hostile fire that you see who's going to freeze up and who you can rely on. And even they don't always last. You can't expect most men to go back again and again to face gunfire. The few who do are likely to be half-crazy. The problem with them is that you never know what they might to do next.

'You'll get your orders. From me. And you'll pass them on to your sergeant – Visser, isn't it? He's all right. Fought against us at Mafeking and on commando with Smuts. You're lucky to have him. And Visser will pass them on to Corporal Reynolds. The chain of command. That's what it was invented for, to overcome fear.

'It's true that sometimes the orders that come down to you are not always the best ones. But as long as you've carried them out that's all that matters. You don't have to be a hero; you just have to carry out your orders, and make sure your men carry out theirs.'

Carter paused. I could see fires being lit outside the kitchen huts. There were the silhouettes of the cooks and kitchen hands moving to and fro across the fires.

'Just about anything can happen in battle,' Carter said. 'Stand your ground. And get your men to stand theirs, then you will have done more than many officers ever do.'

Major Macintyre was striding by across the peaked rows of tents. A barely-controlled look of irritation crossed over Carter's face. Seeing the two of us sitting together, Macintyre abruptly changed direction and came over.

'What did you two think of today's exercises?' he asked, his voice ebullient, falsely jovial.

'The men did well,' I said cautiously.

Macintyre nodded. 'Yes,' he said. 'The whole regiment's coming along nicely.'

'No,' Carter shook his head. 'It was no good, any of it.'

'What was no good?' Macintyre's voice shifted. It was cold and hollow.

'General Malleson and the others, they expect us to fight on our own.'

'Come on, there's thousands of men along with us,' Macintyre said shortly. 'The Royal Fusiliers, the Rhodesians, all the artillery.'

'There're no African troops. No King's African Rifle regiments. They're who we need the most.'

'African troops?'

'Yes,' Carter said. 'They're the only ones with the experience. They've been fighting here in the bush for ten, fifteen years.'

Macintyre gestured with the back of his hand. 'I'll grant you they can fight when their backs are against the wall, but it was the example of white officers that won every single one of the frontier campaigns. Look at what happened with the Nandi. It was Captain Meinertzhagen who led them out of the ambush their chief, the Laibon, had set for them. If it hadn't been for him –'

'There is another story about that incident. The Nandi claim they were tricked. That Meinertzhagen called them to a truce and then ambushed them. They say our men then shot the Laibon in cold blood.'

'There were three separate commissions of enquiry,' Macintyre said. 'Each one of them exonerated Captain Meinertzhagen. They praised him for his quick thinking and determination.'

Carter sat back. He was looking up at Macintyre in the fading light. 'Whatever happened, he didn't do it on his own. It was his Sudanese and other African troops who did the fighting. All I'm saying is that we should have some of them with us now.'

Macintyre smiled thinly, the lines on his face drawing tight under his neatly-combed hair. 'You're an old-fashioned thinker, captain. The days of the colonial skirmishes are over. This is a real war. A modern war. A white man's war. Everything now depends on us.'

He turned and stalked off into the growing darkness. A half moon came up over the hills. All through the camp there were the shadowy movements of men lining up for their evening meal.

'You know he's never yet been in a battle?'

I looked at Carter, finding it difficult to hide my astonishment. 'But all those years, in India? The Afghan frontier?'

'He was never given a battlefield command. He needs to succeed here – for his career.'

'You were in India together,' I said hesitantly.

'Yes. We were in the same regiment for a while. He was a cadet officer directly under me.'

'And under Major Reading?'

Carter looked at me. 'How did you know that?'

'Everybody – well, it's common knowledge.'

'It *is*?'

I nodded.

'That was then, a long time ago,' Carter said quietly. 'Now, I take my orders from him.'

5

I DREAMED OF HELEN AT NIGHT, coming to me through a gate. She led me inside. Slowly she would reveal herself to me, layer upon layer slipping off until we were both naked. Laughing secretly together in the darkness of night. The smooth curves of her body moving over me, underneath me. Her slim waist in my hands. Her soft thighs opening, her legs wrapping around me; the electric touch of her fingers running through my hair, drawing me deeper, deeper into her.

It was impossible, I couldn't forget her. The woman of my dreams was married to somebody else.

She did agree to have tea with me. It was a disaster. She kept fiddling with the lace napkin in her lap. I tried, but I couldn't find any way to impress her. It was clear that she regretted having come out at all.

The conversation between us was stilted and uncomfortable. In the moments between our sentences, I could hear the bone china cups being placed delicately back on saucers; the silverware tinkling ever so self-consciously against the hard gleaming edges of the crockery.

Suddenly I was painfully aware of the two of us being alone in a room full of other people. Here she was, a married woman, with her husband away at the war; alone with me – a man who hadn't even volunteered to go. I didn't care what the hard eyes staring at the teacups and silverware might think of me, but I saw what she must be feeling. For her, she was surrounded by the possibility of a shrieking whirlwind of judgment and condemnation. I didn't think anyone knew us there. I couldn't be sure, though, and I was suddenly furious with myself for putting her in that position. But then, I told myself she had, after all, agreed to come.

It was silence that we were battling. The potentially disastrous gaze of the other people around us, and the silence that lay between us – in the things we didn't dare say to each other.

'I'm sorry,' I said suddenly, wanting the whole afternoon to end. 'I shouldn't have brought you here.'

'Yes. It was a mistake. But not yours. It was mine. I can't imagine what I was thinking when I agreed to come.'

She let me accompany her on the tram back to her house in Yeoville.

'Here,' she said, when we came to a small wooden gate between brick pillars. From the sidewalk I could see a stone bungalow with a tin roof painted dark green. There were shuttered windows and a curved veranda with purple wisteria climbing the square stone pillars.

We stood there together for a while on the street. A strand of her hair had worked loose.

'I'm sorry if I ruined the afternoon,' she said. Her eyes were dark under their curved lashes. She reached up nervously and touched the downy hairs at the back of her neck.

'No,' I began. 'It wasn't like that at all –'

She turned and lifted the iron latch.

'I've got to go in now.'

I felt myself suddenly loose and falling, away into empty space, scrabbling for some way to hold on, uncertain of what to do, but refusing to let go.

'I'll call. We'll –'

She turned. 'No,' she said. She turned back towards me. 'Please. You must understand. We can't.'

Part of me knew that I shouldn't be doing it, but I couldn't help myself. I tried again a few more times to get hold of her, but somehow she always seemed to be out. I went around to her house once, but there was no answer when I rang the bell. I knew that she could see the gate from the front door, but the house remained silent. All I could see over the top of the gate was the clear purple reflection of wisteria in the windowpanes beyond the shaded porch.

After that, I saw there was no point. I stopped calling. But at night I couldn't stop myself from dreaming.

Our camp was the centre of a small city that had grown up to serve the war. Just outside the perimeter were the thousands of African porters who lived with their families. At night, we could see their cooking fires and hear their drums and the occasional bursts of laughter. Some, mostly the youngest of them, had come with the illusion of finding adventure. But most had been forced by poverty and the hunger of their families to come for the money, little as it was.

For now, around camp, their work was light and there was not much for them to do. It was only later, when the long march deep into the interior of German East Africa under General Smuts started that their ordeal of disease and exhaustion would begin.

In a radius of a few miles around us were camped the Rhodesian regiment and the East African Mounted Rifles, drawn from volunteers among the local white settlers. An English regiment, the Loyal North Lancs, was nearby too. There were also the Indian sappers and gunners and the Pathans, Baluchis and other Muslim troops in the 129th and 130th Baluchis from the Punjab, and from the tribes on the North-West Frontier. They had been fighting this war for months before we came. Many of the Baluchis were veterans of the colonial wars on the Afghan frontier and were some of the toughest soldiers in the Empire. When the war began they had been sent to the Western Front, and had witnessed the horror of their comrades being slaughtered in the mud at Ypres for an entire winter before being transferred to Africa.

They marched out from the camps around us on regular patrols. We watched as they came back in, with fixed bayonets, bringing their prisoners, German askaris with their hands tied behind their backs. Long grass ropes were looped three times around each prisoner's neck. They would come in in long lines, a dozen or more hungry, thirsty and defeated men being led through the bush in single file.

But the times we stared at the others most was when they went out to meet the distant artillery fire that we could only hear. We lined up at the gates and watched them as they marched bravely past. We watched as they returned, grim-faced and exhausted, their walking wounded hobbling along with bloody bandages, followed by those shivering, gaunt-faced men suffering from malaria and covered in the bloodied shit of dysentery. The worst cases followed them, in rows of bloodstained stretchers. The mules came last, bodies strapped to their packsaddles – the faces of the dead jolting and hanging open to the sky; their blood clotted and mingling with the salt sweat of the animals' flanks.

Outside our camp there would be the sound of spades digging in the earth, laying to rest the Christian and Muslim dead brought in and the wounded who had died on the journey home or in the hospital. Then would come the mournful, drawn-out notes of a single trumpet playing the Last Post. Smoke would rise above the Hindu section of the Indian camp attached to ours as they burned the bodies of their slain, the huge plumes coiling black against the wide orange beauty of the sunset.

Still we waited for the unseen Generals to choose our time and place of testing. More stories came and went through the camp, each one larger and grander than the one before. Neither officers nor men were immune to the conceited charms of rumour. We could not help hoping that the one *we* had heard was true. That, yes, something was going to happen to us. This was what it would be, and we had been the first to know.

We were surrounded by war, but we had not yet faced the enemy. No one said anything but each day of waiting diminished us. We had not yet been judged ready to join the fighting. That judgement galled us, and at night the murmurs of discontent flowed through the neat, shadowed rows of tents.

Every morning we were woken before dawn to man the trenches around camp, holding our rifles at the ready on top of the sand bags and staring into the cold darkness. We strained our eyes through the barbed wire and piled thorn branches, waiting for the Germans to attack. We battled against the hallucinations of fear and tiredness that were the leftover flickers of nightmares. A shadow would flutter in the bush in the cold half-light and you would be just about to raise the alarm, but somehow you waited those few moments longer and the bush stayed still and dark. You thought you heard a twig break or the rustle of a branch against a khaki uniform, or perhaps the clink of a rifle barrel against the edge of a bayonet. This time, you were certain of it, you recognised the sound from the exercises you had done in the thick bush. The Germans were there just a little way away. You had a few minutes at most before they came screaming through the bush…

They never did come. Every morning they must have been waiting for us in their own fear-filled dawns on the other side of the bush. Most men hated having to stand to before first light, but I came to look forward to the solitude and to testing my patience against the silent menace of those cold, dark mornings.

I would hear the breath of the men in my platoon stretched out along the line of the trench. Sergeant Visser always contrived to be next to me, and next to him, Burger. Like Visser and Major Van Hasselt, Burger was an Afrikaner who had also fought on commando in the Boer War. I never quite understood why Burger had volunteered to leave his farm and come to fight for his old enemies, the British. 'He wants to see more of Africa before he grows old,' was the explanation Visser had offered when I had once found an opportunity to ask.

Burger and Corporal Reynolds were often together. Corporal Reynolds had immigrated to South Africa from his shared room in a terraced house in Islington. The son of a furrier and a bonnet-maker, he had seen few opportunities to escape his life if he stayed in London. He had tried his hand at a dozen jobs before joining the army, and there he had found his true vocation as a non-commissioned officer. He seemed to love the task of mediating between the officers and the men and would always be found somewhere in camp, moving up and down on his short, stocky legs, his booted feet splayed out at an angle, as he rushed from one crisis to the next. Reynolds would never become an officer, his class was against him. His particular genius was the absolute determination and precision with which he made sure that specific tasks were carried out. If a wagon were stuck in the mud or a row of tents needed striking, then Corporal Reynolds was your man. Within minutes of his being given the order, one would witness a small, hand-picked team of men moving towards the problem with Reynolds striding out ahead. He would pitch in with his men, yelling, bullying, cajoling until they were sweating and covered in dirt, and the wagon was standing free and clear in the grass at the side of the road or a neat pile of tents lay on the ground folded with geometrical precision.

I was never quite sure what the men thought of Reynolds. He worked closely with them, but he was also the closest conduit to them of the absolute power the army held over their lives.

He was not afraid to use that power and he tolerated no unmilitary behaviour from the men. Sleeping an extra two minutes after dawn was 'a bad business', as would be his discovery of a minute spot of unpolished boot leather. At a higher level, going AWOL or failing to clean a rifle would be known as 'monkey business'. It would cause him to shake his head as he referred the offender to an officer for punishment. A case of being drunk on sentry duty or of stealing ammunition would be known as 'monkeyfuck business'. Such genuinely serious breaches of discipline would bring out Corporal Reynolds' deepest sense of outrage and betrayal. The offender would be subjected to the most vicious tongue-lashing and physical punishment that Reynolds could impose before being handed over to face a court-martial.

Visser, Reynolds and Burger, the three older men in the platoon, were a sounding board for me. They seldom said anything openly, but I could tell from the tone of their voices, or from certain expressions on their faces, what the mood of the platoon was.

After them down the line in the trench came Johnson, his lazy, cynical eyes sharp with this new duty. Johnson was perhaps the strangest man in my platoon, or in the whole regiment, for that matter. He was a sad, lonely misfit of about twenty-four. We were all surprised that he had passed the medical examination. A skinny, physically weak boy, he had hollow cheeks that were pitted with purple acne scars. He smoked constantly and his thin, bony fingers were stained a dull orange with nicotine. In the training camp he had shirked the physical exercises of the morning Swedish drill, and consistently came last in the field exercises. The only thing he did well at was at shooting practice. It was a mystery to us why he had joined up. He complained constantly in a loud, whining voice that grated on everyone's nerves. I had seen him slouching around the camp and the decks of the troopship on his own, muttering to himself. The other men mostly scorned him, but to everyone's surprise he, like Wallis, had struck up a friendship with young Stephen Kirkpatrick.

Whenever they were seen together, it was Kirkpatrick who did most of the talking. Johnson would be lifting a cigarette to his lips, and then blowing the smoke out while listening to whatever it was that Kirkpatrick felt like talking about. It was a strange friendship, but I suspected that their kinship had its roots in the frustration both of them felt: Kirkpatrick towards his father and the pressure the old soldier put on his son to succeed, while Johnson seemed to exude anger with the whole of life.

Beyond Johnson were Steinberg and Campbell, the youngest men in the platoon after Kirkpatrick. They were two of a group of school pals who had joined up straight after matriculating. They were both just nineteen and seemed to think everything they were doing in East Africa was one great adventure.

Further on, leaning up against the edge of the trench, were Hooper, Watson and Williams, each one anxious, each looking at the others for his cue. They were all in their early twenties and had signed up at the Wanderers Cricket Ground in Johannesburg at the same time I had. They were the sort of men who were pouring into the new City of Gold by the thousand from every corner of the Empire. Young clerks who worked at a bank in town, they had come that afternoon to volunteer in a confident, jostling group. The bank had agreed to hold their positions open until the war was over and the army released them. They were the type the bank wanted to have back again – trustworthy young men with fine, prosperous futures ahead of them. Their patriotism was obvious and unquestioning. They were the pure, unalloyed stuff of which Society is made. They had been to the right schools, they worked hard at their careers and they believed in their country, in themselves and in the promise of the Twentieth Century. The three of them were always together, chatting or laughing uproariously at the practical jokes they played on one another.

They always carried out their orders cheerfully, but, unlike with, say, Wallis or even Kirkpatrick, I never knew exactly what they were thinking. I knew men like them from my years in the mining company; men brought up in the ways of a hierarchy. They watched me and the other officers carefully. Underneath their ready obedience, they were measuring the officers and non-coms, probing us for our weak points; never making the mistake of currying favour openly, but always searching for ways in which we might be of use to one of them in moving up the ladder.

I could see Visser glancing over at them from time to time. Corporal Reynolds was further down the line, keeping an eye on Kirkpatrick, and, as an afterthought, on Campbell and Steinberg.

Then there was Gerald Wallis. Over the weeks that we had been here, I had come to see that Wallis was the unofficial leader of the platoon. His friendship with the much younger Kirkpatrick had at first struck me as unusual, perhaps worse. It was only when I realised how unhappy and insecure Kirkpatrick really was in the army that I understood that Wallis had seen that too – before any of us officers had. The truth of the matter was that Wallis might never have been a soldier before, but he understood better than most of the other men what lay ahead of us when we got to the front lines. Kirkpatrick needed someone to look after him, and Wallis had decided discreetly to take on that role.

Wallis was thirty – older than most of the other men – and carried himself with an air of easy self-confidence. In the little time we had spent together as a unit, he had challenged my leadership and that of Visser and Reynolds on a number of occasions. He was an independent thinker, not well suited to the rigid discipline of the army. He had a certain arrogance, but the most striking thing about him was that he was not afraid to act on his decisions, no matter what anybody else might have thought of him.

Wallis had immigrated to South Africa some years back to find work on the mines. Before that he had spent a number of years seeing the world. He had worked for a year or so on a fishing boat up and down the Atlantic seaboard of the United States. From there he had found his way into the offices of a shipping company based in the Persian Gulf. After that he had served a stint on a rubber plantation in Malaya. Somehow he had ended up helping to build railway tunnels through the mountains of Japan. He was an average-sized man, but strong and fit from the active, physical life he had led. Wallis was a survivor, somebody who had pulled himself out of a thousand tricky and dangerous situations, and had come back for more. He was a self-taught man who could speak at least a smattering, often more, of half a dozen languages. Wallis knew more than a little knife-fighting, including, I had heard, some brutal tricks with a Malay kris, and could sail a wide variety of vessels. He read constantly, he could tie a score of complex knots and he could repair just about anything he set his hand to.

He had even achieved some minor successes in the New York stock market with the meagre earnings he had saved from his various adventures.

He was an ordinary soldier. I was a lieutenant. Our different positions in the army meant that we could never be friends, but I couldn't help respecting him. It was his variety of experience that I found so refreshing in Wallis. He had set out to see the world for himself, and he was not afraid to take his own measure of what he found. Wallis was only a year younger than I, and sometimes when I thought of the years I had sat at my desk at the office just in range of Mr. Bradley's sight, when I remembered how, day after day, I had submitted the hours of my youth to his probing, intrusive gaze, I admired Wallis – even envied him – for having had the courage to choose his own life.

Despite his natural leadership qualities, I knew that Wallis would never be promoted to sergeant or even corporal. He made too many officers uncomfortable. He could never be trusted to do things the army's way; the independent, rebellious streak in him was too obvious, and too deeply ingrained.

I once asked Wallis why, having already survived so much danger in his adventures, he had joined the army. 'I've lived both above ground and under it, and I've seen a lot of the world,' he told me, 'but I've never seen a war. I've only got one life to live and this is likely to be the biggest war I'll ever see, so I decided I might as well join up.'

The army was new to me, but I was beginning to learn how it worked. Its energy was in its symmetry. It was when I thought of my Latin classes at school that I understood that this way of seeing the world had begun with the Romans, with their orderly military camps. Every night when the Roman legions halted, they built a camp for safety, each night the camp was exactly the same as the night before. The tribune's tents were pitched in the same position every night, the centurions' tents always nearby. The gates were always erected facing the four points of the compass.

The ordered symmetry inside the walls was safe. For the army there was nothing of value outside the defensive walls of the palisade, only the darkness of night and, all too often, the dull gleam of the enemy's weapons.

Men like Wallis had volunteered to fight for their country, but it came as a rude shock to find themselves in the army first, before they could even come near to war. They brought with them their knowledge and experience of the world outside the ordered safety of the stockade. The army didn't like that, but it tolerated them because it needed more and more men every day.

Somehow the army, which was uncomfortable with men like Wallis, had found a place for me. When I finished my basic training, much to my surprise, I was sent to officer's training. Apparently, my managerial experience was the main consideration. The fact that I was over thirty, that I could shoot at a target reasonably well and that I had learned to speak some German had counted in my favour too.

During the officers' course we were taught things I had never even imagined before. We learned from our *Notes for Fire Unit Commanders* that a rifleman must lead a galloping horseman at 4 feet per 100 yards. I could design a perfect trench in my notebook, and I learned at exactly what angle a urine funnel should be stuck into a soakage pit. We memorised the *Disadvantages of Cover* in planning an attack. When we were sitting in a ring on the ground around the instructor's blackboard balanced on rocks in the veld at Potchefstroom, each one of us could recite them off by heart: *May delay advance and cause crowding; May offer a good aiming mark; May prevent free use of rifle; May tend to delay the advance through men being loath to leave good cover.*

The books and manuals we read in the officers' course were like dictionaries in a foreign language. The definitions were there, clear for anyone to read, but what did *enfilading fire* really mean? What would it feel like to be commanding a platoon that was being cut down, man after man, from the side? And how did one *deploy* men? What could you do to *protect the left flank*?

What would it be like, I wondered, when the bullets were flying? Who would I be able to trust to do the right thing, even after our training? And would my men trust me?

At the end of the course, they gave us each a copy of the official *Field Service Pocket Book 1914*. It was small enough to fit into the pocket of our tunics, and was protected by a leather cover with a clasp to hold it closed.

'This is your lifeline,' the training officer told us, holding up his own battered copy. 'Anything you're unsure about, you can be certain that some other officer has been unsure about it before you.'

'Don't try and reinvent the wheel, consult the bloody manual.' He bent over and flipped through the pages with exaggerated haste. 'Here it is,' he said. 'The wheel. Oh, it's just like the army, designed to roll along smoothly –' I never heard the rest of the definition; it was buried in the burst of laughter that went up all around.

I had become Second Lieutenant Fuller. The order of the words reflected the world of the army. I was an officer before I was a man. I was a junior officer, my position neatly poised between the senior officers and the NCOs and the men. Above me, in a series of immutable layers, were Captain Carter, Major Macintyre and Major Reading. Those three men were as far as the army needed me to see; above Reading the officers blurred into a swirl of brass badges and red collar-tabs.

Below me were my own men; the NCOs first: Sergeant Visser, Corporal Reynolds, then the enlisted men: Kirkpatrick, Wallis and the others in my platoon. I had to try hard to keep the rest of the men in the regiment outside my own platoon from fading into a mass of khaki shirts and sun helmets.

This was the way the army wanted things to be. My place in its hierarchy was precisely calculated. It had nothing to do with who I was as Michael Fuller. As a subaltern, or second lieutenant, I was the pivot between the officers who would make the decisions and the men who would carry them out. The senior officers would give the orders. I would hear them from Macintyre and Carter. Men like Wallis and Kirkpatrick would hear them from me. Above me were all the men most likely to survive the war; while below me were all the men most likely to die.

Matthews' platoon was assigned next to ours in the line. As the first grey light of dawn began to grow I would see him there with his own sergeant, Willis. Beyond Matthews and his men lay Lieutenant Martin Scheepers and his platoon.

In the darkness on those mornings, it would first grow colder, and then the birds would begin. A few faint calls in the receding darkness. Then, as the first light broke the horizon, hundreds of them would erupt into a symphony echoing from trees that were still dark against the grey horizon.

I often thought that would be the best time for the Germans to attack. We would never hear their footsteps coming through the bush over the deafening splendour of the birds' singing. We redoubled our watch. It was only when the eastern horizon turned to amethyst and flame behind the lacy black silhouettes of the thorn trees that we began to relax. The sun never failed to cheer the men. As the light grew golden and the warmth of the first rays fell on our shoulders, I could sense the spirits of the platoon lifting. The attack had not come; there would be hot tea and hard biscuit soon and another day lay ahead.

It was after the first full week of manning those trenches at dawn that I first met Jemadar Aziz Khan. Jemadar was the Indian Army equivalent of lieutenant. I knew that he and Captain Carter had struck up a friendship, and that Captain Carter regularly went over to the Indian section of the camp to talk to him. Khan had also fought on the border with Afghanistan where Captain Carter had started his military career. The two of them always seemed to have something to talk about.

My meeting with Jemadar Khan did not take place under such convivial circumstances. We were coming back to camp after standing to in the trenches at dawn. Our platoon was marching in front so I didn't see what triggered the whole thing. It was a minor incident, one that should have hardly been noticed, but the Baluchis had just returned from a long march and a shameful incident at the nearby Mbuyuni ridge. In the confusion of a German counter-attack in the thick bush, they had come across what they thought was an enemy regiment. A loud cheer ran up and down the line and the Baluchis launched into a headlong charge. The enemy they were charging turned out to be the Rhodesian regiment. One of the Rhodesians was shot, and it took some angry minutes of shouting and blowing of whistles by officers on both sides before the charge was halted. It was a humiliating mistake for the proud Baluchis, and they were still smarting from the memory of it. That they had fought a number of battles alongside the Rhodesians made it worse.

Corporal Reynolds told us later that he saw Doyle, one of the men in Miller's platoon, trip and bump into one of the Baluchis who were marching in the other direction. The Baluchi, a private known as Rahman, pushed him out of the way. It was partly out of irritation, and partly an instinctive, self-protective reaction. Doyle stumbled and fell into the damp, dew-covered dust, twisting his wrist. He picked himself up, holding his arm to his side and lashed out: 'Why don't you shoot me instead, you clumsy black bastard?'

A shocked, furious hush fell on the Baluchis who had gathered around. For a few moments, no one did anything and then, with a loud cry of mingled rage and hurt, Rahman lunged forward and punched out at Doyle. Doyle pulled his head away and Rahman's fist glanced off his cheek.

Conradie, one of the men in Matthews' platoon who was nearby, handed his rifle to the man behind him and punched straight back, smashing Rahman squarely in the nose.

Muhammed Din, an enormous muscular fellow, lunged forward. He caught Conradie behind the ear. As the force of the blow spun Conradie around, Muhammed Din whacked him another one on the jaw. Our men and the Baluchis started squaring off for a fight when Corporal Reynolds and one of the Baluchi havildars – sergeants – named Lal, managed to elbow their way simultaneously to the centre of the fracas.

'What's going on here?' Reynolds demanded, standing with his hands on his hips, looking first at Doyle, who was nursing a bruised cheekbone and a twisted wrist. Then Reynolds turned his head to glare up at Conradie towering over him.

Conradie's knuckles were covered with blood and he was holding both sides of his swelling face. Nearby, Havildar Lal was berating his own men.

Jemadar Khan and I managed to make our way through the fracas and arrive at the same time.

'He attacked me,' Doyle snarled, looking at me.

'He pushed me first,' Rahman retorted, turning to Jemadar Khan. He held the back of his hand up to his swollen nose. His voice sounded thick through the blood that was still gushing out of his nostrils. 'I don't know why.'

'It was the coolie who started it,' someone shouted out from the group of men gathered around Reynolds.

'Ja, I saw it, Doyle did nothing. That's why I hit the coolie,' Conradie mumbled through his battered jaw.

Jemadar Khan was glaring at me. His eyes were dark with rage. 'My men might have started it, lieutenant,' he said, his voice hissing with anger. 'But it seems like your men have every wish to continue it. If you do not stop your men from behaving like this, I cannot promise that I will be able to control mine.'

'Bloody coolies –' Fielding started saying. Reynolds swung around and smashed him full in the face.

'Shut up!' he yelled. He swivelled around to face the rest of the men. 'And that goes for all of you cunts. Unless you want to end up on a charge, and a few hours of field punishment number one chained to a tree in the fucking African sun.'

Both sides were still facing one another. The crowds of men were tense; they jeered at each other with their fists clenched. Corporal Reynolds and I began hauling the angry men out of the way, shoving them backwards. To my surprise, Wallis joined in. He pushed Conradie. Conradie drew his fist back, but then thought better of it. He dropped his hand and submitted to the older man's control.

Sergeant Visser now was shouting at the men, up and down the line. Jemadar Khan and Havildar Lal began doing the same thing on the Baluchi side. They were joined by two corporals from the KAR. The Asians didn't like being pushed by the blacks, even if they did outrank them. Some of the Baluchis twisted angrily back again. But the discipline of rank held. Slowly the Baluchis began to move back as well.

Finally a gap was created between the warring parties and order was restored, but the damage had been done. As we lined up our men and marched them off, I could feel Jemadar Khan watching our every movement. I wondered what Captain Carter would have to say about the incident.

As I suspected, it didn't take long to find out. Early that evening, Matthews and I, and Lieutenant Miller from the 6th, were called in to the officer's *banda* by both Major Macintyre and Captain Carter. Major Reading was there too.

'What the hell happened?' Captain Carter demanded.

'Apparently Doyle tripped and fell against one of the Baluchis, Rahman or something like that he's called,' Miller said. 'He shoved Doyle. It was completely unnecessary. Conradie lost his temper, and hit Rahman. From there things deteriorated.'

'Deteriorated?' Captain Carter stared at Miller. 'They almost got out of hand. We can't have this sort of thing going on. It's the Germans we've got to fight, not one another.'

'It's not the first time Conradie's been involved in fighting,' Major Reading added. 'There were at least two other incidents at the training camp. Once with a civilian who had come to shoe the horses; and then he almost beat up young Steinberg once. When we questioned him about it at the disciplinary hearing, he had nothing to say. We could not help getting the impression that both incidents happened only because both the blacksmith and Steinberg are Jews.'

'It seems he doesn't like anybody much,' Carter said.

Reading turned to me. 'What do you think, Lieutenant?'

'Conradie is a trouble-maker, and so is his friend Doyle,' Matthews burst in before I could say anything. 'They've threatened some of my men, too. I recommend putting them both on a charge. It will act as an example –'

'Bullshit!' Miller blurted out. 'I've spoken to my men. I'm satisfied that the Baluchi started it. If you ask me, he got what was coming to him.'

'Thank you, Lieutenant,' Reading said, looking over at him. 'And what do you think?' He turned to me.

'Conradie *has* been a problem before,' I said. 'But not Doyle, not until today –'

'You can't charge the one and not the other,' Major Macintyre interrupted.

'Charge them both,' Carter said. 'And we'll speak to the colonel of the Baluchis about disciplining his men.'

Macintyre turned to face him. 'You know as well as I do that that will do nothing. The English officers in the Indian army are worthless old fools.'

'They're besotted with their sambo houseboys,' Miller added. 'A good kicking is the only thing those wogs understand.'

'You don't know what you're saying,' Captain Carter moved forward threateningly. Miller started backing away.

'Get a grip on yourself, Carter,' Macintyre snapped. 'Just look at you – the way you behave –'

'*What right* –' Carter swung around to face Macintyre.

'Stop it. Both of you,' Major Reading shouted. Macintyre and Carter glared at each other across the light and shadow of the kerosene lamps.

Major Reading went on, more quietly. 'At the end of the day, we have to remember that it *was* only a fist-fight. And there's a lot worse that lies ahead of us. I would hesitate to make too much of it.'

'I agree,' Miller added. 'It'll stand as a lesson to those coolies not to –'

'Thank you, Lieutenant,' Reading rapped out. 'We *know* what you think.' He looked slowly around at all of us.

'Tensions have been running high after that business with the Rhodesians,' he said. 'And the men have been stuck here in camp for days on end now. It's natural that problems will show from time to time. I think it's best to drop it. I'll recommend to the Baluchi officers that we leave it this time.' He turned and looked at me. 'It's your job to make sure this kind of thing doesn't happen again.'

I saw Helen again, unexpectedly, only a few weeks later. At a wedding of mutual friends. I didn't know she knew them or I probably wouldn't have gone. I don't know how I could have stood knowing that I was to see her again without knowing what I might be able to do about it.

It was only a few days after Edith Cavell had been shot by the Germans in Belgium, on charges of spying and helping British prisoners to escape. Their purpose in executing her was to punish and deter others from following her example, but the Germans could never have anticipated the rage that was unleashed in the wake of her death. Men poured in to volunteer to fight Germany. The pressure was on men like me to join up, and even in the midst of the wedding celebrations the anger at her death drifted through the speeches and the talk of the guests.

No one could be immune to this surge of collective rage, and to the renewed determination to win that bubbled through every conversation. I arrived late at the service and hurried into one of the pews. Church services, even weddings, bored me, and that day I was more pre-occupied than usual, wondering how long it would be before I made the decision to join up.

It was only when we stood up to sing the first hymn that I noticed Helen. I recognised her hat first; when I looked a second time I saw that it really was her. I mumbled the words of the hymn, my heart pounding as I thought of what I should do, of how I should greet her. She was standing between two other young women, so I knew that at least she was there alone, without her husband.

She must have seen me coming in late. At the end of the hymn, as she sat down she turned ever so slightly, and, half-hidden by the wide brim of her hat, I saw the gleam of her eye as she looked at me.

I found her among the throng of guests outside the church. She was wearing a long, cream-coloured dress with a high lace neck, and held a pair of white gloves in her hand. She was standing talking to one of the women who had sat next to her in the pew. The other woman twirled a silk parasol as she talked on gaily. But Helen was watching me, waiting for me.

I hardly knew what to say, where to begin. She was no less nervous than I. I could see a faint blush creep along the edge of her chin when I greeted her.

'This is Jenny,' she said, introducing me to her friend. 'Jenny Peterson.' We shook hands politely, but it was no good. No amount of breeding and good manners could hide the discomfort between Helen and me.

Jenny smiled, her eyes flicking between the two of us. 'How is it that you two know each other then?' she asked lightly.

'We don't,' Helen said firmly. 'Well, not really.'

'We met at a garden party,' I said, suddenly angry with her. 'Some weeks ago. We had a most pleasant time then.'

Helen stared back at me. For a few moments neither of us would yield, but neither of us knew what to say next. She couldn't dissemble, and nor could I. Yet I could only guess at how much she wanted to hide.

'Oh,' Helen said, running her gloves through her fingers. 'Let's not ruin such a nice day. With this damned war on, we all need to be happy as much as we can.'

She smiled at me then. 'Would you walk with us to the reception? It's only a few blocks away.'

She allowed me one dance that night. I have never been a good dancer, and I couldn't help feeling awkward as I tried to keep my movements flowing with the music. Her hand lay on my shoulder with just the lightest touch. My hand touched her waist. I could feel the smooth hardness of her body beneath my fingers. Her skin was pale in the candlelight. Her eyes gleamed, but I could not get her to look at me. She turned away from my gaze, and stared across the room over my shoulder.

She smiled at me when the dance was over, and then hurried away to the table where her friend Jenny sat. She was so beautiful, her movements fluid and graceful. I watched her for a while just drinking her in, the brightness of her dark eyes, the tiny measured gestures of her slim hands; the way a strand of her hair tumbled down her neck. She was another man's wife. I couldn't stop myself from wanting her.

There seemed no way out of this dilemma. It was only late that evening that she gave me my first real understanding that she felt the same way I did. It was after midnight and I walked out into the garden, a little drunk. I stood in the shadow of the trees, the moonlight silvering the edges of the leaves. I felt a little sorry for myself, thinking of Helen and of how much I desired her.

Suddenly, she was standing there in the darkness nearby. 'I hoped to find you alone.'

'Why?' I half-whispered, hardly daring to believe that this was happening.

'I've been leading you a dance. And it's not fair.'

'I don't know what to say.'

'Please don't say anything. Not now. I want to explain, but I don't know if – how – I can. I don't know anymore what I think about you. I just know that I need time to think about it.'

I reached out in the darkness and took her hand. I held it. For a few moments, neither of us said anything.

'You have to know one thing,' I whispered. 'I'll do anything for you.'

She leaned forward and kissed me on the lips. The night was filled with the smell of her. 'You have to give me time. That's all I ask.'

6

SERGEANT HASSANI JUMA OF THE King's African Rifles was the most knowledgeable guide in the whole camp. He was also an essential conduit between the world of white officers and the thousands of black men – soldiers and porters – under their command. Sergeant Juma followed all the comings and goings of even the lowliest porters. He knew who was married to whom, he knew whose brother was sick, and which man was the youngest son of a chieftain who had come to the army seeking adventure rather than the meagre pay which was the most common motivation for young men to sign up as porters. He knew who was satisfied, and who was disaffected and likely to foment mutiny if the food ran low and the German shells kept falling.

Rumour had it that he also made it his business to know as much as possible about what was going on among the white officers and soldiers. Nothing was too insignificant for Juma's attention. He never made the same crude power plays as he did among the porters and the black soldiers, but there was no doubt that when asked for advice, he would be able to gauge the mood and the immediate circumstances of the white officer asking for it, and choose his words accordingly.

'He's a Swahili from the coast. His family has been trading in the interior for generations,' Carter told me one day after we had finished some of our manoeuvres. 'He's the best man to help us find our way through this bush. We wouldn't have the confusion we had the other day if we had him with us.'

'Why don't we?'

'I've asked if he could be assigned to our unit. Major Reading was keen on the idea, but Macintyre refused to have him along.'

Helen was in her garden. She was wearing a pale cotton dress and sandals on her slim bare feet. The palm fronds above us were silver in the moonlight and the iris petals in the flowerbed glowed black. She looked long and hard at me, dark-eyed in the night, and then, brushing a strand of her silky hair away from her cheek, she bent her head to kiss me. A single shot rang out in the darkness, echoing far across the sleeping roofs of the city.

I turned away from her to see where it had come from and men were shouting in the gardens around us. I woke to hear the sound of Sergeant Visser screaming. 'Put that light out!' There was the sound of bare feet running on the dusty lanes between the tents.

'Sniper!' someone else yelled.

'Keep down!' It was Corporal Reynolds this time. 'Keep your fuckin' heads down!'

I grabbed my rifle and, bent double, I clambered out of my tent into the cool night air. Millions of stars glowed overhead. In front of me, I could just make out the faint outline of the snow-covered peaks of Kilimanjaro in the moonlight. I heard the soft flutter of a nightjar rising in alarm nearby. Then three shots rang out from our men crouching behind the thorn *zariba* at the edge of camp. Two in quick succession from one rifle; a single one from another, sparks flaring from their barrels. Then two more rifles opened up, their muzzle-flashes bright in the darkness.

'Stop firing. You'll give your positions away!' It was Captain Carter's voice. Men from my platoon and others were running and then stopping, hiding behind tree trunks, wagons, artillery pieces. I could see Kirkpatrick a little way away, sheltering behind a field ambulance. He was in his underwear, holding his rifle awkwardly in front of him, his eyes wide with fear in the darkness. Wallis was a little way beyond, crouching behind a tree trunk. He was alert, scanning the darkness in front of him for any suspicious movement. Next to him was Burger, lying spread out on the ground, his heels pressed flat to make less of a target, sighting down his rifle barrel into the dim bush.

An eerie calm fell over the darkened camp. We waited for an answering shot from the dark mass of thorn scrub. Long minutes passed in which I could hear nothing but the rasp of my own breathing. The sniper was too cunning to fire back now and give his position away; in fact, I was sure he had already gone, slipping away through the bush.

Keeping down and darting from one point of cover to the next as we had been taught to do at the training camp, I worked my way over to the crude wooden gate that served as an entry point to the camp. The men in a King's African Rifles platoon had been detailed to do sentry duty that night, and one of them, a young Sudanese volunteer, lay huddled on the ground next to the gate.

It was Captain Carter who had moved ahead of the rest of us and reached the wounded man first. He was kneeling over him, wearing only his shorts. His rifle was on the ground next to him. The sniper's shot had torn most of the man's jaw and tongue away. He was gurgling as the blood welled out from his throat.

Sergeant Hassani Juma and his Corporal, another Sudanese called John Akul, came running up. The wounded man was one of theirs. They had been inspecting the perimeter on the opposite boundary of the camp when the German sniper attacked.

'Is he going to die?' Corporal Akul's voice was low and hoarse. His tall body was bent over anxiously. His face was a grimace of fear in the starlight.

Captain Carter looked up at Akul. He said nothing. He lifted the man's head and held it in the crook of his arm. He put his thumb somewhere on his neck, under the slippery mass of meat that had been a young man's chin. He found the artery he was looking for and pressed hard.

'Hold on,' he whispered, as the blood spilled over his hands and onto the cool sand. 'Hold on.' And then over and over again. 'You're not going to die. You're not going to die.'

'Where are the medics?' Sergeant Juma yelled.

The bleeding began to slow.

'Coming, coming,' came the answering yell out of the darkness.

The medics ran up carrying a stretcher and bandages. One of them knelt down and began bandaging the young soldier.

'Hold on. Just hold on,' Carter said to him as the medics padded and folded the bandages over what was left of his jaw.

Corporal Akul leant over the young man. He muttered gently in Dinka. He stroked the youth's head with his large, powerful hands. I could see tears gathering in his eyes.

One of the medics looked up from his work at Corporal Akul. 'He'll make it.' Then he turned to Captain Carter. 'You stopped the bleeding just in time. Saved his life.' The medic shook his head. 'He'll never speak again though. Fucking snipers.'

The young soldier was barely conscious. He stared up at the face of Corporal Akul and beyond him to the starlit emptiness of the night sky above.

In the end, I couldn't stop myself. I went to the library to find her among the shelves of books bound with cloth and leather. My nerve failed me at first. I wandered alone for a while through the corridors. The sun streamed in from the windows overhead. The smell of fine dust hung in the bright morning stillness. The books stood like rows of uneven piano keys waiting for the warm, fluttering touch of fingers.

I watched her eyes hold mine as I walked into the high-ceilinged reading room where she worked. The soles of my shoes squealed once or twice on the polished wooden floor, each high-pitched sound cutting across the rows of people reading hunched over the long oak desks. My heart was beating in the echoing space all around me.

'You have no right to come here,' she whispered hoarsely.

'No,' I whispered back, startled by the depth of her anger. 'No right at all.'

She started walking towards the exit. I followed her, barely conscious of the readers looking up at us, one by one, their gaze following us like ripples across a pond.

She shoved the door closed behind her back, almost trapping me in the jamb.

'Then why?' Her voice was suddenly loud in the foyer.

'Because you are the most beautiful woman I have ever met. And I can't wait for you any longer.'

Then I found I was holding her in my arms, the softness of her hair brushing against my cheek, the gorgeous smell of her filling my whole world.

The days in camp dragged on. Every morning we were up before dawn and standing to in the perimeter trenches. All day we trained in the brutal sun. The heat and the lack of sleep began to wear on the men until the inevitable happened.

Late one morning I was dozing in the heat. I had spent most of the night up on sentry duty with my platoon. A messenger came to my tent. He woke me up and handed me a folded scrap of paper. The man was sweating from running. I opened the note. *Come to my tent urgently. Do not tell anyone. Carter*.

I folded the note carefully and slipped it into the pocket of my battle tunic. I stepped out of my tent and walked hurriedly past the other officers. Macintyre was sitting nearby with his boots up on a campstool. He was cleaning his revolver.

'You're in a hurry, lieutenant.'

'Yes,' I said, not wanting him, of all the officers, to know where I was going.

'All quiet last night, I assume?'

'Relatively.'

'Did you see the Baluchi patrol come in last night?'

'They came in about three in the morning. Jemadar Khan was the officer in charge. Sergeant Juma was their guide. Corporal Akul was his assistant.'

Macintyre nodded. 'The patrol was late. They were supposed to be back yesterday afternoon before sunset. They were delayed by a skirmish with the Germans. Their colonel was about to send out a search party.'

He lifted his revolver and squinted through the barrel. Then he looked up at me. 'There's a report that they weren't challenged at the outer perimeter sentry post. Your men were manning that post.'

'They were.'

'I'll need to know why there was no challenge to the Baluchis. And tell Captain Carter I'll need an explanation from him too.'

'What the hell happened?' Captain Carter asked Kirkpatrick.

'It was only for a moment, sir,' he said. 'I just closed my eyes…' He hung his head and stared at the ground. 'I… couldn't help it. I was so tired, sir.'

'We're all tired,' Sergeant Visser said. 'You know what the penalty is for sleeping on guard duty, don't you?'

Kirkpatrick looked up, his eyes were wide with fright.

'Yes, Sergeant.'

'For God's sake!' Wallis burst out. 'There's no need for this! You can't think of having the boy shot.'

Visser spun around. '*Hou jou bek*! Shut your mouth! You're just as much to blame.'

'*That's all the more reason you can't have him shot*,' Wallis' voice was strangled, halfway between frightened pleading and demanding rage.

Visser stepped towards Wallis. He grabbed him by the front of his shirt, twisting the fabric in his huge meaty fist, and lifting Wallis half off his feet. 'I thought I could trust you,' he said, his voice low and hard. 'That's why I put you on guard duty with the boy. You were supposed to make sure this didn't happen.'

'But it happened only once,' Wallis said.

'*Only once*,' Carter said. 'It only takes one German attack to have this whole damned battalion wiped out. We're at war. We can't afford to make even one mistake. One mistake can mean the deaths of hundreds of men –'

'But – but, it wasn't him who fell asleep,' Kirkpatrick said. 'It was me. He was looking the other way.'

Visser turned, still holding Wallis by the shirt. '*Ja*,' he replied. 'It was you who fell asleep. And who didn't see the Baluchis come in. We haven't forgotten that.'

Kirkpatrick face was pale and haunted. His voice was quavered as he spoke. 'So you see, you can't make him take the blame.'

Carter's gaze flicked from one man to the other. 'All right, Sergeant,' he said. 'Let him go.'

Visser unwound his powerful fist and let Wallis down.

'Please, Captain,' Wallis went on. 'You can't have him shot.'

Carter sat in his camp chair looking at Wallis and then at Kirkpatrick in the darkness of his tent. 'No,' he said. 'We're not going to have him shot.'

Relief flooded both men's faces.

'But there are plenty of officers who would have. You must know that.'

'Yes, sir,' Wallis said.

Kirkpatrick's face was still white. He was breathing heavily.

Carter looked coldly around at the two of them. 'Get out,' he said.

The two men saluted and left the tent. Sergeant Visser and I waited for Captain Carter to speak.

'Jemadar Khan came to me in confidence as soon as he could after the patrol came in.' Carter looked at the two of us. 'We knew each other a little in India.'

'He's also got youngsters among his men,' Visser said. 'I've seen them.'

Carter nodded. 'But the mood in the Baluchis is not good. They're angry about what happened the other day. Many of their officers will be determined to make an example of white soldiers now. There'll be pressure on Major Reading and the others to do something with Kirkpatrick and Wallis.'

'They won't shoot him. They can't –'

'They can,' Visser said. 'They bloody can. It's in all the rule books.'

'It's Macintyre that Major Reading and I are most worried about,' Carter added. 'He's been a goddamned failure all his life, and now he's hell-bent on proving himself in this war. A reputation for stern discipline will look good on his record. I'm afraid Kirkpatrick and Wallis are in real trouble.'

The sun was a blaze of white in the wide blue sky. Heat wavered over the desolate expanse of red soil. On the edge of the perimeter of camp, a tall palm tree towered against the sky. There was no shade around its thin, dry trunk. The sun's rays beat down on the hard ground.

The lone palm tree was in sight of the whole camp. Every single one of the troops, black, white or Indian was able to see the two figures chained to its base.

Captain Carter had lost his temper when he heard what had been planned for Kirkpatrick and Wallis.

'I won't see my men chained up like monkeys,' he had yelled at Macintyre in the officer's *banda*. 'Not for three days in a row.'

'You bloody well will,' Macintyre spat back. 'And they can count themselves lucky. In France they would be shot.'

I felt a mixture of anger and guilt seething inside me. I had checked Wallis and Kirkpatrick's post only a quarter of an hour before the Baluchi patrol came by.

'Surely, Major, there's some other way?'

'This is war. They have to learn to carry out their duties like real soldiers.'

'That kind of punishment only teaches fear,' Carter seethed. 'Not respect for their duty.'

Macintyre sneered. 'Duty, Captain? Well now, that is something you would know about.'

Even Major Reading couldn't stop the punishment going ahead. We found him alone in his tent.

'I'm afraid the colonel has backed Macintyre's decision.'

'But you're on his staff,' Carter said. 'Can't you find a way to stop it?'

Reading shook his head. 'Only on medical grounds. The doctor has already ruled those out.'

'There must be something you can do,' I said.

'Not this time. It's too late. What they did is too serious. And Macintyre found out about it before I did. Once he started the wheels of army discipline rolling, there was nothing I could do.' Reading reached down and shuffled among the books and papers on the trestle table that served as his desk. He pulled out a worn copy of the *Field Service Pocket Book*. He unclasped the leather strap holding the book closed. 'You must've read it for yourselves. *When a sentry in time of war is sleeping upon his post. Maximum punishment – Death.*'

Reading looked up at the two of us. 'I managed to get that nonsense out of their heads early on in the discussions, but there's no more I can do. After all, they *were* sleeping on sentry duty. The colonel's reasoning is that we have to be seen to be doing something about it. We might have been able to overlook it before the fight broke out between your men and the Baluchis. But now we can't. The mood among some of them is near-mutinous. Most of them are Muslims. So are most of the German askaris. A lot of the Baluchis are unhappy about fighting against their fellow believers. And now, on top of that, they caught the same men who called them coolies and niggers sleeping on sentry duty. We can't leave it alone now, after that.'

'Wallis and Kirkpatrick weren't involved in that incident with the Baluchis at all,' I said.

'I know,' Major Reading said. 'But there's nothing any of us can do now to stop it.'

'It's a mistake,' Captain Carter said. 'It'll break their spirit. They'll be no good as soldiers after this.'

Her garden was filled with flowers – a mixture of tropical plants and good old English staples. An enormous frangipani grew above a bed of daisies, a blood-red bougainvillea fought with ivy for space on the stone wall in a sun-filled corner at the side of the house; pansies grew at the base of a tall spreading palm tree. Hyacinths grew in the shade of a cedar tree and there was a birdbath where a flurry of yellow weaver birds flew up into the trees, their bright eyes startled by our presence.

'It's my refuge,' she said.

Inside the house was dark and cool. Persian rugs lay on the polished wooden floors. There was a faint smell of wax, and the odor of jasmine that drifted in through the open windows from a sunlit hedge outside. A clutch of umbrellas and carved walking sticks stood in a large blue Chinese vase at the door. There were books everywhere. They were crammed into the low bookshelves on either side of the fireplace, and piled up on side tables and in the corners of the house.

'They're mostly my husband's,' she said. 'He reads a lot.'

I nodded, uncomfortable now that the subject we had avoided talking about all afternoon had finally been brought up.

I found myself looking out of the small bay window that faced the garden. I suddenly realised how nervous I was.

Helen was standing behind me. 'His name's Peter,' she said quietly.

I turned around to look at her.

'It's his house too. I'll go. If you want me to.'

She reached out to block my way. Her hand was trembling slightly. 'No,' she said. Then, quickly, as if I hadn't noticed, she pulled it away. Her eyes held mine.

'Do you want to stay?'

'Yes,' I said, taking her into my arms. 'Very much.'

A patch of light shone through the curtains and fell on the polished floorboards. I bent my head to kiss her again. There was a tantalising edge of lace against the smooth skin of her breasts. We both moved slowly in the afternoon heat. Tiny beads of sweat formed on her nipples. I leaned forward, closing my eyes, surrendering myself to the feel of her flesh and the taste of her.

The soft shock of her mouth over me, the flickering of her tongue.

The coolness of her delicate fingers. The breath catching in my throat. Her tongue running across the inside of my lips.

Her brown hair spread out sideways like a fan, her arms stretching out in front of her. Her hands clasping and unclasping, pulling at the sheets.

I leaned over and kissed her.

She put a finger gently over my lips.

'Don't say anything. Not now.'

She was sitting opposite me, cross-legged on the bed. Her stomach flat and smooth, her waist narrow, her hips just slightly rounded. The fine triangle of her pubic hair was just visible above her slim ankles; her knees lay almost flat on the rumpled sheets.

'I found a picture of her,' she said finally. 'It was lying under the bed. It must have fallen out when he was packing his suitcase. I found it two days after he had already left for France. She's quite pretty.'

Helen lay back on the pillows, staring at the ceiling. Tears ran slowly down the side of her face. I tried to hold her, but she turned away.

'I wrote to him, but it was a long time before I heard anything. I was alone in the house for all those weeks with just her picture. I put it in an envelope and hid it in the bottom of a drawer, but it didn't help. I didn't know who she was, but her lovely face haunted me. Every memory I had of Peter was overwhelmed by her eyes, by her fine long hair that was so neatly combed. He was gone, away, to the war, possibly even to his death, and all he had left me with was the picture of the girl he was sleeping with. I couldn't confront him, of course, so the wondering about her was the worst. Who was she? Where had they met? How long had it been going on? What had he told her about me?

'In the end, the letter came. He didn't deny it. He said that it had all been a mistake. It was over between them. It was one of the reasons he'd volunteered to go to the war, he said. To get away from her. He asked me to be patient. He was sorry, so sorry, he said. Couldn't we start again, when he came back from the war?'

We were silent together for a long while. She let me take her hand; her palm was cool and dry. Outside, the sun was setting. The air was still warm, but the room grew dark as the last tiny points of light slipped off the edges of the brass of the bed stand.

'But he never did say why he planned to take her photograph with him, when he went away to the war.'

We made love twice more that afternoon. The shade from the trees in the garden falling slowly over the shuttered windows, both of us growing more comfortable with one another as we started to learn the new touch of our bodies. Her elbows, for example, were surprisingly bony, quite unlike any other pair of elbows I had ever negotiated my way around. The rough skin on them contrasted with the soft perfection of her breasts, and I found myself rubbing the hardness on one of her elbows while she dozed in my arms. She woke and felt me doing it. 'Stop it,' she said and twisted inside my arms and pushed herself away from me.

'You don't like them, do you?' She asked, looking up at me. Her hair was in disarray over her face, a few strands of it caught on the swollen moistness of her lips.

'Don't like what?' I asked innocently.

'My elbows,' she replied

'Your elbows are perfect.'

'No they're not.'

'Yes, they are. Absolutely perfect.'

She sat back on her heels. She brushed a few loose strands behind her ear.

'But there is one other problem.'

'What is it?'

'It's too embarrassing. I can't tell you.'

A look of horror passed over her face. 'You have to tell me.'

'I can't.'

'You have to.'

'All right. The problem is that, well, you've got hair on your lips.'

She jumped at me and we both exploded into laughter, collapsing backwards on the bed. She grabbed at my wrists and pinned my hands down against the pillows.

'Your ribs are bony,' she said looking up and down my body, and you've got a thin neck.'

She leaned forward to kiss me. Our tongues met, and I let go, sliding downwards across the sheets, deep into the fullness of her body

'There's hair on your lips now,' she gasped.

Her voice was hoarse in the darkness beside me. Her hands were soft on my chest; her lips were brushing my ear.

'I never expected this,' she said, her voice a whisper as if she were suddenly frightened to speak too loudly. 'The night after I met you, I couldn't sleep. I was furious with myself. I felt that I had made myself appear cheap, flirting with you.

'You didn't contact me, and I tried to think, "well, that's it, a bit of silliness that he didn't take seriously, and it's over. I won't do it again." Of course it wasn't the truth, so trying to think like that didn't do any good.

'I couldn't help it. All I wanted was to see you again, somehow, somewhere. I was furious with you for not finding me, and I was ashamed of myself for not being stronger.'

She squeezed tighter against me, the softness of her body pressed all the way down against mine. She held my head tight in her hands, and turned my face towards hers.

'Quick,' she said. 'No time to think. Tell me again. How do you feel about me?'

I could see Wallis and Kirkpatrick across the open space of baking hot ground. They had not been allowed to wear their sun helmets. They were chained by their wrists and ankles to the tree. There was a thick smear of blood on Wallis' wrist where the metal was chafing the skin. Kirkpatrick's nose and cheekbones were turning scarlet and beginning to peel in the hot sun. Sweat was pouring off his temples. His uniform shirt was stained with dark patches of sweat.

Two porters were standing at the edge of the clearing. One of them pointed at Kirkpatrick's face. The other laughed. Kirkpatrick kicked out angrily in their direction. The weight of the chain jerked his foot sideways. Both porters laughed. Then they turned and walked slowly away. They didn't look back.

Number 1 Field Punishment was to be imposed for a maximum of two hours a day for three days in a row. This was their first day. The effects of thirst and heat exhaustion were bad enough, but it was the humiliation that was the real point. There were two more days to go.

It was Major Reading and Captain Carter between them who found a way to cut the punishment short. And it was to Sergeant Hassani Juma and Corporal John Akul that they turned for help.

That evening, after Wallis and Kirkpatrick had been released, and marched back to the large tent that served as a detention barracks, I happened to be speaking to Major Macintyre in front of his tent. Sergeant Juma came up to where we were talking.

Major Macintyre was sitting in a camp chair under the fly that extended out in front of his tent. He was wearing long khaki shorts and an open-necked shirt.

'What is it?' he asked Juma irritably.

'A problem, sir.'

'I guessed as much. What is it?'

'Corporal Akul reports that our men are laughing, sir.'

'About what, sergeant?'

Juma hesitated just a moment for answering.

'About Wallis and Kirkpatrick, sir.'

Juma let the statement stand for a moment to sink in. 'The porters are also laughing,' he added for good measure.

Macintyre sat back in his chair and looked at Juma. I could see he was examining the African sergeant carefully, trying to work out what the man had to gain by coming to him like this.

'Captain Carter sent you over here, then?' he asked.

Juma hadn't expected this.

'N-no, sir.'

'But I saw him speaking to you this morning.'

'Yes, sir. He was – he was asking about the man in my platoon. The one the sniper shot.'

Macintyre hesitated. I found myself trying hard not to smile; it was obvious what Reading and Carter were doing. Any further pleas for mercy for Wallis and Kirkpatrick would just make them look weak, or worse, favouring their own men, but Macintyre could not ignore the bald statement that white men were being humiliated in front of black men. It was a given in this war that the white man's prestige must be maintained at all costs. I had heard this same issue discussed a hundred times at dinner in the officer's *banda*. Everyone understood that the future of the colony – perhaps of all the colonies – depended on the white man maintaining his position of superiority in this war.

It was a stroke of genius by Reading and Carter. The issue of white soldiers being shamed publicly in front of black soldiers was a real one. Macintyre would be forced to act and report it to the colonel's staff where Reading would take up the issue. But in acting, Macintyre would lose face himself.

Macintyre stared at Juma. His eyes were cold and hard.

'Discipline must be maintained whether Captain Carter or you like the way it's being done or not.' He waved his hand angrily.

'Dismissed, Sergeant.'

'Thank you, sir.'

The next morning, Wallis and Kirkpatrick stayed under guard in the tent. The chief medical officer on the colonel's staff had issued an order that, in view of the unseasonably hot sun, to continue with No 1 Field Punishment was too risky for the men's health.

7

WE WERE WORKING OUR WAY through the crowds of people on Commissioner Street. The sky was blue, but shadows from the gathering rain clouds slipped over the cast-iron balconies on the front of the buildings. They drifted across the metalled surface of the road, tumbling light and shade across the gleaming new tramlines.

I was struggling with a large paper bag. It was filled with packets of sugar, flour, a pat of butter and a host of other groceries. I almost dropped it as we crossed the road. I found myself laughing out loud at my clumsiness.

We were halfway across the street. She turned and looked at me. 'What is it?'

'It's just funny how things work out. I wanted to take you out to a film to have a good time, to impress you. Instead we end up looking for groceries.'

She watched my face for a moment. I felt my heart being drawn up into her eyes.

'Can't you see? This is the most obvious sign I could have given about how I feel. I don't need you to do something special. I don't need you to try and impress me. What I want to know is whether I can be comfortable with you doing something silly and ordinary, like going shopping.'

The risk she had taken in trusting me was so enormous that at first I was almost overwhelmed by it. My heart was in my throat at the wonder of her every time I was permitted to unwrap the nakedness of her body. Slowly, over the weeks and months she drew me up into the wild, intoxicating journey of entering into her life through the perfume of her skin and each soft new curve of her body.

We had so little time to take that journey; we entered into it recklessly, driven by the need to go as far into each other's lives as we could before the war came and took everything away from us.

I knew I would have to volunteer sooner or later – the fighting was going badly and the pressure was building on men like me who hadn't signed up yet. But now I had a reason not to go; so I delayed and tried not to think about what would become inevitable.

Late every night after I had finished my work in the office, I would walk over to her house. The streets of Johannesburg were dark. The tall jacaranda and eucalyptus trees loomed over me, their branches and leaves silhouetted against the stars in the night sky. The wonder of her and what was happening to my life because of her was so close that it seemed almost unreal. I walked on through the darkness in a sort of daze, feeling my way carefully along the empty moonlit roads, and it was only when I saw Helen's face at the garden gate that I knew it was real.

We lay half asleep, drifting in the cool night air. The bed sheets were twisted and rumpled. They lay half-across our naked bodies and half-tumbled down on to the floor. The curtains billowed in the hazy darkness.

Helen slept stretched out and endlessly soft against me, her head tucked in against my arm. Her hair tickled my cheek as her breath rose and fell. The smell of her and of our lovemaking drifted up into my heart, calming, soothing me.

Somewhere in the darkness I had fallen asleep. I woke to the soft sound of her crying. Tears were on her cheeks. For a while I said nothing. I pretended to be asleep. But in the end I asked the question that I been hiding for months.

'What are you going to do? About him?'

She turned and lay on her back. She stared at the ceiling.

'We can't talk about that, not now.'

'We can't pretend – not forever anyway. One day he'll come back.'

'Or you'll go.' There was a sudden catch of bitterness in her voice.

'To the war, yes. But not because of anything else. I'll never leave you. Not unless you want me to.'

She turned away from me.

'No. I don't want that.'

'Then what?'

She sat up. She put her face in her hands, sobbing for a moment. Then she drew a breath. It calmed her. She looked at me in the darkness.

'I want to be free. I don't want to be betrayed again.'

I sat up in bed. The anger and the hurt exploding in my chest.

She turned her head away from me.

'This is all that matters to you, isn't it? The fucking.'

I threw the sheet off. I got up and walked over to where my trousers where hanging. She watched me as I stepped into them. Rage made my movements jerky and hard.

'I'm sorry,' she said.

I turned my back to her. I was groping for my shirt in the moonlight. I faced her as I slid an arm into the sleeve. 'It's not enough.'

'What is enough for you then? What do you want from me?' Her voice was loud, each word harsh and exploding in the darkness.

'I want you to choose. To choose. Between him and me.'

Smoke from the cooking fires hung over the camp, turning the sky over the bush a pale lilac with streaks of gold. The exercises were finished for the day, and I went over to where my platoon had their tents. Hooper, Watson and Williams were sitting on the sandy soil, scooping stew out of their mess tins.

I greeted them in the dusk light, and, amid a banging of cutlery and mess tins, they started standing up to salute.

'Easy,' I said, holding up my hand to halt any further moves in the elaborate pantomime that was unfolding in front of me.

They clattered back down again, putting their mess tins down beside them.

'Heard any news about the rugby, sir?' Watson sang out cheerfully.

Watson's most obvious distinguishing characteristic was his thick mop of red hair. He was also the son of one of the wealthiest directors of a bank. The story was that his father had been involved in the financial structuring of the War Bonds sold in the Dominions to help finance the war. I liked him the most of the three. He cared far less about social position than the other two – perhaps because he could afford not to, but it still made a refreshing change to the self-conscious snobbery Hooper and Williams sometimes exhibited towards the other men in the regiment. He was also the leader among the three of them.

They were obsessed by sports – the results published on the back page of the newspapers of the most obscure tennis or golf tournament played somewhere on the globe would keep them talking and arguing for days. I didn't share their vicarious fascination with the manly strivings of others on the sports field, but there was a certain charm in the enthusiasm it generated within them. There was a boyish innocence in their belief that a well-hit ball or a stoutly tackled opponent was the surest measure of human experience.

'No, Watson,' I said. 'As it happens, I have been marching through the bush of East Africa all of the last week.'

He smiled disarmingly at me; the same smile, I felt sure, that he had turned on any number of outraged clients and dissatisfied managers.

'Of course, sir. I just thought that, well, you officers might have information that we men don't get.'

'We do, Watson. Lots of it. Not about rugby, though.'

'No, sir. Quite so. I'm sorry.'

I began to walk away. A few paces on, I relented. Some messages had come through, just that afternoon. Not all of them had been strictly military business.

'Western Province won. The score was 19 to 12.'

Watson broke into a large grin. 'That is good news. Thank *you*, sir.'

'Yes, sir, good news. Thank you,' Hooper and Williams echoed.

I left them where they were and started walking back to the tent I shared with Scheepers. It was my favourite hour in Africa, when the heat was cooling down and you felt good after a day's sweaty work. I loved the aromatic smell of smoke from the thorn hardwoods that curled around the tents. In the distance at the edge of camp, I could hear some of the porters singing a Swahili song. Further away, an *imam* was calling the faithful to prayer, the rhythms of his voice echoing over the darkening thorn trees.

Among the rows of 61st Pioneer and Baluchi tents I caught glimpses of men taking out their prayer mats. They unlaced their heavy leather boots and began performing their ritual cleansing with their precious water ration. They washed their nose and mouth and faces first and then their bare feet. They were careful to allow a few drops of the clear water in their canteens to tumble and spread out along the tiny veins of the earth, churned now into grey, thirsty dust by the thousands of marching boots. One by one, as they finished their ablutions and readied themselves, I saw men turning and kneeling. They bowed deeply in the direction of the Qibla, towards Mecca, their bodies and their prayers following the ancient lines of memory and faith.

Nearer to me was the comforting sound of water being poured into buckets as our men began their own business of washing the sweat and dust off their faces and from behind their necks. I could hear the gentle clinking sound of the lid of a kettle being replaced, and the dull *thuk thuk* of someone stirring a pot.

'Pass me that razor, won't you,' I heard Wallis ask someone in a muffled voice in the row of tents behind me.

A huge white light, like a searchlight, flashed into the fading dusk. A tall spurt of red earth shot up into the air from the rows of tents where the Baluchis were camped. Then in a sudden, rolling crash came the thunder of the explosion, shattering the air around me. I dived and half-fell, half-rolled onto the ground. My ears were ringing.

Screams came from behind the rows of tents, and loud shouting in Urdu, Afrikaans and English – commands, swearing and harsh yells of agony.

I looked up. All over camp, men were shouting. Carter was in front of me in the lane between the tents. Sergeant Visser was next to him.

'What's going on?'

'Looks like some askari bastard crept in,' Visser shouted above the commotion. 'He put a mine under one of the Baluchi cooking places. It went off when they lit their fire on top of it.'

We ran over to where the commotion was coming from. Stretcher bearers were running in from every direction. Two men were sitting on the ground in front of us. One of them was holding his bleeding, twisted shin. The bone was shattered and his foot hung at an angle to his leg. He was groaning as he rocked back and forth with the pain. The other was sitting back, his turban askew, blood pouring from underneath it down his face.

Corporal Reynolds, Kirkpatrick and Steinberg were running over to them. Sergeant Visser and Wallis, still with white shaving foam all over his face, were close behind. Hooper and Williams held their rifles. They were looking out beyond the perimeter. I glimpsed Watson behind a row of tents. Corporal Reynolds was waving at the stretcher bearers to come over to where the two wounded soldiers were.

A frying pan was stuck; handle first, into the sand. Prayer mats lay tumbled and forgotten, scattered on the ground like pages torn away from the spine of a book. Fragments of burning and blackened wood lay between them. A piece had lodged itself in the fold of a tent and was burning a growing hole in the dirty white canvas.

'Water! Bring water,' Jemadar Khan screamed from out of the growing darkness.

A soldier came running with a canteen of water. He shook it over the flames. Another rushed up and threw a bowl of dirty soapsuds on it.

We hurried closer. The medics already had the soldier with the mangled leg on a stretcher and were sprinting towards the hospital tent. Two more lay on the ground, twisted, blood pouring from their bodies. Havildar Lal was bending over one of them, trying to stem the flow of blood.

There was a dark hole in the ground where the cooking fire had been. Muhammed Din was kneeling down cradling Rahman in his arms. Rahman was dead, his tunic smeared thick with blood, his turban unravelled crazily, the long fabric falling over his body like a shroud. Muhammed Din was weeping, the sobs shaking his huge body; his tears falling onto his friend's face.

Jemadar Khan was standing barefoot in the fading light, staring at the scene in front of him. He turned, and was surprised to see me and Carter.

'So. You came to help us?'

'We're too late,' Carter replied.

'None of the others came.'

'Revenge,' Carter said, pacing up and down in the cool shade of the grass *banda* that served as an officer's mess. The rest of us – Matthews, Scheepers, Miller and I, were sitting on the rough plank benches around the edge of the large hut. Reading and the other two majors had called us in with some of the Baluchi and Rhodesian officers to discuss what we should do about the sniper and the bomb. The Germans were beginning to threaten us more frequently now. Three nights ago, Johnson had struck a match and held it to light one of his cigarettes – a tiny orange flame in a sea of darkness, and two quick shots had rung out from the bush outside camp.

'This time the sniper missed,' Reynolds bawled at him in front of the other men. 'But he's there, waiting for his chance. The chance that monkeys like you are hell-bent on giving him.'

Then the Rhodesians had almost caught one of the spies in their camp the day before. He was posing as a porter, but someone saw the glint of steel under his ragged shirt. It was a German bayonet. They chased him, but the man was strong and agile. One of the Rhodesians got close enough to make a grab at him. The askari slashed his bayonet in a fast, skilful figure-of-eight, slicing the Rhodesian across the inside of his left hand and severing the tendons in his right forearm, then turned and forced his way through the thorn *zariba*. He left bloodied chunks of his skin behind on the long white thorns as he fled, but he had disappeared into the bush long before anyone else could get close enough to grab at him again.

'We must respond,' Carter went on, banging the bottom of his fist into the palm of his other hand. 'It's bad for the morale of our men to be forced to sit here waiting for the next sneak attack and not be able to strike back themselves. We must show the Germans that they cannot act against us with impunity.'

'What do you suggest?' It was Major Reading.

'A quick raid by half a dozen hand-picked men. We move through the bush at night and get near their camp. We strike hard. Then we run before they know what's hit them.'

Reading smiled. 'And who would lead this raid?'

'I would be willing to,' Carter said.

'What about you, Major?' Reading looked over at Van Hasselt. 'Would you do it?'

Macintyre glared at Reading, infuriated by the obvious omission. Van Hasselt gave a thin smile. 'Of course, but if Captain Carter wants to –'

'Captain Carter's right. And I want to go too,' Jemadar Khan said angrily. 'After all, it was one of our men they killed.'

Major Reading lifted up his hand. '*Stop*,' he said. 'No one's going out on any revenge attacks.'

'We can't just sit here, day after day, doing nothing,' Carter said.

Major Reading looked at him. 'You'll let the colonel and me make the decisions about who does what, Captain. And you'll be told as soon as they have been made.'

The next morning after our fight, I went to the Wanderer's Cricket

Ground to sign up for the war. I told myself I couldn't avoid doing it any longer. No matter what had happened between Helen and me, and no matter what might happen, the war was bigger than us both. As a man, and as a subject of the British Empire, there was no longer any getting around it – I had to go to the war.

The truth was, of course, that as I stood in the line that fine, sunny morning, waiting to sign my papers, I was ashamed of myself. I could have waited, but I knew that I had chosen to volunteer that morning because I was punishing Helen for still loving her husband.

They gave me two weeks to sort out my affairs before I had to take the train to the training camp.

That afternoon I went to see her. My heart was pounding as she opened the door for me. Inside her house was cool and shaded; outside the sun was beating down as hard and bright as remorse.

We stood there for a while. The polished wooden floors reflected the sunlight from outside. Through the window I could see the courtyard garden behind the house. Water spilled out of the crumbling stone fountain, her favourite climbing roses gleamed pink against a brick wall. A shiny beetle crawled across the edge of the open window.

'You're going, aren't you?'

'I have to.'

She closed her eyes for a moment. Then she nodded.

'About last night. I am sorry. I shouldn't have said it.'

'It doesn't matter.'

'Yes. It does matter. More than ever now.'

I took her in my arms. Somewhere from deep within me, I heard my own voice, helpless with love, tearing itself out of me, calling across the space that ran between our pasts, and the questions that lay across our future.

'I love you, I love you, I love you.'

Then her fingers were touching my cheek. She was softly saying my name, over and over again. Her voice was filled with happiness.

'I love you too. Will you ever understand how much?'

8

SALAITA. THAT WAS THE name on everyone's lips. The rumours at last were becoming reality. It was almost certain now that Salaita Hill would be the chance to prove ourselves. From what I had seen on the campaign maps it was situated roughly half-way between our camp at Maktau and the town of Taveta on the border between British East Africa and *Deutsch-Ostafrika*. The town and the area around it had been taken and held by a few hundred askaris at the beginning of the war. The only practical route into German territory was through what was known as the 'Taveta Gap', a narrow corridor of flat land that lay open between the northern end of the Pare Mountains and the southern slopes of the Kilimanjaro foothills.

Salaita Hill was the crucial barrier to our progress through the Taveta Gap. The front lines had shifted when the Germans took Taveta and marched as far east as the territory around Salaita. For nearly two years now, the slopes of that small mound of rock and earth with its askari defenders had marked the outermost border of our civilisation. Beyond it lay the unknown expanses of enemy territory and the tempting promise of the victory that we so craved.

We had been chosen to dislodge the enemy forces on Salaita and spearhead the British advance into the heartland of German East Africa. The whispers had been gaining momentum for a few days. The Loyal North Lancs, the Rhodesians, the Baluchis, they would be joining us in an offensive to drive the Germans and their askaris from their arrogant perch.

'It'll hardly be much of a scrap,' Lieutenant Matthews said one evening in the officer's *banda*. 'I wish they'd give us something bigger to get our teeth into.'

'A few hundred kaffirs squatting in the mud on the top of a hill,' Lieutenant Miller added. 'We'll chase them off in an hour.'

'It'll take longer than that,' Carter said. 'Don't forget the East Africa Brigade launched an attack on Salaita a year ago. They were beaten back decisively.'

Van Hasselt smiled. 'You forget, Captain that most of us are Boers. We kept your army running around the veld for years. A few natives with their rusty old rifles are not going to delay the South African Brigade for long.'

'We'll drive those flat-nosed monkeys yelping out of their burrows with a whip,' one of the officers from the 6th added.

Carter was listening, the blood rising into his cheeks. 'Von Lettow-Vorbeck and his askaris are a force to be reckoned with. For Christ's sake, don't underestimate them.'

I noticed Major Macintyre said nothing. But his eyes flicked across in the lamplight, watching Captain Carter.

The following day was scorching hot. Heat waves shimmered above the bush. Two aeroplanes roared over camp, shaking the tents and flagpoles, whipping up dust and then shrinking into tiny dots as they climbed against the white mass of cloud over Kilimanjaro.

Corporal Reynolds glared up into the air, shading his eyes with his hand, watching the arc of the planes disappearing into the horizon. Wallis and the others stopped what they were doing to gaze at the planes in the faraway sky.

Sergeant Visser brushed the thin coating of dust off the front of his bulging, sweat-stained tunic. He took a drag from the cigarette pinched between his heavy thumb and forefinger, and glared up at the sky from under his sun helmet.

'More reconnaissance missions,' he said. 'They're not going to help. We need to get out there and look at the damn hill. I want to see for myself what I'm leading my boys into.'

For a long time we could still hear a thin thread of sound in the distance. Then the *whirr* of insects in the noonday heat of the bush drowned it out.

Twenty minutes later the sound grew again out of the blue sky. There was only one plane.

'Poor bastards,' Reynolds said.

A company of Baluchis was sent out to find the pilot and his observer. Their orders were to burn the plane to prevent it from being used by the Germans. They were led by Jemadar Khan. He chose Sergeant Juma and Corporal Akul to find secret ways through the thick bush behind the German lines.

The images of horror in the distant blue sky drifted down to us in pieces – the mute evidence of the twisted wreckage, snippets of conversation from Jemadar Khan, and the pilot's own fragments of memory drifting, falling through his head, over and over, as he lay in the hospital tent.

A well-aimed rifle bullet had pierced the cooling pipes of the engine of the aeroplane, ricocheted through the light canvas of the fuselage and killed the observer in the front seat. The engine spluttered twice and then stopped. The pilot had watched the earth come towards him as he floated down through the cool layers of air towards the undulating savanna below. His body trapped inside the fuselage was light and fragile, hollowed out with fear like the bones of a bird. He felt himself jerked and thrown about as the plane smashed into the hard earth, snapping a tree trunk and then spinning and buckling around the next.

The observer's body was hanging out of the wreckage. The pilot was wandering alone in the bush. His hands were bleeding from where he had torn himself out of the wreckage. He was concussed and badly bruised from the crash. He limped through the thorn trees, unable to find his way through the mass of game tracks cut into the red earth. One side of his flying goggles had been smashed and was filled with blood. The other was covered in dust and grease.

Jemadar Khan and his Baluchis found him sprawled out against an anthill, breathing heavily and in pain. He saw them coming, dim shapes through a red fog. He tried to run, but fell.

Two of the Baluchis rushed over to him. One of them was Muhammed Din. He gave his rifle to the other soldier and picked up the pilot. He carried him all the way back to camp, cradling him in his enormous arms. Four of the others carried the observer's broken body in a stretcher.

That far-off explosion of liquid fuel and burning wood and canvas sent its shockwaves all through our men. For more than an hour those of us waiting in camp watched the column of black smoke rise up into the distant sky and then slowly burn itself out. The Baluchis sent a few scouts ahead to report that the pilot was alive, and the news of what had happened spread quickly through the camp.

I didn't even know the pilot or the observer, but the shooting of one of our planes frightened me. The Germans had no aircraft at all here in East Africa. Those fragile Be2C biplanes, obsolete already on the Western Front, were supposed to be one of our greatest advantages over the Germans. To see or rather, to hear, one of them plucked out of the sky like an annoying insect was unnerving. We knew, now, that our own confrontation with the enemy was growing nearer. I needed to know what I could count on and what I could not when we finally faced them. That afternoon of the shooting down of the plane I decided to confront Captain Carter with my questions about his past.

Sometime late that afternoon, I approached with a list of supplies for the company. We sat down at a folding camp table outside his tent and began going through them. I didn't know how to begin. The arrival of Jemadar Khan and the rescue party solved the problem for me.

We heard the commotion and looked up to see the column passing through the gates heading towards the hospital tents.

'You see what I'm getting at?' Carter said, looking up from the pile of lists that the quartermaster had drawn up. He nodded over at the straggle of tired, smoke-blackened men led by Jemadar Khan and Muhammed Din. 'I learned this in Afghanistan – even our most modern weapons don't make us invulnerable. It's quite probable that that machine was brought down by a black man armed with an obsolete rifle dating back to the Franco-Prussian war.'

He shook his head. He picked up a handwritten list of boots and sizes and was about to start reading from it.

I watched him for a moment before I sprang the question I had wanted to ask for weeks.

'What exactly was it you learned in Afghanistan? There was something else, wasn't there?'

Carter started forward over the camp table, pushing the papers onto the ground. He jabbed an emphatic forefinger at me. 'Lieutenant, you have no right –'

We stayed like that for a long moment. Finally, he lowered his hand and slumped back in his chair.

'There's no point,' Carter said. 'You've heard something already. You're going to hear the rest of the story from somebody, so you might as well hear it from me.'

He put his hands together in front of him; his thumbs pressed against his lips. He glanced down at the ground for a moment before looking up again.

'Don't think I'm trying to set the record straight, or anything like that,' Carter's voice was hard. 'I said what I had to at the court-martial. I've never had any reason to say anything else.

'I was a young subaltern on campaign on the North-West Frontier – the Waziristan border. A minor rebellion had broken out among the hill tribes – the sort of thing that usually never even makes the papers. I didn't understand the details of what had sparked it off; something about taxes, coupled with a village border dispute over land and sheep grazing rights – a problem any decent colonial administrator could have sorted out sitting cross-legged on a rug and drinking a few cups of the local tea for an hour or two.

'It was a mistake to have allowed it to reach the stage of armed rebellion. Once it had gone that far, though, troops had to be sent in. The border up there means little to the Pathan tribes who live in the area. They have ancient connections amongst each other. They take little or no account of what we think as to the difference between Afghanistan territory and the British Empire. There was a danger of the unrest spreading – becoming something far more serious and widespread than just an outbreak of tribal unrest. It had to be crushed before it got out of hand.

'It wasn't my first time commanding a platoon under fire. Months before, we had had to fight our way into a besieged stone hut where a chieftain's daughter was being held after being kidnapped by her jilted suitor.

'Then I was with a column of troops caught in an ambush by bandits in one of the narrow rocky passes in the area. We spent five hours in the blazing sun that day, with bullets whistling around our heads. I was mentioned in dispatches for bravery under fire for taking over one of the Gatling guns when the gunner was shot. I fired bursts whenever I saw movement. We were outnumbered and without my bringing it back into action, we would have been overrun.'

He looked over at me to judge my reaction. I might have looked a little sceptical. It seemed too clichéd. The North-West Frontier, Afghanistan, Waziristan, hill tribes... it could have come straight out of one of Kipling's more sentimental adventure yarns. *The sort of thing that usually never even makes the papers.* A strange detail to throw in. I suddenly doubted the trust that I had decided to place in him. I didn't want to be lied to.

'I was an up and coming young officer, and I was pleased to have been selected. It was my first important campaign. The uprising had started in a few villages in the remote mountains, but it was spreading. It had reached that dangerous and volatile stage where the origin of the trouble no longer mattered. It had taken on a life of its own. Men were picking up arms in every village throughout the countryside. Worse, we had information that gangs of tribal warriors armed with *jezails* and even Lee-Enfields were coming across the border from Afghanistan in growing numbers.

'Every day there was news that the headman of another village had declared his allegiance to the rebels. It was a matter of weeks – days, maybe – before the prestige, even the stability of the Empire itself would have been threatened.

'Something had to be done. The colonel of our regiment received orders from Lahore and late that same afternoon he gathered us together on the parade ground in Peshawar. We marched out that night – unusual, but the situation was becoming grave. The rebels were gathering an army in the hills and it was our job to smash it before it threatened first the trading routes and then perhaps even the cities of the Punjab themselves.'

Carter paused here for a moment. He picked up a fountain pen off the camp table and began fiddling with it. I was suspicious and said nothing, and waited for him to continue if he so wished. I sensed something at war within him. I couldn't tell whether he was deciding how gullible I was, or whether he could trust me. But he couldn't back out now, and he went on.

'It was three days' march into the border foothills. In the steep valleys it was difficult to tell whether we were on our own land or had crossed the Durand Line into Afghan territory.

'The column bivouacked on the side of a mountain, and the colonel selected me to lead a reconnaissance patrol further up into the high country.

'It was something of an honour for me, such a young officer, to have been selected to lead the patrol. I was fully conscious of what it meant and very proud of myself for it. We set off at dawn the next day, marching over the exposed stony ground. Somehow we must have crossed the border into Afghan territory without knowing it. It was about noon – the sun was high in the sky, anyway – when the first shot came. One of my men dropped dead right there at my side, a bullet through the heart.

'I don't remember what happened next except for the fact that I froze up with terror when I heard the sound of the shot.'

Carter stared across the table at me as he said this.

'I stood there, unable to act. The one thing I remember was my sergeant looking over at me and saying, 'Come *on*, sir.'

'I saw the men looking at me for orders, too, but I couldn't say anything. If I had acted quickly and decisively, we might have been able to avoid the disaster that followed. They were angry and determined men, those Pathans, and they had planned their attack perfectly. They opened up with their rifles from the hills around us. It only took a few minutes. My men milled around helplessly, taking cover where they could, behind rocks and in shallow depressions in the ground. I watched it happen around me as if in a dream. Something had snapped in my mind. To this day, I don't know what it was. There was nothing conscious about it. I don't know how to explain it. I was not *reminded* of anything that had happened. I just couldn't stand to hear gunfire any more. It was as if I had used up my chances. I had this wild notion that the bullets that had missed me when I had been manning the machine gun in the previous ambush were coming back to get me this time.

'I fell on the ground, paralysed by fear. My sergeant dragged me behind a rock, just as the Pathans descended on us with their swords and long knives. It was utter chaos. Panic set in and my men tried to flee. Over three-quarters of the men in my platoon were killed or wounded before they managed to scrabble their way down the hillside. Somehow the sergeant managed to rally a few of them and get me and the survivors back to base.

'The Pathans came to the perimeter of the camp that night and threw a sack over the fence. It was filled with the noses and ears of the men, dead and wounded, whom we had left behind on that stony hillside.'

Carter paused. He was looking down at the table in front of us.

'Of course there was an inquest. Because I was so young I was censured, but not stripped of my rank as I had expected.

'The sergeant faced a separate court-martial. I was one of the witnesses. I said I couldn't remember much about what had happened, but that he had taken over. Somehow the sergeant was punished. They accused him of something like "tardiness in taking action".

'He just stood there at attention in the court as they read out the sentence. I felt ashamed, because I knew that it was my terror and the panic that had resulted from it that had cost those men their lives. The sergeant had really been the hero of the day. When I collapsed he took action, and saved what he could of the situation. I owe my life to him and to the men who didn't panic, who fought back so bravely.

'I didn't say enough in my sergeant's defence, partly because the fear had blurred my memory and partly because I was scared of implicating myself even further. It destroyed both his career and his reputation. He became known as the sergeant who had let his officer down. It is the knowledge that I didn't stand up for him in turn that makes it worse. I know it's not much, but the only thing I can say in my own defence was that I was very young. I was at the beginning of my career and soldiering was all I ever wanted to do. The thought of losing my prospects in the army was intolerable. I accepted what the court-martial said, and even came to half-believe in it for a while.

'But they were wrong. And after I had spent some more time in the army, I saw that. Years later when I was on leave back in England I went to the cottage where my sergeant had retired. He met me at the garden gate. He had become a thin, white-haired old man. He was frail and he looked far older than his sixty-one years. The strain of his humiliation had taken its toll on his health. We spoke about what had happened, and I apologised. His hand rattled the teacup in its saucer and he smiled thinly. He said he understood, but I knew he didn't. There are certain things – betrayals – that you can never be forgiven for. I've learned that now. Time doesn't heal all wounds.'

Carter looked up at me. 'I must add one thing, though. I never failed again. And I have fought in many battles since then.' His voice had regained its usual combative, powerful edge. 'There is not a single soldier in the world who isn't ashamed of something he has done or not done in the heat of battle. Shame is the hidden wound of battle. We carry it with us always.'

I regarded him evenly. 'I wasn't judging you,' I said.

'No?'

'Well, yes, in the beginning, when you started telling me.'

Carter's gaze was steady. 'I wasn't making any kind of excuse when I talked about shame and battle. I was stating a fact. It is something you will come to learn.'

I understood then why people hated him. You would have expected with a past like his, he would have tried harder to make friends or at least allies.

'Why did you stay in the army? Your career and your reputation were damaged. Why didn't you resign, make a fresh start in business or something? People do it all the time.'

'I thought about doing just that,' Carter said 'but in the end I knew I had to face up to what I had done. We've each only got one life to live. I decided not to run away from mine. Also, I learned something from what happened – that there is only one moral way to lead men into battle. To live with your conscience you can order men to go only where you are willing to go yourself.'

For a moment neither of us spoke, and then Carter leaned over and began picking up the lists that had fallen onto the ground.

'But what about Major Macintyre?' I asked. 'What is it between you and him?'

Carter smiled – a thin, bitter smile.

'Those years in India. He was so ambitious then, desperate to succeed. At first everyone thought of him as the brightest, most capable of all the cadets, but I caught him cheating in his officer's exam. It was a terrible shock, because I also had thought so highly of him up until then. I had to report him, though. I had learned in my own life that you can't have half-trained, dishonest officers leading men into battle – men's lives are at stake. I believe the incident held up his chances of promotion for quite a number of years. He couldn't stand it that a coward – someone who had collapsed on the battlefield – could be allowed to make a judgement about him. Certainly because of me, though, he was never given a battlefield command, and he never made anything of himself in the army. Now, here in Africa, he wants to undo the past and revenge himself on me at the same time.'

9

AT LAST WE HAD BEGUN TO LEARN something of war. From the snipers and the sneak bomb attack we had felt the hot, trembling brink of fear, but we didn't know where its centre lay, or understand yet what fear meant to each one of us. We had no idea what we would do when we were faced with it. More than anything, we had hoped that in coming to war we would one day be able to say that we knew fear; that we had seen it in our lives and that we had triumphed over it. Some deep instinct in us wanted to go close to the very edge of life, so that we could come back knowing we had lived life to its fullest. *And what if you did not come back?* You could not think that way – even we, innocent of blood and of the cost of it to our own lives, knew that much.

We marched out on pre-dawn reconnaissance missions towards Salaita, once, twice – each time convinced that this would be the day. On the second occasion, we forced our way through the thick bush as the sun was coming up behind the thorn trees on a clear pink sky. We were advancing while the heat of the sun broke through the beauty of the morning. Still we marched further, blind and sweating in the thick bush, unable to see more than a few yards around us.

I was supposed to lead, so I dared not show my confusion. I kept on, following what I hoped was the direction Captain Carter had ordered me to take. Sergeant Visser was at my side, plunging through the grass and thorn trees, on and on, as I had been ordered to do, hoping that we would not stumble into an ambush.

No one said anything. For long minutes the bush was silent, the heat pressing down around us. There was just the creak of leather and the rustling of boots crashing through the undergrowth. There was a bugle call to halt. Then another, further away, where the Rhodesians were, calling on them to attack. Thunder broke out behind us, and then the sound fell in front of us like huge sheets of steel crashing down. The shelling was landing where Salaita was.

'Whose is it?' Kirkpatrick asked, crouching down in the bush, his voice hushed. 'Ours or theirs?'

'It's all right,' Sergeant Visser said. 'It's outgoing. It's ours.'

'How can you tell the difference?'

Visser looked sideways over his rifle at Kirkpatrick. He took a moment before replying.

'You'll learn. Just keep your head down now.'

'But –'

'Shut your fucking mouth,' Corporal Reynolds hissed from his hiding place in the bush a few yards away. 'Your job this morning is to look out for the Germans.'

A commotion broke out ahead. There was shouting in Swahili from the German askaris, and then the loud, flat *bang-bang* and the puffs of smoke from their black-powder rifles. Sporadic firing broke out here and there along the line. Men were dropping to their knees, lying on their stomachs, working the bolts of their Lee-Enfields, shooting back at the Germans.

I saw one of the men in our regiment huddled down behind a large rock, his rifle on the ground next to him. His eyes were screwed shut under his sun helmet and he flinched every time a shot rang out. Major Macintyre came striding through the long grass, deliberately ignoring the bullets that whizzed in the air around him. He came up to the frightened soldier and stood over him.

'Get on your feet,' he screamed at the man. A loud shot rang out from an askari rifle nearby and the soldier hunched down even further. Macintyre exploded in rage. He grabbed the soldier by the front of his tunic and hauled him to his feet. He drew his arm back and slapped the man across the face, then shoved him backwards. He sprawled in the dust, a thin line of blood trickling from his nose.

'*Pick up your fucking rifle and shoot back,*' Macintyre roared. The man scrabbled forward on his hands and knees and picked up his rifle. His hands were shaking. The barrel wobbled, but he turned and faced in the direction of the enemy.

Another volley of shots rang out. Macintyre leaned down and yelled again. His voice was drowned out by the gunfire, but I saw the frightened young soldier's shoulder jerk from the recoil of his rifle as he fired the first shot of his war.

There was chaos all around me. My heart was pounding, but nothing had brought the battle close enough to me for me to feel fear. It wasn't real yet. It was almost as if I were watching the whole thing happen to someone else.

I saw Major Macintyre striding down the line. I knew this was the first time he was encountering hostile fire, distant and sporadic though it was. I could feel the sweat of fear at my temples and the cold hollowness in my gut, but he seemed to thrive on it.

A few more shots rang out and then the askaris were running, dark ghosts disappearing back into the bush. *Crrack, crack,* the sharp sounds of our Lee-Enfields opening up everywhere. The firing breaking out along the line.

'They're running!' It was Lieutenant Matthews' voice. 'Can you believe it? They haven't got the guts to face us. They're fucking running already.'

'*Hold* your positions!' It was Major Van Hasselt's voice. 'Don't go after them.'

There was more firing, and bugles. We moved forward in the bush until we came to a clearing. I could just see Salaita through the grass and thorns. It was a low hill with sangars – defensive breastworks made of stones – dotted across its gentle slope. A German Imperial eagle and a green banner with the white crescent moon of Islam flew above the stone fortifications on its crest. Jemadar Khan had told me that the fact that the Germans had tried to appropriate that holy symbol for themselves and their askaris had enraged the Baluchis. There appeared to be trenches in front of the hill, with a thick cordon of barbed wire in front of them. The massed layers of coils were tied on to stakes, thorn trees and anthills. But if they would bring up the artillery and bombard it, it could be cut – and then we would be through. Germans and askaris were running up and down the slopes, carrying boxes of ammunition, readying themselves for a fight.

There was some more firing in the distance from the north where the Rhodesians were – machine guns. It went on for a while and then stopped. There was no answer from Salaita. I could just see a few men on the slope of the hill. The rest were behind their stone sangars, waiting.

The stillness of the bush. Heat. One by one, the insects began to call again in the depths of the bush. A few minutes went by. We were tense, waiting in the heat for the order to advance. Then a bugle rang out, its sound limp and muffled in the long grass and the thorn trees. Withdraw.

'*Why?*' I heard Burger asking Sergeant Visser. 'We *had* them. We could have taken that damned hill. There were so few of them. They'll bring up reinforcements now. We'll never get another chance like this.'

Visser wiped the sweat out of his eyes with the back of his hand. Then he shook his head as he stared at the hill, and the Germans watching us withdraw.

We returned to camp that afternoon exhausted from the long march of twenty-five miles, but elated with the fact that we had finally seen something approximating a real battle.

'We were so damned close,' Lieutenant Miller said. 'You could smell the stink of kaffir. It was more than sweat. It was fear, and it was everywhere around us in the bush. Next time we'll splat a couple of them straight between the eyes. I can't wait.'

'When our guns opened up, it was just magnificent,' Halford, a young second lieutenant with the 5th said.

'Bloody good fun,' somebody else added.

'It was fantastic to get a chance to see action,' Matthews said. 'I was getting tired of sitting around in camp all day.'

Sergeant Visser stopped and turned to look at him. 'We didn't see action,' he said. 'You can take my word for it. All that talk about guns. The Germans don't even have any to fire back at us. If we had been at the end of a bombardment, we would have come back with a different story. Then we might have smelled some of that fear on us, and maybe some shit in somebody's pants.'

Matthews burst out laughing.

'Don't laugh. It happens to a lot of men under fire. Especially the first time.' Sergeant Visser turned and started walking towards the rows of tents, leaving us to follow in his wake.

That night I noticed something of a disturbance among the younger members of my platoon. I walked over near to where the four of them were gathered crouching in the darkness. Their full attention was centred on whatever it was that they had on the ground in front of them. When I came a few steps closer I saw it was an abandoned puppy, no more than a few weeks old. It was thin and starving. Without someone to feed it, it would certainly die. Johnson was giving light to the area around the dog. He had a box of matches in his hand, and he was striking them one by one, holding the burning match in his fingers until the very last second. He would shake it out just before it burnt his fingers, and quickly strike another one. Kirkpatrick was holding a sliver of beef under its nose. Steinberg and Campbell were mixing a little leftover gravy and water in a mess tin, and when Kirkpatrick tired of holding the gristly piece of beef out, one of them would thrust the entire mess tin at the tiny animal, hoping that it would begin eating. Then Johnson's match burned out.

'Come *on*, Rob, quick,' Kirkpatrick said. 'Light another one. She can't see to eat.'

There was the sound of a match being struck and then a wavering orange light flared up. It illuminated the puppy on the ground wailing in terror and the faces of the young soldiers staring down anxiously at it out of the darkness.

I watched them at it for a few moments. Finally the puppy calmed down. It twisted its head to one side and began to lick at the piece of meat Kirkpatrick held out for it.

'Look at that,' Johnson said, in his slow, drawling voice. I could see him in the flickering matchlight, smiling and shaking his head. 'The bloody little dog really likes it.'

'Maybe she wants some of this too,' Steinberg said, wiggling his mess pan.

'No, she wants the meat,' Johnson said, holding the match to one side so he could see better. 'Haven't you got some more there, Steve?'

'*Get rid of that dog!*' It was Carter's voice. He had come up on the men without their knowing it.

'What do you mean, sir?' Johnson asked.

'Take the dog outside the perimeter of the camp and leave it in the bush. It cannot stay here.'

'But sir –'

'Do what I tell you!'

I looked at Johnson's thin, scarred face in the torchlight. He hesitated, not believing what he had been asked to do. He looked over at Kirkpatrick. He was still holding his hand out and the puppy now was licking the back of his hand. Johnson looked over at Carter again, and then slowly he reached out and picked up the puppy. He stood up and, clutching it to his chest, he disappeared into the darkness.

'The rest of you clean your mess tins,' Carter said sharply, 'and get ready to turn in. The train to the front leaves for Voi at dawn tomorrow.'

I turned and walked back into the darkness. There was nothing for me to say to the men now. I waited for Carter to move on, and I confronted him in the criss-crossed shadows of the tents.

'Why did you have to do that?' I asked.

Carter turned on me, one eyebrow raised. 'Whatever can you mean, lieutenant?'

'The dog,' I said. 'Why did you have to make them get rid of the dog like that?'

'We've got a war to fight. We can't have *pets*. We're an army, not a travelling circus. Besides, a stray dog like that, it could easily have rabies, or something else. There are thousands of men crammed in together here. An outbreak of disease at the beginning of the campaign would be disastrous.'

'Yes, of course that's true, but surely you could have found a better way of doing it?' I hesitated, torn between my outrage and the knowledge that I might be going too far in questioning my senior officer. Then the anger got the better of me. 'It was Kirkpatrick's dog. It was unnecessary to order Johnson to do it so deliberately,' I said sharply. 'You know as well as I do that he and Kirkpatrick are friends.'

'Lieutenant,' Carter replied coldly. 'Your concern for your men's emotional well-being is touching, but you too will have to learn that nothing can be allowed to interfere with an army's discipline.'

He walked away from me, then stopped and turned. 'You don't understand this yet, Fuller, not properly anyway, but it's discipline that will keep them alive.'

The moon, almost full now, hung over the bush. Lying in my tent, I could hear the cough of a lion in the distance, and then the sound of Wallis and Kirkpatrick's boots crunching as they came back from their turn of sentry duty. They certainly would not be sleeping on duty again.

Helen, Helen, Helen. I would take out the photograph she had given me on our last night together and look at it two or three times a day. I couldn't help it. I had to remind myself of her, of the tiny, faded scar on her finger, of the long smooth curves of her legs tucked beneath her floral dress, of the way she would flick a few errant strands of hair back when she was being at her most earnest. I missed her so much already, it was an almost physical ache.

On my last night before going to the war we had dinner at the Carlton Hotel, both of us trying to be light and relaxed among the potted palms and the gleaming silverware.

Just before the waiter brought the dessert she passed me an envelope across the white starched tablecloth, slipping it between the fresh cut lilies and the red glow of the half-empty glasses of wine.

I reached out to take it, but she hesitated for a moment, holding it in her slender downturned palm. Then she pushed it forward again. The feel of her skin was soft and electric as I slid it from under her fingers.

'Open it.'

The envelope was not sealed. She watched as I pushed my finger under the creamy whiteness of the paper and pulled the flap open.

It was the photograph. She was sitting on a stone bench with carved gryphons in her mother's garden. She was wearing the hat she had worn when we first met and she was smiling into the camera.

'It was taken just before I met you,' she said. 'It's the only one I have to give you.'

'You are so beautiful.' I looked up from the shaded tones of the picture and found her eyes across from me, gleaming in the candlelight.

She smiled, and looked down at the table. It was what she always did. I knew she only half-believed me when I told her how beautiful she was. I didn't know how to convince her.

It was our last night together. It struck me that there must have been tens of thousands of couples all across our world, huddled together in the same circles of frightened intimacy, each one of us wondering what terror and what comforts the future might hold. It was important to get things right, to make sure there was nothing left unsaid that needed to be said.

'Why did you hesitate?' I asked.

Helen ran her finger around the edge of her wine glass. 'I panicked for a moment,' she said finally. 'A single photograph has already caused so much trouble in my life. What if you go away to the war and forget about me? Then you can throw me away like a scrap of… I don't know what. Maybe you won't even bother to take it with you. Or some other woman will find it and tear me up into tiny little shreds. I promised myself that I would never give anyone the power to destroy my life ever again.'

I watched her face through the candlelight. 'I won't forget you.'

She hesitated for a moment before answering. 'You might, but tonight I decided I'm willing to take that chance.'

When we got to her house we fell into one another's arms, bumping elbows, hips and knees in our haste to take one another's clothes off.

Then in the darkness afterwards, my back naked against the cool iron of the bedstead, she turned away from me. I could feel the first wetness of tears spilling onto my skin.

'I'm sorry.'

She turned back towards me. 'Don't be. You have to go. I know that. I don't pretend to like it, but I can see that you can't not go. Not now, not any more, after so many men have already gone.'

She fell silent. I leant down and kissed her. She kissed me back, the tips of her hair brushing my cheek, and then we lay back together on the bed, the warmth of her body pressed against mine. There was no need to go over it again. I had chosen to leave her and go to the war.

For a long time we lay together, moulding our bodies into one another, feeling the beating of our hearts and the electric touch of our skin. We were no longer sleepy. She turned and covered me with her slim nakedness, putting her mouth over mine, and for long minutes we inhaled each other's air and smell like deep-sea divers of the soul, entirely dependent on each other for every precious breath of life.

She moved slowly downwards on top of me, kissing me on my chin, my neck, my chest, brushing her lips over my nipple. She was trying to hide the tears, but I felt them sliding hot and wet across my skin. I took her face in my hands and kissed her on the eyes, one by one, taking her tears onto my tongue, drawing them into my mouth and letting them run down my throat.

10

'WE CAN'T DO THIS,' CARTER SAID, his face hard and etched in the yellow light of the hurricane lamps. He was standing over the sheets of paper outlining our battle plan. 'The Germans will see us coming for miles. They'll slaughter us.'

Macintyre glared at him. 'General Malleson has approved the plan. He told me himself that the best intelligence puts the German force at 300 blacks, a couple of machine guns and a few white officers.'

'Malleson's –'

'Watch yourself, Captain,' Major Reading snapped.

Carter looked over at him, and then back at Macintyre.

'You *must* know that can't be right,' he went on. 'We were there on the plain in front of Salaita only three days ago. There were at least that many German troops on and around that hill. I myself positively identified a number of units from both the 14th and 15th Field Companies alone. Now, they'll have brought up more. We know that the 10th, the 13th and the 6th *Schutztruppe* are somewhere between Taveta and Salaita. They can be brought up within an hour. Also, you saw for yourself that the main trenches are not on the slopes. They are in the bush at the base of the hill. We could hear the Germans laughing at us when the order came to withdraw. They know we're coming for them now, and they've had plenty of time to reinforce themselves.'

'Are you questioning the orders of the Commander-in-Chief?' Macintyre snarled, the badges of his rank and the polished leather of his Sam Browne belt gleaming.

Carter ignored him. He looked straight at Major Reading.

'Do you know that there is no Field Ambulance section attached to our Brigade, and that only one stretcher and bearers has been assigned to each company?'

'Yes,' Major Reading said.

'Damn it, Carter!' Macintyre broke in, slamming his fist down on the rough plank tabletop. 'We've just come from the divisional briefing. The attack has been carefully thought out.

The enemy are present in minimal strength. The artillery will soften them up. The Germans will be cut to pieces before we even get to Salaita. We'll take the hill easily, before any reinforcements can arrive from Taveta. There will be very few casualties among our men. You can take my word on that.'

Carter stood in the flickering lamplight, seething. He looked back at Major Reading. 'Does General Beves know about these orders?' he asked.

Reading looked at him in the lamplight. 'Yes,' he replied. 'Yes, he does. He passed them on to me himself at the briefing earlier this evening.'

The junior officers gathered around the map on the makeshift table looked around at one another.

'Any more questions?' Major Macintyre snapped.

No one said anything. Van Hasselt was looking down at the map, turning his wedding ring round and round on his finger as he studied the lines on the paper. Matthews looked pale and strained. Even Miller, normally so contemptuous of the enemy, said nothing. Carter glared over at Reading, and at Macintyre at the far edge of the circle of light.

'These orders *will* stand, gentlemen,' Major Reading said, his voice low and firm. 'I have to tell you that we've been given instructions to move out at 05h00 tomorrow.'

The night was cold. We shivered outside and very few men slept. We had marched most of the morning. We spent the rest of the day bivouacking alongside the Baluchis at Serengeti camp further down the railway line. Most of the men had to sleep out in the open under their greatcoats, but the officers had been lucky enough to be given tents. I was sitting outside our tent, unable to sleep. Scheepers was inside, writing a letter to his father on his knee. The stub of a candle dripped wax on the edge of the camp cot. A gecko hung pale as a curved thorn against the tent wall. A praying mantis swayed inside the circle of light, raising its spiked forelegs from time to time against the sputtering sound of the flame.

Watching him I found myself thinking, remembering all that I had left unsaid to my own father.

Just *write* it, I wanted to say. *Now*. While you still have the chance.

It seemed unreal that we were now at this point. Everything in my life had brought me here, to this night. Tomorrow and what it would bring seemed a thousand years away. To try and imagine too much was a mistake. Tomorrow we would journey into the centre, come what may. Tonight, yes, there was fear, eating at my gut and filling my heart and lungs like water. I could feel the unsettling hints of something that I had never felt before, something that I knew could spread inside me – a black, overwhelming panic that would blot out everything if I let it. I would have to hold it in, no matter what. I could not bear to imagine the shame of breaking and running – of failure. The shame that Carter would have to endure for the rest of his life, no matter how many times he had redeemed himself since then.

The battle plan was absurd. I had seen for myself the stone fortifications, the German trenches, the thorn barricades and the wire. I had glimpsed the German machine guns, and I knew there were more that I had not seen. A frontal assault. Even with our numbers it was madness. And yet, even having seen this, I would carry out my orders. I would follow Major Macintyre and Captain Carter and I would lead our men to face the possibility of their deaths, each one of us officers knowing from the start that not enough had been done to protect their lives.

I thought of what Carter had told me. *To live with your conscience, you can only ask men to go where you are willing to go.* But what did that mean to me? I had never been tested. What could I ask men to do when I did not know my own limits? I had written to Helen earlier, as dusk was falling.

My Darling,

I'm here at the edge of it now. There is no turning back. I think of you all the time, especially now, on the eve of my first battle. Every day I feel the terrible emptiness of being without you, and of not knowing how long it will be for. The honest truth is that, no matter what the newspapers say at home, I have come to see that it could still be years before this war is over. That is the worst part, knowing that so much of my life, our life, will be spent apart.

You are the only person I can say this to, but I am frightened tonight as I write these words to you. I don't know if I will ever come back tomorrow, but at the same time – I don't quite know how to say this properly – I do want to go. I want to see what it will be like.

I will come back. I know somehow that I will be all right. But I'm going to say this all the same, so that I've said it no matter what happens. You must never forget how deeply, how passionately I love you.

I can never say it enough. I love you. You mean everything to me.

Yours forever,
And ever,

Michael.

So it was we all tried to make our peace with the world that night. Earlier in the evening, shortly after the officer's briefing, I had glimpsed Van Hasselt in his tent. He had stooped his large body over and was kneeling on the rough ground at the low camp cot. An old Dutch Bible and his revolver lay on the blanket nearby. There was a photograph of his family in front of him. His balding head was bowed and his big hands were clasped in prayer.

Kirkpatrick, Steinberg and Campbell were sitting in a circle on the sand in the moonlight just a short way from my tent. Johnson was with them too. He sat hunched over at the edge of their group, smoking and staring out at the night. They spoke in hushed whispers. Their excitement carried across the cool night air in the rise and fall of their murmured voices.

Wallis and Burger were lying on the ground just beyond, overcoats and a canvas waterproof sheet spread over each of them.

'They're cannibals, the askaris,' Campbell was saying. 'When they catch you with their bayonets they cut your hands off and roast them.'

'Come off it,' Steinberg said.

'It's true. One of the East African settlers in Belfield's Scouts told me about it. He said they even chew the fingernails.'

'I heard from Thompson that one of the Rhodesians got lost on patrol the other day,' Kirkpatrick said. 'They found his body in the bush with his arms cut off and his eyes torn out.'

Johnson's voice was raised above the others. 'I heard that too. They started it. So now we're to take no prisoners when we storm the hill. Everyone's saying those are our orders. No prisoners.'

'Make sure you get to the hill alive yourself, before you start worrying about prisoners,' Burger growled across the darkness from underneath his greatcoat.

'Get some sleep,' Wallis added in a muffled voice. 'You'll need that more than anything tomorrow.'

Across the way was Watson, sleeping next to Hooper and Williams. I was worried about Watson. He was the first man in the regiment to come down with malaria. Quinine had cleared it up partially, but on parade he had been pale and shaking. It seemed he was suffering a relapse. I spoke to him about it, but he shook his head and looked down at the ground. 'I'm fine,' he said through clenched teeth. 'I want to be with the regiment tomorrow.'

Sergeant Visser was sitting on his own a little way off. I could see his large belly and the sudden glow of his cigarette end as he sucked on it. He lifted a mug to his lips every now and then. It was the last of his rum ration. After a while he got up, and slipped. He dropped the cup. It rang against a stone.

'Shit!' I heard him whisper under his breath. He bent down to pick it up and swayed backwards as he straightened up.

He wandered into the darkness. A few moments later, I heard the strong, steady stream of his pissing, releasing the pressure of the rum that had gathered in his bladder.

'*The artillery will soften them up,*' Major Macintyre had said. Carter didn't believe him, nor, it seemed, did Sergeant Visser.

'*The Germans will be cut to pieces before we even get to Salaita.*'

I could hear Sergeant Visser sitting down heavily and fumbling in the darkness with his greatcoat. So, the black seeds of fear were inside him too, but he would get some sleep or, at least, some moments of oblivion tonight.

A few yards away I could see the triangle of Carter's tent lit by the glow of a hurricane lamp. I was sure he was going over the rough sketch map he had made of the area around Salaita Hill.

'*I never failed again, and I've fought in many battles since then. There isn't a single soldier in the world who isn't ashamed of something that he carries with him from the heat of battle.*'

Matthews was walking down the alley between the tents. He was heading for the pit latrines for the second time in an hour or so.

'Something in the water,' he said when he saw me, and then slunk away. His face was gaunt and drawn.

The Baluchi camp across the way was quiet. The men were sleeping, or at least trying to, knowing already what lay in store for them. Jemadars Khan and Zaman had been among the officers at the briefing. Their dark, thin faces were sombre under their turbans as they listened to the outlining of the Operational Orders. The Baluchis and the Rhodesians and the Loyal North Lancs were to wait east of Salaita in reserve near the Njoro drift. They would be near the artillery and provide support for us in the event we needed it.

'It'll be a day resting in the sun for you,' Miller had joked with some of the Rhodesian officers after the briefing.

'Let's hope so,' Wilkins, a major from Bulawayo, said without smiling. He had looked over at Khan and Zaman, but none of them said anything. The Rhodesians and the Baluchis were old comrades-in-arms by now.

I saw Major Reading walking through the rows of tents, his hands clasped behind his back, his shiny knee-high boots crunching on the cool sand. He nodded at a group of men. 'Evening, boys,' he said to another. I saw him look over at Sergeant Visser sitting on his own, and then he turned away. He walked past where I was sitting.

'Evening, Lieutenant.'

'Evening, sir.'

He stopped and turned towards me. 'We're relying on men like you. The older officers. To keep the line steady.' He looked at me. 'No matter what happens, discipline must be maintained down the line. If discipline falters, the attack will fail.'

'Yes, sir.'

He nodded in the darkness. 'Get some sleep.'

Rain started falling in the middle of the night, slicing down through the darkness, splashing into the puddles and streams that flowed across the dark, red earth. Lightning filling the sky and then the thunder crashing, rolling through the huge empty blackness of the night.

Helen leaning down over me, pinning me down by my wrists and the deep gorgeous smell of her filling my heart as I breathed her in. Her hair covering my face, touching every corner of my universe. Her voice hoarse and secret, for me alone. Yes, yes, yes.

Her fingers caressing the roots of my hair, electricity in their tips. And the two of us tumbling over, her backwards, me slowly forward. Then me entering her, pulling her shoulders towards me. Opening my eyes to find her eyes shining, watching me.

'Look,' she said, breathless, pointing at our shadows, huge and dark, moving against the whiteness of the wall. Leaning down to kiss her, to smother her with my mouth, trying to fill her with me, and, then, the explosion into her, feeling each spasm flooding into her depths. My God, my God, losing myself deep inside her and then collapsing, my face into hers. The mingled sweat and smell at her temples, her hair pulled up and backwards.

No. Pulling me towards her. Stay in, stay in. The flickering brown darkness of the candlelight around us. Breathing her in, breathing me out, soft and wet; lips touching.

Her half-rising, resting on her elbow. Looking at me. Her finger touching my arm, my shoulder, running down my ribs. Her eyes gleaming in the darkness.

It was too late now for regrets. Tomorrow the line must be steady. Tomorrow.

11

WE MARCHED OUT JUST AFTER FOUR in the morning, light-headed with exhaustion and lack of sleep. The moon had set and the night was dark. Kilimanjaro was invisible behind the mass of rain cloud rolling low across the sky, the pale starlight fleetingly visible through breaks in the fast-moving cloud.

The men were looming shapes struggling around me in the darkness. They were moving slowly – too slowly, it seemed. Orders had been for them to carry full kit: rolled greatcoats, mess tins, haversack with rations for two days, two bandoliers with 200 rounds of .303 ammunition and another 50 rounds in the top of the haversack, a full water bottle, entrenching tools, bayonet, side arms and rifle. Many of the men had to carry wire cutters along with the rest of the gear.

Matthews and I and the men in our platoons fell in behind Captain Carter. He was grimly silent in the weak glow that reflected off the base of the clouds. Major Van Hasselt and Macintyre were ahead of us in the column.

'None of your fucking smoking, hear?' Corporal Reynolds leaned over and whispered angrily at Johnson. 'We don't want Fritz seeing us coming.'

Sergeant Visser stood and checked each man as they staggered past him through the wet grass.

'They're all here,' he said to me. He sounded hoarse and distant. I could smell last night's rum on his stale breath.

We moved out of the wet, clinging bush. We began padding down the soft, sandy road that led to Salaita. 6000 men, guns, machine guns, wagons, horses, ox-carts and mule-drawn ambulances moving forward under the eerie glow of the scudding clouds.

There was just the squeak of wheels, the snort of a horse, the creak of leather boots and the occasional clinking of a bayonet or the edge of a mess tin against a rifle barrel. I could smell the wet earth and the rain lying in pockets hidden in the grass and already beginning to sink into the parched earth. The rain had brought out the frogs. They were calling to one another along the muddy edge of the road, falling mute as we passed by.

We moved forward in column of fours down the road. It was not a parade-ground march in step, but there was something exhilarating in the tramp of thousands of feet moving forward into battle together. The steady tramp of our boots in the dust was a thread of steel woven into the memory of our army. This was what our training had been for. The collective strength in such a determined advance had overcome the terror of millions of men in the past. The fields of Hastings, Agincourt and Waterloo had all felt the tremor of the same relentless progression. We were a single, almost forgotten, army lost among the thousands of legions of the greatest war the world had ever seen. On that cold, outermost edge of night our sheer mass carried us onward, towards our enemy.

Rolling behind our columns of men and horses came the artillery: 4-inch naval guns salvaged from ships wrecked by the Germans earlier in the war, 12-pounder guns and a battery of howitzers. Four armoured cars drove slowly, clashing their gears among the spans of oxen dragging the gun limbers. After the aeroplanes, they were the most modern of our weapons. Powered by Rolls-Royce engines, they carried a machine gun in a rotating turret and were armoured with heavy steel plate. The Germans had nothing to match them. Their askaris were terrified of them and called them 'the charging rhinoceros which spits lead'. We felt cheered and emboldened by their presence. They seemed invulnerable. Their complex machinery and iron bulk loomed over us, casting the comforting shadow of someone else's mortality.

In the rear straggled the ragged lines of hundreds of black porters, many of them barefoot and naked to the waist, shivering with cold and struggling with cases of ammunition, extra food, water, tents carried on their heads. Along with them came the black transport drivers and more heavily-laden pack mules, the covered ambulance wagons with red crosses painted on the white canvas jolting over the ruts in the road, and the groaning, crank-started Ford and REO trucks filled with medical supplies, more ammunition and more water.

Hoarse whispered commands came down from General Beves to the officers and the sergeants. They echoed up and down the line in the darkness. We branched off into bush and marched north-west of the road. The main body of the column stayed on the road while we struggled through the thorns and tall grass.

The bush broke the rhythm of our marching and the men soon began to sweat under their load. We had passed the lowest ebb of the night. The very first grey light of morning was beginning to grow. The men's spirits picked up, but we could hardly see where we were going. Thorns and branches grabbed at our uniforms. The damp sand gave way under our feet and packed around the bottom of our boots. I watched the youngest men, Kirkpatrick and Steinberg, struggling. And Campbell, too, marching with his rifle slung over his shoulder, his thumbs hooked behind his haversack straps as he leaned forward into the weight of it. I saw red-headed Watson stumble over a rock in the dim haze and fight to push himself up again. Wallis grabbed at the back of his haversack and jerked him to his feet. The others marched on, flowing around them. Some clutched their rifles and looked ahead at the dark horizon; others kept glancing down at their feet, watching their steps in the cold half-light.

Matthews worked his way over to Captain Carter. 'This gear,' he whispered. 'It's too much. The men are already beginning to tire.'

Carter turned and glared at Matthews. 'Those are the orders. They will carry it.' Carter turned and pointed towards a clearing in the thorn trees. 'Keep their minds on moving forward, towards the objective.'

We marched on in the darkness, forcing our way through the bush for two hours. Despite the pre-dawn cold, the men were perspiring freely and their khaki uniforms were blotched with patches of sweat. The clouds thinned. A single line of orange lit up the blackness of the sky behind us. Birds began singing. Kilimanjaro loomed for a moment, grey and streaked with faint lines of bronze, then disappeared again behind the clouds.

The sun was coming up when we halted at the edge of the Njoro drift. We were 3000 yards from our objective, Salaita Hill, though we could not yet see the hill and its German defenders above the thick bush. 3000 yards. How many steps was that? Less than 4000 for a man of my height, perhaps 100 fewer for a man as tall as Carter. By the end of the day we would have taken every one of them.

A blaze of crimson and gold poured out over the bush behind us. The air smelled fresh and cool. A warthog and its young darted out from behind a clump of thorn trees. She stopped and stared at me for a moment. Then they turned and fled, skittering through the grass with their tails held high.

The Rhodesians, the Loyal North Lancs and the Baluchis were halted just a few hundred yards south of us, spread out along the banks of the dry riverbed. I could hear them laughing and joking among themselves. There was no longer much point in maintaining absolute silence. The Germans must have known now that we were coming. They would be waiting on Salaita, facing into the rising sun. I imagined them standing in the red dust of their trenches and crouching behind their stone sangars. They would be gripping their rifles, staring through the coils of barbed wire to the bush beyond. Their mouths would be dry with fear, wondering just when it was we would come and what we would bring with us.

A rest was ordered. The men threw off their haversacks and bandoliers and collapsed among the smooth rocks and on the dry sand of the riverbed. A mass of thorn bushes hung over the steep banks. Watson put his head back and fell asleep. Kirkpatrick and Steinberg were sprawled out full-length in the dirt.

Sergeant Visser's eyes were hard in the first golden light of morning, despite the red lines in them and the stench of sweat and rum that hung over him. He walked from man to man, taking their rifles and checking them, sliding the bolts open and shut with a sharp metallic *clack*. All along the riverbed, the sergeants were doing the same thing with the men in their platoon. I could see Willis moving up and down among his men, and beyond him, Sergeant-Major Harvey squinting down the barrel of one man's rifle.

Sergeant Visser leaned down and shook Watson awake. The boy's face was pale and drawn under his shock of bright red hair; he hadn't slept last night. He was exhausted. Watson sat up and shook the sleep out of his head. He looked embarrassed at being so tired already, but I was relieved to see that the worst of the malaria was receding under the quinine.

The sound of an aeroplane buzzed in the distance. It came out of the low sun behind us. The diamond-pattern of the strut wires between the wings caught the morning light like cold silver flame. The pilot wagged the wings at us as he passed over. The shadow of the plane was long and black, flowing over the swaying tips of the tall grass. The men waved as it flew overhead, craning their necks to follow its arc in the new blue sky of morning. The 3000 yards that lay ahead of us was nothing more than a few seconds in the universe of the plane's speed. It turned and circled twice in the air above Salaita. There was the distant sound of the German machine guns firing up into the air at it. Then the plane straightened out and flew back over us. I watched it pass over our lines and drop a message somewhere near General Malleson's HQ.

I could see Macintyre talking to Carter. Carter stood stiffly in front of Macintyre for a few moments; then he turned and made his way down the dry riverbed through the rows of men lying in the sand. 'On your feet!' he said.

He came over to me. 'Form up your platoon. We are to advance in mass.'

'Into this bush?' Sergeant Visser's face was shocked. 'In *mass*?'

'Do it,' Carter snapped. His own face was drained and white. 'Now.'

Visser turned away and began moving down the line, pulling the men by their haversacks, pushing them, forming them up in the river bed behind Matthews' platoon. We waited below the steep edges of the bank of the narrow watercourse. The bush in front of us was dense and impenetrable. We could see nothing but grass and thorn branches.

The order came down the line. The South African Brigade was to advance first. We in the 7th would lead. The 6th were on our right, and the 5th in the rear. Thousands of men clambered up over the river bank and crashed into the bush.

I couldn't help it. My heart was beating wildly. I found it difficult to breathe. Carter was next to me. A few yards down the line I saw Major Van Hasselt take a last-minute glance at a photograph of his family and shove it back inside his tunic. He buttoned it up hastily. He scrabbled at the flap of his leather holster and drew his revolver.

Helen. No, no. There was no time now for that. Our platoon was next. We scrabbled up over the red dust of the river bank and tumbled headlong into the thick bush. Carter was in front, already shoving his way into the thorns and tall grass. I could see no more than two or three yards on either side of me. I could just make out the shapes of Lieutenant Matthews and of Major Macintyre, pistol in hand, shoving his way through the undergrowth. Sergeant Visser was behind me on my right. Johnson was there somewhere, bent over his rifle, ducking and plunging into the bush. Then Corporal Reynolds. Burger, Hooper, Williams and Watson, sweat pouring down his exhausted, haggard face beneath the brim of his sun helmet. Wallis was furthest away, Kirkpatrick was close behind him.

A burning slash cut into my nose and across my cheek. I jerked back. A needle-sharp acacia thorn the size of a finger had slashed into my face. The sweat made it sting.

'Forward. Keep moving.' The bush was so thick. I had lost sight of Carter already, but I could hear his voice, raised now and angry. *'Move, move, move.'* I could just see Matthews and some of his platoon coming up on my right.

We were slowed at every step. Hard, sharp thorns grabbed at our shirts, and tore at the exposed flesh of our legs below our shorts. We had to keep moving. Men were shoving at the bush with their rifle butts. In a tiny clearing I glimpsed Scheepers hacking at a branch with his bayonet and Sergeant Willis pulling a man entangled in a thorn tree, dragging him out by his collar. Tiny red patches of blood appeared on the rips of his shirt where the hooked thorns had torn his flesh. He half-tumbled, half-fell on the ground. Willis picked him up again and pushed him hard in the small of the back, sending him stumbling forward.

The bush crashed and seethed around us. I had no idea how I was supposed to command my platoon in this impenetrable undergrowth. I could see almost nothing. I could just hear the shouts of officers and sergeants.

'*Move, move, move.*' It was our only hope. I knew the Germans on their hilltop must be watching the bush sway with every yard of our clumsy advance.

A heavy crack came from behind us. The first of our naval guns was opening up. A rushing, whistling swirl of air overhead, and a shuddering distant crash in front of us. Loud cheering erupted from the bush all around me. Another shell, and another. Crashing into the ground ahead of us. Through gaps in the thick bush, I could see earth spraying up and clouds of smoke rising over the flat-topped acacias.

Another shell, and another. The howitzers and the field guns were beginning to open up. They were firing ranging shots: one long, one a fraction shorter. An artillery officer perched high in a thorn tree was watching them land through his field glasses. He would calculate the angle of their trajectory and order an adjustment to the angle of the barrel until the shells began to find their target.

I felt a sudden wild surge of joy as the barrage grew louder. *We would take the hill.* Our guns would destroy them first. No one could withstand the shattering thunder crashing down on them from our naval and field guns. Their high-explosive shells would split open the Germans' defences and the shrapnel from the howitzers would tear them into pieces of bloody meat. The noise roared all around me. At last, the doubts of not knowing what war was like had been confronted. I was plunging now into the very screaming, thundering heart of it.

I yelled at the outlines of my men struggling in the thick bush. '*Move, move, move.*' I hardly noticed the thorns now. '*Keep going. Forward.*' I wanted to go, go, go – all the way to Salaita, lurking somewhere there in the bush in front of us. Run – all the way to the fucking top. I saw Johnson next to me, Sergeant Visser, Wallis, Corporal Reynolds. Kirkpatrick, white-faced, gripping his rifle to his chest. Hooper, Williams, they were there, even Watson was somehow managing to keep up. We were rushing forward together, a pack of men ready now to do anything. To shoot, to stab, slash, throttle, kick, punch, bite. Our guns spat thunder and fire behind us. The shells screamed overhead and slammed into the enemy's ground. Tearing their flesh and crushing their bones.

The blood was pumping in our hearts. We were moving. We would do anything. Anything to kill.

There was a clearing in front of us. An open patch of dry yellow grassland, tall and waving in the cool morning breeze. The sweat was pouring off me now. I dimly noticed Carter in front of me. He was standing, looking at Salaita and drawing great sucking breaths of air.

'Halt,' he yelled out, raising his hand and waving it in the air. We paused. All down the line in the thick bush at the edge of the clearing, men came to a stumbling, panting halt. There, at last, was Salaita. A low sloping hill barely protruding out of the savanna. Stone sangars and breastworks lay across its slopes. At the crest of the hill was a small stone fort. The German eagle and the green and white moon ensign of Islam were still flying proudly against the blue sky. Baobabs and thorn trees were dotted in the grasslands that lay between us and the hill. At the foot of the hill lay another thick patch of thorn trees.

Hooper reached into his tunic and pulled out a camera. He unfolded it quickly and held it up high above his helmet. He snapped a picture.

'Put that thing away,' Corporal Reynolds snarled at him between heavy breaths.

'What the hell are we waiting for?' I yelled over the shelling at Carter. The hill is just there. Let's go. Now, while we've got the advantage.'

'Permission,' Carter shouted back. 'We're waiting for permission from General Beves to open out our formation before we enter this damned grassland.'

He pointed up to the hill. I could see men rushing up and down its slopes. Another group of Germans stood together near the stone breastwork at the crest of the hill. I assumed they were the officers.

'They're watching us. The moment we move into that clear space we will be in full view of them and their machine guns. We need to open out our formation to minimise casualties.'

Our guns stopped. A sudden, unearthly stillness fell over the battlefield.

'What's going on, sir?' I heard Kirkpatrick ask Lieutenant Matthews. His voice was hoarse with excitement.

'We're waiting for orders.'

It was already past 08h00. The sun was high. A gleam of white heat in the sky. I saw Major Macintyre glancing down at his wristwatch.

'We should just bloody go.'

'Wait,' Van Hasselt said. 'They must give us permission to break open our formations before we advance into that.' He pointed at the flat grassland.

'Bugger the formations,' Macintyre said. 'We've got the niggers hiding now. The guns started it. We just need to finish it. The sooner the better.'

Heat waves were beginning to build up over the bush. Men began swigging at their water bottles, the cool, fresh water spilling out of their mouths and dripping down their chins. The only sound in the bush was flies buzzing, not yet stupefied by the heat.

The orders came.

The general says the enemy has no guns. Carry on in mass.

I looked over at Carter; his face was expressionless. I saw Sergeant Visser working his way over towards me.

'It's madness; you know that, don't you, sir? They're going to murder us, going across that clearing in mass. We should open out the formations. Make the men less of a target.'

'Those are the orders, Sergeant.'

He looked at me. I could see the sudden rage in his eyes. He was struggling to hold it back. 'I *know* that, sir. But Corporal Reynolds and I will do our best not to let the men bunch up when the Germans start firing. We were hoping you would do the same.'

'Yes, sergeant,' I said, chastened. 'Of course. I'll do my best.'

Visser nodded and moved back into position. Down the line there was the staccato, clinking sound of rifle bolts being opened and slammed shut as the men checked their weapons one final time.

My hands were trembling. *Craaack. Whoosh.* A single shell whistled overhead. It slammed into the crest of the hill. A cloud of white smoke and dust rose and streamed away on the breeze. The crescent moon on its green background was still flying, but the German eagle had been brought down by our shellfire.

Cheering, hoarse and exultant, broke out. Some of the men raised their rifles defiantly, the barrels glinting in the bright sun. From behind us a thunderous roar hammered out from our guns, shaking the ground and filling the air with a rush of sound and hot steel. Clouds of white smoke and dust erupted on the slope of Salaita obliterating it from view for a few moments. Then, as the sound caught up, the echo of their explosions rushed back, engulfing us in a wild, thrilling wave of our own power.

A pause. Another roar from our guns sweeping over us. Somewhere in the din the order was given to advance. The lines of our men broke through the last of the dense bush that edged the clearing. We in the 7th were leading, the 5th and the 6th were echeloned out behind us to the right. The grass clearing opened out to us, soft and easy after the dense thorn bush. Our legs were pumping as hard as they could, driving us forward, on to the enemy. The lines of men stretched out on either side of me, rifles at the ready, sweeping through the wavering savanna grass.

A man's head disappeared. A fountain of crimson blood soared into the air and his headless body pitched sideways into the tall grass. Two men from the 6th dropped, their arms flapping outwards, their rifles tumbling in an arc through the air. Another man spun around and was flung against a thorn tree. He hung in the low branches, spread-eagled with the force of the bullets. His body jumped and shuddered as more bullets hammered into him.

The advance halted. Everywhere men were throwing themselves to the ground trying to take cover. Machine-gun bullets cut through the air around me. A single anthill lay a few yards away. Two men were sheltering behind it. Puffs of hardened earth and red dust flew off its crown and sides.

'Get the fuck away from there!' I heard Lieutenant Scheepers shouting at the men. They seemed not to hear him. They remained frozen in terror crouched behind the anthill clutching at their rifles. The Germans had counted on this happening. Their machine guns were ranged on the anthill. Their bullets would strip it bare in seconds and tear the men to pieces, but they could not move for fear.

I saw Carter leopard-crawling, struggling on his elbows and knees, towards the anthill. He grabbed one of the men and dragged him away behind him through the long grass.

Scheepers was moving towards the remaining man when the German pom-pom guns opened up. The first few shells landed well behind us. Then more came and more, landing right in amongst us now. Fountains of earth and stone flew up into the air. I watched them come closer and closer to me. They seemed slow and drifting. Fragments of yellow grass, cut by the bullets, drifted down on me. I was conscious of our own guns firing back, but they didn't seem to matter anymore. Nothing could overcome my need to hold onto the ground, tighter and tighter. The ground was as hard and unyielding as rock. I could never get low enough now to escape the shrapnel. I clung on, squeezing my body down, trying to will myself into the ground. I felt like a snake trapped in an aquarium writhing against glass. I could sense my escape, but I was powerless against the incomprehensible might of the earth.

There was a peaceful humming sound as a fragment of shrapnel tumbled through the air over my head. It sounded almost benign, like the whirring of a child's top. There was something almost wondrous in that sound. It had missed. I was still alive. I lifted my head. The anthill was blown to pieces. The man Scheepers had tried to save lay with blood pouring out of his mouth. The other was stooping down behind Carter. He looked dazed, as if he could hardly believe he was alive.

I scrambled up into a crouch. I could hear Carter screaming at the men. He had his revolver in his hand and was waving them forward. 'Keep moving, get into the bush on the other side.'

Scheepers and his platoon went first, following Carter. Sergeant Visser was with me. So were Wallis and Kirkpatrick. Johnson was next to them. He lifted his rifle and fired at the hill. Then, bent double, he darted forward a few yards and fell down behind a fallen log. He fired again, aiming and squeezing the trigger like he had been taught to do on the shooting range. Then he was up again and moving forward.

I could hear the agonised screams of the wounded men. They seemed to come from everywhere. The feathery heads of the grass were wet and red with blood in patches. Somehow everything around me seemed to be taking place in a slow, spinning daze. It hardly seemed possible that less than a month ago we had been in the training camp, running across the veld, playing at being soldiers.

Carter ran back towards me, ducking and weaving. 'For God sakes, Fuller, get your platoon forward. Head for the cover of the bush. This open plain is a death trap.' Then he was gone, zigzagging through the long grass towards Matthews and Miller and their platoons.

Corporal Reynolds had been nicked in the ear. Blood and sweat were streaming down the side of his face. He had Hooper with him. The boy's face was ashen with fear. He was still holding his rifle, but his hands were shaking so violently he would not be able to aim. I thought about his camera. I wondered if he still had it with him.

'Williams,' he said. 'Poor bloody Williams. He's gone.'

'Where is he?' I gasped.

'Christ knows,' Reynolds said. 'I last saw him crawling in the grass.'

'And Watson?'

Reynolds shook his head.

A fresh burst of machine-gun fire hammered over us. We dropped to the ground. Corporal Reynolds dragged Hooper down with him and held him by the shoulder. The boy lay motionless.

'We've got to find them,' I said.

'We can't go back, sir,' Visser hissed. 'We've got to get the rest of us out of here.'

There was a loud, savage hammering above our heads. Another German machine gun had opened up. Our group had been spotted and the gunner was finding his range. Visser was right; Watson and Williams were on their own now.

Wallis was already up and running; Kirkpatrick was following him.

I looked at Visser and at Steinberg and Campbell crouching low against the ground. 'Let's go,' I said.

Bent double, we scrambled through the grass. Reynolds was still dragging Hooper. Burger was behind them, crouching as he ran. Somehow we made it to the edge of the thick bush. Bullets were still filling the air above us, but the German gunners could not find their mark as easily here. We lay flat in the red dust gasping for air. One of our own machine guns had been set up at last. It hammered out a response to the Germans which made them keep their heads down and stop shooting at us for a few brief, glorious moments.

I heard Major Van Hasselt's voice rise above the noise. 'Keep firing. Rake the hill. Make them keep their heads down.'

The remnants of Matthews' platoon were gathered nearby. Sergeant Willis was there. I didn't know the others who were lying spread-eagled in the dust, keeping as low as possible. Lieutenant Miller and his platoon from the 6th were just a few yards further on. In front of him was Lieutenant Halford and a few men from the 5th.

Major Macintyre was crouching behind a tree. He lifted his revolver in frustration and fired three shots into the bush in front of him. Then he turned and slumped back against the trunk. He broke open the revolver and ejected the empty cartridges from the cylinder. He scrabbled in the pocket of his tunic for more ammunition.

The battle plan we had discussed in the officer's *banda* last night was meaningless now. Carter had been right and Macintyre wrong. Malleson and the other generals had misjudged the strength of the enemy and of their black soldiers.

I knew that General Beves was unhappy about the orders for a frontal attack, but at the last minute even he had been caught up in the bungling, ordering us to make this final advance in mass. He should have allowed us to advance in loose formation, making the men less of a target for the German machine guns.

Our regiments were hopelessly muddled now. The faces of the men around me were haggard and cowed with fear. It had taken nothing more than a few minutes for our whole brigade to be shredded. Our charge had been cut to pieces. We were now the ones who were being hunted, huddling together for protection under our pathetic shelter of thorn trees. I realised with a shock that in the short dash we had just made, Campbell had now gone missing. I looked around for him wildly, but he was nowhere to be seen. I could only hope he had found cover somewhere else. There was nothing I could do for him now.

'How far are we from the hill?' Reynolds gasped.

'800 yards at most,' Carter told him.

'They've got us pinned down here,' Sergeant Visser said. Sweat was pouring down his face; his massive belly was heaving up and down as he gulped air. 'We can't see them, but the Germans can watch everything we do. General Malleson will have to send in the Rhodesians and the others to back us up. We can't do it on our own now. We're trapped.'

'We're going forward, sergeant,' Carter said.

Visser looked at him. I knew Carter was right. It was one of the first lessons we had learned at officer's school – when in doubt, go forward. Visser must know it too; but he also knew how hopeless was the situation that lay ahead of us.

Visser shook his head, almost imperceptibly, and turned away.

More machine guns opened up from in front of us. The bullets whistled overhead. Carter had been right about that too. The main enemy trenches were not on the slopes of the hill. They were here, in the bush, not more than 150 yards away. I looked over at Carter, crouched behind a rock, aiming his Webley revolver at the enemy. Red dust covered his usually gleaming boots and stuck on the sweat patches on his shirt. There was no trace of the funk that he feared so much within himself. He had judged the disastrous situation of the battle perfectly, but even though he had disagreed with the orders, he had followed them without question. Despite the doubts his senior officers had about him, he had done his duty without wavering. In following his orders he had led us straight into this inferno. The senior officers who had given him those orders couldn't help us now. We relied on both Macintyre and Carter to see us through this mess.

Heavy firing was coming over from our right. The 6th were getting it harder now than we were.

I could hear faint cries coming from everywhere around me. 'Stretcher bearer! For God sakes, please! Here, here!' The image of Major Macintyre in the officer's *banda* last night flooded into my head. *The attack has been carefully thought out.* Last night. Was it only last night that he had said such a monstrous, incredible thing? I looked at him now, crouching behind the trunk of the thorn tree. His face was grim, and determined. He was showing guts under fire, but I could see he had no idea what he should do next.

And what should I do? I thought desperately. I could see Wallis, Kirkpatrick, Burger, Watson... the remains of my platoon were lying flat in the bush around me as the bullets flew over our heads. Every now and then one of them would turn his head and glance at me.

Another salvo from our guns roared over our heads. The German machine guns stopped for a few moments while the shells slammed into the hillside. Clouds of dust and smoke drifted up into the sky. Their machine guns opened up again, as fiercely as before. There was a loud scream in the bush nearby. High-pitched and broken with little staccato whimpers, it soared up through the bush and rang in my ears, over and over.

There was another burst and the scream was cut short.

'Bloody arseholes are shelling the top of the hill,' Corporal Reynolds said. The blood from his wounded ear was caked with sweat and dust around his nose and lips.

'The Germans are killing us from the bush here in front of us, and all they want to do is knock that Mohammedan flag down on the top of the hill.'

Another wave of shells from our guns came over. They crashed into the hill.

'Let's move. Now!' Carter yelled.

I saw Macintyre glance over at him from behind the tree, furious at his usurping the position of command. Then he, too, turned back and waved his pistol over at Matthews' platoon. Macintyre had missed the critical moment when the shells landed and the askaris would be keeping their heads down. From that moment on, Carter took over command of us on the battle field. Experience and confidence counted more than rank now.

'Keep going forward,' Macintyre shouted before following Carter. 'Forward.'

Sergeant Visser and I gathered the men. We scrambled forward in the few brief moments of respite we had from the German machine guns. Kirkpatrick and Wallis were both lagging behind. Bent double, I sprinted through the bush towards them.

'You must keep moving,' I said, the breath sawing in my lungs. 'If the Germans pin you down, you're finished.'

Kirkpatrick stared at me. His face was white with fear. Wallis refused to look at me. He gazed straight ahead at the hill.

There was an abandoned German trench cut into the red earth in front of us. It was empty.

'Make for the trench,' Carter ordered.

We ran, stumbling, crawling, rolling, getting up and running again for the blessed safety of the deep, cut earth. The Germans saw us moving, firing broke out all around us.

I saw Hooper frozen in a mixture of fear and confusion. A bullet smacked into the trunk of a tree beside him, bark flew off in a shower of dark fragments. He ducked and then swung wildly about, looking for a place to hide.

'This way,' I shouted at him, motioning with my arm in the direction he must go. 'Move this way. Towards the trench.'

Hooper looked up at me, his eyes wide with fright. I watched as he began moving in the direction I had ordered him to. He moved slowly, half-paralysed with fright, his rifle held awkwardly in his hand as if he had forgotten it.

He fell flat as if he had tripped; shot in the back of the head, his sun helmet spinning out in front of him.

I stared at Hooper's body. I felt as if my words were still hanging in the air between us.

'What the fuck's going on?' I heard Wallis scream. I saw him alongside me, half-whirling in rage and the panic he had been holding back rising to the surface. 'Those cunts from the 5th are shooting us in the back.'

'No they're not,' Visser roared at him over the hammering sound of the fusillade. 'The askaris have cut themselves hiding places in the trunks of the baobab trees. They've got us covered from every angle. Head for the trench. Keep moving.'

Bark spat out in a line from a tree trunk. There was a hoarse, frightened scream from my right. A gaping hole had opened up in a patch of grass.

'Help, help me!' It was Corporal Reynolds' voice. I slammed into the ground and leopard-crawled on my knees and elbows over to the edge of the pit.

Reynolds lay in the bottom of the trap. His small body was twisted and crumpled like a child's. His spine was smashed. A rough wooden stake pierced the side of his knee, another two, smeared with blood, stuck up through his stomach. His thumb was broken and twisted in a coil of barbed wire.

His sun helmet had fallen off. One of the spikes had gashed his head. Dark blood ran into the red dust. The exposed bone of his skull gleamed white beneath the torn and ragged flesh. He looked up at me. 'Please, Lieutenant. Help me,' he said softly. At the edge of the wound, I could see how he had tried to train the long, greying wisps of his hair to hide his growing baldness.

'I'll send the medics,' I told him. My throat dry and my voice croaking.

He looked up at me. His eyes were hard and dark with pain beneath the whiteness of bone. He could not live, but it would take him hours yet to die.

'They'll never come. You've got to help me.'

'They'll come,' I lied. 'Soon.'

'No, sir. You know they won't.'

Those eyes staring up at me. They were brown and ringed with long fine lashes. I had seen them smiling at me, laughing with the men so many times. He had almost loved the men. I thought of the way he had dragged and cajoled the terrified Hooper until the very last. Hooper had been dead not more than a minute, and now he was dying too.

I looked down at him. I heard the sound of machine-gun bullets tear into the air above my head. They seemed impossibly far away, as if they no longer mattered. I stared at him for a few long moments. I suddenly didn't care if the bullets hit me. I scrambled up and stumbled the few yards over to the trench. I collapsed inside it.

'Call the medics,' I said. 'Corporal Reynolds is trapped in a pit. He's badly hurt.'

'There are no medics to call, sir,' Visser said. 'The first dressing station is two miles back and there're no field ambulances with us in the forward ranks.'

'There's nothing they can do for him now, anyway,' Wallis said.

'Call the medics.' I said. I felt as if I were in a trance. 'We must get the medics.'

I looked around the trench. The men were staring at me with slack jaws and exhausted faces. I looked around at each of them:

Visser, Burger, Johnson, Wallis, Kirkpatrick... so few of us left already. I thought of Reynolds, and Hooper. If I had not ordered him to run... I felt now as if I were looking at the other men across an abyss. I could never explain. They would never understand.

I turned away from them. Carter was sitting a little way off in the trench. He was watching me.

'We're going forward,' he said.

We followed Carter out of the trench and sprinted for the next row of dummy trenches that the Germans had deliberately abandoned. A wave of fire swept over us, but this time we all got across. Matthews and Miller and the remnants of their platoons had somehow got here first, and they were cowering in this trench. Major Macintyre was trying to rally them.

'We're almost there,' he said, waving his revolver in the direction of Salaita. 'Almost. Just a few more yards.' The men stared at him blankly, as if he had suddenly decided to recite a poem, or to share a recipe for greengage jam. Further off down the trench, I could see Van Hasselt with a few men grouped about him. We were a thin line of attackers who had made it to the dummy trenches. There were not nearly enough of us here to take the hill.

Half a dozen men were holding their rifles at the edge of the trench, crouching as the German fire spat overhead.

'I think they're over there. Can we open up, sir?' one of them shouted.

'No, no,' Matthews screamed.

'Can we have the order to fire, *sir*?' Sergeant Willis was glancing over at Matthews. Sweat was pouring off his face. 'They're getting closer.'

Matthews swung his head violently, looking up and down the length of the trench.'Do *not* fire,' he yelled. 'Shoot only at visible targets. Ammunition is expensive. We must not waste it.'

Another volley of German bullets splattered into the ground around us.

'Ignore that order,' Carter yelled. 'Five rounds rapid.'

We opened up on the bush, firing and working the bolts of the rifles as fast as we could. The German fire halted. There was a hoarse scream and a few moments of respite for us. Then the firing began again, exploding in puffs around us.

Conradie was there in the trench, tall and powerful. His lean, muscular body gleamed with sweat, but his eyes were haunted with fear. Fielding and Smit were sitting beyond him. They looked exhausted. Fielding had lost his rifle. He held a bayonet in his right hand and a rock in his left. In another setting they might have been menacing, but here they were nothing more than the impotent weapons of a frightened, desperate man. An image of him in the field exercises, laughing, talking about black men as monkeys came into my head. That was so long ago now. A lifetime away. There was nothing for him to laugh about anymore.

Smit was sitting next to him. His hands clutched the barrel of his upright rifle; his head was hanging below his hands and to one side. We could have been a platoon of askaris, but he didn't even bother to look up as we clattered and tumbled into the trench.

Their lieutenant, Miller, sat hunched at the side of a trench wall. His eyes blazed with impotent fury.

'Kaffirs,' he said, smacking his fist against the red earth of the trench. 'Fucking kaffirs have done this to us. How could it happen? How? I just want to know how.'

'Shut up, Lieutenant,' Carter snapped.

Miller glared at him, but he fell silent.

Kirkpatrick and Steinberg were there. Steinberg was lying on the floor of the trench, blood seeping from his upper body, staining his khaki shirt dark red. Someone had tried to fix a field dressing over it, but the blood had leaked through it and around the edges. He lay still, his eyes half-closed in pain. There was a fluttering sound coming from the hole in his chest as he struggled to breathe.

Kirkpatrick's face was pale and wasted. He was staring down at the dusty floor of the trench. Hundreds of shiny brass cartridges lay half-submerged in a thick pool of red blood. In the dust on the edge of the blood lay a tiny fragment of skull bone, the smooth curve of it white and wet with membrane and tiny blue veins. Kirkpatrick began to shake with fear. He looked like a frightened schoolboy. With his skinny arms and legs sticking out of his khaki uniform shirt and baggy shorts he seemed even younger than his seventeen years.

Johnson went over to Kirkpatrick and put his arm around his shoulders. *You never know how a man will react to hostile fire.* Johnson, the company slacker, had so far turned out to be the strongest of them all under fire.

'Steve,' he said to Kirkpatrick. 'It'll be all right.'

Kirkpatrick turned and looked at him. His eyes were sunken and hollow with fear. Tears began to roll down his filthy cheeks. He said nothing, but the shaking began to abate. Wallis struggled down the trench towards me. His eyes were open wide in a mixture of fear and rage; his hands were shaking. He jabbed his finger at Kirkpatrick and at Steinberg, lying in his own blood.

'*What are you going to do now?*' he said, leaning forward towards me, his breath coming in angry, terrified gulps.

'We stay here,' I said, my voice was shaking. 'The line must be steady.'

'Here? We stay here?' he was almost screaming. 'They're going to die! We're going to die! You're going to die!'

I pushed him, hard, in the centre of his chest. 'Get back to your post!' I heard myself screaming now, somewhere, far away. 'The fucking line must be steady.'

Wallis half-stumbled, and fell. He picked himself up and faced me. His eyes were dark and menacing.

'*Get back!*' I heard Major Macintyre's voice behind me. At the very edge of my vision, I could see the cold round steel of his revolver barrel lowered towards Wallis.

There were a dozen or so of us trapped in the trench. We could hear the sound of the German machine guns. The return fire from our own men was sporadic. Our whole brigade was pinned down just as we were; islands of bleeding, defeated men trapped in the dummy trenches, behind rocks and in shallow depressions in the hot, red dust.

We were vaguely aware of bugles somewhere far to our left. At last the Rhodesians, the Loyal North Lancs and the Baluchis were being thrown forward. They were too far away and there was no way of communicating with them. General Malleson had delayed sending them for too long. Now they could do nothing for us where we were, trapped.

The slightest attempt to move brought in a hail of German bullets. The sun climbed higher in the sky. There was nothing to drink; most of the men had gulped down the water in their canteens before we had even made that fateful advance in mass through the open grassland.

'Where's Corporal Reynolds?' Miller asked.

'He's dead, he fell into a Hun trap,' Carter said.

There was a loud burst of fire. A man from the 6th came scrambling into our trench. He tumbled down into the bottom and lay gasping for breath.

'They're killing us out there. We had orders to move to protect your left flank, but the Huns and their niggers have got us pinned down. Every time we try to move they slaughter us.'

He began to shake his head. 'It's impossible. It's just fucking impossible.'

'Shut up,' Carter said. 'Shut your mouth.'

The man stared at him for a few moments, and then something inside him snapped. 'Fuck you!' he screamed. 'You're a fucking officer. Do you know what I saw? While the Germans are killing us, a group of officers drove up in a car behind the lines and started unpacking a picnic – a fucking picnic. Wicker baskets, champagne, silver –'

Sergeant Visser hit him. Splitting his lip with the first blow and knocking out a tooth with the second. The man fell backwards against the wall of the trench, blood streaming out his mouth. Visser moved up on him, surprisingly quickly for a man of his bulk. His fist was cocked again. The man dropped his rifle and put his hands up to defend himself. 'No, no, no,' he was mumbling.

Somewhere in the distance, our bugles rang out. It was the order to withdraw.

'Thank *God*,' I heard Matthews mutter under his breath.

Carter turned and looked at us. 'There must be no panic. We must hold this position until the units on our right flank are clear.'

'Hold this position?' Wallis asked, his voice incredulous. 'We're not *holding* anything.'

Just then the German bugles rang out. It was the order to counterattack.

'We are now,' Macintyre spat. His revolver was in his hand. It was lowered, pointing towards the ground, but no one could mistake his meaning. 'You will stand and hold this position. There must be no panic.'

Carter looked over at Macintyre for a second, and then glanced back again, towards Salaita.

There was a sustained burst of machine-gun fire from the German trenches in the bush in front of us. Clouds of dust exploded at the lip of the trench. There were a few screams as more of our men were hit. Then a strange quiet fell all down the line. It seemed to unnerve the men more than anything.

A single cry rang out from the bush. A hoarse shout of rage.

And then the charge began. We could hear the askaris coming, screaming '*piga, piga!*' –'shoot, shoot!' Hundreds of them were crashing through the bush, the waves of sound sweeping out before them, cowing and terrifying our men long before their bayonets reached us.

Carter jammed his revolver back into his holster. He snatched up the rifle the man from the 5th had dropped. He stood up full above the lip of the trench and began firing into the bush.

He was working the bolt of the Lee-Enfield furiously. Ejecting the spent, shiny cartridges and lifting the rifle to his shoulder to fire again, and again.

'Five rounds rapid,' he yelled out the corner of his mouth.

'Five rounds rapid,' Visser repeated. Matthews was firing. Miller was cowering against the side of the trench. Wallis was leaning up against the trench pointing his rifle into the bush. I saw him pull the trigger. Burger was hit in the shoulder. The bullet spun him around and slammed him crazily against the exposed roots of a thorn tree. Major Macintyre was pointing his revolver into the smoke around him and pulling the trigger, over and over.

Kirkpatrick was sitting on the bottom of the trench. He covered his ears with his hands. Visser grabbed him by the collar and threw him up against the front wall of the trench. '*Five rounds rapid,*' he screamed at him. It was useless. Nothing could raise the boy now.

Johnson was up at the edge of the trench and firing, working the bolt of his own rifle. He peered down the sights with a cold fury. His face was expressionless with the concentration it took for him to seek out and kill the enemy.

My own world was overwhelmed by a wave of terror, stronger than anything I had ever felt before. My hands were shaking. The breath was coming in panicky, burning gulps into my lungs. Somehow, I took my own rifle and began firing, shooting into the grey, dusty bush in front of me. I could not aim. I found myself just pulling the trigger and working the bolt.

Our men took heart from Carter's example and did the same as me. First, I could only hear single shots ringing out. Then the firing picked up – *crack, crack, crack-crack*, faster and faster the shots began to ring out.

I could see the first faces of the askaris emerging through the smoke and the thick bush. Some of them wore ostrich feather headdress, others had long tufts of grass for camouflage tied around their heads. They had gleaming bayonets fixed to the barrels of their rifles.

They came, thick and fast, through the bush, but we held them. Their charge faltered. Somehow two of our armoured cars had broken through the German lines. They were driving up and down behind the charging askaris. Their turrets revolved as they scythed the askaris down with their machine guns.

Carter turned to us, and pointed with the barrel of his rifle. 'We'll move back to the next row of trenches,' he said. 'Wallis, you and that man,' he pointed at Fielding, 'put Steinberg in a groundsheet and drag him back with you. We'll try and get him to a field ambulance.'

Carter looked over at Burger. 'Can you run?' he said. Burger, white-faced with pain, nodded. 'Right,' he went on. 'Sergeant, you bring Kirkpatrick.'

He looked over at me and Matthews and Miller. Somehow Miller had managed to regain his composure, at least enough to look like he was in control of himself. 'We'll stay and cover the withdrawal of the wounded and then you subalterns follow with the rest of your men.' Carter looked over us. 'Remember, this is a withdrawal, not a retreat.'

Macintyre was loading his revolver again, hastily shoving the bullets into the cylinder. There was blood trickling down under his sleeve from where a bullet had nicked his arm.

Wallis and Fielding rolled Steinberg onto a groundsheet. They dragged him as carefully as they could and began hoisting him towards the back lip of the trench.

The armoured cars had gone. The German bugles rang out. The askaris came on again, smashing through the bush. The askaris nearest us were the crack troops of the 6th *Schutztruppe*. They were men who had been battle-hardened over nearly two years of war. Their charge was brave and disciplined, and they were mad now with the killing lust as we had been this morning, so long ago. This time there was no stopping them.

They were on to us before we knew it. As we scrambled out of the trench I saw three of them catch Conradie. He stumbled as one of them stabbed him in the back; the other smashed his teeth with the butt of his rifle. The third ripped him open at the stomach with a long, practiced sweep of the bayonet. There was a flash of red opening up and then Conradie's intestines poured out onto the ground. He screamed as his boots tangled up in them. He twisted and flailed and tried, too late, to flee their oncoming rush.

The askaris came on and on. Wave after wave of wild, confident men, fearing nothing any longer.

We broke in the iron face of the askaris' bravery. I could see our men at that critical moment, abandoning our last hope, the machine guns, jumping up, turning and running through the thorn bushes. Within seconds the bush around me was filled with men screaming in fear, dropping their rifles, water bottles and their wounded comrades in their panic to get away.

The entire South African brigade was fleeing in terror. Whole companies, or what remained of them, turned and ran, leaving their dead and wounded behind them. The regiments were hopelessly mixed in the panic to get away. The men ignored the few officers who tried to rally them, pushing them out of the way as they scrambled backwards. Carter tried to grab one of the fleeing men by the straps of his webbing. The man twisted sideways to avoid his grasp and scrambled away.

I saw Major Macintyre above me, firing his revolver. An askari loomed out of the bush behind him. The man swung his rifle butt at Macintyre. He ducked and shot the askari in the chest. Then I lost sight of him as he disappeared into the thick bush.

The askaris were on us now, yelling, shooting, kicking and stabbing. The main group of men had managed to get out of the trench just in time. I could hear them crashing through the bush behind us. Miller and I were left in the trench. I saw the gleam of bayonets and Miller falling, curling himself into a foetal position. He screamed as the first bayonet tore open his nose. The next sliced into the flesh above his kidneys.

I was alone in the trench. The askaris were bearing down on me between the narrow earth walls. The terror rose up inside me, half-choking me with its crippling, burning fire. I shot point blank into the face of one of them. I heard him scream. I saw his face crumple and his eyes roll backwards. I watched him fall, then I turned and scrambled up and out over the red earth walls.

As I ran I caught a glimpse of Sergeant Visser's body lying flat on his back in the long grass. His tunic was torn open and was soaked in the blood that pumped in runnels down the sides of his fat, white belly. His own rifle with fixed bayonet stood upside down, plunged deep into the redness of his chest. I saw Wallis fleeing into the bush chased by two askaris. There was no sign of Kirkpatrick, nor any of the others.

There was a large rock in the bush behind me. I sprinted and dived behind it. My hands were slick with sweat. I was weak with horror and fear, but I turned and somehow I fired again. The askaris kept coming. They were almost on me. I scrabbled back again, my feet slipping on the fine, powdery dust and stumbling over the rocks scattered on the ground.

A baobab tree loomed white out of the red dust and clouds of black smoke. I made for it and took cover behind its thick bulbous trunk. Carter was struggling on the ground with an askari who had caught him. The man had Carter on his back and he was holding a bayonet above Carter's filthy, blood-spattered face. Carter had him by the wrist. He was just managing to hold the blade away from slicing into him. Inch by inch, the blade came closer as Carter gave way to the younger man's strength.

A wave of uncontrollable fury swept over the top of my terror. I ran over to them with my rifle lifted high over my head. I was still shaking as I slammed the butt down hard onto the back of the askari's skull. He grunted and fell sideways. Carter prised the bayonet out of the askari's hand and wriggled out from under his prone body. He jammed the blade into the man's back. He pulled it out and flipped him over. He grabbed the man's curly hair in his left hand and jerked his head back against the ground. The man was still half-conscious and his eyes were wide with terror. Carter stabbed the bayonet downwards. Into the left eye, hard and deep. He turned the blade in the socket, wedging it tight against the edges of the bone. He left the bayonet lodged in the man's skull. Carter scrambled upright. He kicked the dying askari hard in the head; the blood sprayed out.

We looked at each other. Carter's hands were red with blood. His face was drawn and haunted. Hundreds of other askaris were yelling and crashing through the bush close behind us, chasing the main body of the regiment. There was no time for words. I lost sight of Carter in the dense bush as we fled. I was alone again, with the enemy all around. I ran as hard as I could.

The bush was filled with fleeing men. The askaris' charge had stampeded the ammunition mules. They bolted wildly alongside us, their traces and bits jangling loose. Their mouths foaming and their eyes rolling in terror. Loud bangs from the askaris' ancient rifles rang out behind us, or from the sides where snipers were concealed in anthills and in hollowed-out baobab trunks. A man, or two, of ours would fall while the rest of us kept running. I could hear the askaris yelling with excitement as they caught up to one of our slower men and stabbed or beat him to death. There was nothing we could do now to help them. We could only run. We had broken and we had no way left to defend ourselves.

We came to a low rise at the edge of the thick bush. Shots rang out from in front of me. It was a new trap. The Germans would slaughter us now. More shots rang out.

Then I saw them – neat turbans gleaming with regimental badges. Under them were the stern, dark faces of the Baluchis. In steady ranks they held the ridge. They were shooting disciplined volleys back at the askaris, giving us covering fire.

A bugle rang out and the long lines of Baluchis charged forward, their bayonets gleaming in the hot sun. They came through our frightened, broken ranks and descended on the askaris, meeting steel with steel, smashing head on into their wild, exultant charge. They shot and slashed and stabbed and drove the askaris back into the bush.

In a few minutes it was over. It was the askaris' turn to feel pain as their charge collapsed and broke under the determined onslaught of the Baluchis. It was their turn to flee as the Baluchis fired into the chaos of their retreat. It was their turn to bleed. It was their turn to scream and die.

12

KILIMANJARO LAY CLEAR AND distant in the night sky. The stars gleamed cold and white. They seemed different now. Everything seemed different as we began to count the cost of the day.

Exhausted as we were, we had been ordered to dig in around the edge of the camp at Serengeti in case the Germans came after us in our weakened, frightened state. Guards stood to in the shallow trenches throughout the night, waiting. No fires were allowed. We huddled together and ate cold biscuit and corned beef. The tents had been ordered struck. We feared that the moon shining on their white sides would provide a target for the Germans if they came. The wounded lay out under the open sky. Most of them were silent, but a few groaned as even morphine could not stop them slipping deeper and deeper into the swirling currents of their pain. The surgeons had been operating non-stop since morning. They would keep stitching, slicing and bandaging for another two days without a break. Outside the hospital tents the bodies of the men the surgeons could not save lay on the ground. They were covered in blankets, waiting for morning, when they could be buried.

Hyenas were gathering in the darkness. I could hear their low *whoop, whoop, whooop*. Occasionally, I could see their dark, humped shapes as they slunk past us in the night, attracted by the smell of new-killed meat and bones on the savanna. There was the call of a single jackal, deep and faraway in the bush, then another joined him. They were circling the edges of the battlefield, revelling in the iron smell of fresh blood mingling with the dew on the grass.

Men moved like ghosts in the hazy darkness around me. I had survived the day unwounded, but I could only think back on it with a sensation of spinning numbness. I did everything not to give in to my exhaustion – to hold on, searching for clarity in the cloud-like shapes of the umbrella thorns against the stars.

I had collapsed unconscious in the long grass somewhere behind the Rhodesians who were holding the line in support of the Baluchis. Two porters found me and carried me nearly two miles to the makeshift hospital tent strung between two baobab trees. I don't know how long I lay on the ground. I remember coming to and hearing the doctor's voice, curt and sharp: 'Heat stroke. Give him some water.' He dismissed me with a wave of his hand, and turned back towards the rows of wounded men on the rough ground. The blood mingling from their wounds was so thick, the blankets they were lying on were black and slippery with it.

There was hardly any water in camp. The medical orderly had given me a single mug, but it was not nearly enough. Waves of nausea still washed over me from time to time, but they hardly seemed to matter. I noticed them through the surging images of horror that filled my head, as one might notice some tiny detail in the landscape of a valley miles below.

The vague wisp of a conversation I had overheard among some of the ambulance muleteers and the stretcher bearers kept coming back to me. They had been talking in hoarse, low whispers.

'Jesus, you just can't believe what it was like. They were lying all over the place…'

'We couldn't hardly keep up with the work. The grass and the bush was so thick, we kept on finding new ones. Then there was one pile of wounded and, worse, we come across, must've been thirty of the poor bastards lying there. Some of them were groaning. They were covered in each other's blood. We got there just in time, two hyenas were skulking in the bushes nearby when we found them…'

I had my own memories, already crowding in on me. Williams, Hooper, Miller, Conradie, Sergeant Visser… Corporal Reynolds. The world of the dead seemed more real now than the shattered world of the living.

The dead and wounded one could account for, but it was the missing that haunted my thoughts. First Williams and Watson and then Kirkpatrick and Wallis had gone missing from my platoon during the chaos. More than thirty others were missing from our regiment alone. What was their fate? Had they been captured, and were now being tortured somewhere in the bush behind that damned hill? Had they been wounded like Steinberg and left behind to the marauding askaris? Williams and Watson had disappeared right at the beginning of things. The last time anyone recalled seeing Kirkpatrick was leaving the trench with Sergeant Visser. I was not the only one who had seen Sergeant Visser's body, but no one had seen Kirkpatrick.

And no one had seen Steinberg or Wallis, who was supposed to bring him in. Fielding, though, had come back, wounded himself. He was so shocked he could hardly speak. He could not say what had happened to Steinberg, nor why he had left him there. Fielding was a cowed, broken man. I wondered if he would ever be fit for combat again.

I could not find it in me to pity him, though. He had abandoned Steinberg on the battle field. I shuddered with horror to think of what the hyenas would do to him and the other men lying helpless and in pain in the dark. I wondered what had happened to Wallis. Major Macintyre was the most senior officer among the missing.

There were rumours that not all of the missing had been captured or wounded. Men had been seen disappearing into the bush in the confusion as we tried to regroup behind the protection of the Baluchis and the Rhodesians. There were already stories circulating among the men that after their first taste of battle many of the missing were heading for Nairobi, and from there to the coast to escape the war.

The low murmur of men's voices surrounded me: Swahili, Afrikaans, Urdu, Pashto, English. The voices of the men, the terrified whinnying of the horses and the exhausted braying of the mules mingled into one frightened, angry, unintelligible Babel.

Occasionally a shouted order broke through the low rumblings of voices, and disappeared into the muted turmoil of our defeated army as suddenly as it had risen up. In amongst it, I could hear harnesses, gun carriage traces, empty canteens, rifle barrels, bayonets, belt buckles clinking like tiny bells, reminders in the darkness of the dead and wounded we had abandoned to their fate.

The guilt flowed in, sharp and bitter under the numbness. How many of the men in my platoon had survived? Hooper was dead, I myself had seen him killed. Hooper... The question burned in my mind: what had I told him to do? If I had not ordered him to move at that very moment, might he still be alive?

I could not bear to think of the pain-wracked face of Corporal Reynolds. And Sergeant Visser... he was dead. I still hoped they would be accounted for alive – I had been happy to see Campbell come staggering into camp with some bedraggled men from the 6th.

Johnson, of course, had survived. Just as the sun was going down I had found him somewhere among the men lying on his back smoking a cigarette. He had been staring up at the sky, his rifle that he had used to such great effect on the ground beside him.

'You did well today,' I told him.

'Did I?' his voice was cold and hollow. Then he sat up and looked at me. 'Do you know what happened to Stephen?'

'No, I don't.'

He pulled on his cigarette. 'They're calling him a coward.'

'He wasn't that.'

Johnson looked up at me. 'I lost him, sir. I tried to keep him with me, but there were so many of them I couldn't.' He looked down at the ground. Tears began to run down his filthy, scarred cheeks. He wiped at the corner of his mouth with his sleeve.

'He was just scared, that's all it was, sir. It was his first time. It could have happened to anybody. I should have stayed with him.' His skinny shoulders were shaking.

'You did your best,' I said. 'If it weren't for you –' But he had already turned away from me.

Burger had made it too. I had found him when they were dressing his wounded shoulder.

'What happened to the others?' he asked.

He looked up at me when I had finished telling him. His eyes were wide and flecked with rage. He spoke slowly, the morphine and the pain blurring his words. 'It was true what that man said about the picnic, and the champagne. He wasn't the only one who saw it.'

Macintyre, Williams, Wallis, Kirkpatrick, Watson – they were all missing.

Men were still coming in. A porter, wrapped in a faded, ragged strip of cloth, shuffled past, his face copper in the moonlight. His left arm was shiny and wet. His hand swung loose at his side; he held his upper arm tight above the elbow with the other. He must have been hit by German pom-pom fire landing close behind our lines. Two young white soldiers from the Loyal North Lancs followed behind him, supporting one another. The nearest boy limped with one boot; the other had a field dressing tied around his ribs. His head was lolling over onto his companion's shoulder.

Nearby Burger was talking to Lieutenant Scheepers. Burger's arm was in a sling now, dressed and clean. The two of them were speaking in Afrikaans, their voices low, the sharing of their language taking them beyond the hierarchy of rank.

'Your platoon got the worst of it,' I heard Scheepers saying. 'Carter and Macintyre and Fuller led you closest to the hill. Your platoon and two others were in front of the rest of the regiment.'

'And much good it did us,' Burger said.

'What happened with that young boy? What's his name –?'

'Kirkpatrick.'

'Some of the men say they saw him lying on the ground, shaking with fear. Others say he was taken prisoner by the Germans. It doesn't look good, his father being who he is. They're talking about him, the war hero's son who turned yellow.'

'Let them talk,' Burger growled. 'They were running themselves.'

'It's not that simple. You have to understand. There's his father and his reputation –'

Burger turned away, cutting him short. Scheepers watched as the older man disappeared into the night. Then he himself turned and wandered down towards where the rows of stretcher bearers were still coming in.

A group of officers was standing in the darkness as the wounded streamed past them. They were talking in low, anxious voices. Van Hasselt and Carter were with them, so was Major Reading. In a daze I wandered over to join them. They were standing around two stretchers lying on the ground. I could see the Sam Browne belt and the blood-stained officer's tunic.

Only half of Macintyre's head remained. He had been shot in the face. The bullet had torn away the bone and the flesh. Williams' body was next to him. He had been shot full in the front of the chest, the heavy bullet from the askari's rifle ripping through his body. He must have been killed instantly.

'My God,' Major Reading swallowed. He ran his fingers through his hair. They were trembling. 'Did anyone see what happened?'

Van Hasselt turned to Carter. 'You and Macintyre were out in the front. I saw you holding the line together.'

'We lost sight of each other after the askaris overwhelmed us,' Carter said.

Van Hasselt looked down at Macintyre and Williams' shattered bodies.

'It was thanks to the two of you that more men weren't killed.'

Carter nodded, his face gaunt and filthy in the darkness.

Words. They seemed empty, hollow sounds, their meaning wiped out by the memories that were in our heads.

'Did anyone see them after the – the withdrawal began?' Reading asked.

'I saw Macintyre fight off an askari,' I said. 'Then I lost sight of him. I lost track of Williams right after we crossed the grasslands.'

'I saw him in the bush,' Scheepers was shaking his head sadly in disbelief. 'He was scared, crouching down under a bush. I never expected him to die like this. He must have been one of the last to be hit before we turned and ran.'

'The askaris must have got them as they charged,' Van Hasselt said.

Major Reading was looking down at the mangled body. 'The first battle. For both of them. And no one will ever know how they died.'

But no one knew what had happened to Wallis, Kirkpatrick and Watson.

There was no sleep for us that night. We kept an anxious watch in the darkness for the German attack that we believed must come. The exhaustion, the horror and the humiliation of the day had brought us near to the edge of panic.

All night we could hear the muffled groans and the occasional screams of pain drifting through the darkness from the hospital tents as the wounded lay waiting for the hard-pressed surgeons to get to them. It was unnerving. Every scream brought back the terrifying images of what we had lived through. If the Germans had attacked that night I doubt whether we would have held our ground. I don't know how any officer would have persuaded his men that they could survive another charge by the askaris.

But it never came. Sometime late that night Carter found me standing guard with the regiment on the camp perimeter. He called me back out of the trench onto the ground behind one of the blockhouses.

'I wanted to thank you.'

I looked at his face in the shadows. 'I just reacted. It doesn't even seem real anymore.'

'It is to me. I wouldn't be alive had you not done what you did.'

'I'm glad you are.'

He reached inside his tunic and took out a pewter hip flask. I took it from him. His hands were shaking as he passed it over. He must have seen my look of surprise.

'I don't usually. But after today I think we both need it.'

I took a swig. The warm, burning taste of whisky coursed down my throat.

'Take another one,' Carter said. I swallowed again and handed it back to him.

'It's terrible isn't it? About Williams. And Macintyre.'

Carter shook his head slowly. 'Williams' death is a tragedy. But he died bravely, facing the enemy. That will be a comfort to somebody.'

'Will it?'

'There's nothing else to offer them.'

He passed me the flask. I drank again. Carter took a deep breath in the cold night air.

'Macintyre and I, we hated each other all our lives. And I –' he looked away and a shudder of something – regret, abhorrence, shame made him turn away from me. 'I didn't like him either,' I said, wondering at this strange reaction from Carter. Then I found myself remembering the torn hole in his face, and the full horror of everything that had happened came rising up inside me. It was a black, unstoppable convulsion that ran through my body. '*So many of them*,' I found myself saying in a distant, faraway voice. 'How could they have killed so many? Just about my whole platoon.'

'Stop.' Carter's hand was on my shoulder. His hands were cut and bleeding. He was shaking. 'Stop it.'

I sat on the cold ground and drank his whisky with him, trying to piece together the fragments of memory from the battle that swirled in my brain. We sat for a long time, the alcohol and the horror sinking into our minds.

'Look,' Carter said at some point. We stood up and turned in the direction he was pointing. A column of Baluchis were coming in through the gate. They were stepping proudly in line, their faces hard and fierce in the starlight.

Our men, defeated and haggard, turned and watched as they came in. Many glared at them in exhausted silence, but a ragged, weak sound of clapping broke out here and there among the ranks. There were even a few rasping cheers.

The Baluchis marched past heedlessly, their heads held high. Jemadar Khan was leading them, followed by Muhammed Din. He was carrying a heavy bundle wrapped in canvas. More men behind him were leading mules carrying similar bundles. They marched up to where our officers were standing.

Jemadar Khan halted his men and saluted. He turned and pulled off the canvas cover of the bundle Muhammed Din was carrying. He was holding two of the machine guns we had abandoned. Muhammed Din lowered his thick, muscular arms and the machine guns clattered down onto the ground in front of Major Reading.

'With the compliments of the 130th Baluchis,' Khan said, and then, his eyes flashing: 'May we remind you that we are not coolies. We are sepoys.'

13

WE BEGAN DIGGING THE GRAVES as soon as it grew light. One by one, we placed our dead in the ground. They had brought in poor Hooper's body overnight. His face was peaceful in death, the skin smooth and white, but the fragile skull bone at the back of his head had already been cracked and gnawed by hyenas. They laid his corpse next to that of Williams.

Macintyre's body was there too; the horror of his shattered face covered now, in daylight, by a blood-soaked blanket. I was glad of that. I turned away, trying to forget the gruesome image that the memory of last night brought welling to the surface. I thought of the woman I had seen on the station platform. I wondered who would tell her and what they would say.

Of Sergeant Visser and Corporal Reynolds there was no sign. They would never be buried. Only six bodies from the 7th had been recovered; thirty or more lay somewhere lost in the bush.

'In the midst of life we are in death…

The priest's voice wavered as he read from the back of his book. His prayers drifted out into the cool morning air. They mingled with the grating of the spades and the scattered thuds of earth falling on cold, stiff bodies.

'… commit their bodies to the ground; earth to earth, ashes to ashes, dust to dust; in sure and certain hope…'

A few of the men wept, tears rolling down their cheeks as the words brought some distant comfort and release. For me, there were only the silences between the words. In them lay guilt and the memories that words could never explain.

Someone began to sing a hymn. I looked over at Carter. His head was bowed and he was staring at the ground. Reading's eyes were filled with tears. Van Hasselt held his sun helmet awkwardly, his eyes closed, his thoughts lost inside his large, powerful body.

Afterwards, when the piles of red earth lay silent in the growing heat of the day, Carter came over to me. 'You all right?' he asked.

I nodded. He was watching me under the brim of his sun helmet.

'There's a long way to go yet before this war is over,' he said. 'Yesterday was just the beginning.'

A hospital train came in later in the morning. It shone in the sun as it came to a halt in a screech of brakes and steam. Up and down its length we loaded the wounded onto its bright gleaming carriages. The train brought with it the smells of another world, the world of women, fresh water, clean sheets. The train brought mail, too. I watched as the lucky men amongst us were handed their letters. No one opened the envelope right away. They carried it a little way away and opened it only when they were alone. I waited, my heart pounding, hoping for something from Helen, until the very end, but there was nothing for me. I was not the only one. A small group of us turned away, not daring to look at one another – or at the men who had been lucky.

'It happens all the time,' Captain Carter said. 'The mail always gets lost on its way up to the front. It'll come on the next train. Or the one after that.'

'Yes. It's just a matter of time.'

An hour or so after it had arrived, the train shunted and screeched and took the wounded away, leaving us staring along its length as it gathered speed and disappeared down the line. Once the noise of the locomotive had faded, we were ordered to form up. We marched back to the camp at Mbuyuni, silent except for the sounds of our new world: the constant clanking of steel on steel, shouted commands in the distance, and the buzz of flies in the shimmering heat.

Rest. Hot food. Sleep. From these beginnings, courage begins to grow again. Within two days of being back at Mbuyuni our broken regiments were beginning to talk of the next battle. Major Reading ordered more marches into the bush, more firing practice, and endless bayonet drills, slashing and stabbing at rows of straw men set up on the parade ground. There was no light-heartedness about the drills now. The men sweated and strained at their work. There was rage, and the memory of our comrades' deaths in each hard thrust and in each deep slash.

It was fear that lay at the heart of our determination. We had learned the first lesson of war: we knew now *what would happen next* – and we feared that more than anything. Not a single one of us could say that we had seen fear and triumphed over it. To think like that was an absurdity, a meaningless abstraction. The only thing each one of us wanted to do now was to survive our next battle. And we had learned that we could not survive if we did not know how to fight.

I sat down in my tent a dozen times and tried to write to Helen. I had survived the battle, as I promised her I would. It was a promise I saw now I had no power to keep, or even to make. Before Salaita, I could believe that I had some intuition that I would be safe. Now I knew that was not true. The best I could do was to go on, to assume that I would not be killed. I could find no more certainty than that. To try and imagine beyond that point was madness. I was sure in retrospect that Helen must have seen through my attempt to hide from reality.

But how could I ever tell her what I had seen? Where could I begin? When I had arrived here, so long ago it seemed, I had wanted to share with her everything that I was going through. Now, I could think only about how to hide it from her. After Salaita, I feared the memories I would take back home with me. That alone was reason to hate the Germans and their askaris.

I could not write to Helen of hate, nor of fear, nor of the fresh blood thickening around Corporal Reynolds' soft grey wisps of hair. What could I write to her about? These were the things that marked out my life now. For days after the battle I wrote nothing. I could not bring myself to tell her of what I had seen. I could not speak to her of my days of rage and my nights of guilt. Outside, I was an officer doing his duty. But inside I was overwhelmed by the memory of horror and, in wanting to hide that from her, I hid from myself instead.

They merged the remains of my platoon with Matthews'. They gave me command of it. Matthews was not pleased. I did not know what to think. Instead, I contented myself with watching alongside Matthews as Johnson and Campbell trained with the bayonet, sweat dripping off them, their faces screwed up in concentration.

'We'll get them next time,' Johnson said when I came over to them for the third or fourth time that day.

Campbell swung around from the ripped straw dummy. His bayonet shining in the sun, his youthful face hard now.

'We'll never let them do it to us again. We'll make them pay for every fucking one of us.'

Campbell turned and, in a single, smooth motion, he slammed his bayonet into the dummy; the wooden pole shook with the force of his blow.

Colonel Freeth had written to the Red Cross with the names of thirty-three missing men, but the Germans had not responded. Some of the men listed as missing I knew must be dead: Sergeant Visser and Corporal Reynolds were just two examples. No one had found their bodies yet, and as each day passed it became more and more unlikely that they would ever be recovered and given a decent burial.

The strangest of all was that there was no news of three of the men in my platoon: Kirkpatrick, Wallis and Watson. No one remembered seeing them being wounded, no one remembered seeing any of them after the rout began, and no one had found their bodies. Search parties were still being sent out to scour the battlefield and the bush surrounding it. Every day they ranged further and further, but still they found nothing. I could only hope for news from the Red Cross – that they were still alive and well and in German hands.

In the daytime, I went about my tasks as best I could. At night I had stopped dreaming of Helen. Instead, I would wake with the faces of my men staring at me in the darkness. On the second day, Major Reading had called me in.

'You're a credit to the regiment, to all of us, despite what happened,' he told me. 'A fine example to the men.'

I thought of how it had been, of the awful, burning terror that had made my hands shake as I held my rifle. 'It was Captain Carter,' I said. 'He was the one we followed.'

'Yes, his conduct hasn't gone unnoticed either. You and Carter, and Macintyre. You were the ones who were at the front of whatever assault there was. The three of you took your men as far as the edge of the dummy trenches. And you held them firm, for as long as you could before the brigade broke and ran.

Colonel Freeth is very pleased with your conduct at Salaita.' Reading shoved his hands in his pockets and stared at me. 'Had it not been for the way it turned out, you would all be up for medals.'

'What about the men in my platoon?'

'No word so far. I'm sorry.'

The news spread like wildfire. It was a breath of hope after so much failure. General Jannie Smuts and thousands of reinforcements were on their way. Once Smuts was here, the big push into German territory would begin at last. Smuts was still on the ocean voyage up from South Africa, but he was only days away. The trains began coming into Voi and the camps beyond, bringing the reinforcements for both divisions. They were mostly black troops: a regiment of King's African Rifles, three Nigerian regiments, a battalion of our coloured troops from South Africa, the Cape Corps, a detachment of soldiers from the Gold Coast. There was a white colonial regiment, the 25th Royal Fusiliers, and a number of Indian units: the Kashmir Rifles, the 29th Punjabis and the 17th Cavalry. Day after day, the troops poured in until there were thirty thousand soldiers of the British Empire waiting to advance across the frontier and sweep the Germans before them.

As the reinforcements poured in, we began to believe again. The excited talk flowed up and down the rows of tents. This time, with all of us together under Jannie Smuts with his famous luck, we could not fail. This time we would take Salaita and drive the Germans back, crushing them at last. We would take revenge for our dead and for our defeat.

But huge dark, rolling clouds began building up on the horizon. They broke up slowly, dissipating into the darkening blue skies, leaving the dusk clear and fresh. The rains were due in a month, or less. If we did not advance soon, our entire army would be stuck for weeks, unable to move in the mud and the endless days of tropical downpour.

At last Smuts arrived, disembarking at Mombasa and coming directly up to see Salaita.

Carter and Reading and I were among the officers selected to accompany him and his staff. We set off in a convoy, Smuts himself sitting straight-backed in the staff car, his clear, hard eyes and neatly-trimmed grey beard dominating everyone around him.

We stopped the convoy of cars along the road before we reached Njoro Drift. He got out first and walked to a gentle rise with a pair of binoculars hanging around his neck. He raised them to his eyes and scanned the bush and the small hill that had cost us so much. The Germans and their askaris were still there, no doubt watching us through their own binoculars, wondering what his arrival in East Africa meant for them and the fortunes of their war.

It seemed so strange to me, to be standing in the midst of this peaceful bush where only a week ago we had been forced to endure such horror. Here and there were a few broken trees or a shallow depression of bare rock and scorched ground where a shell had landed, but there was nothing else to show what it was we had gone through. It scarcely seemed possible that this quiet bush had been filled with the screams of the wounded and the endless thunder and crack of artillery and rifle fire. I stood there, watching the great general peering through his binoculars with his sharp, calculating eyes. Every now and then, he would turn to one of his aides and mutter something in a low voice. He would shake his head and then raise the binoculars to his eyes once more. He was seeing for himself the ground that we had blundered over, committing to memory every detail of the tactical errors that had led to our flight of terror.

It was the landscape of our humiliation. We would carry it with us for the rest of our lives, but the land itself had already forgotten us. Where I remembered the odour of fresh blood and the sour reek of fear, there was only the fine powdery dust under our feet and the hint of rain in the distant clouds building up over Kilimanjaro.

Smuts stood there for a long time, staring at the ground that lay between him and his opponent, General Von Lettow-Vorbeck. None of us dared disturb his thoughtful solitude. Finally, he climbed down from the rise he had been standing on and strode towards his car. An aide pulled open the door for him. Just before Smuts climbed into the car, I saw him turn towards one of his staff and hand him the binoculars.

'Damned kaffirs,' I heard him say, and then he climbed in and slammed the door shut. We got into our own cars and in a cloud of dust followed him back to camp. I glanced over at Carter and Reading. Their faces were expressionless, but I knew what they were thinking. Even Smuts was trapped by the same illusions of racial superiority, even he had not understood the inescapable meaning of Salaita hill.

When we got to Mbuyuni, Smuts said a few curt farewells and his convoy of staff cars immediately headed down the road to Nairobi. There, with his maps and typed reports spread out across the gleaming tables where the other generals had merely banqueted, he instead would lay plans, and mark out the first steps of our new war.

14

NOW THAT JAN SMUTS WAS HERE at last, there was confident talk of our upcoming 'new offensive.' There was talk, at last, too of what we all wanted – revenge. Major Reading had outlined Smuts' plan to us. 'The 1st Division under General Stewart will march east around Kilimanjaro. We're to advance from the west under General Tighe. Von Lettow will be trapped between us.'

'What if he slips out?' Carter asked.

'We follow him.'

Reading looked around the room. 'We have to leave before the rains start. Stewart's column marches out tonight. We follow within three days.'

'I wonder how it will turn out,' I wrote to Helen, at last finding the courage to probe the edges of my fear. The mail had been held up. I still had not received a letter from her, but I couldn't keep silent any longer. I wanted her to know that I was all right.

I scribbled in the light of the same candle stub lieutenant Scheepers had used when writing to his father the night before Salaita. *'Things have happened so quickly these past few days. I can't tell you everything now, but I do know that I will never see the world in quite the same way again.'*

I crumpled up the paper and started again. Slowly, I began to write, choosing each word carefully.

'I have faced my first test under fire. I have come out of it pretty well. Of course I can't tell you everything, but I'm all right, unwounded and ready to face whatever comes next. You won't receive any letters from me for a while, but don't worry. It won't be because I am hurt, or because I have forgotten about you – that would be impossible! It is because something big is about to happen. I can't say any more, but I will be fine. It's important for you to know that.'

The same lies again, tumbling out from underneath my pen. I stopped writing and stared at the wavering light on the tent wall. The images of Salaita swirled in my head. Corporal Reynolds skewered by the rough wooden stakes, his eyes holding mine from the bottom of the pit; Captain Carter hunched over, his face contorted, stabbing wildly down into the askari's eye sockets; Kirkpatrick and Wallis staring at me in rage and terror – the guilt of it washing over me because I didn't know what to do, how to lead them. And still there was no news of them, or of the trembling, malaria-stricken Watson.

I closed my eyes for a moment, trying to clear my head. I had to fight to hold on to my other memories, to the world I knew before Salaita.

Watching Helen in awe one night across the table from me at a dinner, so aware of her every movement, her small, perfectly-formed hands, the fullness of her lips as she spoke, the silky tendril of dark hair framing her face.

Afterwards, late at night, just the two of us sharing a drink on her porch. Helen holding her glass in the tips of her fingers. She was lounging gracefully against the wicker back of her chair, her face half-hidden in the yellow light and the shadows from the streetlamps across the road.

I opened my eyes and looked down at the sheet of paper in front of me. I could not afford to do anything to frighten her. I could not imagine losing her now. I understood why the men whose letters I had to censor wrote such cheery nonsense. To tell the truth was to risk too much. The truth would make you come out sounding bitter, crazy. One day, perhaps, would come the time for telling it. But for now the only business was survival. In order to carry on here you had to believe that there was something for you to go home to. Nothing, not even the truth, could ever be allowed to threaten that.

Officers' letters were never censored. They trusted us to know what we couldn't say.

I started writing again. *'The truth is, though, that not everyone in my platoon came out of it. Without you, and the memory of you, I don't know how I would have survived. I'm not talking about the actual fighting itself, but the horror that lives on in my head afterwards. Just to think of you, and of how much I love you has kept me sane. You have given me the strength to carry on now, despite the things that surround me here.'*

The men were trained and rested. They could hardly wait to meet the enemy again. Excitement filled the camp as the men made their preparations to depart. Smuts' plan was daring and far better than anything that the drunken buffoons before him had come up with.

The High Command had tried to keep what had happened to us at Salaita quiet, and so far it had not reached the newspapers, nor was our defeat public knowledge in Britain or South Africa. But we knew the whispers had been passed down the railway line as far as Mombasa that after all their talk, the South Africans didn't have the guts to stand up to the German askaris.

What had happened to us at Salaita had begun to take on a life of its own. It was not the numbers of dead and wounded, or the scale of our defeat that mattered – it was tiny by comparison to what men were enduring on the Western Front. What mattered to the generals was the story of what had happened to us. Britain and her allies needed the news of a success in Africa to help bolster the war effort. Instead, we had given them a humiliating defeat. Even worse, it had happened to white troops armed with the most modern of weapons against black troops fighting without artillery and with obsolete rifles.

It was the facts themselves which now posed the greatest danger to our commanders and to their reputations. They needed a credible case to present to the newspapers and to the politicians when the story of our defeat did become public. Every day, while we junior officers and the men trained in the blazing sun, messages and despatches about what happened at Salaita flew backwards and forwards between our senior officers and headquarters in Nairobi.

It was one, unexpected, message amidst that anxious flurry of words that came to define my war. A single moment of truth among so many lies and evasions.

The despatch came two days before we were due to leave on the long flanking march that would meet Stewart's army. Shortly after it arrived, Major Reading called me and Carter in. The message had come via headquarters in Nairobi from Major Pretorius' Intelligence Section. It was the first news of the missing we had heard since Salaita. Major Reading's voice was flat and expressionless as he read from the typed sheet of paper he held in his hands.

'*Privates Wallis,*' he began, and then went on. '*Kirkpatrick, and Watson have been seen moving west towards German territory.*'

This changed everything for us. They were deserters, cowards. But they were our men. All three of them were in my platoon, under my direct command, and above me was Carter and above him had been Macintyre. A few days ago, the two of us had been respected and admired by the High Command. But now the ominous stink of failure hung over us.

I stared at Reading. I didn't know what to say. I could feel the blood rising into my cheeks.

'But can this be confirmed?' Carter asked. 'Only one of the missing has definitely been accounted for so far. Poor Anderson. He was found with his throat slit, but no other wounds. He must have been hiding alone in the darkness until the askaris found him. The others might have been killed too, or captured by the Germans. We haven't had the final report from the Red Cross yet.'

'The sighting was quite definite. Major Pretorius' informants among the Masai and the Ndorobo told him that three British soldiers, one of them ill, had been hiding in a village nearby for some days. Three days ago they left and were seen heading into German territory.'

'What would they be heading into *German* territory for?' I asked.

'It's the route we would least expect,' Reading answered. 'We would imagine they would head east for the coast or north for Nairobi and we would look for them there. They hid in a village for some days before they set out. That's when Pretorius' informers spotted them. They must have gambled that we wouldn't guess they would go west.'

Carter nodded his head. 'It makes sense. Everyone must know that most of Von Lettow's soldiers have abandoned the north-east of their colony. There's a good chance the country might be almost clear now through to the Belgian Congo. If their luck holds and they don't get seen by one of our patrols or picked up by the Belgian army while crossing the border, they could make their way through the jungle to Stanleyville. They could find passage on a river boat to some remote Belgian settlement on the banks of the Congo River. There they could become any one of thousands of white men lost in the forest. Very few questions are asked about a white man's past in that part of the world. The colour of his skin is his passport and his guarantee of safe passage. With a bit of luck and a cautious mouth, they can rely on the continent itself to shelter them until the war is over.'

'Still,' I insisted. 'I don't see how we can be sure that they're our men.'

'The descriptions match,' Reading replied. 'Our informants say that two young boys and an older man have been seen on the run. One of the young boys has red hair. That must be Watson. The other young soldier is short and has blonde hair. It must be Kirkpatrick. The older man has dark hair and speaks a little Swahili and some Arabic. A lot of men have picked up some Swahili in the last few weeks, but Wallis is the only man in the entire East African Brigade who knows some Arabic. He knows French as well.'

The information was damning. I wondered, though, how Watson was keeping up with the other two. His malaria had been real enough. Then I remembered the report said they had waited some days in a village before moving out. That sounded like Wallis, making sure that Watson had recovered somewhat before leading them out across the savanna.

My head was spinning with the implications of it.

'Their running away is a humiliation for the whole brigade,' I heard Reading say. 'They have let down their comrades and been disloyal to you, their officers. And they have betrayed the regiment. With this and with what happened at Salaita, we've become the laughingstock of the whole division. Perhaps I shouldn't be telling you this, but there has been all sorts of talk and finger-pointing at headquarters among the British officers – especially after the Cape Boys were so steady during the attack the other night at Ngare Nairobi.'

Reading jammed his hands deep into his pockets. He went over to the window and looked out over the rough bush airstrip.

'But that's not the main issue with these runaway men. The real problem, is that, as you probably know, young Kirkpatrick's father is General Kirkpatrick. He fought under Kitchener at Khartoum, and was highly decorated for that action and for his bravery at Spion Kop. He is well-known at Buckingham Palace and throughout the Empire. He is also a friend of General Smuts.'

He paused, to let that fact sink in. It wasn't necessary for him to say more. Then he went on. 'If the Germans get hold of Kirkpatrick, they will publicise it. The last thing we need is the story of a war hero's son deserting under fire coming on top of the news of what happened at Salaita. Especially after all that business of falling asleep on sentry duty.'

Reading turned back towards us. 'I don't have to remind you that showing cowardice in the face of the enemy is a serious offence. The maximum penalty is death.'

Carter's eyes flickered down towards the floor and then he forced them up again. He swallowed, his Adam's apple sliding underneath the sheen of sweat on his skin.

'A lot of officers believe in the firing squad,' Reading said. 'As an example to the rest of the men.' He watched us for a moment. 'But I'm not one of them. You can't use fear to make men brave.'

Outside, one of the aeroplanes was coming in to land. It seemed to hover above the ground, its double wings dipping one way and then the other before it bounced onto the hard earth. The three of us watched as it bumped and wobbled further away down the field and the sound of the engine died down.

'The Germans won't shoot them,' Carter said. 'At the very least, Kirkpatrick will be too valuable to them.'

Reading didn't move.

'So you see, you have to help me. You have to get to them before anyone else does. Now that Macintyre's dead, you've been put directly under my command. And that means Wallis, Kirkpatrick and Watson are under my command too now.'

Reading was staring at us. His eyes were hard and unmoving. 'I just might be able to do something to stop a firing squad. But only if you bring them to me first. If any other officer gets his hands on them before me, there will be nothing any of us can do. Their fate will be entirely in the hands of strangers. Men who will see sacrificing them – making an example of them – as one more step towards winning this war.'

'Surely with Kirkpatrick's connections –?' I began.

'Possibly,' Reading interrupted. 'I've thought of that. They could also make things worse. The war's going very badly in Europe. Men are being killed on the Western Front in their tens of thousands. Deserters are shot every week there. It wouldn't look good for the story to leak out that officers were showing favouritism here on the colonial front.'

'When do you need us to leave?' Carter asked.

'No later than dawn tomorrow. You must go before the main column sets off.'

We had turned to open the door, when his quiet voice stopped us.

'You know I can't guarantee anything – for any of you.'

15

'WE TRAVEL LIGHT AND FAST,' Carter said to me outside. 'With men who know the country. We'll have to move fast if we're going to find these three.'

I knew immediately who it was that Carter would ask to join us. That day was a mad scramble to find the three of them, and to organise the mules and supplies we needed without answering the multitude of questions as to why we wanted them in such a hurry.

'We're going ahead to scout for the big offensive,' Carter told the quartermaster. Then we strode over to the Baluchi camp in the white blaze of the noonday sun.

Jemadar Khan looked at the sweat pouring off the two of us.

'Yes,' he said. 'You came when my men were dying after the bomb went off, so now I'll come with you.'

I followed Captain Carter's rapid strides towards the King's African Rifles base.

'Major Reading said we should keep this within the regiment,' I said between paces. 'We're running a risk here of too many people knowing.'

Carter stopped in mid-stride. 'All right, then. Which way do we go once we walk out of camp?'

'I will ask Corporal Akul if he will also come with us,' Juma said when we arrived at the KAR base. 'He is the best man in my platoon. He has been a soldier for ten years. He also knows the country we are going into.'

Mail had finally arrived for me. That evening I went over to the officer's *banda* to pick it up. There was a letter from Helen. It had been written a few weeks back – before Salaita.

'I don't know how to say this, Michael, but he's been wounded. Badly wounded. He's written to me from hospital in England. He wants me to come out and see him. He says he wants us to try again.

'I'm sorry Michael. I know you want me to choose, and I know it's not fair for you to get this letter while you are miles away somewhere in – well, places that I cannot even imagine – but I don't know what else to tell you. I have to go to him. I do love him still, despite what he's done. The problem is, that I love you too. But you and I have only known each other now for a few short months, and, well, I can't choose. At least, not yet I can't, not until I've seen him.

'Please try and understand, Michael. Both of you went away to the war, and left me behind. I know that you had to do it – I would have done it too. But I can't live a lie – for either of you. I must find the truth of my own feelings, and I have to go to him to do that.'

At dawn the next day we walked out of the camp gates into the bush. John Akul led our only two pack mules laden with corned beef, biscuit, ammunition and a few medical supplies. The idea was for us not to stand out too much. We knew – now especially after the meticulous precision of our defeat at Salaita – that Von Lettow's spy networks were wider and more efficient than we had given him credit for. We didn't know who was watching us as we passed through the barbed wire gates, and who might be reporting that a slightly unusual patrol consisting only of five ranking men, without any porters accompanying them, was leaving Mbuyuni. It was our hope that he might have added, however, that there were three officers and they appeared to be only lightly provisioned so they were likely to be doing nothing more than checking the far outer perimeter defences after their defeat at Salaita.

We spoke in low voices in the pre-dawn darkness, checking and re-checking that we had what we needed. '.303 cartridges, corned beef, field dressings, large, small,' Carter read out each item from a list that he had put together, and each one of us confirmed that we had brought it. The few men awake early enough to witness our departure watched us with curious gazes. No one remarked on the glint of chain and three shiny new pairs of handcuffs from the military police storeroom loaded into one of the saddle bags.

The five of us knew very little of each other. Yet already, in the grey half-light of dawn, we were becoming a unit as we gathered ourselves and our equipment together under the scrutiny of the men who would be staying behind.

After checking the straps on the mules one more time, Carter pronounced us ready to leave. We stepped through the rough camp gates hewn out of thorn branches. The sentries at the gate saluted as we passed them. I recognised one of them. He was from the 7th, one of Matthews' men. 'Good luck, sir,' he said. It was clear that our secret was not safe, that already the rumours were circulating.

The air was cool and fresh. The dawn chorus of birds grew louder by the minute as we began our journey. Behind us the sun rose, bursting bronze from behind the dark horizon, then blazing pink and gold over the panoply of thorn trees spread out all around us. Carter and Juma were in front, leading the way. Juma knew the pathways from before the war, when he had led trading caravans carrying *merikani* cloth, salt and guns from the coast deep into the bush country looking for ivory and skins. From that very first morning, it was obvious that we would have to rely on him to show us the way through the thick bush.

Khan and I came behind them. Behind us was the tall dark figure of John Akul towering above the mules. I knew nothing about him beyond the fact that he was a Dinka from the Sudan who had volunteered some years back to serve in the King's African Rifles.

We had been thrown together for this mission. Our only common link was that, for our own reasons, each one of us had agreed to follow Captain Carter. We were a band of strangers, both to the land we had come to fight in and to one another.

That letter. It was a few weeks old. She had written it long before I had faced the Germans at Salaita, but it had only arrived in East Africa a few days ago. The world was different for both of us now. I didn't know how much was hurt and how much was anger. I hardly knew what to think at all. I was dazed by it all. I had waited so long for a letter from Helen, and then, it had come – and all I could think of were those terrible, crushing words: '*I have to go to him.*'

The cool beauty of the morning faded quickly. Heavy clouds gathered high around the crest of Kilimanjaro, hiding it from view. The heat began to beat down and to rise up from the ground. Within an hour we were filthy and sweating, our shirts and sun helmets soaked and turning dark, our rifles and packs growing heavier and heavier on our shoulders. We marched in silence, knowing that we had to make up ground as quickly as possible. The only sound was the occasional snort from one of the mules, and the even more infrequent grunt from Juma as he guided us past a tall tree or a large rock that served as a landmark to the ancient pathways through the bush.

Here and there we saw game – kudu, giraffe, even a rhino with her baby turning and crashing through the long grass in terror at our sudden, unexpected approach. We took it as a good sign that we could come so close to a rhino before we startled it. We were still on the British side of the frontier, but such stealthy progress through the bush boded well for our mission.

We saw quickly that John was a marvel with the mules. He led them both gently by their tethers, never pulling too hard, but never once hesitating and letting them believe that he was uncertain of his mastery over them. Every now and then, they would become frightened, perhaps sensing a snake or a scorpion that we had blundered past. They would stop and tug against the ropes. I could see Carter becoming irritated each time it happened. John would bend his tall, muscular body over and whisper into the ear of one of them, and always, perhaps after a momentary shake of the head, and a flick of the ears, the beast would begin to edge forward and the other would follow. Even on that first, easy day of marching, he saved us hours of delay with the animals.

We stopped for a rest once. That was for ten minutes to attend to one of the mule's packs that had worked loose. Carter was impatient even then, sitting to one side on a rock. He took out the map from his pack and began looking at it, trying to judge how far we had to go and how accurate the map was.

We had time to drink some water, eat a little biscuit and catch our breaths before he had jumped up from where he was sitting on the rock. 'Let's move,' he said. 'We must keep on if we are going to catch these men.'

We set off again in the middle of the hottest part of the day, with the sun beating down and the heat rising out of the ground. I watched Carter with his jaw set and the sweat trickling from under the brim of his sun helmet. We moved forward in the bush, following Carter and Juma's lead. Through the afternoon we marched, saying little to one another.

An hour before darkness fell, Carter called a halt. He and Juma had found a shallow depression in the ground that was easy to defend. Except for a few low bushes, it had a clear line of fire all around. Khan and John, old soldiers both, seemed pleased with the choice.

John hobbled the mules and went out to cut fresh grass for them. Carter ordered the rest of us to spend the hour before darkness cutting down the bushes that obscured our field of fire and gathering firewood. He joined us as we worked, hacking at the bushes with his bayonet.

'This is the last decent fire you'll have,' he told us. 'Early tomorrow we cross over into German territory. From then on, there'll be no fires at night.'

We cut the bushes and gathered the wood and, just as the sun was setting, we built a good-sized fire. Juma and Khan were sent out as guards. Carter took out his map again and began looking at it in the firelight.

John and I began to prepare the evening meal. We had kudu venison that we had carried with us from the camp at Mbuyuni and flour to make grilled cakes. While I sliced the meat into steaks, John took the flour and moved a few paces away into the darkness away from the fire, as the African servants at the officers' *banda* would do. He began to mix it with water.

Carter looked up from his map. 'There's no need for that, Akul.'

John stopped stirring. 'Sir?'

'There's no need to step away from the fire. You'll work with the rest of us.'

'Yes, sir,' John replied. His face betrayed no hint of what he thought. He picked up the bowl and came nearer into the circle of firelight. He continued stirring the flour mix.

Carter watched him for a moment and then turned his attention back to the map.

After we had eaten, John and I went out to relieve Juma and Khan. They came in towards the fire and we settled down in the bush to watch.

I took Khan's place in a clump of long grass under a spreading thorn tree. In the flickering light of the fire behind me I could see Juma and Carter bent over his map, talking. Khan was sitting in front of the fire, staring into the flames.

I had asked him once, in the days before Salaita: 'What was it like, the Western Front?' I would never forget his answer.

'We arrived in the winter. It was freezing cold. That night it snowed. I couldn't sleep because of the cold and the heavy guns firing. At dawn the next day the guns stopped and a British officer took us on a patrol, "to show us the ropes" he said. It was the first time I had seen such smooth wide plains of snow. At first, I loved its white empty beauty. Then as we crept through no man's land in the dawn light, I saw where the blood from those wounded in the night's bombardment had remained. It had first burned a hole deep in the snow. Then it had frozen in dark, ragged clumps, each one the size and shape of something one could recognize – a toe, perhaps, or maybe a shattered elbow, or even a heart.' He had looked at me. 'Now that is the only way I can think of snow. I do not even like to think of it on the far mountains of my homeland.'

In the distance to the south, I could see flashes on the horizon, like pale sheets of lightning in the wide empty night. I didn't know whether it was from our guns or from the Germans'. Later we heard that General Von Lettow-Vorbeck had fled down the Pangani River deep into German East Africa, ahead of Stewart's column. Tomorrow our division would join the chase. The march down the Pangani and beyond would be the story of this war, helping to cover over the failure of Salaita.

But what did that story matter to me now? I cared about what happened to the three men who had been under my command, but most of the time I could think only of Helen sailing for England – standing at the rail of a silent, darkened ship slipping across a moonlit sea. The Atlantic route was treacherous, with the U-boats sinking Allied ships, and the army mail from East Africa took months to arrive. The letter I had written to Helen about Salaita would not arrive before she left for England.

She would not read how much I loved her before she left to see… him. How many times had I told her I loved her? I regretted now the times I had not told her, but it was too late. I would have done anything – I would have begged – to convince her that her life lay with me. But there was nothing I could do. My only power in the days and months that lay ahead of me in this war was to make sure I stayed alive. I would have to try not to think how much easier it would be if I had never read that damned letter. In my letter to her I had tried to protect her from the truths of this new horror that had come into my life; in the end, though, it was her truth, her love, that meant everything to me, more even than the war.

The dark expanse of land stretched out for miles. It was too far away to hear the shelling, but for hours the white incandescence on the horizon flickered against the web of thorn branches hanging above me. Then, as suddenly as it had lit up, the horizon fell dark. There were only the cold, bright stars above and the faint night rhythms of the bush.

16

THE FIRST SIGN THAT WE HAD come to the border were the bloodstained, abandoned German uniforms lying on the road. Splintered wooden boxes torn open in haste lay beyond them; brass rounds dropped in the panic of the fighting gleamed in the dust.

It was already mid-morning. The faint smell of corpses hung in the air. The rocks on the hillsides at edge of the road had been smashed by artillery fire. There was dried blood on the jagged edges of the stone. A scrawny ginger cat chased a white butterfly into the long grass. A single lost horse with the remains of leather traces on its breast took fright at our coming. It galloped behind the dozen or more new British and German graves that lay humped like fresh scars cut into the hillside above us.

The clouds on the peaks of Kilimanjaro shimmered in the blue sky behind us. We rounded the last bend in the road. In front of us lay a small trading store and a corrugated iron hut. A torn, dirty white flag flew on a bamboo pole in front of the buildings. This frail token of neutrality was the owners' only protection against the horrors of war. I wondered how they had survived this long. There had been something of a battle for this border post a few days back, and I could not see how their flag would have helped them then. The windows of the store were smashed. Nearby lay a few crumpled sheets of corrugated iron and blackened timbers where a shell had demolished the tiny customs shed.

There were a few tents and makeshift shelters of sticks and grass beside the remains of the customs shed. Next to them a black, red and white striped post had been hammered into the ground. It was the official German marker of the border. Now it was guarded by a handful of exhausted-looking Indian sepoys in khaki turbans. They wore baggy, loose-kneed trousers and puttees. Their African porters and servants were gathered in a filthy ramshackle camp nearby.

A few refugees were gathered on the tiny veranda in front of the store. At the side of the building two women tended a blackened three-legged pot that stood over a smoky fire. As we drew nearer, the Indian family who owned the store came out to peer at us. The man stepped out first, followed by his son, a pimply youth of about twelve, and then the mother and daughter, dressed in colourful but dirty saris.

Khan stepped in front and greeted them.

'I'm sorry sir,' the man replied. 'I am from Gujerat, my wife is Tamil. We do not speak Urdu. English will have to do.'

Khan was clearly disappointed. He had hoped to find a common language and strike up a rapport with them. That was one of the reasons he had joined us. This war in Africa was a war in which a Babel of languages rose up and howled around one another. Information was constantly misunderstood, attacks were misdirected and to be able to speak the same language as one's troops was a luxury few officers enjoyed.

Nevertheless, Khan smiled at the man. 'English is fine,' he said. 'Tell me, have you seen any Germans?'

The man shook his head. A look of fear flitted over his wife's face. They had no doubt been asked the same question many times before, and they had certainly been asked its corollary: 'Have you seen any English?' as well. Whether they had or not, they had learned that even a true answer was no guarantee of their safety.

'Not at all, sir, not a man. Not since the fighting here, anyway.'

'How did you survive that fighting?' Carter asked.

'We went away, into the bush, sir. We came back yesterday, with what supplies we had with us. The only ones the Germans had not taken. That is why you see us like this, so dirty and hungry.'

'Who are these people?' Juma demanded, pointing at the Africans on the veranda.

'They are people who used to live in a village near by here. Until the Germans and their askaris came and burned them out. They depend on us for charity now. Things are terrible here. Why don't you ask them how things are,' the man pointed to the Indian soldiers.

Khan called over the Indian sergeant who was in charge. He was surprised to see so many officers in one group. He saluted and stood loosely to attention while Khan spoke to him and he answered at some length. Khan spoke again briefly and turned to us. 'The sergeant says the shopkeeper is all right. He charges high prices for salt and cigarettes and that seems to be the only complaint they have against him. He confirms the story about the villagers – they've got nowhere else to go now. He also asks if we have any tea for them. They've run out, and so has the shopkeeper.'

Carter took a moment to digest this. 'What about Wallis and the others? Did they see them? This is the main road into German territory. It's likely they would have come this way.'

Khan unbuttoned his tunic pocket and took out a packet of cigarettes. His movements were careful, fastidious, the mark of a man not given to making hasty decisions. Like Reading and Carter, Khan had fought in the countless skirmishes on the border between British India and the frontier tribes. And he had seen plenty of killing here in Africa and on the Western Front. He had learned to take his time and observe carefully.

Khan was only twenty-eight. He had done very well in the army. He was a career soldier who had been fighting the Empire's wars in Asia for nearly a decade. In the weeks leading up to Salaita, he had told me a little about himself. Originally a city boy from Karachi he had always been expected to join the family printing business. That had bothered him throughout his childhood – the thought that his life was mapped out for him. He secretly hated the idea that, if he remained the dutiful son, he would have to live his whole life in the place he grew up. He wanted to see the world, but he didn't want to betray his family. So he joined the army to delay the day when he would have to join the business and marry the girl his family had chosen for him.

What changed his life was one afternoon two years ago; on leave in Karachi he saw a girl in the wide marketplace in front of the mosque. She was buying an English dictionary from the bookseller's stall next to the tinsmith's along the outside wall of the mosque. He couldn't help himself noticing the black glint of her hair under her embroidered headscarf and the way her dark eyes caught the late afternoon sun.

'May I asking your name, please?' he said nervously in his best classroom English, trying to impress her.

She turned and laughed at him. '*Ask*,' she said.

'This is what I am doing,' Khan replied, blushing.

'Nadia,' she told him.

Once a week after that he bought her an orange squash at the *Gates of Paradise* tearoom. His parents knew nothing about Nadia. They were certain that he was content with the girl they had chosen to be his wife. But Nadia's uncle saw them when he was coming home from the Friday prayers. They were sharing one of the small, round marble tables under the straggly hibiscus tree in the courtyard of the tearoom. They had one glass on the table between them. Two wet paper straws stuck up out of the warm, sticky orange squash. It was all the evidence his uncle needed.

But meeting Nadia had changed things for him. Khan was no longer willing to risk losing her to his family's demands. He finally found the courage to confront them the afternoon before he took the train back to the regiment at Quetta.

'What happened?' I asked him when he told me the story.

He smiled. 'That was not easy, but because I am an officer, her parents finally accepted me. When this war is over, we will be married.'

I watched as Khan placed the cigarette between his dry lips. He lit it and his fine, handsome face relaxed as he inhaled the smoke. He scrutinised the tiny settlement, looking once more at the family and at the people they were sheltering. He finished his cigarette and crushed it under the heel of his boot. The leather toe still retained something of its base-camp shine.

He held the shopkeeper in his gaze. 'Have you seen any English soldiers?' he asked. 'There are three we are looking for. One older one and two boys. One of the young ones has red hair. You would not have missed them.'

'No, sir,' the shopkeeper replied. 'Not at all. We have seen no runaways.'

'Who told you they were runaways?' Carter demanded.

The shopkeeper's face remained impassive as he turned to face Carter. 'If they were not runaways, why would you be looking for them?'

'Watch your mouth, man,' Khan snarled. 'This is serious business.'

'But it's true, sir,' the shopkeeper's wife said. 'We have seen nothing. We are loyal subjects of the King. We would never lie to you.'

Khan and Carter said nothing as they looked at the frightened, bedraggled family. I wondered what fate it was that had brought them to this point deep in the bush, surrounded by two desperate armies.

'I think they're telling the truth,' I said.

Carter looked at me, and then over at John. 'Give them some tea,' he said. 'And some to the soldiers as well. Then let's move on.'

The shopkeeper's family stood outside their shop and waved as we marched out. The Indian troops stood to attention as we passed by the German border pole, chipped and scarred by bullets from the recent battle to take control of this insignificant chunk of territory. The fighting had been hard, the graves on the hillside were evidence of that, but I wondered who would ever remember the men who had died here.

As we marched off British soil and entered the immense no man's land that this abandoned German territory had become, I looked back one last time. The Indian soldiers were still at attention, the family was still waving. The refugees on the shaded, dirty veranda were staring after us, relieved that the strange soldiers were going again, leaving them in peace.

We had been on the road for over twenty-four precious hours already and still we had no leads. We were wandering almost blind, relying on the scanty information that had been given us back at camp. Wallis and the others had been last seen in British East African territory heading in the direction of the border. After that, we had no information. We were following the most logical direction that we could assume they would take. Our next destination was a village Juma knew of called Kilele. It was not large, but it was a crossroads in the bush. Traders and caravans had been calling at Kilele for centuries.

The savanna stretched out as far as the eye could see. It was green with trees and brown where the grass had been eaten away by the herds of game. A few low hills rose out of the thorn bush and grasslands. Somewhere beyond them lay the fighting that I had seen in the distance last night. For miles around us now the land was empty, most of the people who lived there having fled the war. There was only the distant haze and the shimmer of heat hovering over the bush.

We were taking our first steps into the outermost limits of our new empire, into the land that our armies had captured for King George. I had heard it said that Victoria had given Kilimanjaro to her grandson the Kaiser for his birthday. Well, we had taken it back. But the soldier's first lesson in the geography of war is that the front line is always shifting. For now, we held this ground, but the only proof of our conquest was our dead and theirs, lying at the foot of the mountain.

It was the same all the way along ,the border. Our hold on the ground we had captured was weak. The border itself was shifting, inexact. The maps we had of the territory, both German and British, were vague. I had seen them dozens of times in the officer's *banda* – huge sheets of paper with the contours of the major mountains and rivers marked in black ink and other, newer marks on top of them in pencil. The new shapes were smudged and wavering. Between the lines, old and new, were huge white spaces with nothing written on them at all.

The bulk of our armies were chasing Von Lettow deeper and deeper into the interior of Africa, and what troops we had to guard our new possessions were spread thinly, like the pathetic handful we had just left behind at the border post. They could have been overrun and wiped out in a matter of minutes by no more than a determined platoon of askaris.

The war had a different meaning here. In Europe men clashed and died over ground that was their home. The network of trenches where English and French and German alike screamed and bled today followed the ancient boundaries and bloodlines that their kings and queens had slaughtered each other over for centuries.

But we, surrounded by the vastness of Africa, fought and died in a war from a world that had no connection with the life of the people who lived here. For them, this land was home. For us, it was *terra incognita*, where such maps as we had meant nothing, where the questions we asked were our own guesses and the answers we received were mostly lies. Even with Juma and John's knowledge, it was a land of danger for us, where we could trust nothing and no one.

None of us would have admitted it openly, but fear was what we felt most strongly on passing by that single black-red-and-white-striped pole standing alone on the beaten red earth.

Deep ruts from the wagons and lorries of the passing armies had scarred the road deeply, making it difficult to walk. John's mules were having a hard time of it. Red dust powdered the tiny leaves of the thorn trees at the edge of the road, the only evidence of the tens of thousands of oxen, men and machines that had passed this way.

After leaving the border behind, we marched for hours down the long dust road that ran straight for miles and miles through the thorn bush, two already tired beasts and five tiny human figures struggling across the savanna. There were a few abandoned huts along the road, but we saw no one. The people who lived here had moved deep into the bush, away from the main highway of the war. There was nothing in the fields either. What the people could not carry with them, the Germans had burned, leaving nothing for our army to forage. There was not even a filthy chunk of manioc or a broken cob of corn left behind. The fields lay scarred and empty, their collapsed furrows dry and blackened with soot.

Towards noon, when the sun was at its hottest, and we were dripping with sweat, we smelled the first sharp, peppery hint. A hundred yards later, we were gagging on the reek of death. A pile of dead horses and oxen lay heaped up at the side of the road, their flesh black and rotting, peeling back from the sun-dried bones and crawling with maggots. A huge black cloud of flies crawled over them and buzzed in the air above. Half a mile further on, another pile of dead beasts lay bloated and decaying. Beyond them lay another and, just a few yards further, another. Abandoned piles of saddles and bridles lay crumbling in the sun at the edge of the road.

The odour of death hung in the air. It was a heavy, foul stench that made you feel dizzy with the awfulness of it and made breathing in the stifling dusty air even more difficult. We tied handkerchiefs around our mouths and noses which made us even hotter, but they kept the worst sharpness of the smell out of our noses.

When we came to the third pile John stopped for a moment and adjusted the handkerchief around his face. His tunic was buttoned up to his neck. His khaki fez, with its black tassel and its bronze '3' in the centre, was stained with dirt and sweat. His gentle brown eyes seemed anxious above the line of the handkerchief. His dark blue puttees were covered in the fine red dust, but I noticed that his rifle barrel was plugged with a tiny scrap of cloth to keep the dust out.

'Tstetse fly,' he mumbled through the cloth. 'There's nothing they can do.'

Carter overheard our conversation. He stopped at the edge of the road and waited for the two of us to catch up. He hooked one finger over the edge of his handkerchief and pulled it away from his face down over his chin.

'What about our animals?' he snapped.

John shrugged. 'I chose the best ones I could, sir. The rest is in the hands of God.'

'The hands of God,' Carter snorted. 'I want safer hands than those. We're going to need that food and ammunition with us.'

John looked upset. 'But we are all in the hands of God, sir,' came from underneath his handkerchief.

Carter laughed. 'Like hell you are, Corporal Akul. Here, you're in my hands. I'm in charge on this mission. If I make the wrong decisions, we all die. You along with me. God's not going to help any of us here.'

Akul turned away and said nothing, but, as we resumed marching into that stinking miasma of heat, dust and the reek of dying animals, I could see from his eyes that he was both shocked and angered by Carter' blasphemous outburst. Of all of us, John Akul was the only one who had anything like a genuine religious life. The rest of us were not devout towards any God. Hassani Juma and Aziz Khan were Muslims in the same way as I was a Christian. It never would have occurred to me that there was any other way of looking at my spiritual life except through the way I had been brought up. Carter might be a cynic, but I had never thought of questioning those beliefs – not until now.

John Akul was different. In the hours that we had been marching in the heat, he had told me something of his story. The most important experience of his life had been his conversion to Christianity brought on by an Anglican missionary from New Zealand, Father Walter, who had received the call to go to Africa when he was well into his forties.

He left his family in the suburbs of Auckland and took a ship to Massawa, the Italian port that lay in Eritrea on the Red Sea coast. From there he had walked alone through the high valleys and the lonely blue skies of the mountains of Ethiopia to the plains of the Anglo-Egyptian Sudan. Father Walter let his beard grow long. He wore sandals on his bony feet and a black cassock. He wandered through the wide baobab trees and the grass villages of the Sahel like an ancient prophet armed only with the rage of his convictions. He carried with him a walking stick, a cloth bag of dates, a water bottle, and a rucksack full of small red leather copies of the New Testament.

He gave one of them to John when he came to his village in Bahr El Ghazal. He was sowing seeds upon fertile ground. John had admired Father Walter and his lonely courage from the first moments he had seen him striding towards his village through the distant heat haze.

Most of the villagers had either ignored Father Walter or treated him as a transient curiosity, which in many ways he was, but John and a few other young men befriended him from the beginning. When they weren't out tending their cows, or sitting around in circles under the trees discussing them, they would go over to Father Walter's humble grass lean-to and speak to him about his strange God. The young men were curious about a God who was powerful enough to have persuaded Father Walter to do what most Dinka would have found unthinkable – to abandon his family, his cattle and his kinship ties to wander unknown through a foreign land.

Inspired by the gift of the Bible, John had learned to read and, some months later, he agreed to become an Anglican, and take the Christian name, John. Father Walter baptised him by being immersed in the papyrus swamps of the *toic*, called by the Arabs the Sudd – the barrier. Here the Nile meandered into ten thousand streams, forming the enormous expanse of swampland where the Dinka migrated with their cattle every year during the drought-stricken Hungry Months.

Father Walter was a confirmed pacifist, but ironically it was his appearance and his talk of faraway lands both in Africa and across the seas that had made John restless to see the world that lay beyond his village and the seasonal migrating paths of the *toic*. It was this restlessness that made him decide to walk south to Juba, where there was a King's African Rifles outpost, and there he volunteered to join the force.

Even though he had become a Christian and had joined the white man's army, John had not rejected his ancient African religion – despite Father Walter's urgent appeals to him to abandon what he saw as its heathen rituals and dangerous temptations. I had seen John reading his worn, red leather Bible, but he also wore around his neck a leather amulet a diviner had given him to protect his life against German bullets.

The sun bore down on us as we walked – Carter and Juma in front, the other three of us behind them. John walked with his Lee-Enfield slung over his shoulder. It looked tiny on his tall, muscular body. He was restive and thoughtful as he led his two mules that brought up the rear of our party, no doubt the fiery and plentiful words of Father Walter ringing in his ears against the blasphemy of Captain Carter.

Every now and then, I could hear snatches of the conversation between Carter and Juma drifting back from in front of me. They would speak in brief, staccato bursts, trying to avoid the smell of the rotting carcasses by not breathing through their noses.

'When do we get to Kilele?' Carter demanded.

'After we have crossed the Pangani. Late tomorrow maybe.'

'No sooner?'

'No, sir, that's the best we can do.'

Carter bit his lip.

Juma narrowed his eyes. 'They'll make a mistake somewhere.'

'I don't like this walking aimlessly along the road.'

'This is the quickest way to Kilele. Everybody stops there.'

'Three white men on their own? Wallis isn't stupid.'

'They have to get food from somewhere. Even if they didn't stop, somebody at Kilele will have news of them.'

Carter had first come to know Juma when the KAR regiments came up the line with the other reinforcements. Juma was a short, restless man, always smartly turned out. He seemed to take special pride in his appearance, both for its own sake and as a way of confirming his authority. His dark grey eyes were constantly moving, restlessly taking in information, thinking it over and then looking again to confirm. Nothing escaped him.

Juma had joined the army as soon as the war began. I once asked him why.

He looked at me. 'My brother followed the caravan routes as we had always done and as my father had done and my grandfather before him. One day, just before the war started, he was travelling on the same path that he always followed. He crossed the border that the Germans had marked. They found him on their side. He had no papers so they said he was a spy. They hanged him because of what was drawn on a map.'

Juma had welcomed the chance for revenge when war broke out. He left his wife and children in Mombasa to join the army. He occupied a unique position in the army. He acted as a bridge between its white leadership and its African soldiers. Despite the strict racial hierarchy that existed in the army, Juma and the other black NCOs had more power in certain ways than most of the white sergeants, and he was one of the most adept at using it. The white officers were reliant on Juma, and a very few others like him, either to provide them with their intelligence or to confirm what they had received. Without this local knowledge, the plans the senior officers made were meaningless. There were, of course, the few white officers who chose to disregard their black NCOs, but the best of them knew, like Carter, that they were virtually impotent without their black aides. This gave the black NCOs a part in making decisions that was resented by their white counterparts. It was a difficult racial game to play. There was no question of black NCOs issuing orders to white troops, or even usually of daring to make suggestions to white officers, but with a few words of agreement or of caution, men such as Juma could influence an entire battle plan. They never made the decisions, but according to what they said, towns could be attacked or bypassed, villages burned to the ground or the inhabitants left in peace.

They could choose to reveal their knowledge of a herd of cattle hidden in the bush, or they could say nothing. They could choose to recommend that certain water holes be poisoned and others left fresh and sweet.

Their power to influence the lives of the local inhabitants was immense, and men such as Juma, who never openly abused it, were the most powerful.

From the moment he had arrived at the camp in Mbuyuni, Juma had been continually coming and going on intelligence-gathering missions into the bush, continuing to run his trading operations on the side. He hated the Germans, but he also used the opportunities the army gave him to court favour with the local chieftains that he knew would prove valuable trade after the war was over. No matter which side won, one day the white men would retreat to the comforts of the colonial cities of Nairobi and Dar es Salaam and leave the bush tracks to men such as Juma. In the meantime, officers like Carter had come to know him and respect the information he gave them. In return, Juma himself was learning which of the white man's borders he could cross safely and which he couldn't.

We marched across the open plain, stopping in the shade of an umbrella-thorn tree at midday for a rest and for a meal of army biscuit and lukewarm water from our canteens. Late in the afternoon, we turned off the road and struck out south and west on a tiny path that Juma knew. The path was narrow and overgrown in places with thorns and thick elephant grass taller than our heads. It was overhung by raspy, sharp-edged leaves that slashed at our faces and necks. The footpath was very old, its surface beaten smooth by the tens of thousands of feet that had passed over it.

We took off the handkerchiefs from around our faces and breathed again. We were glad to get away from the dust of the road, and the stench of the piles of carcasses. As we had progressed further down the road, we had seen the first graves of men placed just a little away from the piles of animals. They were designated with simple, freshly-hewn markers. Wooden crosses for the dead Christians, smooth posts for Muslims, Hindus and the pagan Africans.

The names of those who had died and the dates of their deaths were carved like fresh pinkish scars into the newly cut acacia wood, but nothing else was done to mark their graves. We knew that most of them had not died in fighting the Germans, but had suffered agonising, humiliating deaths from disease: malaria, dysentery, blackwater fever. Whites and Indians died more quickly and easily than blacks, but disease affected us all. It was a far bigger danger than the possibility of taking a German bullet.

When we passed the first of these graves, Carter stopped and looked over at us. 'Never miss a day of quinine, not a bloody day, unless you want to end up like these poor bastards.'

After we turned off the main road, leaving the memory of those men and the stench of the dead beasts behind, our journey started to become more bearable. After an hour of walking in the cool late afternoon air away from the road and the path of the armies, we began to see signs of human life. A broken calabash, a dry cob of maize tossed at the side of the path, and finally, footprints that were only a few hours old.

We had entered the edge of the Pangani river valley and the scenery around us was green and lush. There was a lot of game moving in the bush alongside us, and even though I was tired, I began to enjoy the walk, allowing myself to relax and be carried along by the steady rhythm of our feet that our group had allowed to develop and which we fell into a few minutes after we set off after each halt.

We were just coming out of a thick patch of bush when out of the corner of my eye, I saw John let go the leads on the mules and grab at his rifle, wrenching it across his body into a ready position. Seeing him act, the rest of us dropped flat on the ground or down on to one knee, forming a rough defensive circle. We waited for the shots to ring out from around us. Our trigger-fingers were tight with fear as we scanned the bush for the danger.

My heart was pounding, and my hands were trembling, making it difficult to keep my sights still on anything. Khan was lying next to me. Even though he had flung himself onto the ground, his uniform was still neatly arranged around his slim, muscular body. He had assumed a perfect shooting position, his legs spread out to steady him, his heels pressed down against the ground. His rifle was held still and tight up against his shoulder, his face under his turban was calm. He was waiting for something to happen. I felt a stab of shame at my own sweaty agitation when compared with his experienced battlefield calm. My feelings were a strange mixture – scared by the sudden, invisible threat that surrounded us, but also excited. A part of me was just waiting, wanting something to happen.

Out of the corner of my eye I could see Juma holding his rifle and peering into the bush around him. I could hear his fast, shallow breathing just next to me.

'There!' John lifted his arm to point.

'*What is it*, Akul?' Carter shouted out, the barrel of his Lee-Enfield sweeping in a controlled arc in front of him. 'What do you see?'

John stood up, putting his rifle to one side. 'It is my mistake. There is no danger. It is just some *wakimbizi*, some refugees, under that bush there,' he pointed at a clump of dense vegetation just a few yards away from the track.

They were hidden under the bush. None of the rest of us, not even Juma, would have seen them until they had been pointed out. They were a family group; an ancient grandmother, her daughter and three children – two toddlers and a teenage boy, huddling together, terrified.

We relaxed, looking at one another, embarrassed to think we had been so spooked by such a frightened little band. Khan was the first to breathe a sigh of relief and put his rifle up.

'Hold it!' Carter barked. 'Keep your rifles at the ready until we're sure. Don't take anything for granted. We wouldn't be the first patrol ambushed by Germans hiding behind native women and children. What else do you see, Akul?'

John peered into the bush around us.

'Nothing else, sir. Only the women and their children.'

'Anybody else see anything?'

We shook our heads.

'It's all clear, sir,' Juma said.

'Right. Akul and Khan, bring them over here. Keep them covered,' he said to myself and Juma.

John and Khan got up and went over to the bush where the family was hiding. At first, they refused to move. John walked away a few metres and put his rifle down on the ground. Khan did the same thing. I looked over at Carter. I was expecting him to order them to pick their weapons up again, but he watched, his rifle held at the ready.

First, the teenage boy emerged. He was wearing nothing but a pair of dirty shorts around his skinny waist. He was shaking with fear as he approached. John reached into the pocket of his long khaki shorts and took out a small piece of army biscuit. He held it out for the boy. The boy reached up his hand and took it. He put it in his mouth and began to chew, never taking his eyes off John. Then the grandmother and her daughter came out, keeping the children behind them. They stood around in a forlorn group. John and Khan both broke pieces of a ration biscuit and handed them to the children. The tiny hands grabbed at the food.

The rest of us walked over to where they were standing. The two women and the teenage boy eyed us warily. The children stopped chewing and stared up at us in fear.

'What do they know?' Carter asked John.

'They're waNdorobo. They don't speak much Swahili. According to the old woman they're not from here. They come from much further east. The Germans burned their village and they ran away into the bush. They've walked here, hoping to find somewhere safe to hide, but it seems that instead, they've come across soldiers everywhere, and found nowhere safe.'

'If they've seen so many soldiers, maybe they know something.' Carter said. 'Ask them how far away the Germans are.'

John leaned forward. *'Waulive wa Geremani wako mbali aje?'*

The old woman shook her head. The teenage boy moved his arm as if he were going to point, and then dropped it, as if he had thought better of it.

Juma was the first to notice. He stepped forward and slapped the boy on the side of the head. *'Waulive waGeremani wako mbali aje?'* he demanded.

The boy crumpled up and fell on the ground. His mother dropped down next to him, holding his head in her hands. She began to talk rapidly.

'What's she saying?' Carter demanded.

'It's not clear,' Juma said. 'They saw many soldiers, white and black, passing by on the road a few days ago.'

'Germans or British?'

'She's not sure,' Juma told him. 'But she thinks they must have been w*aAngrezi* – English soldiers.'

'Why does she think that?'

The woman kept looking at us, but she leant sideways and grabbed at the side of her leg while she spoke.

'They were wearing short pants. Like us. The Germans cover their knees, she says.'

Carter glared at her. 'Has she seen any Germans, then?'

Juma relayed the question.

'They've seen them everywhere in the bush. One group even gave them some food a few days ago, but they haven't seen any since then. Some other refugees told them that they were following the river, and the *waAngrezi* were behind them.'

'And what about our three? Have they seen or heard anything about three British soldiers travelling on their own through the bush?'

Juma asked first, but the woman didn't seem to understand. Then John asked, more gently. She still didn't understand. Juma's eyes were flicking from one to the other.

'I think they know something,' he said, 'but they are scared to speak. They don't know which answer is the one we want, and which answer might mean trouble for them. They cannot guess our intentions, so they say nothing.'

Carter was squatting down next to them. He and John and Juma formed a deliberate semicircle around the boy. John's quiet gentle way was getting nowhere.

'There is only one way,' he said. He looked at the boy for a few moments, holding the boy's frightened eyes in his steady gaze. Then his hand shot out and he slapped the boy again, twice, not hard, almost lazily, and barked out the question. The boy slumped back on his hands in the grass, looking dazed, a drop of blood oozing from a swelling on his lip, and began to speak.

'They've seen them,' John said, translating the boy's words for us. 'Two days ago. It's the red hair they remember.'

'Which way were they heading?'

The boy shook his head, and stared down at the ground, waiting for the blows that he knew were coming next. Juma raised his hand again.

'Leave him be,' Carter said. He felt the shame we all did.

'How could anyone know in this thick bush?' He stood up. 'Give them some biscuits, Akul, and let them go. They've told us enough.'

He stood up and shouldered his rifle. 'Let's get to Kilele, and see what they know there.'

17

THAT NIGHT WE REACHED THE BANKS of the Pangani. Juma led us along the edge of the river until we came to a place that he knew, where the channels were shallow enough for us to ford the river. We still didn't know whether Wallis and the others had crossed it or not, but it seemed logical that they would have. Despite the tiny snippet of information we had gleaned from the refugees that afternoon, guesswork was still all we had to go on.

'Is it safe here?' Carter asked.

Juma was standing at the river's edge, staring at the water running past his boots. 'It's the only place to cross for miles. It's the quickest way across the river to Kilele.'

He looked up. 'We used to camp here every year with the caravans. It was here that I first met the man whose daughter I would marry. The next year we met here again. He and I drank coffee boiled on the coals of the thornwood fire. She was called Zainabu after the desert flower. She was only fourteen – his youngest child. We sat up talking together until the moon had disappeared. That night, sitting here, I agreed with her father to wait two more years.' Juma looked at us and smiled. 'But Zainabu made me wait four.'

Carter looked away from him. He watched the brown water swirling over the rocks. 'We must cross at first light tomorrow,' he said.

We lit no fire, but made a simple, well-guarded bivouac in the bush away from the riverbank. There was corned beef and biscuit to eat. The others wrapped themselves in their blankets and dropped off to sleep until it was only Carter and me still awake and keeping watch.

'There's a good chance they'll face a firing squad,' I said. 'When we bring them back.'

'If the Germans find them, they might shoot them too. Certainly Kirkpatrick will never recover from the things that will be said about him.'

'It'll just be enemy propaganda.'

'Enough of it would be true.'

'At least the others would have a chance to defend themselves.'

'No,' Carter sat up and put his elbows on his knees. 'They would have no chance. That I can promise you. There's too much else at stake. Their story will be used by the Germans and by our side. At the end of it there'll be nothing left for them to say to defend themselves.'

'And,' I said angrily, 'there's also the question of the regiment's honour.'

'You heard Reading. There are men who will shoot them to defend it.'

'And we're bringing them their victims.'

'We're soldiers. Doing our duty.'

'But there're no guarantees. Major Reading said that himself.'

'Exactly. Reading's the best, the only, chance they've got now.'

'You trust him a lot.'

'He was kind to me in India. When everything went wrong.'

An unpleasant idea suddenly occurred to me. 'Are you doing this to impress Reading, and the other officers?' I asked. 'In the hope that things might be different in the future? Because of your career?'

'Fuck you, Fuller. That's going too far.'

'Is it?'

'You'll have to decide that for yourself. But whatever you decide, don't forget that I'm in charge on this journey. You'll do exactly what I tell you to.'

There was no need to answer him. For a long while we stared into the darkness. I could never forget the images of the dozens of bodies lying among the rocks and thorn trees. Men I knew well, good friends some of them, splayed out in strange, unnatural postures, looking peaceful until I saw the pools of oily blood beside them or the white, shattered bone sticking out from gaping red holes. I thought of how close I had come to deserting my own post out of terror.

'What if Reading can't do something, and they do face a firing squad?' I asked finally.

Carter turned to me in the darkness. 'It's too late to ask that question. We've got a job to do now. Our orders are to bring them back, and I'm going to make sure we do that.'

The moon rose from the bush behind us, casting a silvery light over the languid expanse of the river. The currents swirled and flowed under the shadows thrown by the trees on its banks. A single date palm, perhaps a relic of some ancient Arab trading expedition, stuck up out of the bush on the other side of the bank.

I thought of Helen, for the thousandth time that day. And of everything that would be gone from my life without her. I had tried not to think about her, to concentrate on the business of the mission that I was on. It was impossible.

I saw her laughing, her arms wrapped around her knees, glancing at me out of the corners of her eyes from where she was sitting deep in her wicker chair on the long stone veranda of her house. I saw her splashing barefoot through the red mud in the garden, the rain slicing down silver against the green of the garden behind her, her arms wet and covered in goose bumps, her eyes half-closed against the power of the rain, her yellow cotton skirt clinging to her slim, elegant ankles. I saw her hair like a dark fan, clinging to her face as she slept in the afternoon after we had made love.

I closed my eyes, trying not to think of her. It was too painful to imagine that I might never see her again.

I lay on the ground covered by a blanket, surrounded by the soft light and the sound of the river. I could hear the occasional distant snort of some animal in the bush or the splash of something entering the moonlit water farther upstream.

Somewhere out there were the Germans and their askaris. I listened carefully to every sound, hoping that I might recognise the telltale clink of a rifle barrel against a button or a bayonet scabbard against a rock before it was too late. I was learning to live on the edge of fear, hiding from my own breaking point.

I had never expected war to be like this – every day you found yourself living in the midst of beauty, fear and horror. After a while it became difficult to untangle them. That was the allure of war, the way they fell into one another so smoothly and seductively. What you were going to do with the rest of your life had ceased to matter. The rest of your life was a gamble, anyway. It didn't count for much at the moment.

I was one of those who still had the luxury of the rest of his life. I had not died at Salaita, like so many others. In my dreams, I could never understand how it was that I had survived and they had not. But in my waking moments, the world was different. There were the moments of fear, the real fear that I had learned face down in the dust with the bullets and shrapnel flying over my head at Salaita. I could not help the joy rising inside me when I remembered firing into the askari's face. Over and over, I saw him screaming and falling back. My heart would begin to pound when I thought of it. I was able to kill. The askari had died. I had not.

18

THE SURFACE OF THE RIVER LAY still in the dawn light. Underneath, the current was swift, but Juma's knowledge served us well. The ford was shallow. One by one we crossed in the first pale light of day and slipped into the cool depths of the bush. It was easy walking in the early morning. Now that we were moving into German territory we had to be on our guard, but for those first few hours, the bush seemed a benign presence around us, sheltering us from the watching Germans. It was a treacherous illusion. We had to keep reminding ourselves of the dangers that lay in the beauty. As the day grew hotter, we became more exhausted and we paid less and less attention to what was happening around us. It was a constant struggle to stay alert.

We reached the first sign of Kilele at mid-morning – an empty, burned maize field. The blackened stalks were bent and twisted against the red soil and the white ash. A few crows pecked at the dry ground. A lizard skittered across the hot sand and disappeared into the grass at the edge of the field.

'We have to be careful,' Juma turned and whispered. 'They must be watching us. There is thick bush surrounding this path just ahead. It's a perfect place for an ambush. We'll pretend to go down that one, but we'll turn off onto another one I know. It'll bring us into the back of the village.'

'If we are attacked,' Carter said quietly, 'Hit the ground and open up rapid fire. It doesn't matter whether you see anything or not. Just carry on firing. Force them to keep their heads down. That's the best chance we have of fighting our way out of it.'

There was a series of soft *clack-clacks* as we checked the mechanisms of our Lee-Enfields.

We set off down the path, following Juma, looking from side to side as we walked. We held our rifles at our waists, ready to pull them up to our shoulders and fire into the thick bush. The trees loomed over us, casting dark shadows. Sunlight broke through the gloom, dappling the ground. Each patch of light wavered and looked like the khaki of a German askari.

The birds and the insects had fallen silent with our passing. We could hear the breaking of twigs and the rustle of leaves. Ten minutes ago we had been relaxed. Now, our nerves were on edge. The slightest sound – a beetle whirring across a face or a grasshopper scuttling over a leaf would spook us.

We passed through the thick bush and came to a clearing. At the far edge a jumbled pile of bones lay in the bright sunlight. In horror we moved towards them, keeping our rifles trained on the forest that surrounded us. The remains of human flesh curled and hung off the bones, spilling onto the ground in dark tendrils. Torn rags of clothing, oily with old blood, lay around them. The curve of a skull bone gleamed white. The fine, eggshell bone was crushed where bullets had entered and where later the teeth of wild animals had gnawed at the edges. My mind was spinning as I counted at least nine skulls.

'How old do you think they are?' Khan rasped, his throat dry with tension.

'Several weeks,' Carter hissed. 'They look older because the hyenas have been at them.'

John was looking carefully at the ground. 'The people in the village must have scared them off. If not, the animals would have eaten them all.'

Juma said nothing. He pointed towards the edge of the pile. It was the skeleton of a child. The ribcage had been smashed by a heavy bullet.

'Who the hell did this?' I heard myself ask.

'The Germans,' said Juma. 'Who else?'

'They must be near,' John added. 'We must be careful.'

'How can you know that?' Khan asked.

John was standing over the pile of bones, shaking his head. 'The people left alive in the village are scared. And hungry.'

'He's right, of course,' Carter said. 'Something has to be very, very wrong for Africans not to bury their dead. The Germans must have terrorised them.'

'Let's get out of here,' Juma said.

A short way further along the pathway we came to an abandoned hut. The door had been smashed in with rifle butts. It was hanging off its leather thong hinges. The grass roof had been pulled down. A dead cow lay on the ground nearby.

It was still tethered by the neck. One leg had been hacked off. The half-dry, half-rotted skin hung in shreds on the hard bone. The reek of death and a cloud of flies hovered in the warm air. A thin, mangy dog whined and slunk behind a banana tree as we approached.

Two more huts stood empty and ransacked on the other side of the path. A broken chair lay upside down outside one of them. A single broken china plate lay in front of it. Beyond them, a hut had been burned down. A gutted circle of mud and sticks and a few gnarled, fire-blackened timbers remained. Anyone caught inside would have been cremated by the fierce heat of the fire.

There was another burned hut further along. We walked past it and then the pathway opened out into the centre of the village. In front of us was a rough circle of earth. It had been beaten flat and hard by the passage of bare feet over the decades. It glinted like a pool of white light in the midday sun. A few abandoned calabashes and earthen pots lay scattered across its expanse. They cast small rounded shadows on the ground. A trail of water lay spilled in dark stains around one. I could almost see the woman dropping it off her head in panic as she joined the others to flee at our approach.

In one corner of the clearing was the tiny marketplace. It consisted of nothing more than a few blackened bananas, shrivelled mangoes and tamarinds piled up on mats. Further along there were some dried fish, dirty piles of salt, and withered cassava roots.

A few huts were gathered around the outside of that abandoned circle. I could see they had once been neat and well-maintained, and had only recently fallen into disrepair. Their deserted silence was eerie and frightening. We advanced into the centre, rifles at the ready, looking around us with every step. The same lean yellow dog with its ribcage showing crouched down at the edge of one of the huts. It raised its hackles and snarled at us as we approached.

Juma raised his hand to shade his eyes against the bright sunlight.

'I don't like this,' Carter hissed at him. 'We're walking into a trap.'

'What else can we do?' Juma said. 'They're waiting for us anyway.'

Juma stepped out alone into the centre of the empty village clearing. He turned around and shouted in Swahili. I couldn't understand what he was saying, but he kept on repeating a name: 'Mbogo, Mbogo!'

He stopped shouting. There was no response. We were surrounded by silence, empty even of the sounds of birds and insects.

'What's that?' Khan yelled out. He swung around, raising his rifle to his shoulder.

'What do you see?' Carter was looking around the empty perimeter.

'There,' Khan pointed. 'There it is, behind that hut.' He aimed the barrel of his rifle.

I saw it too, a brief movement behind the crumbling mud wall. Behind it, there was another. I caught the glimpse of a heel disappearing behind the hut.

I raised my rifle to my shoulder.

'Don't shoot!' Carter yelled.

'They're all around us,' John said. 'If we're going to fight, we must shoot now.'

'Hold your fire!'

They poured out from behind the huts. Ten, twenty, thirty or more villagers, men and women. Each one of them was armed with a crude weapon. Spears, bows and arrows, axes, machetes. There were even two men armed with ancient, rusty trade rifles. They surrounded us.

John was right. We could have shot our way out of it up until that point. It was too late now. If it came to a fight, one or two of us might escape, but the rest would be killed.

The villagers' faces were thin and hostile. They were pushing and shoving against us. One of the women shouted out and the others took up the call. The angry shouting rose to a crescendo. The sound of their rage surrounded me, shutting out everything else. I could not speak to the others or hear anything they said. I could see Juma, and John through the crowd, towering above everyone. The two of them had the worst of it. The villagers blamed them for bringing more white soldiers to their home.

They pushed and shoved them the hardest. I saw a woman elbow her way towards John through the crowd. She stopped in front of him, her face contorted with rage. She gathered herself together and spat upwards at his face, flinging her whole body forward as she did so.

John's face was angry as he looked down at her, but there was nothing he could do except take it. Someone pushed me from behind. The crowd roared as I stumbled forward, almost losing my balance.

It was a matter of moments before they attacked us. My mind raced as I tried to think of an escape. I tripped over the dozens of calloused bare feet that kicked at my shins. I lowered my rifle against my chest, hoping that I could somehow push a space into the crowd big enough to allow me to open fire and shoot my way out. An old man was screaming as he waved a machete in my face.

A single voice rang out above the shouting. The crowd became still, staring at us. Sweat was running down their faces. The older men and women were breathing heavily from exertion.

A man pushed his way to the front of the crowd. He came face to face with Carter.

'You are English soldiers,' he said.

'Yes,' Carter replied, out of breath.

'Why have you come to this village?'

'We need to know if there are Germans nearby,' Carter said, as boldly as he could.

The man stared back at Carter. 'I am asking the questions.'

Carter held the man's gaze. 'We are looking for Chief Mbogo.'

'He brought you here,' the man said angrily, pointing at Juma. 'He knows me. My name is Walele. Before the war we gave him shelter in our village. Now he repays us by bringing soldiers here.'

'I am in command,' Carter said. 'I brought him here.'

Walele turned to Juma. 'You brought them to see Chief Mbogo?'

Juma nodded. 'You know yourself how old my friendship with the chief is. We have known each other all our lives.'

'Come,' Walele said. 'Let's go to Chief Mbogo.' He turned and began walking. The crowd opened out before him. We followed him. Carter and Juma were in front. The throng followed us across the empty space of the village clearing.

We came to a hut. Walele stopped a few yards away. The door and the tiny openings in the mud walls were shut up against the bright sun.

'Chief Mbogo is waiting,' Walele said. Juma bent down and began to unlace his boots. The rest of us followed suit. We would enter the hut barefoot, as a mark of respect.

'Rifles too,' Juma said. 'Akul will have to stand guard over them outside.' We handed our rifles to John. He stacked them in a pyramid a few yards away from the wall of the hut. He turned and faced the crowd. His own rifle held ready at his waist. We put our boots in a row alongside him.

Walele walked forward. He swung the door open and stepped inside. The interior of the hut was dark. Carter and Juma crossed the empty space in front of the hut. They bent their heads under the eaves and stepped inside. Khan and I followed. We were bent double as the stench hit us. My first instinct was to straighten up and flee, but somehow I controlled my reactions. The acrid reek of death forced its way into the centre of my head. I could hardly breathe. My eyes were burning from the power of it. I forced myself to look up in the murky darkness of the hut. Chinks in the straw roof sent weak bars of light streaming down to the smooth mud floor. A decomposing body hung by the neck from the rough wooden rafters. The limbs hung stiffly down. The wrists were torn and jagged where the hands had been hacked off. The grey, once-distinguished head had fallen back against the thick rope of the noose. The lips were pulled back and the teeth were white in a snarl of frozen pain.

We stumbled out into the daylight, choking on the horror of what we had seen, and on the foul stink of death that filled the hut.

Juma was pale. He shoved his feet into his boots. His hands were shaking as he laced them up. A thin trace of saliva dried white against his lips. 'He was my friend, and my father's before me,' he said, shaking his head. 'We traded with him every season.

I have known him since my childhood. They killed him. They killed him like that.'

'His son joined the King's African Rifles,' Walele said. 'He came across the border to visit and one of their askaris found him. He told the Germans. They came here six weeks ago, and surrounded the village. They were too late to catch his son, but they burned our crops and took Chief Mbogo and his wives and his family prisoners. They destroyed their huts. They took the family to the edge of the village. They shot them all. They made the Chief watch and then they brought him here and cut off his hands. They left him to bleed all night and then hanged him in the morning.

'It would be a lesson, the Germans told us. To the rest of us. We are traitors to the *Kayizari*. To the Kaizer, they said. We were not permitted to bury him, or his family. His body must hang and the others must stay where they lay, they told us, as a warning to others.

'They left their camp a few days ago,' Walele added. 'They marched out when they heard the English were coming. The next day we saw the dust of the English army on the road. Then nothing. After two days we began to hope that maybe they had gone. Then you came.' He pointed to the villagers. 'They have seen too many soldiers. They were ready to kill you or to die themselves.'

Juma dug the grave for Chief Mbogo himself. Some of the village men tried to help, but he pushed them aside.

'No,' he said, sweat pouring down his face, when I offered to help. 'I want to do it.'

The rest of us walked to the clearing. We dug a deep hole for the remains of Chief Mbogo's family. The villagers came to help us, but they were weak from hunger, and it was dark by the time we had patted down the last of the red earth. The crickets began to call in the cool twilight.

It was too dangerous to spend the night at the village. The Germans could have been anywhere, and we feared that even if they were gone, their spies might be watching us.

As we were preparing to march out, a group of villagers brought us some manioc and bananas as a gift.

'No,' Carter said to Walele. 'We can't take them.'

'It's rude to refuse,' John said.

Carter looked over at him and then reached out to take the meagre bundles of fruit and vegetables that the villagers were holding out to him. John unstrapped the saddle bags on one of the mules. He took out some rice, and some large tins of corned beef. John handed them to the group of villagers gathered around us.

Juma's face was grim as we set off down the path through the thick bush. Walele led us for a mile or so through the undergrowth.

He stopped at the edge of a valley that was thickly carpeted with bush.

'From here on the path is safe,' he said. 'The Germans do not know it. It will take you to a waterhole. You can sleep there tonight. From there you will have to find your own way.'

'Thank you for your help,' Carter said, holding out his hand to Walele.

Walele took his hand in return.

'We are looking for some of our soldiers,' Carter said. 'Three of them. They are led by an older one. One of the younger ones has red hair. The other is blonde.'

'They are traitors.'

'No,' Carter said. 'They are soldiers who ran away. There is a war on.'

'You will shoot them. Like the Germans hanged Chief Mbogo and shot his family.'

Carter narrowed his eyes. 'I just want to know if you've seen them.'

The sky began to grow dark after we had left Walele at the edge of the high ground and we began our descent into the valley. He had taken us some distance away from the village before he finally showed us the path. In the growing distance behind us we could hear the faint echoes of the village dogs barking at the thunder and at the lightning flashes on the horizon.

We marched through the bush for an hour before the thunder cracked and rumbled above us and the cold rain began to fall, an unrelenting torrent lashing down out of the night sky. We stumbled through the cold, cutting wetness of it for hours. Our heavy boots slipped on the sticky mud that the pathway had become. At every step, wet thorn branches slapped against our faces and grabbed at our ankles. We were quiet as we fought our way through the darkness and the battering rain, the memory of the day's horror filling our heads. I thought of Chief Mbogo's tortured, decaying corpse swaying in the beautiful dappled light of his hut, and of the dried, half-eaten remains of his family lying in the long swaying grass of the clearing. I had been at war only a few weeks. Already I had seen so much death. I could no longer recall each one of them. But they came to me themselves – in a sudden flash of unguarded memory while I was lathering my face before shaving or picking a stone out of the sole of my boot.

Grotesque, ravaged corpses, torn and bleeding, they came to me demanding that their deaths and their pain should not be forgotten. I could not promise them that. I had thought war might teach me something of life, but already all that I wanted was to forget what I had seen. I wanted to forget the dead, to forget the way they had died. I tried to speak to them in my dreams, to explain how it was; that I was sorry, but still I could not find a meaning in any of their deaths. Nothing helped; they came back to me, night after night.

I glanced around at the others: Carter, Aziz Khan, Juma and John, each one of them hunched over and marching through the rain, wet and exhausted, their rifles slung over their shoulders. Unlike me, they had been professional soldiers for years. How many deaths had they seen in their lives? How many corpses disturbed their sleep? They never spoke of them. Carter was the only one who had even hinted at their presence in his life.

She sat up on one elbow and looked down at me. 'This war. It's going to change everything.'

'Not everything,' I told her. 'It'll never change us. It'll never change what I feel for you.'

She lifted one hand and pulled it back through her hair. She looked at me, her eyes bright in the darkness, gleaming with tears. She held my eyes for a long while until she began to move. I watched, transfixed, as she slid across me and the soft, dark strands fell down over her face.

Late that night, the rain came. I woke to hear the soft sound of water running down the eaves of the roof, pouring onto the earth. She was leaning over me, the smell of her surrounding me.

'You've given yourself away,' she said softly, her voice hoarse with sleep.

'What do you mean?' I asked sleepily myself.

'You were talking in your sleep,' she said. 'About a woman. You mentioned her name.'

My heart started pounding. Not her again. It couldn't be. The wasted years, Katherine had called her time with me. I couldn't bear the thought of losing Helen because of her.

'It was my name,' Helen said. She kissed me, light and girlish, and then suddenly the brightness slipped away. 'If you weren't going away, it would have been the happiest moment of my life.'

We reached the waterhole late that night. The rain still poured down. We found a place screened by some bushes were we could make a miserable bivouac and slumped down, shivering and exhausted.

'Akul and Khan,' Carter shouted above the sound of the rain drumming on the ground. 'You'll take the first watch.'

The two of them walked into the bush to position themselves. Carter, Juma and I tried to find some place out of the mud to try and rest. Sleep was impossible in the pouring rain. We found ourselves huddling close together under a tree that provided some slight shelter from the relentless downpour.

'That Walele,' Juma said. 'I think he knows which path Wallis and the others took.'

'What makes you think that?' Carter asked.

'That woman, the one we found the day before, the one whose son told us he had seen them. When you were in the hut with the body of Chief Mbogo, I saw her among the crowd watching us.'

'For God's sakes,' Carter said. 'Why didn't you say something then?'

'I wasn't sure. It was only now while we were marching that I knew I was sure.'

'So, that's why they knew we were coming. She told them, and they were waiting for us.' Carter stared at us in the rain, water pouring off his helmet and down onto his shoulders. 'Jesus, that family must have walked through the night, while we were sleeping.'

Juma nodded.

'And Walele knew that we were British soldiers all along.'

Juma shrugged. 'He couldn't be sure about that. He got the news from an old woman and her hungry, frightened family. He would want to see for himself who we were.'

'But why did he lie to us? There's no reason for him to protect Wallis and the other two.'

'He didn't lie,' Juma said. 'He just didn't say that he had seen them.'

'I asked him,' Carter said. 'He could have given me a straight answer.'

'I think he wants us to find them.'

'But then why didn't he tell me he had seen them?'

'I think he has learned it is better not to say too much to soldiers. He showed us this path.'

'We don't even know where it leads.'

'It is the same path he showed Wallis and the other two.'

'How can you be sure of that?'

'I was thinking, all the time we have been walking. He doesn't know who we are, or what we want. He is thinking that maybe the next soldiers that come along will say to him: "Why did you tell them about the three soldiers? You are a traitor." And then they will kill his family and hang him like the Germans did to Chief Mbogo. It is better to say nothing, but show us the right path without anyone seeing. He doesn't care about Wallis or about us, but if we find them and that means that British soldiers will leave his village alone then he wants us to find them. But if other soldiers come then and they are not happy, at least there is no one to say he told us anything.'

'But he stopped the crowd. Why didn't he just have us killed?' I asked. 'He could have done that and had us buried. No one would have known anything then.'

'I was thinking about that too. It is a sign that the Germans are finished here. The people know it. Walele does not want us in his village, but he could not take the risk of allowing his people to kill British soldiers. Even if he managed to keep it secret for a while, eventually someone in the village would talk. Someone else would tell someone else, and then the British would send soldiers, lots of them, to their village.'

Juma looked at us through the pouring rain.

'The people here remember what happened to the Nandi. When you are the new chief of one small village that is hungry and poor it is very foolish to make an enemy of the British Empire.'

19

THE RAINS WE FEARED HAD BEGUN. For three days we marched in the rain following the red streak of the path that twisted and turned in front of us. Water surrounded us everywhere, day and night. We trudged through the blinding wetness of it, soaked to the skin and shivering with cold. Our uniforms grew heavy and began to stink with the constant damp. Our fingers grew soft and numb and our belts became stretched and slippery.

The mud clung to the soles of our boots in thick, heavy clumps that dragged at every step we took. The inside of our boots turned soggy. Our feet wrinkled and turned pulpy inside them. The blisters on our feet grew and the layers of skin peeled off. When Juma took his boots off at a halt, tendrils of blood curled out of his disintegrating socks and dripped into the wetness of the earth below. I was too frightened to take off my own socks and see what lay underneath.

The photograph I carried of Helen in my shirt pocket disintegrated after the first day. I could feel it sticking to my chest through the thin soaking material of my khaki uniform shirt. There was nothing I could do. To take it out would have been pointless. There was nowhere for me to put it where it would stay dry. I could feel it against my skin, breaking up with each step we took. First the paper of the envelope fell to pieces, clumping into a sodden wad in the corners of my pocket. Then the photograph itself began to crumble. I could feel the chemicals washing off the paper and soaking through the fabric of my shirt. For a few brief moments, they were slippery as soap against my skin.

I turned aside from the path and took what shelter I could under a thorn tree. I pulled the picture out of my pocket and tried to keep the rain off it with the wet edge of my sun helmet. I put it beneath my chest and hunched my shoulders over it, but there was nothing I could do to stop the rain. I looked at it one last time and watched as the huge gleaming drops of rain sliced down out of the sky and dissolved the last outlines of her summer hat and her bright dark eyes underneath it.

I watched her face through the candlelight. 'I won't forget you.'

She hesitated for a moment before answering. 'You might, but tonight I decided I'm willing to take that chance.'

I turned and I saw John. He had stopped and was the holding the mules by their tethers. He was watching me, hunched and alone at the side of the path.

'You are lucky,' he said. 'I have no woman. And no children. Because of my life as a soldier.'

Then he turned and stumbled back into the river of red mud that stretched out in front of us.

Spores of rust took hold in the crevices of our rifles. We learned to sleep in the rain. We sat with our heads on our knees in the darkness and dozed in the few moments when the rain eased, nodding off out of sheer exhaustion for a few moments. We would start awake in a fresh torrent to find the world still drenched, to find that our fingers were still stiff and cold as claws; and that our feet still burned with the damp and the pain.

As the cold, drab light of morning grew, we would force ourselves to stand and stumble into the relentless downpour. It was only Carter's fierce will that kept us moving forward into the blind, grey heart of that deluge. He came behind us, driving us onwards.

He was a man possessed, knowing that it was the only way to get us through those days of endless rain. He would not hear of stopping, and taking shelter until the waters had subsided. He screamed at us as he had at Salaita, to keep moving onward into the icy deluge.

That rain almost broke my will to go on. I could hardly believe my sleepless exhaustion and the constant pain of my waterlogged feet. I had slept so little and was so dizzy with hunger, the boundary between waking and nightmares became blurred and indistinct. The days of endless marching grew longer and longer. We stumbled through the dripping bush, surrounded by the sound and the torture of the drumming rain. My thoughts turned inward towards the memory of my shaking hands, and of the terror I felt as the askaris charged down on us. *How had I survived?* I asked myself that question over and over. When the tide of battle turned, I was as frightened as any of the men at Salaita. What had kept me from running, until the very last minute when it had been too late to save anything? Why had Kirkpatrick frozen in abject terror, and I had not? What had we experienced in our separate lifetimes, that we had behaved so differently? It was something more than Kirkpatrick's extreme youth. When the shooting began, young Johnson had been the bravest. I could never have matched his reckless, wild abandon. I had found myself balanced midway between the two of them, filled with a hot, choking terror, but not paralysed by it.

And where had Watson gone, right at the beginning of the battle? What was his story? Cowering in the heat and red dust of those stony trenches, we had assumed that he had been one of the first to have been killed. He was ill before the battle even began. The truth was that his courage had failed him, and that would mark him and the others forever. I could not help feeling pity for him and Kirkpatrick. They were little more than boys. How cruel it was that a single moment of weakness would destroy their lives.

Wallis' fleeing was a mystery. I had been right there with him at Salaita. I remembered him leaning against a tree and firing back at the Germans. I lost sight of him in those chaotic moments when everything was lost. My last image of Wallis was of him and Fielding trying to drag the wounded Steinberg out of the trench in a groundsheet. It was at the same moment that the askaris had emerged out of the bush and slaughtered Conradie. It was then that I had found myself alone in the trench staring into the face of that askari. In a few seconds of battle I, in a fit of terror, had killed a man face to face and Wallis had run away. I knew that it might have been the other way around. *Daddy, what did you do in the Great War? 'I shot a man in the face, son.'* I might say, while he could only say now. *'I ran away, son.'*

In the split second that it had taken each of us to act, we had found ourselves on opposite sides of an unbridgeable gulf.

And still we marched, the rain beating down on us, the merciless Carter driving us on. In a glade of deep bush we found some respite from the downpour. We walked for an hour or more in the dark, shaded greenness, grateful for the quiet and the soft damp that surrounded us.

Birds and frogs called in a muted, gentle chorus from the trees and clear ponds. At one point we could see where a leopard had slunk across the pathway minutes before us. Her paw marks lay deep in the mud like live things; the edges of the dark soil still writhing and tumbling into the tiny rising pools of water that her pads had made. New golden hairs streaked with shiny black lay against the trunk of a tree. There were gashes in the bark where her claws had slashed at the wood – red crescent moons, like the cuts of an axe-blade, bleeding crystal tears of rain at their tips.

The rain was stronger that afternoon and into the sudden darkness of evening. We halted in the partial shelter of a large boulder, which could not stop the water falling on us, but it broke the force of the downpour, turning it into a gentle mist that settled around us. As we crowded into the slight shelter that the rock provided I looked over at Khan, Juma and John. They were as tired and cold and wet as I was. We were very near the end of our capacity. Only Carter seemed somehow impervious to the fatigue we felt. All day and into the darkness of evening we had been walking more and more slowly, barely able to lift our feet out of the clinging mud for another step. He had pushed us to the very limit of our strength and still he glared at us as we shifted around beneath the rock, trying to find some way to be comfortable.

John brought the mules in close around us. They looked worn out too, damp and red-eyed. Their hair was beginning to fall out and their skin was bleeding where the wet saddles had rubbed them raw and the flesh had begun to die.

I sat exhausted as John moved about behind me. He bent over as he lifted a rock in the long wet grass, trying to clear a space to squat down. Suddenly he froze.

A cobra that had been coiled up under the rock now swayed less than two feet from his face, watching him with its black, glittering eyes, its tongue flickering in and out. Its head was drawn back slightly, ready to strike.

We stared at it, numb and too slow to act. I looked over at Carter. His face was blank, but he could not hide his feelings entirely.

I knew him well enough now to see that his eyes were wide with the effort of holding his fear at bay.

Khan straightened up and began to unsling his rifle from his shoulder. He lowered the barrel towards the snake.

'Stop!' Carter ordered. His voice hoarse and croaking. 'Don't fire. The noise will echo out from this rock. Who knows who might hear it.'

Khan's face was drawn and haggard, but he flushed dark with rage.

'In this weather?'

He turned towards the snake and raised the rifle to his shoulder.

Carter took a deep breath. 'Jemadar Khan,' he said, pausing at each syllable. 'I am ordering you not to fire.'

Khan turned back towards Carter. He held the rifle with the butt just below his shoulder.

'You can't order me.'

Carter stood quite still.

'Put that rifle away.'

Khan glared over the top of the barrel at Carter, who stared back at him, holding his gaze, looking away from where John still half-crouched, frozen, facing the snake.

Carter sprang forward. In a single swift motion he shoved his boot on the cobra's neck, bearing it to the ground. The snake struck, fast but uselessly, against the thick leather, twisted and writhed its thick, muscular body, desperate to pull its deadly head free. Its mouth opened and closed in a wide flash.

John stood back in amazement as he watched Carter pull his bayonet out of his scabbard and slice the snake's head off in a single sweeping motion. Blood sprayed out over his face and arm and onto John's tunic. Khan had lowered his rifle. He and Juma watched the arc of the knife and the blood. I looked at Carter's face. It was twisted up in fear and loathing as he threw the still-writhing body of the snake a few yards away into the bush.

He bent down and wiped his bayonet several times on the long, wet grass. When he straightened up his face had regained its calm, but he was still panting. He put the bayonet back in its sheath and looked around at us.

'That is the way to kill a snake,' he said.

I doubted whether Khan would have had the audacity or the insanity to pull the trigger. Carter had counted on that. What he could not have depended on was his own reaction to the snake. I wondered if it was only I who saw that his hands were shaking as he wiped the bayonet on the grass.

I watched as Khan tore up some clumps of wet grass and wiped the snake's blood off the front of his uniform. Carter did the same, twisting the green stalks as he cleaned his hands. None of us would ever say anything about what had happened. The moment had passed. We would follow Carter now deep into the heart of the rain, day after day, as far as he wanted to go.

But the rain stopped that night. Sometime in the darkness I woke to the blessed sensation of not feeling rain pouring, dripping, running onto my water-logged skin. Misty clouds scudded across the dark sky. The equatorial constellations shone through like bright jewels. A breeze flowed over the wetness of the earth. It was cold and damp, but it brought the promise of dryness with it.

At dawn we set out again. For the first time in days we could see the sun rising. It lit up the sky behind us, a pale orange diffused by the broken remnants of clouds. In front of us the horizon was a deep turquoise, turning to blue. Kilimanjaro was invisible far behind, but huge banks of white cloud hung on the horizon where its distant peak lay. As the sun rose, pale wisps of steam began to rise off the sodden earth. The long tufts of elephant grass, beaten down by the days of rain, began to spring up again. The water glistened on their leaves in the warm, new sun.

The heat of the day began to build around us, drawing the water out of the ground and high into the deep-blue sky above. The air was humid and we sweated freely, but there was sun and warmth now, which counted for everything.

Our spirits lifted with the drying of the earth. We began to march more rapidly. It was only after a couple of hours that Juma called a halt in the middle of the savanna.

'Where did we lose it?' Carter asked.

Juma shook his head. 'I don't know. It could have been last night. It could have been a day ago, even two days ago. With that rain I can't say for sure.'

'We can find our way back to the village,' Khan said. 'Or at least until we are sure we went wrong. If the weather holds, it'll take us two days march. Perhaps less.'

'Turn back now?' John shook his head.

'What do you think, Juma?' Khan said.

Juma looked out over the arc of land. Heat waves were beginning to shimmer and distort the view.

'The rains have confused me. I don't know this country.'

For hours we continued to march in the growing heat. Each one of us scanned the horizon ahead for some sign that we were headed in the right direction. In front of us lay the undulating monotony of the bush.

We were as hot and fatigued now as we had been wet and exhausted the day before. The rain had done us more harm than we had imagined. We were nearing the end of our strength. My feet had started bleeding. Juma was limping too. John was the strongest of us, but even he had taken to staring into the distance as he walked. The mules were lagging and pulling at their traces. Their hair was coming out in clumps. On one of them the ribs were beginning to show through.

John was the first to see it – a wavering pool of white, merging with the distant horizon.

Juma stopped and stared out across the bush at it. 'I know this *boma*. They built it where the caravans come together. The Germans used to control the trading routes around here from this fort. You come here from the east or the south. From here you can go west to the Belgians, or north to Lake Victoria and then along the Nile to the Sudan.'

John was looking out through the heat waves over the grassland.

'I came this way once,' he said. 'They marched our regiment down south from Juba. They said there was trouble and the king needed his soldiers here. He never sent us back.'

Juma narrowed his eyes against the glare of the sun.

'You've been inside?' he asked.

'Yes,' John said stiffly. 'But it was ten years ago. Or more. There was no trouble with the Germans in those days.'

Juma looked at him. 'I remember those days. We were far north of here near Lake Victoria. We were taking ivory to the coast. The villages were burning at night, and the soldiers were moving in the day. It was the Nandi who had risen up. We had to travel at night and very quietly because it was not safe. Many people of the Nandi were killed by the soldiers – even, they said, their leader, the Laibon.'

'It was a long time ago,' John replied. 'I don't remember well. There have been so many wars. There was also the war against the Wakamba.'

'But you've been inside the fort?' Carter insisted. 'What is there?'

John turned towards him. 'They have no well inside,' he said. 'There is a stream nearby where they fetch water.'

'General Stewart and his column would have passed very near here,' Carter said, following Juma's gaze.

'The Germans must have gone then,' Khan said. 'If they weren't driven out.'

'We can't be sure.'

'They can see for miles around from the walls of that fort,' Juma said. 'Whoever is there will see us coming across this plain.'

Juma led us off the wide grasslands into a strip of thick bush that lay alongside. The bush was dense and it was impossible to move easily through it. The thorns grabbed and tore at our ragged clothes and left long red scratches of fresh blood welling up from under our skin. The heat bore down on us out of the empty sky. After an hour of marching we came to a shallow pan hidden deep in the bush. A flock of sacred ibis were foraging with their dark heads and long curved beaks in the water. There must have been a hundred or more of them. Our coming upon them drove them into a panic. They exploded upwards into the air, their wings beating rapidly in their alarm. Then they stretched their wings and glided in white fragmentary spirals, screeching as they flew higher and higher into the blue sky.

'Damn them,' Carter said, sweat pouring down the taut muscles of his neck as he looked upwards to watch them disappear above us. 'Now they'll know we are coming.'

We went on slowly, picking our way around the thickest bush and the sharpest thorns, trying not to disturb anything else that might betray our advance.

Finally we reached the stream that Juma knew about. The water was running brown from the rain and the mud on its banks was churned up with tracks of animals. It was impossible to tell one from the other and what else might have come to drink there.

We could see the fort through the bush some way in front of us. It was a bleak, simply constructed edifice of long white walls with square, crenellated blockhouses at each corner. No flag flew above any of its battlements. The walls that had once been whitewashed were filthy with mud and dirt. In places, the walls had been damaged, or had begun to crumble from neglect and the recent heavy rains. There was no movement on the towers, and in front was nothing but empty, abandoned ground. The fort lay squat and soundless in the dead heat of midday. The heavy wooden gates were shut tight.

'What do you think?' Carter whispered to Juma.

'The Germans must have gone. If they were here, their flag would be flying.'

'Who would be there now?'

Juma shook his head. 'But there is someone there. The gates are shut up from the inside.'

'I'll go and look,' Khan said.

'No,' Carter said. 'You can't get to the fort without being seen.'

We lay in the long grass at the edge of the clearing.

'I'll go,' John said from the dark shade of the bush behind us where he was holding the mules out of sight. 'I can take my uniform off. They won't know I'm a British soldier.'

'No,' Carter said. 'If they even suspect anything, they'll shoot you as a spy.'

'But the Germans have gone,' John said.

'We're not sure of that.'

'They've gone,' John said. 'They would never stay here without their flag.'

Carter wiped the sweat out of his eyes with his knuckles.

'Akul is right,' Juma said. 'The worst there could be inside is bandits.'

'There's only one of him,' Carter replied. 'And four more of us if things go wrong. We will wait and watch.'

For hours there was no movement from the fort. We sweltered as the sun moved across the sky. There was almost nothing left of our biscuit and corned beef and we had not eaten that day. Still we kept watch. The gates stayed shut. No one appeared on the ramparts.

'What the hell could this mean?' Khan whispered as the afternoon wore on.

'They saw the birds,' John said. 'They're expecting us to attack. They are frightened because they are too few.'

Carter glared at him. 'I told you. We wait. Our coming must have caught them by surprise. Whoever is in there will have to take the risk of coming out to get water sooner or later.'

20

THE STARS BURNED FIERCE AND BRIGHT. The cold black sky was clear and new-washed from the rain. We had not moved all day, and we shivered now in the night as we kept watch over the fort through the darkened bush. The walls were pale and luminous in the night. From far away came the echo of a lion's hoarse grunt. It was joined by another. And another. They lingered in the distance for a while until the male rolled out into a full-throated roar. The mules snickered and pulled at their traces, their eyes rolling white with fear. John held them tight. He bent over and whispered into their ears. If they began to bray in the stillness of the night they would give our position away, to both the lions and whoever was hidden in the fort.

We tensed as the sound of the roaring drifted over us. It was moving behind us. There was an answering grunt closer by.

The roaring stopped. I could hear the gurgle of the stream.

One of the mules bucked and kicked out into the darkness. It was wild-eyed and shivering up and down its flanks. It was on the verge of braying and giving away our position, either to the men in the fort or to the lions.

'They've smelled our animals,' Khan whispered. 'They're hunting them.'

'They must have smelled us too, but still they are circling through the bush,' Juma said. 'Lions are usually frightened of humans, but in the last year they have found the wounded and the sick. This war has taught them a liking for human blood. Tonight they are coming in for an easy kill.'

Carter got up from his hiding place and walked over to where John was holding the mules. He took the halter of the mule that was shaking with fear. 'Unload it,' he said to John. 'Put what you can in the other one's saddlebags and lead it away to a hiding place downwind.'

John bent over and whispered into the mule's ear. He stroked the side of the neck and the withers as he took off the saddlebags. The mule calmed and stood still for a moment.

Then a spasm of violent shivering took hold of its entire body. John held the chinstrap and stroked its forehead, but the animal would not stop shaking. It breathed in loudly.

Even the insects had stopped their rhythmic crescendos. Every unseen creature in the bush was straining its senses to the limit to follow the low, padding arc of the lions' hunt.

The mule bucked again and rolled its eyes as it tore against its halter. John stroked it one more time. He handed the lead to Carter.

Carter waited until the other mule was out of sight. He pulled his bayonet out of its sheath. Bending down, he slashed once backhanded across the mule's throat, using the full weight of his body. He severed the mule's larynx and jugular vein in the same stroke. Blood spewed out in a fountain, flowing and dripping off his arm. The mule fell to the ground. Its legs straightened and its hooves kicked. Then it lay still. From underneath its head, a thick pool of blood was spreading out, shimmering in the starlight.

'Let's move,' Carter said.

We followed him through the bush, along the route that John had taken with the other mule. It took us across the front of the fort past the dark closed gates. There was no help for it, we were moving ahead of the wind now. Slight as it was, using it was our best chance of outwitting the lions.

We bent double, flitting across the open grassland between bushes, boulders and anthills. Nothing moved on the fort. If anyone on the walls saw us, there was no sign of them. We caught up to John in a thicket a few hundred yards away from the western wall of the fort. He must have been a few yards in front of us as we moved across the grassland, but I had not seen him or the mule at all.

We gathered ourselves together in the thin shelter of the bush. The roaring had started up again. It was coming from where we had been minutes before.

'They've found the mule,' John murmured.

'What if the wind changes and they come for us?' Khan said.

'We move again,' Carter said. 'We keep moving and hope that no one in the fort hears us.'

The wind held steady. All night we listened to the lions grunting as they fed on our mule. As dawn came near they quietened down. We could see their muscular shapes slinking low through the bush as they left the remains of their feeding to the scavengers. Within minutes, we heard the first hyenas chuckling and rippling through the bush. They rushed past where we were hiding and loped across the open stretch in front of the gate, their humped shoulders rolling through the grass.

The first cold grey light filtered through the thorn branches. The sound of the hyena's jaws crunching the heavy bones carried over to where we huddled, hungry and shivering with our rifles in our hands, fighting to keep off sleep. The sun broke over the horizon behind the fort. We lay in its cold, black shadow listening to the snarling of the hyenas and jackals fighting over the last scraps of our mule's flesh.

Carter stared ahead at the dawn, his fingers tight around his rifle. The sun rose high and golden. It would be another day of empty blue skies. Tiny black dots of vultures circled in the sky. One, two came rushing down, their wings twisting and spreading wide as they banked at the last minute before landing at the remains of our dead mule.

The gate creaked open. The tarboosh of a German askari emerged from the side of the gate. The askari scanned the bush in front of the fort before stepping out into the sunlight.

Khan had his rifle up against his shoulder. It would take nothing more than a gentle squeeze of the trigger.

'Hold it,' Carter hissed.

The askari was carrying his rifle and three water bottles.

'We can take them easily,' Khan said.

Carter glanced over at me. 'Fuller, you and Khan, follow the askari down to the river. Bring him back here. We need to find out what's going on.'

John scrabbled in the saddlebags and handed me one of the sets of handcuffs we had brought with us. I shoved them in the pocket of my uniform shorts. Khan and I waited until the askari had disappeared into the bush on the other side of the clearing before we set out after him. We skirted the open clearing and entered the thicket just a little way downstream of where we had lain concealed the night before. There was a stain of blood on the ground and a jawbone lay cracked and white in the long grass. Two vultures were pulling at the tiny fragments of flesh that still clung to the smashed remnants of the ribcage. They hardly noticed our presence as we crept past.

The askari was squatting in the mud at the edge of the stream. His rifle was upright in his left hand and he was holding one of the water bottles under the dirty brown water with the other.

Khan pointed at me to move to the right side of the askari. We crept towards him picking our way around fallen branches and leaves. The handcuffs rubbed against my thigh, heavy as a stone. I couldn't help noticing how still the bush had become, a glaring witness to our presence. But the askari remained where he was, the rushing sound of the stream drowning out the noises of the bush around him.

We drew close. He was a young man, not much older than Watson or Kirkpatrick, perhaps nineteen or twenty years old. I could see black stubble under his chin and a patchy moustache against the dark skin on his upper lip.

The askari was crouched over filling the first water bottle. He lifted it dripping out of the stream. He put his rifle down on the ground while he screwed the cap shut. He picked up his rifle and turned to scrutinise the bush around him. I shrunk behind a tree. I could see Khan through the bush from where I was. If the askari rose and turned, he would see Khan too.

I watched the askari as he searched the bush for signs of danger. Despite his youth, he was clearly a well-trained, experienced soldier. If he saw one of us first, we would have to kill him. He would not give us a second chance. Khan already had his rifle up against his shoulder and was aiming it at the askari's back.

The man turned back to the stream and plunged the second canteen into the water. Khan motioned to me. He mimed the action of the askari putting his rifle down and screwing the cap closed. Then he jammed his hand forward.

I watched the dappled light on the brown water, and the bubbles frothing up as the water rushed into the neck of the canteen. I had never been in such a situation before – hunting another man in cold blood. I was so close I could shoot him point-blank in the back of the head. He would die without ever knowing what it was that had killed him.

I wanted to do it. The memory of blood and the fear of Salaita rose up in me. I hated this young askari who squatted before me. It was his comrades who had slaughtered us there. Now he would pay – for everything. He was powerless in front of me. That made me want to kill him even more. A fine sheen of sweat broke out at my temples and my hands began to tremble. Khan was watching me, but I didn't care. All I could feel was the anger rising inside me.

I lifted my rifle to my shoulder and aimed down the sights. The smooth brown skin on the back of his neck filled the steel V of my sights. I shifted the barrel slightly upwards. Now I could see the sweat stains on the khaki fabric of his tarboosh. They were encrusted with fine white lines of salt. Beneath them lay his soft, tightly-curled black hair. Beneath his hair lay the smooth brown skin and the fine network of veins on top of the white bone of his skull. The same white bone above Corporal Reynolds' eyes as he had stared up at me out of the pit.

The askari's head wavered in my sights. It was the point I had learned to understand on the shooting range at the training camp. It was the critical moment when you were in total control, when you stopped trying too hard to hold the target in your sights. You let go the intellect, and instinct took over. The shot would be straight because your whole being was concentrated on the target. You squeezed the trigger with the pressure that was no stronger than the beat of your own heart in your tiniest capillaries. For the purest control it had to be the smallest pressure you could exert. So, so easy…

My eyes blurred and filled with sweat. I had waited too long. I would have to rest and begin to sight again. I looked up from the barrel. Khan was staring at me in horror through the bush. I felt a hot flush of shame. I lowered the butt of the rifle from my shoulder. The askari was pulling the second water bottle out of the stream. As the anger rolled away, fear came rushing in. Now we would have to act. I was exhausted and almost numb from lack of sleep. What if one of us fumbled in the first rush? Two of us would overpower him, but at least one of us might die in the attempt. And if things went wrong we would have to kill the askari.

As quickly as it had risen up, the hatred flowed out. I feared him now. He was young and strong. He could kill me.

I watched him place his rifle carefully down on the mud, within reach if he should need it. He lifted the second water bottle and began to screw the cap on.

Khan and I sprang forward. The askari heard the crackling rustle of branches behind him. He dropped the water bottle and spun around to face us. He scrabbled on the ground for his rifle. Khan slammed his boot down on the man's hand, grinding it into the mud. I slipped behind him and jabbed the barrel of my rifle longways underneath his chin. I pulled it hard against his throat, choking off his air. He was gargling and retching as he reached up and pulled against it.

Khan kicked the askari's rifle into the stream. He reached down to grab the machete at his belt. The handle was broken and bound up with knotted string, but the blade was curved and gleamed silver at its edge where it had been sharpened like a sword. It would take off the arm or the head of a man with a single blow. Khan threw it into the stream. It splashed and disappeared.

He punched the askari in the solar plexus. The man groaned and curled up. He lay still, hanging heavily on the barrel of my rifle.

Khan slung his rifle over his shoulder and stepped forward. He took the man's arm in a lock, twisting it hard.

'Quick,' he said. 'The handcuffs.' I put my rifle down and reached into my pocket.

The askari twisted around and slammed Khan in the face with his elbow. Khan stumbled backwards, blood dripping from the edge of his eye. He fell heavily on the ground. The askari kicked up into my ribs, knocking the breath out of me. I stumbled back, gasping with the sudden pain that shot upwards through my body. The askari scrambled up and grabbed at my rifle. He fumbled with the bolt. Cold terror washed through me. I put my head down and charged forward, knocking him backwards into the stream. We both fell over into the water. The askari swung at my head with butt of the rifle. I ducked. He swung again. I was groping behind me on my belt for my bayonet. Somehow I got it out. I plunged it into the water above his stomach. I felt it go in, smooth and then suddenly hard as it scraped against bone. I tore it out, frantic with fear. Red oily blood floated up into the water. I stabbed again. The askari groaned. He fell backwards into the water, dropping the rifle. I thrust my hand over his face and held it under the water. I shoved my knees into his chest. I could feel the hard, frenzied spasms of his lungs as they burned for air. His hands grabbed at my arm, but they were weak now as his own blood welled up to the surface of the stream. I held him under the water. The bayonet was in my other hand. I jabbed it clumsily above his shoulder. It slid sideways into the muscles of his neck. I thrust again. The blade went wide, shearing off into the water.

Khan splashed through the water next to me, and grabbed at the man's head. The two of us held him there. There was a single moment when he suddenly went soft under my knees. His will to hold his breath gave way, and he sucked water into his lungs. He struggled weakly, shuddering against our hands under the water, until he collapsed and fell back.

The flesh at the corner of Khan's eye was bleeding and badly bruised. We let the man go and stood up, careful not to meet each other's eyes. The corpse rolled over in the stream and lay face down in the water. I picked up my rifle and watched as the pink blood and water poured off it.

My mouth was dry. I felt dizzy and exhausted. My back ached and the muscles in my thighs and my arms burned from the sheer effort of killing. The breath was burning in my lungs as I gulped for air.

As if in a dream, I slid my bayonet back into its sheath.

'We had to do it,' Khan said to me. 'That's right, isn't it? We had no choice.'

Carter watched as John stowed the empty handcuffs in the saddlebags. He turned to look at the two of us.

'And what the fuck do you suggest we do now?'

'You'll have to let me go into the fort,' John said. 'Before the others realise he's dead. It's the only thing to do. I'll find a way in.'

Carter said nothing for a while. He turned away to look at the walls of the fort. Finally, he nodded.

John handed his rifle and the halter of the mule to Juma. He took off his boots first. He wore no socks. His feet were hard and tough where mine and the others were spongy and bleeding. He stripped off his shorts and shirt and wrapped an old dirty cloth around his waist.

Juma gave him a knife that he always carried with him. It had a curved, sharp blade and a delicately-worked handle of Somali silver set with an oval of green malachite.

John nodded his thanks. He hid the knife in the folds of the cloth. He turned and was about to set off through the bush towards the clearing.

'Stop,' Carter hissed. John turned and looked at him quizzically.

'Your right shoulder,' Carter said.

John reached up and touched the skin of his shoulder with the tips of his fingers. There was a dark callous there the size of a coin. We each had one from the carrying straps of our rifles.

'It'll give you away,' Carter said. 'You'll have to hide it.' He reached in the saddlebags and threw John another, larger piece of cloth. 'Throw that over your shoulder.'

'It's too new and expensive,' John said. 'They might think something is wrong.'

'They'll know if they see your shoulder.'

We moved as close as we could to the fort without being seen. From our hiding place we watched John as he crossed the open grassland – a tall, dark figure alone against the grass and the cloudless sky. Shut up behind those gates there was no way we could help him. Everything would depend on his keeping a cool head. That, and, if it came to it, Juma's Somali knife.

Watching him go, I wondered if I would have had the guts to enter that fort by myself. I had known war as a soldier fighting alongside others. I had never had to face it alone. Even the killing of the askari I had shared with Khan. Doing it had felt different, even to shooting the man at Salaita. I had killed a man this morning with my own hands. The memory of him shuddering and then falling limp – nothing would ever make me forget that. I was still tired from the hard labour of killing.

The guilt of what I had done was already eating away at me. The only people who knew about it were the men with me. They would say nothing. That much already we had shared as soldiers, as fellow killers. I would never – could never – tell anyone else about today, about what Khan and I had done together. I could not even tell Helen. I would always keep this hidden deep within me. I didn't want Helen to know that I knew what it felt like to have a man die in your hands.

Every day that passed in this war, I had something more to hide from her. The gulf between us was growing. This war was changing everything, destroying so much. I began to wonder if there would be anything left between us, if there would be anything for us to share together in the soft darkness of night, when this war was finally over.

John came to the wooden gates. Already the sun was high. It threw dark shadows across the iron bindings of the latch and hinges. He knocked once, twice. No one came. Our rifles were trained on the door, but at that distance there was little we could do to help him. If we fired we were as likely to hit John as we were to shoot anyone who might attack him.

John knocked again. This time the door opened and he stepped inside. The door was closed again. The fort stood in the gathering heat of the day. We waited, our rifles trained on the door for want of any other place to point them.

It was late in the afternoon when the gates opened and two askaris came out. John followed them. Neither of the askaris was holding a rifle and neither was John.

'What the hell's going on?' Khan said under his breath.

'Hold the askaris in your sights,' Carter whispered. The three of them walked some way away from the gates. John waved in our direction and indicated that we were to come over.

Carter turned to me. 'Fuller, you and I will go. Juma and Khan, you two keep us covered.'

We strode across the grassland to where John waited with the two askaris. John saluted as we came nearer. The askaris drew to attention alongside him and saluted as well.

'What's all this, Corporal?' Carter demanded.

'They're surrendering, sir. There are these two and a white officer who is sick inside. I think he is dying.'

John shifted the weight on his feet. 'The first thing they did was check my shoulders. They wanted to shoot me.' John looked over at me. 'I knew their water must be finished, so I told them Lieutenant Fuller and Jemadar Khan had killed their fellow, and that you would kill them too, one by one, as they tried to fetch water. I told them if they surrendered, they would be treated well. So they decided to surrender.'

Carter was staring at the two askaris standing to attention. He looked back at John. He smiled and shook his head. John looked at me and suddenly the three of us were bent almost double, laughing with relief while the askaris sweated in the sun and wondered at their fate.

That lonely, abandoned fort passed into the possession of the British Empire by the simple act of our tiny patrol walking through the half-opened gate. The askaris were split up. One led the way through the gate; the other was placed between Khan and me.

The inside of the fort was as ghostly and abandoned as the outside. The doors and warped wooden shutters of the barracks and jails hung half open. Their hinges creaked in the slight breeze.

In one corner of the fort a loud buzzing of flies rose out of the angular shadows of the walls. A huge pile of chains, manacles and iron collars lay twisted open and heaped up on top of one another. Flies were swarming and feeding on the thin streaks of dried, blackened blood that lay spattered on the iron links. A large bunch of keys hung on a nail driven into the mud wall.

One of the askaris spoke to John in Swahili. 'Criminals and traitors,' John said. 'The officer ordered the askaris to let them go when they heard that the British were coming. They were frightened of an uprising.'

'Did Stewart's column stop here?' Carter asked.

John relayed the question to the askari. 'No,' he said, turning to face Carter while the askari looked down at the ground. 'There was nothing here for them to stop for. The main German force evacuated the fort a few days before, heading deeper into German territory. They attacked the British further south.

These men could see the flashes of the guns at night and again at dawn. The British followed them. They never came to the fort. There was just the major who is ill and the three of them.'

'Take us to see this major,' Carter said.

The askari led Carter and me across the hard red clay of the parade ground in the centre of the fort. A flagpole cast a shadow across the glaring brightness of the sunlight. At the other side of the fort, a battered tin pot of green bananas lay boiling over a charcoal fire. Behind it a wooden door was half-ajar. We stepped inside. For a moment or two, the dark interior was invisible as our eyes adjusted.

We took a few steps. The askari pointed at a door that led off the cool darkness of the corridor.

Carter pulled up the crude, cast-iron latch and eased the door open. There was a small iron-barred window with thick steel shutters high up in the wall. Next to it was a thin loophole for firing out onto the grasslands beyond. Narrow bars of sunlight streamed into the room. I could see a man lying on a bed in the corner. He was emaciated and unshaven. He lay on his side, his knees curled up into his stomach. The smell of sweat, watery faeces and days-old dirty sheets made the air dank and thick with decay. A German pith helmet and a Luger pistol in a cracked leather cartridge belt hung on the rusty iron bedstead. The pistol was in easy reach, but the German made no effort to pull it out. His skin was sallow and dry and his once-bright grey eyes were sunken into deep pits. He watched us as we entered the room.

'So the British have arrived,' he said in heavily-accented English in a low, quavering voice. 'It has taken you long enough.'

He coughed, the spasms shaking his body. Then he looked up at us. 'I had expected there to be more of you. I had thought I might see perhaps even General Smuts himself, once the ally of the Kaiser, now serving his old enemies.'

Carter took a step across the room. He scooped up the pistol and cartridge belt.

'Whatever you think about General Smuts' career, you are now his prisoner.'

'There is no need,' the German said. He raised his hand out of the soiled bedclothes and pointed to where Carter held the pistol awkwardly at his side. 'I knew you were coming for me. If I had wanted to shoot you, I would have been waiting. I would have killed you both as soon as you opened the door.'

He let his hand drop. He closed his eyes and opened them again. 'You should have noticed that the askari let you both go through the door first. And you should never have allowed him to do so. You were so anxious to see what lay beyond the door that I think you forgot to take the most elementary precautions.'

I glanced over at Carter. His eyes were blazing. 'What are you doing here?' he demanded.

The major looked at us wearily. 'It was clear that I had cholera and that it was far advanced. I could not continue the march with Von Lettow-Vorbeck; he ordered them to take me back to Dar es Salaam for treatment,' the German shook his head. 'I don't even know if any German doctors are still left there. They managed to bring me as far as this before I collapsed. When they put me in this bed I told them that if the English came they were to trick them into coming into the room first. I told them I would not let the English take me alive, that I would shoot as many of you as I could before one of you killed me.'

'Your name?'

'I am Major Schirmer,' the German said, raising his head. 'Major Max Schirmer. Of the 6th *Schutztruppe*.'

The two of us stared at him.

'I was shocked too,' Schirmer said, 'to see the maroon and white helmet flashes of the 7th Transvaal Regiment come walking in my door. I was there at Salaita. I watched you break and run. Now, it seems, you have come for your revenge.'

'It was an orderly retreat,' Carter said.

'Then why did you abandon your dead and wounded? We buried more than sixty of your men. I myself found the body of one young boy. We found the metal name tag around his neck – Steinberg. It was sad to see such a young boy lying dead on the field of battle. Jewish, like me. He reminded me of my own son.' Schirmer paused, and lowered his head, looking down over his own emaciated body. 'The boy died of his wounds. Slowly. Perhaps, if he had not been left behind, he might have survived.'

'What did you do with his body?' Carter demanded. His voice was cold with fury.

'We buried it of course, along with some of the others you left behind when you ran. The ones that the wild animals had not eaten. We did the best we could. Some of the wounded had been attacked by the hyenas. I saw one man – Smit was his name, it sounds German too, of course – with his nose and ears torn off by the animals. He was still breathing through the holes in his face when we found him. We gave him the best medical treatment we could. He is with the Red Cross now I believe.'

I thought of those last moments I had seen Steinberg alive, bleeding into the red dust; his eyes filled with terror and pain. My God, how we had failed him, and Smit and the others, too. The stories about Salaita would have been spread through the German army, perhaps they had even reached the German press back home by now.

'We found a diary in the pocket of his tunic,' Schirmer went on. 'I didn't know the British army allowed its soldiers to keep diaries.'

'We don't,' Carter replied.

'I thought so. But the diary was very interesting. In it, this young boy had written of a Captain Carter who had ordered them to take no prisoners among the Germans in the attack.'

Carter stared across the room. 'It's not true.'

'So, you are this captain?' Schirmer's face flickered for a moment through the dull sheen of his exhaustion. 'I wondered what kind of a man would tell his men such things. And now you are standing here in front of me. How interesting life can be.'

'I never gave those orders,' Carter seethed.

Schirmer's exhausted, watery eyes held us. 'It does not matter now. As one of my fellow officers pointed out on reading the diary, your men did not take any prisoners anyhow.'

He smiled a wan, sickly smile and then lay back on his greasy pillow. Carter stared back at him across the bright sunlight that streamed into the darkness of the room. I couldn't imagine where Steinberg might have gotten such a notion. Then I remembered the conversation between him and Johnson and Kirkpatrick I had half-overheard the night before Salaita. 'We're to take no prisoners,' he had said. 'Everyone's saying those are our orders.'

Somehow those rumours and wild speculations must have been transformed into something more in their minds. It was not only that our defeat was never to be forgotten; it was worse to know that the story of what had happened to us that day would be filled with nonsense: rumours, half-truths, lies.

Schirmer was breathing heavily now. Even such a short conversation had drained him of his energy.

'The hyenas didn't kill the wounded,' Carter said. 'It was your askaris.'

Schirmer held his gaze. 'It was you who ran, and left them behind.'

Outside, in the dark corridor, I could hear the askari shifting on his feet. He had been trained to drill, and shoot, and stab with a bayonet, but no one had explained to him what his role might be when the officer he was supposed to protect was dying in a squalid room in front of his enemies. Especially when one of them had killed his comrade only hours before. It was clear that he held Schirmer in respect and had a certain affection for him.

'We didn't come here to reminisce about Salaita with you,' Carter said.

'No, I imagine not,' Schirmer replied, his voice hard beneath the hoarse weakness of his breathing. 'I'm sure you would all like to forget what happened that day. We, on the other hand, will always remember it.'

Schirmer turned slowly on his bed. 'Anyway, I know why you are here. You came to find your runaway soldiers.'

21

WATSON'S GRAVE LAY IN THE SHADE of a baobab tree. It lay a little way from the walls of the fort. The grave itself was nothing more than a heap of red earth, dry and crumbling already in the African sun. A crude wooden cross had been hammered into the soil at one end. It was made of two sticks of acacia wood tied together with a thong of raw goatskin. Fragments of hair still clung to the drying skin. Large black ants were scurrying up and down the wooden base of the cross, gnawing at the edges of the thong. Already the roots of the long grass were creeping forward across the cleared space. In a few months, the grave would be overgrown.

'We came across them just before we reached this fort. They had been in the fort, looking for food. They walked out of the gate right past our hiding place,' Schirmer had told us. 'They had no sense of the bush. They were stumbling along, without keeping any sort of watch. We could have shot all three of them in a matter of a few seconds. But we hesitated. We could not imagine that there would be three British soldiers so lost and alone in the bush. We recognised the helmet flashes, and we assumed that they were a reconnaissance party and the rest of your regiment would be a short way behind. There were only four of us and after what had happened at Salaita, we could imagine that our treatment from you would not be gentle.'

Schirmer pointed to the door. 'Thawabu, the askari outside, was hiding behind a tree. The young British soldier with the red hair saw him, and panicked. He was ill with malaria. He was shaking as he fired at Thawabu and missed. It was unfortunate, but my askari had then to shoot back. He never misses.

'The other two spun around. They were ready to fight back.'

Schirmer paused and looked at us. 'Perhaps they are not quite the cowards that you think they are,' he said. 'But then, I have found that most men are not. They need good officers to find the best in themselves.'

Carter said nothing, and Schirmer went on with his story. 'I was lying on a stretcher, hidden away in the bush by my men, but I managed to shout out at them in English.

'"You are surrounded," I told them, even though there were four of us, three really because I would have been of little use in a fight, lying on my stretcher as I was.

'I watched them as they stared around. The very young one looking up to the older one. The older one looked suspicious, so I yelled again. "You are surrounded. Surrender now, or I will give the order to shoot."

'The older one nodded at the younger one. They put their rifles down on the ground. I saw the younger one kneel down and take his friend's head in his hands. The older one tore off his shirt. He tried to stop the blood pouring out of his friend's chest, but it was no good. He was already dead.

'My three askaris surrounded them and brought them to where I was lying in the bush. "Where is the rest of your force?" I asked them.

'At first, they both refused to say anything. They both looked confused and frightened. I could see that they were hungry and tired. They were men at the very edge of their endurance, who had just lost one of their companions. His blood was still drying on their hands from where they had tried to save him.'

'"I'll have you shot if you don't talk," I said. As I expected, there was no response from either of them. I ordered two of my askaris to take the younger one and shoot him first. They moved forward to take him by the arms.

'"You can't take him," the older one shouted out. "Take me."

'The askaris stopped, holding the younger soldier between them. They looked at me, waiting for my orders. Up until that moment, I hadn't seriously considered shooting the younger one. I didn't know what I would do if my ruse failed to persuade the older one to talk.

'"Shoot him," I said. The askaris turned and started leading him away into the bush.

'The other soldier and I were much the same age. There was something I found to admire in him. In another world we might even have become friends. He was obviously a man who had seen something of the world. He didn't panic; he was trying to decide whether I would have the nerve to carry out such a ruthless act. I watched him as the askaris and their prisoner tramped away through the long grass.

'"Stop," the older British soldier shouted out. "I'll talk."

'I had been on the verge of ordering the askaris to halt. But he gave in to his fear a split second before I did.

'"We're not a patrol," the British soldier said, looking straight ahead at the bush around us. "We're deserters."

'He said they had been walking for nearly two weeks in the bush now. "We've had enough," he said. "There's no sense in any of it. We want nothing more to do with this war."

'"You cannot escape it so easily," I replied. "None of us can."

'"It's too late for us to turn back now. We have to go on."

'"You forget one thing," I told him. "You are my prisoner. You are not going on anywhere."

'He looked at me then for a long time. It was his turn now to size me up. "You don't want us," he said. "For a start, you do not have any food for us, and we will slow you down. If you take us as prisoners, you will never get to a hospital in time to save your life."

'He was right, of course. About getting to the hospital and also –' Schirmer looked up from his pillow. He smiled grimly at me and Carter. 'And also about my own fear. I had found his weak point; he had found mine. I did not want to die a useless death from disease in the bush, far from anywhere.

'Together we buried the young boy who had been shot. Thawabu himself insisted on making the cross and placing it at the head of the grave. There was no need for it to have happened. The boy was a deserter who died because in the end he tried to fight when he could not win.' Schirmer shook his head.

'I never expected it, but something inside me had changed. I felt as sad about his death as I had about any of my own men's deaths. We said some prayers around the graveside. Then I let the other two go on their way. My men brought me here to this room. We intended to move the next morning, but that night my condition worsened. I am still here, waiting to be well enough to travel.'

Schirmer closed his eyes. He seemed to drift off. How long had he been in this room? A week or five days perhaps. And before that? A few weeks ago he had been a strong healthy man, part of the immovable force of men and steel that had crushed us in waves at Salaita. Now he was wasted and dying. It was too late to save him. The disease had gone too far. Even his decision to let Wallis and Kirkpatrick go had not helped him. Was there some justice, some hidden pattern, in all of this?

None that I could see. The man who had shot Watson was alive and well outside the room. He was our prisoner now, and his life was in our hands. And we were the same men who had stabbed and drowned his comrade two hours before. None of it made any sense.

Schirmer was dying too. For a brief moment, I almost envied him. Already, as he lay in front of us on that filthy bed stained with his own shit and the dark blood that welled out from inside him, I could sense the lightness growing in him. He was beginning to shed the horror that those of us who still lived would have to carry with us.

Carter was staring at him. 'Where did they say they were heading?'

Schirmer stirred feebly on his mattress. 'You're not going after them, still, are you?'

'I bloody well am.'

'They are good men,' Schirmer said. 'Two good men whose crime is to have grown tired of war. Leave them be. Have we not all grown tired of this damned war?'

'You're an officer, you know as well as I do that I have to carry out my orders. Where are they heading?'

Schirmer stared back at Carter for a while. Finally he began speaking in low, hoarse syllables.

'They said they were heading north and east for the Belgian Congo. From there they would travel down the river to Leopoldville and take ship to Liberia. From there, neutral America is their goal. They want to start again; as new men. Not be cowards running from a war for the rest of their lives.'

Carter stared down at Schirmer. 'Wallis – the man who in another world might have been your friend – I ordered him to take Steinberg back behind the lines to safety. He might be alive today if Wallis had not run away.'

Schirmer turned his head towards the wall. He spoke in a weak, unsteady voice.

'I can't change what happened at Salaita,' he said slowly. 'But, if you must find them, then, yes, as an officer I understand. My askaris saw them off. They will know the path the men took. I cannot help you more than that.'

'That's all we need.'

Schirmer turned back to look at us. He closed his eyes and lay back on his bed. 'You are a good soldier, Captain. A very good soldier, and I respect that. I was a good soldier too. But – I wonder what kind of men that has made us.'

We buried the askari that Khan and I had killed next to Watson, hacking out the red soil and the hard rocks with bayonets, machetes and our bare hands. The giant, exposed roots of the baobab tree lay beneath the soil like the whitened bones of some ancient, long-forgotten beast. We – Khan and I, his killers, and his friend and comrade, Thawabu – laid the askari's body between the roots and covered him up with the stones and soil that we had laid aside.

The man's name was Patrick Saida. He had come from a village near Moshi, the same village that Thawabu had come from. Unlike many of the German askaris, he was a Christian. We made a crude cross for him too. There was nothing else to use, so we tied the arms of the cross with the man's own bootlaces and placed it next to Watson's cross. Enemy alongside enemy. German alongside British. Black alongside white. Both men buried with the barest of ceremony in the soil of Africa. Neither death deserved such a poor, scrabbling burial, but then, our forlorn group of ragged, hungry enemies made up the strangest of funeral parties.

The two askaris stood among us and mourned their comrade. Carter led us in the saying of The Lord's Prayer. None of us could fully remember anything else appropriate. He and I recited it in English, the askaris and John said the words in Swahili while Juma and Khan looked down at the ground.

For ever and ever. Amen. We stood around the graveside.

Juma said a few words in Arabic quietly when Carter finished speaking. He and Khan swept their hands across their faces briefly in the Muslim custom. Sweat was still pouring down our faces from the effort of digging the grave in the full heat of the day. I could hear the insects calling back and forth in the cool shade of the deep bush. A few tears fell down Thawabu's face. He looked away, gazing over the long grass to the walls of the empty fort gleaming in the sun.

Carter would have to write the report of what happened. He would also have to write to Watson's family about their son's death. I tried to imagine Watson's parents receiving the envelope and unfolding the letter. His father would be a stern, but harassed senior manager at a bank or insurance company. He would be an honest, upright citizen with few, if any, secrets in his life. His mother would be one of the thousands of aging Johannesburg socialites, secure in their husbands' positions and in little else. Their love for their son would be the redeeming quality of their lives. They would want for him only the best. They would want for him that he had been brave and resolute in defence of his King and the Empire. That their son had not would be a blow they would never recover from. To learn the truth of their son's conduct and the fact that he had deserted would shatter not only their world view, but also their belief in the person they had each loved more than anyone else.

Carter would write the letter when this was over, when we had captured Wallis and Kirkpatrick, when they had faced their court-martial. Half the words he could find in the standard letters that went out after every soldier's death in battle; the other half he would have to find for himself.

There would always be some part of Carter that would remember what it had been like as a terrified, confused young subaltern on the Afghan frontier. I hoped he would remember that when he wrote the letter to those lonely, grief-stricken people. But I was no longer sure. His heroism at Salaita had given him a second chance, and with it, Carter had become a man invested with that most awesome of responsibilities – the opportunity to reinvent himself. In his need to forget his past, there would always be now the temptation to write another story. The story that the army would want, the story that only a good soldier would tell.

We took Schirmer's Luger and the askaris' rifles. John tied them to the saddle of our remaining mule. The antiquated rifles would not be much use to us, but we could not leave them in the hands of the askaris. The Luger would be more use. It was a modern, long-barrelled naval model and had a full belt of ammunition.

Schirmer was unconscious when we went back to find him in his room. There was nothing we could do for him. We left him there, dying alone in that pitiful room. There would soon be a third cross under the baobab tree. I wondered how many such anonymous graves there were of both black and white soldiers scattered across the savanna of East Africa, and what people would think, a hundred years from now, coming across three forgotten skeletons lying side by side in the red earth.

It was late afternoon by the time we walked out onto the grasslands in front of the fort. Thawabu and the other askari led the way. Once we had gone, we would leave them in peace. They were no threat to us now, and Schirmer had, at most, a few days left to live. We had left them some morphine and a syringe to ease the death agonies of his cramped, bleeding bowels. Once he was gone, they were free to make their own choices. The war was over for them. Von Lettow had given up any hope of winning his campaign. He and his army were fleeing deeper and deeper into the heart of the continent trying to tie up as many British troops as possible in order to keep them out of the war in Europe. These two had been left behind with a task to fulfil. It was no fault of theirs that Schirmer would die before he could reach a doctor. Once that happened, there was nothing left for them to do. We had taken their guns, and there was no hope of their ever catching up with Von Lettow's army now. *Deutsch-Ostafrika*, the country they had chosen to fight for, had ceased to exist. History had left them behind, to tend to a dying man here in this rotting, abandoned fort in the wilderness. The best thing they could do when that responsibility was gone was to disappear, to wander back to their villages and find some way to live a new life in the peace that would emerge out of their defeat. I envied them their freedom, and their chance to go home again. I wished now that I had never come to this war. I wanted nothing more than to find my way back again, away from the war, and back to Helen.

They led us through the bush for a mile or so until we were looking due west. We could see a range of brown hills in the distance. Their peaks were grey and blue in the afternoon light. Behind us lay Mount Meru silhouetted by the low sun. Further back we could see the heavy cloud banks over in the direction of Kilimanjaro.

'*Aruscha ist in dieser richtung,*' Thawabu said pointing to the south. 'North is Victoria Nyanza. West is Ngorongoro. And then the Belgian territories. The British soldiers went west. That is all I can tell you.'

Carter nodded. 'Get him to a doctor soon,' he said to Thawabu. 'He needs one.'

Thawabu said nothing. He stood and watched us as we filed past, one by one, into the growing dusk.

22

THAT NIGHT WE COULD SEE FIRES in the distance behind us. The furthest were nothing more than thin lines of red bleeding into the darkness.

Closer by, perhaps two or three miles away, huts were being set alight on the hillsides. They blazed up in the darkness, red and gold like tiny jewels and then disappearing into a glow of sparks, leaving an eerie darkness, even blacker for the fire that had blazed so fiercely. A few minutes later, another hut flared up, flames leaped into the night. And another. And another.

The war was closer to us than we had known. Was it Germans or our own soldiers doing the burning? Or was it perhaps some local feud that had been set off by the ripples of our war? We had no way of knowing.

We lit no fire ourselves. We ate some dry biscuit and drank a little water. We had eaten nothing else that day. There was very little left to eat, and the lack of it was beginning to tell. Barely an hour after we had eaten our ration of biscuit, I was dizzy with hunger. I noticed that Khan's eyes were glazed over, and Juma hung his head between his knees when he thought no one was looking. Only John and Carter seemed unaffected by the gnawing faintness that our hunger brought on.

The fires on the hillside burned far into the night. We gazed into the darkness, mute voyeurs of that distant violence and death. The fires and the killings that no doubt accompanied them were as anonymous and inexplicable as any this war had produced. I thought of the burned huts and the skeletons of the dead we had seen at Kilele village. Would their story ever be told? Would the story of Schirmer's or Watson's or of Patrick Saida's deaths ever be really told? And – I tried to push the thought away, but it would not leave me – what about our own fate? Would we die on this mission in some meaningless conflagration in the darkness? Would there ever be a story to tell of us?

Towards dawn the fires died down and the hills lay half-hidden in the mist, which began to melt away as the sun came up. We saw nothing and no one to tell us who had carried out such cruelty in the night. They had moved on, leaving nothing but the faint smell of ashes on the morning breeze.

We stalked slowly through the bush that morning, afraid of coming across a column of German askaris marching to join Von Lettow in the south. Fear and tension were everywhere around us. Charred corpses lay humped under the ash and embers of their huts. Their fingers were black claws, upraised and clenched in the last agony of death. Near one body we found broken spears, their points bent and twisted. Near another there was an old trade musket, smashed and useless. The people here had fought back with whatever they had.

'My God, what happened here?' Carter asked.

'There was an uprising against the Germans here just before the war,' Juma said.

'It was revenge,' John said. He shook his head slowly, staring down at the mangled, burnt corpses. 'Perhaps the askaris remembered their comrades who were killed in the wars from before, in the rebellions against the Kaiser. Perhaps the people themselves attacked first, hoping for their own revenge after seeing the Germans at last were running.'

We caught a glimpse or two of frightened people fleeing the smouldering remains of their homes. They hid themselves or ran when they saw us: just more soldiers armed with guns.

Juma set off after one group – a young man and two children, who darted out from a behind a tree as we grew closer.

'Leave them,' Carter hissed. 'The last thing we want now is to stumble into the arms of any Germans who may be around.'

We moved on, each one of us alert, our rifles at the ready. At one point we heard the distant boom of explosions, and then nothing.

Khan was beginning to sweat more than was normal even in this heat. He was trying to hold himself erect and keep marching, but his face was sallow and his shoulders slumped with pain and exhaustion. He had a hollow, faraway look as he tried to keep watch on the bush around us. The rain and the mosquitoes it brought with it had done their work. He had malaria.

Carter called a halt. While the rest of us kept an anxious guard, he rummaged through the saddlebags. He took out his own portion of quinine and gave some to Khan.

Khan shook his head. 'There won't be enough for you.'

'I'm not sick.' Carter pushed it at him. Khan swallowed it down, wincing at the bitterness of it. He gulped down some water but white streaks of powder still stuck at the corners of his mouth. After taking it, he looked sicker than before. What he needed was rest, but that was the one thing we could not give him. We had to keep moving on, we could not afford to find ourselves trapped by a German column.

'Keep an eye on him,' Carter whispered to me as we set out again. Khan grew worse with every step. Sweat was running off him freely now and he began to shiver sporadically, some deep quiver taking hold of his muscles and then building to a crescendo, shaking him as he struggled to stay on his feet. Somehow he managed to keep up with the rest of us, but he was stumbling deeper and deeper into his own private hell. I could not guess at what phantoms were plaguing his mind, but as every hour went by the delusions of malaria were becoming more real to him than the war that lay so close around us.

'Nadia,' I heard him muttering once, 'do not leave me, Nadia.' He tripped and stumbled. I lunged forward and grabbed him by the arm. Khan turned and looked at me, haunted, wide-eyed with pain. He shook me off and turned away, lurching down the path.

We came to the edge of a low escarpment. Below us lay an empty plain of grasslands and a dense thicket of thorn bush extending to the horizon. Clouds were beginning to gather in the afternoon humidity and the light was golden as it filtered through. In the distance, a single wildebeest limped through the grass, dragging its wounded leg behind it. We could not see clearly, but in the night some beast, a lion or hyena, must have taken a snap at it, missing but leaving the animal wounded and crippled, waiting for a certain death.

Carter seethed. 'We've come to a dead end,' he whispered angrily.

'We'll have to backtrack,' Juma said.

Khan was sitting a little way apart from the rest of us, his head hanging down between his knees. Carter glanced over at him.

'We'll have to rest for the night soon,' John said. 'He is too tired to go on.'

'We can't rest here,' Carter said. 'If they catch us here, we're trapped. We have to –'

John was holding his finger to his lips. He pointed down to the far edge of the cliff face. Three more wildebeest had emerged out of the edge of the bush. Behind them, the mass of the herd was roiling through the bush.

'Something's frightened them,' John barely whispered, his lips framing the words. We lay down at the edge of the cliff, rifles out in front of us, pushing our bodies as low as possible, hiding ourselves behind whatever cover we could find.

I pulled Khan down in the long grass next to me. He was shaking violently. His eyes were closed and his body twisted in pain. He would be no use to us. I took his rifle and placed it away from him at my side. It was better for him not to have a weapon than to risk allowing him to fire it accidentally.

We watched as the wildebeest came pouring out of the thicket, galloping awkwardly as they rolled out into the grassland. Behind them were two zebra weaving in and out among the thorn trees, heading across the edge of the thick bush along the side of the herd.

John watched them for a moment and then pointed for us to look more closely. They were not zebra. They were mules, painted with white stripes. Looking carefully, I could see the pack saddles on their backs and German askaris leading them. Behind the mules, we could just catch glimpses of the rest of the column making their way through the cover that the thick bush provided. It consisted almost entirely of black soldiers. A few white officers and NCOs were scattered among them.

I could see why the Germans had been so effective at keeping our troops on the run after them. They were moving quickly through the thick bush and, had they been any further from us, we would have missed them. The zebra camouflage looked clumsy from close by, but it had fooled us for a few moments. At a distance, it would have been almost impossible to tell.

We watched as they threaded their way through the bush below us. They looked ragged and fatigued, but we had learned that askaris were experienced soldiers. If there was any sign that would give our position away, we could count on their finding it.

These were the men who had burned the huts last night. The Germans and their askaris were far from defeated, but they had been forced to retreat. They would be vicious and sullen, bent on revenge for the humiliation of having to run. If they found us, we could be sure that they would show us no mercy.

The wildebeest broke into a gallop, running across the plain as the full column of German troops advanced in the late afternoon sun. Hundreds of animals flowed out of the bush and careered through the long grass. The drumming sound of their hooves rose up through the air to our hiding place. I could hear their constant lowing and the snorting of their breath, and smell their rank, cow-like stench.

A spout of blood shot into the golden light. One of the animals tumbled head over heels. Its horns dug a furrow into the dark earth as it fell. Another bucked wildly up into the air. The shock wave of two explosions, one after another, rocked the stillness of the bush. A spray of earth, stones and grass flew up into the air. There was another dull boom, the compression from the sound thudding over our heads where we lay. The animals were snorting and neighing in terror as they ran, fleeing in every direction, tumbling into one another in their panic. *Boom.* Another explosion. A large bull wildebeest was thrown sideways into the grass, a smashed rear leg spraying blood and jerking crazily.

'A bloody minefield,' Carter said, 'waiting for one of our columns to come this way. The Germans knew it was here and they were skirting around the edge of it.'

'The burning huts last night,' Juma whispered. 'They wanted them to be seen. They wanted any of our troops in the area to see them and follow them into this trap.'

We watched in horror as the flow of the magnificent beasts carried them over the unimaginable thing that had emerged out of the earth beneath them. They surged across the grassland, shoulder to shoulder in their uncomprehending terror. They reared and snorted and flung their horns through the air in great scything arcs that would tear the guts out of the leanest, most agile lioness and her flailing claws, but they were unable to escape the explosions that tore the earth away from under their hooves and ripped their fellows apart faster than any big cat had ever done.

Even the askaris stopped and watched, partly awed, partly horrified by the destructive power of the trap they had laid for the English invaders. Rage flooded through me as I watched them beneath us. *Sergeant Visser, Corporal Reynolds, Steinberg... I could see them there on the grasslands in front of us. They clutched their rifles tight to their chests. Their faces were pale and slack with fear as they walked across the minefield, knowing what lay in front of them. They were powerless to step aside from the blast that would rip their legs off, the white-hot metal slicing deep into their guts. Slow and deliberate, they walked towards us.*

I knew they were not there, but it was all I could do to stop myself screaming out to them to halt to stop coming forward, to stay where they were and avoid the horror that awaited them.

I felt a sudden, wild urge to open fire on the askaris and their German officers in the bush below, to cover them in a firestorm of hot lead. I wanted to keep firing, pulling the trigger and working the bolt over and over and over until I had destroyed them all, driving them into the ground in a pulp of lead-mangled flesh and smashed bone. Only by destroying them could I protect my own memories. Only with their violent, screaming deaths could I force Steinberg and Corporal Reynolds and all of them out of the minefield and back into the shallow graves where we had buried them in the red earth of the savanna.

I watched them go, one by one, passing within range of my rifle. My finger was tight on the trigger and sweat dripped down into my eyes. Somewhere in the last few weeks, I had become a disciplined soldier. I knew enough about war now to know when to act and when not to. To know about war – that had been a long journey. It had begun under those scudding clouds on the sand road that led to Salaita Hill. I stared over the blue steel of my rifle sights at the men in the bush below. Somewhere along that same journey I had learned what it was to hate.

'I'm scared,' Helen had said on our last night together. 'About what will happen to us when you go.' I could hardly remember that night now. I was losing touch with the world she alone had been able to give me. The smell of her hair, so clean and unimaginably soft. A flower she had drawn idly in the corner of a page. The touch of her fingers on the back of my hand when she saw something that excited her, a huge, ridiculous hat taking pride of place in a shop window, a little bird scurrying across the edge of a roof, its tiny, stick-like legs moving so fast, the wonder of the silvery darkened figures flowing across a cinema screen, making her laugh. Her eyes, turning in the darkness of the theatre and watching me, wondering if I shared her delight.

Our world – it seemed so far away from anything I could imagine anymore. I craved that world so deeply, but I could no longer remember what it had been like. How would I ever be able to go back?

I came to war for what I had believed were the finest of reasons. I came to war determined that I would not hate, because I believed that hatred was a choice.

But war had taken away my choices. Sergeant Visser, Corporal Reynolds, Steinberg… I hated because of them. I felt dirty, smashed up, filled with pity and sorrow, and guilt, and fear that what had been done to them might be done to me.

The only cleanness was in rage, and in the unleashing of it. I looked over at where Carter lay in the grass nearby. His eyes were cold and hard as he watched the Germans below. He was calculating, subordinating his fear to his will to win at all costs. He was my mentor, my leader, my captain, my commander. From those first terror-filled moments at Salaita he had taken me forward and because of him, I had lived. From him I had learned everything I knew about war. Because of him I would live through this war. In order to survive all I had to do was to follow Carter into the heart of war, into the pure, untrammelled rage that lay within every one of us. A rage that was as deep and certain as love had been in the world that we had left behind.

The herd of wildebeest was gone. They had vanished into the thick bush at the far edge of the grasslands. Seven or eight animals lay bleeding and damaged in the long grass. Two of them were struggling on smashed legs, falling and getting up again as they tried to follow the rest of the herd. Soon hyenas and lions would smell the blood and the fear and would come prowling in search of food. They would circle around the wounded wildebeests once or twice before they closed in, each slow, careful step taking them deeper and deeper into the minefield. There was good, fresh meat waiting there, but we could not take the risk of walking through the minefield ourselves.

The Germans were disappearing too, moving further into the bush towards their rendezvous with Von Lettow-Vorbeck further south, deep inside German territory. Smuts and his men would follow them, and might stumble into this minefield. There was no way we could warn them. If we left signs and a German patrol found them we would be threatening our own mission. We knew that the mines were crude, handmade affairs fashioned out of old corned beef tins and the fuses from dismantled artillery shells. The best we could hope for was that they would corrode and become useless in the weeks of rain that lay ahead.

As we watched the last of the Germans vanish into the thorn bush, I saw Carter slip his map and a pencil out. At best, the map was incomplete, at worst, it was wildly inaccurate, but Carter was determined that nothing should pass him by.

Beads of sweat stood out at his temples as he stared over the map. He closed his eyes for a moment as he massaged his eyelids. I noticed the tremor in the hand that held the pencil.

Juma was watching him too. 'You should take some quinine, sir.'

'No,' said Carter. 'I'm fine. Give it to Khan.'

23

JOHN SAW IT FIRST – A TORN AND mangled British army boot. He picked it up and brought it over to Carter.

Carter turned the fragments of leather over in his hands. I could see what looked like toothmarks on them. What remained of the sole was worn out.

'Hyena,' John said.

Carter handed it back. He looked over at John and Juma. 'What else can you find?'

Khan lay down shivering in the shade of a tree. I was carrying his rifle and his spare ammunition. He had managed to keep walking with us, stumbling along through sheer effort of will. I watched Carter's reaction every time we had had to stop or slow down for Khan to catch up. He himself was beginning to show the first signs of malaria, but he kept us moving. We couldn't leave anyone behind, but to slow our progress any further would hamper our mission. At some point, I knew, Carter was going to have to choose.

But for now, we had a fresh, vital clue. John, Juma, Carter and I spread out through the bush, searching for something else which would tell us what had happened.

John and I came across a mound of freshly dug earth. The other boot was lying a short distance away. It too, had been chewed by a hyena.

'Look here.' Carter was a hundred yards away from us. We pushed our way through the dense thorn bush to where he was standing with Juma. The ashes of a fire lay heaped on the ground. There were a few scorched animal bones scattered nearby. The half-melted neck of an empty brandy bottle stuck out from the ashes.

'Whoever made such a big fire felt secure in the area.' Carter was nudging the ashes with the toe of his boot. He kicked the neck of the brandy bottle and a cloud of white ash sprang up.

'It must be German,' Juma was squatting on his heels beside the ashes. 'None of our troops would have come this far yet.

Not in big numbers, anyway. Scouting parties don't make fires like this.'

'How old do you think it is?'

'Four or five days,' John said.

Juma nodded his agreement. 'We saw another party of them yesterday, at the minefield. The Germans are on the move everywhere across the country now, but a few days ago they felt safe enough to make a big fire, cook meat and drink brandy. It was a mistake. General Stewart and his column can't be that far away.'

'That doesn't help us,' Carter said. 'It just means that the Germans will be on the alert now. They may get their hands on Wallis and Kirkpatrick, or on us.'

'They must be walking more slowly now,' I said. 'At least one of them has lost his boots.'

John had moved a little way off. His tall body was bent almost double as he searched through the undergrowth. Juma stood up and joined him. Carter and I began searching the ground on the other side of the remains of the fire.

The heat wavered through the trees. A flock of yellow and black-headed weaver birds, tiny as large butterflies, dipped and rose through the air. I could hear the long, wavering drone of a single fly. John and Juma's boots cracked and shuffled among the twigs and leaves on the dry ground.

Carter had his head bent to the ground as he walked. There was a dark band around the crown of his sun helmet. A single drop of sweat glistened on the point of his chin. I had caught both John and Juma glancing at him earlier in the day.

If the malaria got worse and he was struck ill we couldn't carry both him and Khan. With two sick men, we would be hard pressed even to give up and go back the way we had come. And if the mule died, or another of us fell sick?

I could hear Khan moaning in the agony and delusion of malaria. We had not wandered far from where he had lain in the shade of a large thorn tree. John was some distance away in the bush. I could see him squatting and poking at the ground with his bayonet.

He pulled out another boot covered in earth. The other was just visible beneath.

'I don't think they're moving slowly,' Juma said.

Carter nodded. 'They must have watched the Germans at their campfire, and stolen two pairs of boots. They've got German boots now. They'll be hard for us to track.'

Carter took off his helmet. He wiped his brow with his sleeve. 'Their mistake was not to carry the old boots with them or bury them much deeper. They're in a hurry. They'll make more mistakes.'

Khan was delirious. He could no longer walk. Sweat soaked his uniform and he was shivering constantly. We loaded as much as we could of what we were carrying onto the mule and took turns carrying Khan in the stretcher Juma had fashioned from cut poles and a groundsheet. He was heavy – the inertia from his illness made him a dead weight. Carter's face was pale and he was sweating even more, but he took the first turn at the stretcher, along with John.

We set off into the bush, following a path that Juma knew. We were exhausted. We had eaten nothing since the night before. The *screee screee* of cicadas shimmered in the heat around us. We fell into the seesaw, dizzy pace of walking that had become so familiar to us. There was danger all around but we could hardly concentrate. I knew that we were approaching a critical point. Our growing weakness meant that the dangers we had faced were nothing compared to what lay ahead. A few days ago, we had been a small, lean, confident unit of men, able to move skilfully through the bush and fight our way out of most situations. Now we were moving painfully slowly, an easy target for an ambush. We had to carry Khan. Wallis and Kirkpatrick were likely to be moving far more quickly than we could. There was a good possibility we would never catch them and we would have to turn back, our mission unfulfilled.

We walked for hours, stumbling into the white heat of the sun. At some point we came to a muddy depression filled with filthy, days-old rainwater. Carter called a halt. We slumped down under what shade we could find. The smell of water filled our nostrils. The mule hobbled forward to drink, but we could not take the risk of catching whatever diseases the dirty water might carry. We had to be content with a few sips from our water bottles.

Carter and John put Khan's stretcher down in some shade. I saw Carter reach up and wipe the sweat off his face. A thick smear of red blood spread across his forehead.

'What's the matter, Captain?' Juma asked.

'What do you mean?' Carter snapped.

'The blood. Your face.'

Carter looked at him. Then he held out his hands; the palms were blistered and bleeding from carrying the stretcher. They were shaking.

'I think that's what scaring you,' he said. He squatted down at the water and washed the blood off his hands. Then he took off his sun helmet and bent his face towards the filthy water. His knees buckled and he tumbled forward into the puddle.

John rushed forward and grabbed him by the scruff of the neck. He pulled his face out of the mud.

Carter twisted out of his grip and stood up. 'What do you think you're doing, Akul?' he yelled.

'You fell, sir.'

'I slipped.'

'I thought –'

Carter turned and gestured at the mule. 'Get some quinine out of the saddle bags. That's all I need – a dose of quinine. It's a minor attack, nothing to worry about. Khan's the one you need to take care of.'

John opened the saddle bags and took out the white powder wrapped in paper and oilskin. He took out one for Carter and two for Khan.

He went over to Khan. Somehow he got him to sit up. Khan stared at us with glassy eyes as John tipped the quinine into his mouth. He put the neck of the canteen to Khan's lips and poured the water down his throat, washing the bitter white powder down.

I watched Carter take his quinine. The powder was tinged with pink from the blood on his hands as he forced it into his mouth. He saw me watching him. He seemed about to say something. He turned suddenly and looked away – too late. I had caught the fear in his eyes.

24

A FLOCK OF GUINEA FOWL EXPLODED up out of the long grass at the side of the path. They cried raucously and then glided up across the horizon that lay between the shadows of the bush and the last brightness of the blue sky.

'Damn it,' Carter had cursed under his breath. 'Anybody who sees that will know where we are.'

'Wait,' John held up his hand. We fell silent. John was standing erect, straining to hear. He raised his rifle to his hip. He began to edge into the bush. Juma and I put Khan's stretcher down, and unslung our rifles. Carter drew his pistol. His hand was shaking as he pointed it into the bush. We watched as John crept forward. He bent into the grass and came up again without his rifle. He crept forward, intent on the ground in front of him. In a single swift movement, he dived and came up holding a young guinea fowl in his hand. He took its head in one hand and wrung its neck with an effortless flick of his wrists. He loped back through the grass towards us, pausing only to pick up his rifle.

John came back to where we were waiting. He took a tin mug out of the mule's saddlebags and put it on the ground. Then he unsheathed his bayonet, and slit the bird's throat. He held its head over the mug and collected the blood.

John stood up and took the mug over to where Carter was sitting. The fever was advancing now and he could no longer easily control the shaking that came over him from time to time. John handed him the cup. Carter looked up at him. He took the cup and, in a single swift motion, he swallowed the warm blood. He screwed up his eyes and, for a moment he held his lips closed. He ran his tongue around the inside of his mouth. He opened his eyes and spat the remains of it out onto the ground.

John put the cup back in the saddlebag. He hung the guinea fowl on his belt and we continued our slow, halting march along the pathway. Finally, when we stopped for the night, John plucked the bird and gutted it. He dug a hole in the ground and buried the feathers and the entrails.

The risk of a fire was too great. The Germans might have seen it. Under the pale light of the rising moon, we mixed some flour with water into a paste. We squatted around the carcass of the bird in the darkness and pulled lumps of the raw flesh off the tiny translucent bones. I rolled mine inside the flour paste and chewed it a few times. I gagged on the smell of blood and entrails before swallowing the disgusting mix down. But it was food, fresh food at that. There was a portion of raw meat and wet flour perhaps half the size of a fist for us each. We had finished the corned beef two days ago. If it hadn't been for John's guinea fowl, we would have had only the handful of flour paste.

Moonlight streamed through the branches of the tree above me. The night was hot. A mosquito whined in the darkness and then mercifully drifted away. I could feel the rivulets of sweat running down my temples and collecting in the small of my back. My uniform was filthy and my feet were an aching sodden mess. My hands, too, were cut and bleeding now, from my turns at carrying Khan. Despite my exhaustion, I couldn't sleep. John and Carter were on guard duty. I had tried to persuade him to sleep, but he had insisted on doing his turn. Juma and I had a couple of hours to rest and try to sleep. Khan was moaning in his fevered sleep. I wondered where his Nadia was. He had not spoken of her again, but she filled his dreams. I thought of where Helen was now, and what she was thinking of.

In the distance I heard the low, chilling call of a hyena. I wondered if it was heading for the corpses of the wildebeest in the minefield. Our pace during the last two days had been so slow that we had not gone more than a few miles beyond it.

'We can't go on much longer, lieutenant,' Juma said, softly in the darkness, as if reading my thoughts. 'It'll kill them both.'

I didn't reply.

'Birds' blood is not medicine,' Juma went on. 'He's going to collapse soon.'

'We've got the quinine,' I said. 'Besides, he's in command of this mission.'

'There's three days left of flour.'

'We'll find a way. Those men we are following must be in a worse position than us, and yet they have kept going. We have to find them.'

'Why?' Juma whispered fiercely. 'What's this all for?'

'We have to. It's our duty, as soldiers. Besides, we want to get to them before the Germans do.'

Juma held his tongue, but I knew what his question meant. It was the beginnings of a mutiny. I looked up at the night sky for a long time. The exhaustion made me feel strangely uncaring, as if what Juma said was something I had heard years ago, something that no longer mattered. Finally, I closed my eyes and waited for sleep.

Later, when Carter woke me for our shift at guard duty, his face gleamed bright and shiny with perspiration in the faint starlight.

'Everything all right?' I whispered.

'Yes,' he said. 'It's quiet.' He put his rifle down on the ground and slumped down next to it. I picked up my own rifle.

'Lieutenant.' I turned to face him. His eyes were wide in the darkness and his face looked haggard and drawn. 'We have to go on. No matter what. You do know that?'

'Yes,' I said. 'I know.' Then I turned and walked into the cool shadows.

The morning dawned orange and pink above the trees. Khan had slept through the night. His condition seemed to have stabilised. I gave him another dose of quinine. He was not fit to walk. He was still barely conscious, but he seemed to have come through the worst of the fever. He lay quietly in the stretcher now, not shivering. We set off, with Juma leading the way, followed by Carter. He, too, seemed to be better. He was still sweating, but he was no longer shivering. Perhaps Carter was right, the malaria was just a temporary illness – one that we might all have to work through.

Our spirits had lifted even though we had nothing to eat in the morning. John and I were carrying Khan and he seemed to grow better with every step we took. The thought that soon we might not have to carry him anymore cheered us, as did the thought that we would soon have another rifle to add to our firepower as we moved deeper into enemy territory.

Slowly we made our way through the thick bush. I was dizzy from lack of sleep and from the hunger that never went away. The trees and thorn scrub around me seemed hallucinatory and wavering. Each mottled shadow, each patch of hot white sun, each wary, startled movement of a bird or a lizard was filled with fear and menace.

John was holding the stretcher in front of me. He was much stronger than the rest of us. Now even Juma was slowing down. His pale, bright eyes had become dimmed and he limped on his blistered feet.

The Germans had taken or burned everything in their path. For days now, we had been wandering through a wasteland of bush – beautiful, but a land from which all human beings had been driven out. The huts burning in the night and the few pitiful refugees we had glimpsed the next day were the last inhabitants we had seen. Even if we did find any people, they were starving themselves, and they would have nothing to give us.

Three days of flour. Even if we found Kirkpatrick and Wallis now we would be faced with an agonising dilemma. Assuming that they were as weak and hungry as we were, we were still strong enough to overpower them – just. But how would we feed them and us, on the journey back?

We walked the whole day, stopping once for an hour in the middle of the day to rest in the shade. Carter seemed to be holding the malaria at bay. He sat in the shade of a tree, his lips half-curled into a snarl as he breathed heavily in the hot midday air. John, Juma and I were taking turns with the stretcher and our hands were bleeding. We squatted in silence, trying to keep our mouths closed to stop the moisture evaporating from the soft tissue in our mouths and from deep inside our lungs. John and Juma lay back in the shade trying to squeeze the maximum benefit from the brief rest. Khan lay like a dead man. I woke him to pour a little water into his mouth. He raised his head and drank a few sips before collapsing again. I sat down. We were too thirsty, hungry and exhausted to waste energy on speaking.

I lay back on the sandy soil beneath a thorn tree. Despite the shade, the ground was hot. A hawk spiralled up into the cloudless blue sky. A line of ants scuttled past on the ground, their black bodies glistening in the sun. I watched them come and go through the hazy, unfocused edges of my vision.

Helen was sitting opposite me across the darkened balcony. The two of us sat up late, talking and laughing while the colours and noise of the party swirled around us. I was slightly drunk, which had the effect of making me relax. It seemed to me that she was floating in the semi-darkness as she lounged gracefully against the wicker back of her chair, her glass held in the tips of her fingers, her enchanting face, framed by her dark hair, half-hidden in the alternating lamplight and shadow that ebbed and swung across the balcony.

When she smiled I noticed just the tiniest beginnings of lines – small and hesitant as a mouse's foot – crinkling the corners of her eyes. I liked seeing them; they spoke of a life being fully lived, and of the gentleness that begins in people's lives after some things have – inexplicably perhaps – just gone wrong. And it made me love her all the more.

The hawk was still circling in the sky. I could still taste the half-warm sponginess of John's guinea fowl dissolving in my mouth and there was still a little flour for tonight. But tomorrow…

'I think the Germans won't come this way,' said Juma – a hazy image in a pool of shade across the hot red earth. I saw him pick up a twig and begin to draw in the sand. 'It's getting too close to the Belgian border. I think most of them will go down this way, south along the Pangani River.'

'What about the ones we saw?'

Juma shook his head. 'Maybe they are lost.'

'Plenty of others could be lost along with them.'

'Yes.'

Carter stared down at the crude diagram that Juma had sketched in the hot sand. He took out his tattered paper map and compared the two.

'What about Wallis and Kirkpatrick?' he said.

Juma shrugged. 'They must be heading west for Lake Tanganyika. There are many places they can get across without any soldiers seeing them. They can cross at night in a canoe or find a place on a dhow somewhere.'

'We have to catch them before they get there.'

'It's three days' walk to the border. They must be moving faster than we are.'

'We'll have to pick up speed then,' Carter said.

Juma looked back at him. 'We have no food. The malaria is even worse on the lake. There are other diseases too. We should go back.'

Carter wiped his hand over the map in the sand. He stood up and slung his rifle over his shoulder. Then he bent down and picked up one end of the stretcher. John and Juma watched as he hefted the weight of the stretcher in his hands.

'Fuller,' he said. 'You take the other end.'

The heat rose in waves over the bush. We walked for hours under the sun. I was conscious of almost nothing except the rough wood of the stretcher eating into my hands with each step we took. They were almost numb with the pain of it now. I scarcely noticed how deeply the jagged edges were cutting into the skin of my palms. Flies tormented us, buzzing at our faces and at the blood on our hands. We walked slowly, light-headed in the heat, the effort dragging at our knees. Still Carter kept us going. Sweat poured off his hollow-eyed, drawn face, but he shamed us by the force of his will. Somehow he managed to keep putting one foot in front of the other.

Some time in the afternoon we came an opening in the bush. A small lake lay in front of us. It was deep and cool. Reeds fringed its edges and a tangled island of water lilies floated in the middle. Green pads overlapped one another. Huge white flowers gleamed in the sunlight.

'Look,' Juma was pointing towards the edge of the water lilies. There was swirl in the water. A few bubbles rose to the surface.

'What is it?' I asked.

'Hippo,' John said. 'Or crocodile.' The water was still again. We stood silent, watching. I could hear the call of birds. I struggled to focus on the ripples gleaming in the water. A dragonfly, huge and crimson, skimmed across the surface. There was another swirl and then two ears stuck up out of the water.

Then the ugly, bristly snout of a hippo; the eyes, black and angry at our intrusion.

John unslung his rifle. He raised it to his shoulder.

'*No,*' Carter said in a low urgent tone.

'We have to eat,' Juma said. 'It's the only game we've seen in days.'

John was watching them both, the rifle held half-way to his shoulder.

'*No,*' Carter insisted. 'We cannot risk either the Germans or Wallis and Kirkpatrick hearing it.'

Juma closed his eyes for a moment. 'We cannot go on like this.'

25

WE ARRIVED AFTER DARKNESS HAD fallen. It was a brick-built monastery that Juma had known about from his days in the trading caravans.

'They were German monks,' Juma had said to Carter as the shadows began to grow long across the pathway. 'They will all be gone now. We are not far. There is a rain-water tank there where we can get clean water. We can rest, at least for tonight.'

'One night,' Carter said. 'And only for the water.'

The monastery was built of red bricks made from clay mined nearby. The buildings were constructed around a courtyard in the style of a mediaeval monastery, with deep, shaded colonnades and Romanesque arches. It could have been only a few decades old, but already an atmosphere of decay hung over the place. The fields surrounding it were overgrown with weeds. The roof tiles were cracked and the bricks crumbling. Tall clumps of grass sprouted between the cracks in the courtyard; a scraggly thorn tree brushed against the doorway.

We approached cautiously, rifles at the ready. We had tethered the mule and hidden Khan on his stretcher amongst some bushes nearby. The fever had abated and he was well enough now to understand what was going on. He was too weak to do more than raise his head, but we had begun to hope that a night's good rest and plenty of clean water would get him back on his feet. Carter's malaria was worse than ever. He clenched his teeth and tried to control the shivering, but his uniform was soaked with sweat. '*He will collapse soon,*' Juma had whispered to me late in the afternoon.

There were still the faint smears of orange light against the horizon as we advanced towards the monastery. Carter motioned with his hand for me and John to move around the rear of the buildings. He and Juma would creep up towards the courtyard.

John and I made our way through an overgrown garden. The dry tendrils of a pumpkin vine trailed across the rough ground. There was a single desiccated gourd half-buried in the soil. I saw John take note of it. We would come back later.

A eucalyptus tree loomed over the edge of the entrance to the courtyard. It was silhouetted against the darkening sky. A water tank stood beneath it. We crept around the damp curve of the water tank. I noticed then how quiet the evening had become. I could hear the slow drip, drip, drip of water falling inside the tank, reverberating against the stone walls. This is what we had come for, a place to rest, a desiccated pumpkin and a half-empty rain-water tank. We could only hope it had not been poisoned by the monks or by Von Lettow's askaris.

We passed a row of darkened windows. The crude solid wooden shutters hung askew, their angular shapes dim in the twilight.

Further on the shutters were closed. At the end of the row, the yellow light of a candle flickered out through the cracks in the wood.

I looked at John. He nodded to me. We approached the window. John bent double and crept below the sill to the other side. I stood ready, my rifle pointed at the window. He reached up and unlatched the shutter. It fell open with a clatter.

'*Hände hoch*,' I yelled. I stepped forward and jammed my rifle into the open window. John spun upwards and did the same.

The room was empty. A single candle stuttered on a wooden shelf beneath a crucifix. A half-opened door led into a dark passageway.

I felt the sharp, insistent press of a revolver muzzle grinding into the skin behind my ear. I looked across the bar of light that fell on the ground from the opened shutter. I could just make out Kirkpatrick's pale face above the Lee-Enfield he was shoving into John's ribs.

'We saw you, Lieutenant, coming from behind the water tank,' Wallis' voice said behind me. 'Drop it.'

I let my rifle clatter to the ground. I nodded to John. He let his rifle go.

Wallis pushed his gun tighter against my skull. He stepped forward. The hard muzzle of his gun dug into the skin under my hair. There was a momentary flash of pain and then I could feel the warm blood begin to dribble down the side of my neck. Wallis kicked at my rifle. It spun out of reach. Kirkpatrick kicked at John's rifle. It rolled across the rough ground, the shoulder strap snagging on the rocks and tufts of grass.

As Wallis reached forward and unbuckled my holster, I saw Juma emerging out of the shadows at the edge of the window. He was heading for Kirkpatrick.

Wallis pulled my revolver out and threw it into the long grass. Juma reached up from behind Kirkpatrick.

Wallis saw it. He turned towards me, his face contorted into a snarl. There was a grunt as Kirkpatrick fell to the ground with Juma's forearm choking him. I felt Wallis crumple behind me. Carter had hit him on the back of the skull with his rifle.

John lunged forward and suddenly he was on top of Wallis, wrenching his arm behind his back. The revolver fell to the ground. John kicked it away. Juma had Kirkpatrick down on the ground. His rifle lay next to him.

For a moment we were frozen in immobility – a still point in the fragile balance of violence. Then Wallis twisted inside John's hard grip. He grabbed at the bayonet on his belt. The blade glinted in the dull yellow candlelight as he jabbed it upwards towards John's ribs. Carter dived forwards, grabbing at the blade. It slashed deep into the palm of his hand, ripping it open. The blood gushed out over his forearm. Wallis pulled back and tried to stab again, but Carter somehow held onto his wrist, slowing the stabbing motion down.

It gave us just enough time. John rolled sideways away from the blade. I pulled out my own bayonet and lunged forward. I slashed the edge across Wallis' hand. The tight flesh on his fingers opened up, one after another, red and gaping in the candlelight. He dropped the knife and rolled over in agony, his hand jammed into his midriff.

Carter staggered up, his face white with pain. Huge gouts of blood dripped out of his hand, soaking the front of his shirt and shorts.

'Hold them there,' he said, breathing hard.

The handcuffs were back in the saddlebags of the mule, but John was already pulling some rope out of the deep pockets of his uniform shorts. He shoved Wallis over on his face and began binding his hands behind his back. Wallis flinched as John tightened the rope around his wrists and his damaged hand.

I ripped open the thin canvas envelope containing a field dressing and strapped it onto Carter's slashed hand. It was bleeding and the flesh was badly torn. The white ends of severed tendons were visible beneath the jagged edge of bone and muscle.

He was going to need a surgeon within hours, or a couple of days at most if he was not to lose the use of his hand. I couldn't imagine how we could get him to a doctor in less than two weeks – ten days if we were lucky.

John had tied up Wallis. He came over to where I was bandaging Carter's hand.

'Is it bad?' he asked.

I looked up at him for a moment in the darkness.

'Finish the bandage,' Carter snapped.

26

THERE WAS FOOD FOR US THAT night – a little maize meal scraped out of the corners of the abandoned refectory, John's pumpkin and the fragments of a few beans that we managed to find lying broken on the stone floor of the storeroom.

We closed the shutters and stuffed the cracks with rags to hide the light of the small fire. The rough walls of the room were pockmarked with the stains of dead insects and perhaps worse. We sat in a dim, flickering pool of light. Smoke swirled around the room, but the discomfort was nothing compared to the thought of eating hot food. Wallis and Kirkpatrick sat sullenly at the edges of the room watching the pot boil.

They were handcuffed and Wallis had bruises on his face where John had slammed him onto the ground. I had cleaned and bandaged the cuts on his finger. Kirkpatrick looked haunted and defiant. Something on his long flight through the bush had changed him. He was no longer the terrified teenager who had panicked at Salaita. His look was hardened. He seemed resigned to his fate now, determined to ride it out as best he could.

Khan lay on the stretcher in a corner of the room. Every now and then he would sit up on his elbows and look around the room. The malaria was abating. With a decent meal and a night's rest, he might even be able to start walking tomorrow.

I had given Carter some morphine to still the pain of his hand. There was nothing I could do about the blood loss. He sat upright, his blood-stained shirt rubbing against the filthy wall. His eyes were glassy from the drug and his worsening illness. John handed him a tin plate and a spoon. He ate slowly, resting the plate on his bandaged hand.

We gave Wallis and Kirkpatrick some food. They ate clumsily with their handcuffs on, holding the plates up and shovelling the food into their mouths. Wallis' eyes flicked over us as he ate.

When we had finished eating, he spoke for the first time.

'You have to let us go, Captain.'

Carter lifted his head and glared at Wallis. 'What are you talking about?'

'Don't make things worse for yourself, Wallis,' I said.

He turned towards me.

'They'll make us face a firing squad. You know that. He knows that.'

I glanced at Carter.

'They might not.'

Wallis' eyes blazed. 'Don't play with us, Lieutenant. We know what's at stake.'

'Major Reading sent us to find you,' I told him.

Wallis was squatting against the wall. He shifted the cuffs on his wrists. There were red marks where they had rubbed against the skin. He looked over at Kirkpatrick. They hadn't thought of that possibility.

'He's your only chance,' Carter said.

Wallis said nothing for a few moments, then he shook his head. 'They want us as their scapegoats. What power does he have to stop them?'

John was squatting at the edge of the fire. He had taken his kepi off. His face looked tired without the stern authority that his uniform gave him. I could see the few premature grey curls in amongst his black hair. For the first time I was conscious of the fact that he was older than me, a man somewhere in his mid-thirties. He reached over with his long, powerful arm and threw a few twigs and a twisted hank of dry grass on the coals. Flames sprang up, making our shadows flicker and intermingle on the filthy walls.

'You are soldiers. You ran away,' John said. 'What do you expect?'

'Yes,' Wallis admitted. 'We panicked. But everyone was running by then. I dragged Stephen here away from a pair of askaris who were about to cut him to pieces with their bayonets. We should have come back after dark, or even the next day, but we didn't. The two of us met up with Watson somewhere in the bush that night and we kept running. Everything had gone wrong that day. We panicked. That was our mistake.'

Juma shifted on his haunches. 'It was a big mistake.'

Wallis stared at him. 'We were scared. We had already suffered once by being chained to tree. So we made the wrong choice in running from a battle. Do we deserve to die for that?'

Kirkpatrick was staring at each one of us in turn. He was daring us to condemn him for what he had done, for those few moments of fear – at the age of seventeen – that had brought him to the point where he lost his nerve.

'This is the army,' Juma said. He pointed at Carter and at me. 'They have been given a duty.'

'*Duty?*' Kirkpatrick's voice was high-pitched and angry.

We turned and stared at him.

'What sort of duty was it to send us on our first battle against those trenches? You officers must have known from the beginning what you were sending us into. How could you do that and call it duty?'

I thought back to that night in the officer's *banda* when Major Reading had briefed us on the plans for the attack on Salaita. I remembered the hush that had fallen on every one of us officers as we looked over that map with its neat squares, its bold arrows, confident sketches and clearly-written numbers. Even then most of us had seen the overwhelming stupidity of the plan. I thought of how, alone amongst us, Carter had stood up against the cruel absurdity of what his young soldiers were being asked to do.

'Yes,' Carter replied, his eyes blazing. 'We did know, but we had no choice. We had orders to carry out.'

'Fuck you,' Wallis said. 'You can't absolve yourself of blame by saying you were following orders.'

Even Khan was awake and listening, his head turned sideways on the stretcher.

Carter's face was shining with sweat in the firelight. He shifted his position, wincing with pain as he bumped his hand.

'I don't expect absolution,' he said flatly. 'I'm a soldier. I carry out my orders. As you should have done.'

Kirkpatrick stared at him across the darkness of the room.

'But I saw what you did at Salaita.'

Carter's eyes were wide with shock for a moment, then he controlled them, narrowing the lids, drawing himself up against the wall.

'What do you mean?'

John had moved away from the fire that had blazed up. Juma and Khan were watching Carter.

'I saw you when the panic began,' Kirkpatrick went on, slowly, his eyes holding Carter's. 'Men were running all down the line. None of the officers could stop them. There was a whole crowd of us scattered everywhere in the deep bush. I was hiding behind a rock when I saw Major Macintyre pull out his revolver.'

Carter was staring at Kirkpatrick. He didn't move.

'He ordered you to do the same,' Kirkpatrick said. '"We've got to stop the panic," he shouted. Then I saw you take out your revolver.'

Carter's head was rigid against the wall. A single point of blood was growing through the whiteness of his bandage.

'One of the men from the 5th came out of the bush. Major Macintyre screamed at him to turn around. The man was terrified and he tried to push past. Major Macintyre shot him. He shot him dead.'

Kirkpatrick swallowed. His eyes were wide in the firelight.

'No one else saw him do it except you and me. Then Williams came running out of the bush. He had lost his rifle, but he wasn't wounded. Major Macintyre grabbed him. He pushed him and turned him around. He pointed his revolver at him.'

Kirkpatrick looked over at Carter. 'You could have stopped him before. The first time.'

Carter said nothing. He was staring across the room. Kirkpatrick looked down at the stone floor for a moment and then up again at me, and at the others in turn.

'I saw Captain Carter step up to Macintyre while he was holding Williams. Carter pulled Williams away. Major Macintyre pointed his revolver into Carter's chest. There was some kind of argument, and pushing, shoving. Captain Carter was shaking. He shoved his gun into Macintyre's face. I saw him pull the trigger.'

Carter looked down at the floor, cradling his wounded hand. Then he slowly straightened up. His eyes looked at me, and then at the others in turn.

'They were only boys,' he said. The breath was strangled in his chest. 'Just boys. That bastard… he had no right…'

For a long time we were all silent, crowded together in that filthy, smoke-blackened room. Carter stared across the room into the fire, saying nothing.

'A few moments later, the askaris came up on us. They shot Williams and left him there next to Major Macintyre. The rest of the men ran away,' Kirkpatrick said finally.

Wallis spoke next.

'I was with him. I saw it too. We're the only ones who know what really happened,' he said. 'And, if you take us back, we'll tell the story.'

Juma stood up and walked over to where Wallis and Kirkpatrick were squatting.

'You're nothing but cowards, runaways.' he said. His face was creased in contempt. 'It will be your word against this brave officer's. No one will believe you.'

Khan shifted on his stretcher and raised his head. 'Yes,' he said. 'I'm afraid they will.'

Carter said nothing more. Sometime that night the malaria took its hold and he sank into a state of semi-consciousness. We made him as comfortable as we could on the floor of the adjoining room. We locked Wallis and Kirkpatrick into a separate room, chaining them to a crumbling brick pillar as an added precaution. Khan was recovering fast and the four of us talked and argued until the first streaks of grey light came in through the rough wooden shutters.

Khan told Juma and John about Carter's failure of nerve as a young subaltern in India all those years ago.

'I first heard his story many years ago,' he ended off. 'It was quite a well-known story in the Indian army, especially because he had been linked before in a romantic affair with an Indian woman. It was a kind of double scandal. Everybody in India was interested in it. The story had all sorts of elements of drama in it, the English officer who dares to cross the colour line, but who then, when he is tested in battle, turns out to be a coward. I don't know how the army managed to keep the whole thing out of the newspapers, but lots of people were talking about it.'

'What happened to the woman?' I asked.

'She left him,' Khan said. 'Most of those affairs fail. It's hopeless to try and lead a normal life, especially in the army with the clubs closed to Indians. There is the gossip and the sneering that goes on behind your backs. Every day of your life as an Indian trying to live among whites in British India you have to face something that happens or hear something that someone says to humiliate you. But Carter always made it clear after what happened in the ambush on the frontier that he would never leave the army. It would look like running away, and he would never do that. So, in the end, she left him, rather than trying to lead an impossible life.'

When Khan finished speaking, John looked over at him.

'And after that battle, was there ever a story of him being a coward?'

'No,' Khan said. 'At least I never heard of any. Not in India.'

The three of them looked at me.

'It's the only story about him I've ever heard. Except that he and Macintyre hated each other. Carter caught him cheating in an officers' exam in India. It delayed his promotion for years.'

Khan looked at me and then shook his head. 'He'll definitely face a firing squad. No defence will be able to overcome what he did at Salaita. Even if he tries to deny everything, it'll be no good. He broke once. They'll believe that he broke again. And shot the man he had always hated.'

'Whatever they do to Captain Carter, they'll also make those two pay – after they've told their story.' Juma jerked his thumb towards the room where Wallis and Kirkpatrick were.

John poked the fire and threw another log on. 'The older one, he should pay, but not the boy. He is still young. He doesn't know what it means to be a soldier.'

'But he is a soldier,' Juma said. 'And they'll judge him as one.'

Nobody spoke for a long while. Finally John said what we all knew was true. 'They will make them face a firing squad also. To put an end to their stories about Salaita.'

Khan sat up in his stretcher. His face was pinched and angular in the dim light. 'I'm not sure what will happen to them,' he said. 'But I do know that if we take these two soldiers back, Captain Carter will be shot. He's the only white officer who cared when my men were killed. He deserves better than a firing squad.'

'It's only us here tonight,' Juma said. The three of them looked at me in the glow of the fire.

'Yes,' Khan said. 'We can decide for ourselves what to do with them.'

27

WE TOOK THEIR HANDCUFFS OFF shortly after the sun had risen. Wallis rubbed the skin on his wrist above his wounded hand. Kirkpatrick stared at us in the early morning light, watching our every movement.

'You'd better get going,' I told him. 'Liberia's a long way off.'

Wallis looked up at me.

'Schirmer,' I told him.

'Is there anything you don't know about us?' he said bitterly.

I held his gaze for a few moments. 'Why you ran away.'

He glanced down at the ground and then back up at me. 'I saw you in that trench,' he said angrily. 'How scared you were. Just be grateful that it wasn't you.'

Kirkpatrick was watching Wallis as he spoke. Then he turned and scrutinised my face.

'Everybody's always believed my father was a hero,' he said. 'I've lived my whole life in his shadow. But that young soldier he tried to rescue died all the same, and my father was terrified when the battle began. My father always blamed himself. In his secret heart I know he believed that if only he'd been stronger, braver; if only he'd fought harder, that soldier would still be alive today.

'That medal they gave him, all the newspaper stories, all those dinners where he still stands up to talk about what he did, they don't mean anything. Everything has become blurred in his head now. I don't even think he can even remember exactly what happened, or why he did what he did all those years ago. The truth of who he was then and whatever bravery he showed in those few moments of chaos – it's all lost to him now.

'My mother and I are the only ones who know how he really feels. We don't dare speak to him about it, but we know those long, moody afternoons; then, later, at night, those horrible, uncontrollable rages – especially when he's been drinking; the whisky glasses thrown across the room and smashing against the wall, the screaming and the trembling fists held up to our faces, the endless threats. Then, the next day, the playful punch on the arm for me and the hug for my mother. It's all lies, his whole life now. Layer upon layer of lies and faint, half-remembered moments from a single battle long ago. The only time he says what he is really thinking is deep in the night when he sometimes talks through the drink. He tells of staying awake all through the cold desert night, of seeing the first pink light of dawn over the silver ribbon of the Nile and of wondering whether he would survive that day. But when we wake him up the next morning and he is sober, he never remembers what it is he said then.'

Kirkpatrick broke off and stared at me, his eyes bright and clear. 'Yes,' he said. 'I ran away at Salaita. And no one will ever forgive me. I have to find some way to live with that. But all my life I have been living with someone else's war. I joined up because I wanted to find my own war. I wanted to have my own memories, and not have to live with my father's any longer.'

John came up to where the three of us were standing.

'Look after him,' he said to Wallis. He put his hand on Kirkpatrick's shoulder. 'He followed you. Because of it, he has lost everything. He will need someone to help him. I will be glad I didn't kill you, if I know that you are the one to help him. Because he has no one else now.'

Sudden tears crept into Kirkpatrick's eyes. The hardness was suddenly gone.

'He's right, isn't he? I'll never see my family again.'

'No,' I said slowly. 'If the army ever finds out you're alive they'll destroy you, and them along with you.'

He looked at me. 'What are you going to tell Reading, and the others?'

I shrugged. 'We never found you. There was a garbled story from some villagers about white men's bones and hyenas. We knew it was the closest we would ever come to the truth.'

Kirkpatrick looked around him slowly, as if testing the reality of this first day of his new life.

'What about Captain Carter? What will he say?'

'He was delirious, even unconscious. Malaria. I've got three witnesses.'

Kirkpatrick glanced at the ground for a moment and then looked back up at me. 'I had to do it to him,' he said. 'It was our only chance.'

I nodded. 'Major Reading isn't much of a guarantee.'

'I wish Carter had stopped it. I thought about what I had seen every step we took in the bush. What Major Macintyre did – that's what pushed me over the edge.'

'You've got to try to stop thinking about it now,' I told him, as kindly as I could. Kirkpatrick looked startled, as the meaning of my gentleness made itself clear.

'What will you tell them – my mother, and… my father?'

'The truth,' I said. 'That you are brave, and that you never abandoned your comrades, right to the end.'

We gave them the food left over from the previous night, and a few bandages and bottles of medicine. There was no quinine left, and that was what they would need most in the months to come.

'Can you give us a rifle, at least?' Wallis asked.

John looked at me. I nodded. He went over to the room where we had put their weapons. He came back with one of the Lee-Enfields and a bandolier of ammunition.

'Trade that for another as soon as you can,' Juma said. 'You don't want to be found with a British Army-issue rifle. It'll give you away.'

Wallis nodded. 'Tell Captain Carter I wish it hadn't had to come to this – and also, I'm sorry about his hand.'

'You'd better go,' Khan said.

There was nothing left to say. They turned and walked into the bush.

28

FOR TWO DAYS WE RESTED IN THE monastery, building up our strength. We rummaged in the abandoned fields and in the empty storehouses for a few more beans and handfuls of grain. We cooked some of it and wrapped it in leaves, to carry with us on the fireless marches back to our lines. John found an avocado tree. The fruit was not ripe, but we found an old basket and loaded it full of the fruit. It was a godsend. The fruit would ripen on the journey as we travelled. We washed ourselves and drank the fresh, cool rainwater from the tank.

Carter grew worse every day. We hoped that the rest would cure him, but he lay now barely conscious on the stretcher that he had demanded we make for Khan. Every now and then we gave him a drink of water. It was the most we could do. We had no quinine to give him and he could not hold down even a thin gruel of maize or beans.

Once, as I was trying to feed him, he looked up at me. 'We have to get them back,' he said. 'We must –'

'They escaped,' I told him. 'That night. Somehow they slipped out of the window.'

He looked at me for a moment. His eyes filled briefly with the old, familiar hardness. 'We – you, must find them. Go on. Tomorrow.'

The nights were hard. The Germans could not have been far away. I couldn't sleep so I took extra turns at guard, staring into the dark bush lit by the cold stars and a thin crescent of moon. I could think of only one thing. Williams was in my platoon. His life was my responsibility. After killing the askari, Carter had turned and gone forward to see what he could do to stop the panic. I might have been there with him when Macintyre turned his revolver on Williams. But instead I had finally broken and run away – like all the rest of them.

The sun was already high by the time we left on the third morning. Just before we set out, Juma handed me a tiny battered notebook and the stub of a pencil.

'Khan is the senior officer,' he said. 'But you are a white man. You must write what happened.'

'But we agreed on everything. The other night. Anyway, keeping a diary in the army is illegal.'

'Write. Not a diary. A report. That way they will believe.'

Juma was leading, followed by Khan. John and I carried the stretcher. We followed the same path we had come down. Our pace was agonisingly slow. We were hampered by Khan's weakness and by the exhausting, heavy work of carrying the stretcher. We limped through the bush. The only blessing was that our pace was dictated by our condition, we were not driving ourselves to the limit as we had been in the search for Wallis and Kirkpatrick.

I tried to write down the stories of crushed bones and villagers' rumours that we had discussed. The story they would want to hear. I kept a record of our slow progress back, to give authentic detail to the story we would tell of our failure. I wrote every night with a pencil in the tiny pocket diary Juma had given me, scribbling in the half-light of the stars.

We walked for three, four days. When we stopped one night I reached up into my shirt pocket to take out the notebook. It was gone. I ran my hands up and down my body. I rummaged in my pockets over and over. One by one, I unbuttoned my pockets and searched again.

I looked over at Khan and over at where Juma and John were lowering Carter to the ground. His wounded hand was grotesquely swollen; streaks of blue and yellow were climbing up his arm. His eyes were closed and the sweat was running off his face, soaking the collar of his uniform.

I beckoned for them to come over. 'I've lost the notebook.'

'The notebook?' Khan shifted his rifle strap with his thumb.

'I thought it was better that no one else knew,' Juma said, after a moment. 'Now, it doesn't matter.'

'What notebook was this?' Khan persisted.

'I was keeping a record,' I said slowly. 'Of how we came back without Wallis and Kirkpatrick.'

Khan held my gaze. He looked over at Juma and then at Carter on the stretcher.

'He had malaria,' Khan said slowly. 'We had to turn back. He was delirious. It would be useful to have something to help our story. Just to be sure that all the questions are answered.'

John had been listening. He went over to our remaining mule. He scrabbled around in the saddlebags. He turned back to face us.

'I think this will answer their questions.'

In his hand were the torn pieces of leather we had found near the German campfire. No one could dispute what they had once been – British army boots, of the exact type issued to Wallis and Kirkpatrick, and with the marks of hyenas' teeth on them. They would be their only mortal remains.

After I lost the notebook, the days went by in a blur. There were no Germans left, they had long since fled east and then south down the Pangani with Von Lettow-Vorbeck. That was our salvation, because we did not keep a proper watch. We were too tired and illness began to creep in on us. I began to feel the slow growing dizziness of malaria, while Juma came down with dysentery. Every few minutes as we walked, he crept into the bush at the side of the trail. By that afternoon, he came back with the first of the dark blood and the mucus staining the inside of his shorts.

Somehow, we managed to keep going. The land around us was the same we had come through – burned out and destroyed. If it hadn't been for the little grain we carried and John's avocados we would have died somewhere in that empty land.

As it was, things were bad enough. Late one afternoon, when the sun was low in the sky behind us, Carter looked up at me from his stretcher.

'We're heading east,' he said softly.

'Yes.'

He closed his eyes. He was so weak, he could not stop his head jolting from side to side with each step we took. A black mass of flies gathered around the pus seeping from the brown stained bandage on his hand. Finally, he opened his eyes and looked at me again.

'They didn't escape.'

'No,' I said.

He stared up at me for a long time. His eyes were dull and faded with fatigue and illness.

'You're free, now,' I told him.

'Free?' His brow creased.

'They've taken your secret with them.'

He looked at me from where he lay in the stretcher. 'I won't betray you,' he said. 'None of you. Not again.'

'No,' I began, 'We all know that –' but he had sunk back into unconsciousness.

We slept that night in a deep, shady grove of acacia trees. Khan and Juma stood guard first. Despite my worsening malaria, I agreed to stand an extra watch with John. The others were weaker than us. They needed sleep.

The two of us crouched a little distance away from the others, keeping watch, staring out into the half-hidden patterns of the bush, like a map of darkness, the empty spaces slipping away into the night. The stars were cold in the sky above us. Once or twice, I saw John move across to where Carter was lying. I saw him hunched over, trying to get Carter to take some water.

I hardly slept. I was awake as the night began to end. The sun lay just beneath the horizon, burning the blackness of night to indigo. The last of the stars hung still and alone in the sky, fading as the darkness drew back. Slowly, the air grew colder and the palest wash of orange filtered up over the darkness of the land. The acacia trees loomed above me.

The birds began to sing. The first calls sounded harsh and melancholy in the cold darkness, slowly becoming beautiful as one, two, a dozen started, merged and blended into a soaring chorus of whistles, squeaks, warbling, chattering. Their calls spiralled up into a crescendo, filling the air, the sound itself seeming to draw the light into the darkness.

As dawn was breaking John came to where I was crouching under a tree.

'Come,' he said. The sky was tinged with the first pink light of day as I followed him back to our pitiful bivouac. Khan and Juma were sleeping on piles of fresh cut grass strewn over the red sand. Their rifles were resting upright against a tree trunk. A centipede squirmed across the dew-covered sand that lay between them.

John and I walked a little further, to the edge of the tiny clearing. We stopped and crouched down together beside the body of Captain Carter.

'I wanted to show you first.'

I looked up to find John's dark eyes holding mine.

He handed me a packet of letters and other papers. In amongst them I knew must be the photograph and the letter I had seen him reading in the firelight by the side of the train on our very first night in East Africa.

'They were his. I found them when I checked for his heartbeat.'

For a moment, neither of us said anything, uncomfortable with the death that lay between us.

'Out of all of us – out of all of them, you were his friend.'

'Yes,' I said, realising for the first time, and too late, the truth of it. 'Yes, I was.'

29

THE WIND BLEW THE DAY WE buried Captain Andrew Carter. And then the rain came – a silver storm flashing, pouring out of the wide dark sky. Andrew. I never called him that once while he was alive. He had always been Captain Carter or Carter to me. I wondered, for the first time, what his family had called him.

John threw the last of the muddy soil over his body. The four of us stood over his grave, heads bowed in prayer in our different ways. I was conscious only of the sounds of the bush around us.

'We should move on,' I said, after a while. 'We have a long way to go.'

John had already strapped Carter's rifle to the saddle of the mule. He waited for the rest of us to gather up our own. One by one, we slipped onto the pathway following Juma's slow, agonised lead.

The rains poured through the day and most of the night as we walked. One night we found ourselves at the fort. Next to the graves of Watson and the askari was a third grave – Schirmer's. The three crosses were dark in the rain. The goatskin thongs and the bootlace had almost rotted through on two of them, and some animal or bird had gnawed and tugged at the third. The wooden arms of the crosses hung at different angles, the rain dripping off their rough-hewn ends.

Schirmer's leather belt still hung off the end of his iron bedstead. The mattress, filthy and black with human leavings, lay abandoned on the frame. The syringe we had left lay cracked in the corner, the ampoules of morphine empty beside it.

I was shaking with fever, feeling myself grow weaker and weaker. We took shelter in the rooms of the fort and risked making a fire to warm ourselves and to cook some of our dwindling supplies of corn and bean fragments. As we ate, huge, shiny cockroaches slipped in twos and threes over the broken window sills. They crawled between our boots and under our knees as we sat cross-legged on the floor.

Echoing down the unlit corridor we could hear the scuffling and the dry scratching as rats gnawed at the residue of blood and shit on Schirmer's mattress.

'Stewart or Tighe's column must be near,' I said, half-deliriously. 'If we leave at dawn tomorrow –'

John's eyes were dark in the dying firelight. 'I'm not coming.'

Juma was watching me. Khan was looking down at the stone floor.

'So,' I said carefully. 'I'm the last to know.'

'How could you not be?' Juma said.

'It's your war,' John said. 'Your white man's war, and I'm tired with it.' He picked up a chip of dry wood and flung it into the corner of the room. 'I'm tired with all your wars,' he said bitterly.

'Then why did you come?' I asked angrily.

John swung his head towards me. 'I came because Captain Carter asked me.'

'So, no one forced –'

John stood up in one swift, angry movement. He towered over me. 'Look at me. *Ten years*,' he shouted, jabbing his finger into his chest. 'I have been a soldier more than ten years.' He strode towards the door. He wrenched it open, and turned back to face me. 'You have seen only one battle, and you talk and shout in your sleep like a frightened child.' Then he walked into the night, and was gone.

John took the mule and Carter's rifle and his own, and some extra ammunition. In lieu of the pay owed to him, I suppose. I couldn't find it in me to begrudge them to him. He had left his village in search of the world. He would return with nothing but two rifles and, if it survived the journey, a mule. The rifles were worth hardly anything to us, but to him they carried the promise of two lifetimes of meat for a whole village.

'I'm sorry it had to end like that,' I said to Juma as we prepared to set out the next day.

He shrugged. 'He has finally chosen his own life, but he is angry because it took him too long.'

'But why now?'

'You remember we talked of the Nandi?'

I vaguely remembered Macintyre saying something about it – some minor border skirmish.

'Akul was one of the soldiers sent against the Nandi. They were led by a British officer, he was known as Kipkororor because of the ostrich feathers he wore in his helmet. They say he called the Laibon of the Nandi for peace talks and then shot him dead.'

Now I remembered what I had heard about it. 'No,' I said. 'The Nandi ambushed the soldiers. They had to fight back. The chief was killed in the crossfire. It's all in the report.'

Juma was watching me carefully. 'Now you understand why I wanted you to write in your book.'

'But this is different –'

'So is the story Akul told me about that day. He was one of the soldiers with Kipkororor, waiting in the ambush for the Laibon.'

'There is no proof of that.'

'No,' Juma said. 'Nothing. But it is the story Akul tells.'

'And you believe it?'

'Do you still *doubt* it? Even now, after everything?'

'But how can you be sure? He would have hardly understood what it was all about. He must have been so young –'

'Just like Kirkpatrick.'

I stopped. Juma's eyes were hard.

'Akul never forgot. He carried the shame of it with him always. Until last night. Then it became too much.'

The three of us began to pack up what we could. There was food for a few days and enough ammunition to hunt with, if necessary. There was a small neat pile on the ground next to where the mule had been tethered. It was something John had left behind last night.

Khan went over to it. He bent down and picked something up.

'Look,' he said. 'He left these for us. For our story.' Juma was holding out the fragments of Wallis and Kirkpatrick's boots.

We found the first sentry two days later. I was shaking uncontrollably, barely able to put one foot in front of the other. I don't think I would have lasted much longer. The sentry was standing against the trunk of a large tree. His rifle was lifted up against his shoulder, aiming at the centre of my head when we saw him.

'It was your turban, sir,' he said to Khan. 'That stopped me firing. I knew the Huns don't have them.'

'Bloody fool,' Khan said, his voice barely a whisper.

It was Tighe's column, the 2nd Division, we had stumbled into. Our own men, the 7th were in the Force Reserve further down the line.

The whole column was bogged down in the rain and the mud, unable to move forward. We staggered in out of the rain accompanied by our sentry. He took us to his commanding officer – a thin, exhausted colonel with the Rhodesians – who called for a truck and sent us down the line to where Major Reading was waiting for us.

His uniform was hardly less threadbare than our own. He looked over the three of us standing in front of him in his damp tent. His face was drawn and tired.

'My God,' he said, looking at the three of us. 'What happened?'

'Malaria,' I said. 'We had to turn back.'

Reading nodded slowly, his eyes moving across us. 'They'll want you in Nairobi, Lieutenant. For a full report.'

30

OUR JOURNEY WAS OVER. The army took control of our lives again. Juma and Khan were sent to the hospital tents for black troops and I went to the regimental sick tent attached to the 7th.

We passed through the camp just as a tropical downpour began. Bedraggled, exhausted groups of porters sat on the ground. Many of them were little more than walking skeletons. Their eyes were sunken and haggard as they huddled around the sputtering cook fires smoking under makeshift shelters of grass and banana leaves.

The rows of tents where the soldiers slept were ragged and threadbare, stained with mud and mould. Unshaven men with haunted faces moved slowly in the red mire. They were thin too and their uniforms were rotting and torn. I could not recognise any of them as they stared at me as the truck slowly churned its way through the sludge, wheels spinning, spraying clumps of soft dirt up into the air around them.

Their eyes were bloodshot and yellowed through the silver rain. A young man was about to enter his tent. He lifted up the canvas flap.

'*Johnson*,' I shouted above the roar of the engine. He turned and looked. I waved. He stared at me.

'It's me,' I shouted hoarsely. 'Lieutenant Fuller.' He turned back, looking down at the ground without recognising me, and slipped into the darkness of his tent.

Martin Scheepers came to see me that night. He stood for a few moments at the foot of my bed. The skin hung in folds around his chin, and his blue eyes were sunken and hollow. A single hurricane lamp flickered in the damp darkness. Clear water ran down the seams of the tent and dripped into the mud.

'You didn't find them.' It was a question.

'They're dead.'

'And Captain Carter?'

'Malaria.'

Scheepers took a step towards me. He put his hand on the railing of the bed.

'We took Salaita, you know. Four weeks later. Without a single casualty.'

'How –?'

'The Germans had withdrawn. They were waiting for us further down the valley, at the twin hills of Latema Reata.'

Scheepers' eyes held mine in the flickering half-light.

'This time we didn't run. We fought the whole day. In the end, we charged in the moonlight, with bayonets. We held the slopes with some of the Rhodesians and the KAR until dawn.'

The rain drummed on the roof of the tent. A chill breeze shook the thin canvas.

'We lost so many that day, and more since then. Campbell was one of those killed that night at Latema Reata. Major Van Hasselt had dysentery. He died only two days ago.'

'And Johnson?'

'He's been promoted, to corporal. He was one of the first men onto the slopes of Latema. If he goes on like this, he'll be an officer before long. He's the best we've got.'

That night the rain hammered on the tent in the cold darkness. I couldn't sleep properly, slipping in and out of consciousness. The past kept coming back to me, sweeping over me in sudden flashes of regret and then in unexpected moments of happiness. Fragments of recent memory flowed through my mind. I remembered doing the most ordinary things, as when I was struggling to pull on my polished leather boots, or when I was aiming my new, gleaming rifle at a straw dummy painted with a clumsy grinning black face and a red German uniform kepi at a rakish angle, or at night with the still and now menacing bush all around.

Jumbled up with them came things that I hadn't thought about in months, years, it seemed.

Helen was sailing for England – standing at the rail of a silent, darkened ship slipping across a moonlit sea. The Atlantic route was treacherous now with the U-boats sinking Allied ships. The army mail from East Africa took months to arrive. The letter I had written to

Helen would not arrive before she left for England. Even if it did,
I knew that it was too late. I could change nothing anymore.

Then there were memories from my childhood, things Helen had told
me. Things that could be spoken about once only and then understood
always, layered now into the silences of our lives.

She picked up her shoes, and kissed me on the lips. I slid my hands
out from behind my head, and ran them slowly down her back.

'You will write from the bush?' she asked.

Now there was so much silence between us. We stared at each other
across an empty, darkened room without saying anything. There was
so much I wanted to say to her, but nothing came out of my lips.

The army moved swiftly. Two days later the orders had
already come: I was to go by train to Nairobi to account for our
mission. The other two were to return to their units when they
were well. That morning, just before I left, I was hardly able to
walk, but I had to do it. I went to see Khan and Juma where they
lay side by side in the hospital tent.

They lay there, two thin, exhausted men against clean white
sheets, their heads propped up on pillows. It was only now, in
the confines of the hospital tent that I saw how close they, too,
had come to death.

They looked up as I limped in slowly, exhausted and feeling
almost as ill from the amount of quinine the doctor had forced
me to take as I did from the malaria that was growing in my
bloodstream.

Juma stared at me. In his drawn sallow face, his eyes were
bright and keen as always. Khan nodded gravely.

It seemed strange that everything had come down to this
sterile, empty parting.

'I'm going,' I said, 'to Nairobi.'

It was the moment I had thought about all the way on our
journey back. I had wondered what it would be like. In my
imaginings, I had expected John to be there too.

The doctors and nurses were pretending to be busy with the
other patients, but in reality they were fascinated by this strange,
shattered trio that had wandered in out of the bush. I stood
there, at the foot of their beds.

'You are going to give your report,' Khan began coldly.

'Yes,' I replied.

'What will you tell them about Akul?' Juma demanded.

I glanced at the doctor bending over a patient two beds away. My heart was pounding. The rest of my life was balanced at the mercy of either of them. And theirs at mine.

'Akul is dead.'

'Dead,' Khan was looking at me without blinking. 'From malaria, like Captain Carter and so many others.'

'It'll be in the report.'

'And us?'

'We were all there,' I said. 'What I saw, you saw as well.'

They both stared at me without saying anything.

'Do you still doubt me?' I whispered. 'After *everything*?'

31

THAT NIGHT IN THE CLATTERING HOSPITAL train on the way to Nairobi, I sat up shivering with fever but wanting to stare into the darkness of the bush. The orange glow from the fires of the sentinels guarding the line were reflected in the windows, turning and slowly falling behind as the train moved through the night. The rivers beneath the bridges were swollen now with rain, rushing torrents of dirty water flowing across the land. Water was falling everywhere, turning the dry dust to red, churning earth the colour of blood in the night.

The nurse offered me a sedative, but I did not trust myself to sleep. I preferred to stay awake despite the growing agony of my malaria. There had already been so many betrayals in the daylight hours, I could not bear to think of what it was I might reveal by speaking out in my dreams.

At some point in the night, during a moment of quiet clarity amidst the shifting layers of my illness, I remembered the oilskin packet that John had handed me when he had brought me to see Carter's body. I had not opened it, thinking that it was disrespectful to the dead.

That seemed unimportant now. What mattered was to know whether there was anything inside that might undermine the story I would tell. In my increasingly fevered imagination, I wondered whether Carter might have written something or left a clue of any kind that would betray us all.

I unwrapped the stained oilskin bundle, holding it down in my lap so that none of the doctors or nurses might see what it was that I was doing.

Inside there was only a thin sheaf of old letters and a single photograph protected on either side by two loose sheets of cardboard. The cardboard sheets were smeared with thumbprints and the evidence of much handling, but the photograph was clean and well preserved. It was of a young Indian woman standing in a park somewhere. There were some tumbled ruins in the background. She was wearing a sari.

Her eyes were bright and laughing. She was smiling at the man behind the camera as the light streamed in from the trees above her. She was smiling at Andrew Carter.

Folded next to it was a short letter. It filled a single piece of expensive creamy white paper. Written neatly in a feminine hand were the following words: *'You must know that I will always love you. But it cannot work between us. I'm sorry, but I just can't go on like this.*

Yes, you're right. We were happy together – for a while, such a very short while. We tried to forget who we really were. We tried to forget that you were white and I – was not.

I've met someone else. An Indian man. And I can't let the past I had with you destroy the life I have now. Loving you has almost done that to me. Please, Andrew, do not write again.'

In the end, I did collapse. My last memory was of an endless procession of fires in the darkness wavering outside the train window, of ghostly figures moving to and fro across their flames, and then – oblivion.

A white cloud hanging in the darkness above me, falling, tumbling all around me. Voices, and then silence.

A movement at the corner, somewhere else, in the other world, outside. A hand and a letter sliding through space and resting on the shelf beneath the window.

Eucalyptus trees looming over me, their branches and leaves silhouetted against the stars in the night sky.

Helen smiling at the rail of the ship, smiling, smiling as she slipped away into the night.

In the impossibly far distance outside there was the sound of people moving on the road, talking. A woman's voice beginning to sing in Swahili – a mournful, lonely tune that went on for a few phrases and then petered out. Someone laughed, and suddenly their voices were coming near, touching the edge of the room.

I woke to find Major Reading standing at the foot of my hospital bed.

'At last,' he said, smiling. 'I thought we were never going to get any sense out of you.'

I stared at him, slowly focusing my eyes.

'Sense?' I asked.

'It was blackwater fever. You nearly died. The doctors only said they were sure you would make it when they heard you crying out in your sleep. That's when they knew you were coming out of the coma.'

'What was I saying?'

Reading looked at me strangely. 'Something about heading east. None of it made any sense.' He stopped for moment, to think. 'There was some talk about betrayal.'

'Betrayal?' I said, the terror sliding up my chest.

'Yes,' Reading said. 'It was very odd, and confused.' He shook his head. 'But you stood firm at Salaita. If we'd only had more men like you.'

I closed my eyes, trying to let the panic subside. When I opened them, Reading was smiling at me again.

'You're tired. I must go. By the way, I brought a letter for you. I put it on the little table under the window.'

My darling Michael,

I want to tell you everything that is on my mind – everything that I have been thinking and feeling these last few months, but to do that would take up pages and pages.

But I have to tell you this, at the very least. I realise now that I have been running away from myself for too long. But coming here was the right thing to do. It wasn't easy at first, but at last I saw that I don't love him anymore.

It's over with him. We'll get a divorce and he won't contest it.

What I have learned is that I want to be with you. No matter what. No matter how long this war takes to end.

I don't know where you are, or how long it will take for this letter to find you. I don't know even how you will react to it. But you must know that when this war is over and you do come home, I'll be there, waiting for you.

With all the love you can imagine.

And more.

Helen

It was more than I had allowed myself to hope for. It was everything, and I wanted to see her again, more than anything, but I wondered what it would be like when we met. The war had had changed so much. What would I be able to tell her? Where would I begin?

Once I might have wanted to tell her about Salaita and the fear that nearly overwhelmed me there. Once I might have tried to make her understand what it had been like to see the askaris charging down at us while we – Wallis, Kirkpatrick, Carter, Macintyre and I – stood together in that hot, dusty trench and waited for them to come.

But there was only one moment now that defined my war. When Kirkpatrick had spoken out – and then the long hours that night which followed when Juma looked up at me in the firelight and said *'we can decide.'*

But could I ever tell her – could I ever tell anyone – about the choice we had made at the end of them?

32

AS THE WEEKS IN THE HOSPITAL dragged by I wrote the report and handed it in. I slipped the torn fragments of boot into the brown manila envelope. Major Reading came to see me a few days later.

'I asked you to help me once,' he said.

I sat up in my bed. He held up his hand. 'A lot of men saw you leave camp that morning. And the rumours, they've been very persistent.'

'What rumours?'

He looked over at me suddenly. 'No one is questioning –' Reading smiled awkwardly. 'They're going to put them down as "missing, believed killed." All of them, the same day – at Salaita.'

'But what about Akul? His regiment was never even with us.'

'I transferred him as a guide to the 7th Transvaal a few days before Salaita. He was assigned to Major Macintyre.'

'Very neat,' I said. 'But what about the men who saw us go? The rumours?'

Reading cleared his throat. 'Every war has its rumours. But now everything is in the records. No one can dispute them.'

He looked down at me. 'The Americans are coming in soon they say, but the war's still got a long way to go, and we have to win. This report. It's a question of morale. All that business with Kirkpatrick and his father... sometimes... well, I'm sure we can rely on you, as an officer? What happened at Salaita, it's best left untold. Especially now that we know they're dead. There doesn't seem to be any point in going into it. I'm sure you can see that?'

I nodded.

'It would have been Carter's job to write the letters to their next of kin, but, with him gone, it's up to you.'

He reached into his leather briefcase and handed me a manila folder. 'They can be quite difficult, these letters telling people how their sons died. If you have any difficulty with thinking of what to say, use these. They've got the right phrases in them.

Once you've done the letters, send them on to me. I'll need to have a look at them before they go out.'

He started walking out of the ward. The soles of his boots squealed on the polished floor. Then he stopped and turned to face me again.

'They would have shot them, you know – both for desertion and for cowardice in the face of the enemy.'

Some weeks later, I got a letter back from Wallis' parents. They thanked me for my concern for their son. They were glad, they said, that he had officers like me to stand by him in his last moments. Watson's parents wrote back to me as well. They were happy, they said in their letter, to hear from me that their son had not suffered in the battle. The Red Cross promised to pass on the news I sent them of Schirmer's death and of Patrick Saida.

I kept my promise to Kirkpatrick, but I never heard anything from his parents.

It was Carter's letter that I agonised the longest over. The first letter I sent was to his parent's address in Fulham. It came back unopened. Scribbled on the back of the letter was a handwritten note: 'She passed away three months ago. Please contact Harris and Dangerfield, the solicitors handling the estate.' I took it to mean that his father had died too.

I had hoped to find somebody else who understood that he was more than just an officer who had once failed his men, but the army's records showed no other address for him.

There was no one to write to about John Akul either. I thought of him heading north across the savanna. He would probably be moving only at night for fear of being caught as a deserter, his tall, powerful body moving through the starlit paths through the long grass. Like all of us, he had his memories and his betrayals to take home with him. I would never forget his agonised face that last night as he yelled out at me: *Ten years*. It was a long time to spend fighting somebody else's wars. Even so, in the end, he had not betrayed us. He had left us the fragments of boot. I wished him well.

33

SLOWLY I BEGAN TO RECOVER. I dreaded the thought of going back into the bush to fight, or of being sent to Europe. All I wanted to do was go back to Helen. My fate was in the hands of the doctors. For the time being, though, I enjoyed myself as much as I could. I was still terribly weak, but soon I could sit up in bed, and then I was able to walk. At first, I could do no more than a few steps between the beds in the ward, but every day I could go a little further, until I was able to venture into the corridor. And one day, for a few short paces, into the garden of the hospital itself.

I heard from Khan and Juma. They too were both in hospital, recovering, enjoying the precious moments of rest from the war that their illness had granted them. They had discovered Charlie Chaplin in a film shown to them in the hospital.

Helen sent me letters often, and I wrote to her even more often. Every day I found something I wanted to share with her. It felt like being in love again for the first time in my life. Knowing that she loved me was all that mattered to me. Helen was that second chance I had not expected in my life. At times I would remember what we had gone through and I could hardly believe that I had survived to come back to all this joy.

One day, I was in the garden, hobbling on a stick. Another officer, suffering from malaria and dysentery, was showing me the fuchsias in the garden. 'Not very soldierly, I know,' he smiled apologetically, 'but plants just grow so wonderfully in this country. Not like back home in England where the frost attacks everything.' He knelt down at the edge of one the flowerbeds. 'Look,' he said. 'This variety is the hybrid, derived from *magellanica* and *fulgens*. Very common in –'

Major Reading was standing at the doorway leading out into the garden.

'They've found Wallis and Kirkpatrick,' he said. 'A Belgian patrol caught them trying to cross into the Congo. I'm here to tell you that you're under arrest.'

The doctors insisted I was too sick to be moved from hospital, so they posted an MP at my bedside. Khan and Juma were placed under guard too. In the next few days they would be bringing Wallis and Kirkpatrick to Nairobi. By all accounts they would need the hospital too.

'I'm afraid there won't be much of a reunion, though,' the MP told me drily. 'We've orders that none of you are to see each other until your trial.'

For two days I heard nothing more. The doctor forced me to stay in bed. 'If you start walking around,' he said. 'They'll want to put you in detention barracks.'

I wrote to Helen, a cheerful letter about fuchsias, not wanting to alarm her, and, more importantly, not wanting to give the army anything more to condemn me with. I knew that, now, they would read my letters. Most of the time, though, I lay in bed and wondered what would happen to us all.

Finally, Major Reading came to see me. On the doctor's orders they put me in a wheelchair and he pushed me down the corridor into a small room where we could talk alone. The MP was unhappy about being left outside, but Reading insisted. He closed the door and then turned to me.

'What the hell really happened out there?'

When I was finished telling him, he said nothing for a long time. 'They want to have a secret tribunal,' he said. 'I've tried to fight it, but I lost the battle. It's a time of war, and these are extraordinary circumstances. So it's going to be secret, I'm afraid, which means they can do to you what they want. And no one can do anything about it.'

Reading was watching me as I absorbed this news. 'What do you expect them to do?' he asked. 'You lied to them.'

'But you yourself had a hand in my report. You changed the details about Akul for example.'

Reading's eyes were cold and hard. 'I don't know what on earth you're talking about. Everything I wrote is on record. I have nothing to hide.'

I stared at him in disbelief.

'I want to see those records,' I shouted.

'The officer representing you at the tribunal can ask for them.'

'You've fucking changed them.' I was weak with rage.

'I can charge you with that,' Reading snapped. 'I advise you to shut up. If you carry on like this, it will only get worse for you.'

'But you were the one who sent us to bring them back.'

'You said in your report that you didn't even *find* them. You present evidence that they are dead. And then the Belgians catch them alive. What do you expect the army to do now? What do you expect me to do now?'

There was nothing more to say. There was only one thing I wanted to know from him.

'What would you have done? Would you have brought them back?'

He walked over to the window and looked out for a few moments before turning back to face me.

'I trusted you Michael, and you betrayed me.'

'And now,' I replied angrily. 'It's your turn.'

34

EACH OF US WAS MANACLED, hand and foot. They were taking no chances. The courtroom, if you could call it that, was a small wooden shed, sweltering in the heat. They led me in first, followed by Juma and Khan. They looked haggard and exhausted, but I knew they were both well enough to fight again. Had it not been for this tribunal, they would have been sent back to their regiments. Our troops had advanced far down the Pangani, but they still hadn't caught Von Lettow-Vorbeck. There was still plenty of fighting to be done, and men like them were needed.

They both nodded at me. I didn't know what they had told Reading and the other officers, and they didn't know what I had said. We had made our choice and it had backfired. They were black and I was white. The tribunal would blame me more than them, but it would have less compunction in sentencing them to death. That was the way of our world. We had tried to find a different way together in the bush. The four of us had put our differences of race aside that night, and decided together as nothing more than men to show compassion, to let Wallis and Kirkpatrick go free.

No, we hadn't failed. I wasn't ashamed of the choice we had made together, and, looking at them across that courtroom, I saw that neither of them regretted it either. But we knew that our moment of human solidarity counted for nothing in this courtroom. The men judging us would see our truth as nothing more than treachery to everything they believed in, and they would not forgive us for it. I was glad that John Akul, at least, had escaped. I felt sure they would never catch him. Standing there in the courtroom, sad old Mr Bradley's warning came back to me: *once you've taken their shilling, then they own your soul.*

At last, they brought in Wallis and Kirkpatrick. They looked better than I expected. Both men held themselves defiantly, looking contemptuously at the three surprisingly young officers sitting at the table in front of us. Those three men held our lives in their hands, but Wallis and Kirkpatrick had risked everything already. They had nothing more to lose. They had discovered within themselves a kind of courage that the men on the tribunal would never understand. Between those men and us lay of gulf of human experience that could never be bridged. Our pain and all that we had shared was invisible to them.

Kirkpatrick looked over at myself and Khan and Juma. 'They shouldn't have brought you into this,' he said. 'We're the ones who ran away, not you.'

'We broke their rules, too,' Khan said.

'If they hadn't caught us, then you would all be free.'

The head of the tribunal banged a wooden gavel on the table for us to be silent. Despite my nervousness, I almost laughed. What did he believe, this man? That he was somehow presiding over a court of law? That he was dispensing justice in the secrecy of this crowded, anonymous room?

The trial was perfunctory. The officer leading the prosecution read out a few statements and the long list of charges under military law. *Failing to carry out orders, desertion, cowardice in the face of the enemy.* The phrases were lifeless, the words had no meaning compared to what we had lived together, but he had arranged them neatly, in a pyramid of blame, so as to leave us no chance of escaping the force of their penalties. His logic led inexorably from imprisonment to death by firing squad. I knew he was doing his duty, but I could not help wondering how many hours he had spent alone with his pen and his conscience, arranging our fate so precisely, and what he thought when he saw us, real, living men standing chained in this tribunal room before him.

It took all morning to get through the preliminary formalities, and then all afternoon for the prosecutor to read out his list of charges and pin the specific accusations on each one of us. The tribunal adjourned for the evening with yet another dull thump of the wooden gavel. The MPs were brought in and we were led out separately in our chains to our respective places of imprisonment. I was still in the hospital with my MP, but the other four were led to cells.

As we were walking down the corridor towards the ward, the MP said to me. 'You were at Salaita, weren't you sir?'

'Yes, but why do you ask?'

'Someone brought a newspaper from back home. There are questions being asked now about what happened there. There might even be an enquiry in parliament. They say our men broke in front of the blacks, and ran away. People back home are angry about it. Some are saying they behaved like cowards.'

I turned on him. 'Have you ever been in battle?'

'No, sir, well, I mean – not yet anyway.'

'You can tell everyone you know that our men weren't cowards. Not a single damned one of them.'

We turned into the ward, and he led me to my hospital bed. I held out my hands for him to remove the chains.

'I'm sorry sir, but I can't. They have to stay. Those are my orders.'

35

THE NEXT DAY OUR DEFENCE BEGAN. I still felt weak and dizzy from the blackwater fever, and it was an agony to stand in front of the tribunal. Major Reading was called by the officer supposed to defend us to testify on our behalf. I had not seen him since we met in the hospital, and we stared grimly at one another before he began to answer the questions put to him.

'Yes,' he replied to the first question. 'I was – am – the officer directly in charge of all of these men.'

'And what orders did you give them?'

'When?' Reading asked sharply. 'After the battle or before it?'

'We're not concerned with what happened before the battle. There was no breach of discipline before that.'

'Yes, there was,' the prosecutor interjected. He pointed at Kirkpatrick and Wallis. 'One of these men was found asleep on sentry duty. The other failed to notice a patrol coming in.'

Reading stood for a moment. 'I can see you've done your work well. But they were punished for that.' He turned to the men of the tribunal. 'That reference should struck out.'

The prosecution continued this time. 'What orders did you give after the battle?'

'I sent these three men and two others to search for Wallis and Kirkpatrick and Watson who had gone missing after the battle at Salaita Hill.'

'And why did you do that?'

'I was carrying out my duty as an officer, and asking them to do theirs. Once we found that Wallis and Kirkpatrick and Watson were – missing, we wanted to get them back, and bring them to trial.'

I looked over at Kirkpatrick. I could see he was ready to explode, but Wallis was restraining him.

'And what happened to the other two men, Carter and Akul?'

'They're dead.'

'Dead?' One of the men on the tribunal sneered. 'Just like these two in the report written by Lieutenant Fuller, and signed by yourself? How do we know now that any of what he, or you, say is true? Perhaps both Carter and Akul are alive, as might be young Watson. Who knows where they might be, or who might find them? Perhaps we should wait a few days to see who the Belgians find secretly crossing Lake Tanganyika in the bottom of a dhow this week?'

Reading fumed silently at this onslaught. He had only my word, and that of Hassani Juma and Aziz Khan, that Carter, Akul and Watson were dead. And he knew that all three of us had already lied to him once. He could not trust us with the truth; and we could no longer tell it to him. Not unless we wanted to betray John Akul into the bargain.

The man on the tribunal looked at me. 'It seems that everything in your report is nothing more than lies.'

'Not all of it,' I replied.

He laughed bitterly. 'So where is the truth in it?'

I could not say anything.

'Why, lieutenant, why did you lie? Why did you make all this up? And betray all these men, and not only them, your regiment, and your country? Why?'

Juma and Khan were looking at me. I had to try and give them a chance.

'After Captain Carter died, I assumed command. It was my decision alone to let Wallis and Kirkpatrick go. These two men,' and I pointed at Juma and Khan, 'tried to dissuade me, but I overruled them. I decided to let them go, and then to lie about it afterwards. They had nothing to do with it.'

There was an edge of hesitation in the voice of the man on the tribunal. 'None of this was in your report.'

'You said it yourself, that was lies. This is the truth.'

'You still haven't answered the question as to why you did it,' one of the other men asked.

'Because after Salaita Hill, I did not believe that Wallis and Kirkpatrick would get a fair trial. And even if they did, I knew that they stood a good chance of being shot for the simple human act of having been frightened on the battlefield. The punishment they faced was out of all proportion to the supposed crime they had committed. At that moment, I had the power to choose. And I chose to let them go, and take their chance of freedom.

It was better than bringing them back to an almost certain death by firing squad.'

'But you didn't know for sure they would be condemned?'

'No, and that was the risk I took.'

No one in the room said anything for a long time. Finally, the first man on the tribunal looked at me and said: 'And just who the hell do you think you are, to directly disobey an order in wartime? To put your conscience ahead of the army and ahead of all the millions of other men who are fighting bravely in this war?'

It was a fair question, and it was one that I had asked myself hundreds of times, since that night at the monastery.

'I learned at Salaita that not every order deserves to be followed.'

Slowly I watched the anger grow on their faces. I could see they regarded me now as dangerous, a threat to everything they stood for.

Inside of me, the old fears had taken hold. I felt weak and queasy, as I had at Salaita. I could see both Wallis and Kirkpatrick watching me. I glanced over at Juma and Khan nearby. Somehow, I wanted the respect of all of them. What we had shared was the only good thing that had emerged out of this war, and I didn't want to lose that. I looked over at Reading, but his face was blank. He refused to look at me.

'And,' one of them asked, 'would you do it again?'

'Yes.'

They regarded me in silence for a while, until finally one of them spoke.

'Well, Lieutenant Fuller, *Second* Lieutenant Fuller, to be exact. That's just not good enough. Is there nothing else you can offer in your defence, and in defence of these men around you?'

Hassani Juma stepped forward. 'In fact,' he said. 'It was not Lieutenant Fuller's own decision. We all took it together. You should know that.'

'And what about Captain Carter, your commanding officer? Did he approve this – joint decision?'

'No,' Khan answered this time. 'It was just the four of us. He was too ill to make a decision.'

The men on the table looked at Juma and Khan. 'What you

two have said doesn't change anything. Lieutenant Fuller was still the man responsible for carrying out his orders – as were you. And you've just revealed that he lied again, this time under oath.'

The man seemed desperate, as if he were being asked to make an impossible, almost incomprehensible decision. And he wanted to be clear in his own mind that he was doing the right thing. 'Isn't there something you can produce in your own defence?' he asked finally.

Juma was silent for a long moment as he looked at the three men in turn. 'I think I have something else you should see,' he said. His chains clinked as he reached into the deep pockets of his uniform shorts. He pulled out a small wad of papers folded tightly together and held them up for the tribunal to see.

'You want to know so much about what happened after the battle, and about who was a coward and who was not,' he said. 'But Captain Carter wanted you to remember what happened *before* the battle. He wrote it all down, and he signed it, so that no one should forget who said what. So that when the battle was lost, and your young men killed, your government should know who to blame.'

'Let me see those papers,' the man on the tribunal said. Juma shuffled forward and gave them to him. I caught his eye as he shuffled back away from the desk.

'Akul gave them to me. He found them on Carter's body that morning. He gave them to me after he had given you the photograph.'

'So you didn't trust me, not even then?'

'Like Akul, we had all seen too much of your white man's war, and we needed something that might protect us when we returned.' He looked at me for a long moment. 'No, we didn't trust you,' he said. 'Not then.'

The men on the tribunal spent long minutes reading through the papers.

'What is this?' The first man on the tribunal finally snapped, 'some kind of joke? What bearing could these pages possibly have on the outcome of your trial?'

'These are a load of baseless allegations directed by a bitter captain against his senior officers,' the second man added. 'A junior officer who had already once in his career been convicted of showing cowardice in the face of the enemy. He should never have been given any sort of battlefield command. He was a man who could not be trusted.'

'These papers are worthless rubbish,' the first man said. 'The rantings of a proven coward.'

'You did not know him,' Hassani Juma replied. 'He was a man, and those papers tell the truth about Salaita.'

'These papers!' The first man on the tribunal exploded. 'They don't mean a damn thing.' He took the pages and rapidly tore them to shreds, then he threw the fragments on the floor.

'You can't do that!' The voice was Kirkpatrick's filled with outrage. 'That's evidence you've just destroyed.'

The officer leaned forward onto his table and stared at Kirkpatrick. 'This is a secret tribunal. We can do whatever we like. And no questions will be asked.' Then he added cruelly. 'Perhaps your father should have told you about them. He sat on many in his own day.'

He banged his gavel. 'This court is adjourned. Tomorrow you will assemble hear at 09h00 to hear our verdict.'

For a moment we stood in stunned silence. Then I heard Major Reading's voice, quiet, but clear, in the tiny courtroom.

'I don't think so.'

'What do you mean?' The officer on the tribunal's voice was filled with incomprehension.

'Those papers were just a copy,' he said. 'I have the originals. Captain Carter gave them to me before he left on his mission with these men.'

'So what?' The man's voice was cold and deliberate.

'They matter more than you think. There are questions being asked about Salaita back in South Africa. I have taken the precaution of sending the originals to a journalist I know. He will publish them unless I tell him not to. And I can assure you gentlemen that, while you may not be officers who are acquainted with the battlefield, the information they contain is sensational. They will cause an eruption, not only in South Africa, but across the Empire. There were many failures at

Salaita, and, well, it is better for everyone that truth contained in those pages should not be known.'

'What are you trying to do Major? Are you trying to subvert this court?'

'My request is simple,' Reading replied. 'Let these men go free, and Captain Carter's papers will never be published.'

The men on the tribunal stared at Major Reading incredulously. 'I can't believe I'm hearing this,' one of them said. 'From you, a trusted officer on the general's staff.'

Reading flushed. 'That is exactly the point. Even Prime Minister Botha has been struggling to keep Parliament from finding out the truth about Salaita. Something like Captain Carter's report would be a disaster not only for the war effort, but for South Africa's reputation in the world and, dare I say it, for the white man's prestige in Africa. It would not be good for any of our careers for this information to get out.' He paused for a moment. 'I long ago gave up any hope of further advancement, so it matters little to me what whether I am associated with the shame of our defeat. But for you men, so young still, there are many years ahead. Make no mistake, I can make sure that the right information finds its way over time to the right ears.'

'Are you asking us to participate in a cover-up?'

Reading seemed a little annoyed, even flustered. 'This is, after all, a *secret* tribunal. What do you think it was convened for in the first place?'

36

THE NEXT MORNING OUTSIDE the courtroom, the MPs took our chains off. We shook hands and hugged each other. We could hardly believe what had happened. The officers on the tribunal were silent on the other side of the door.

'Where's Major Reading?' Khan asked suddenly. 'I want to thank him.'

'He's gone,' one of the MPs said. 'He left through another entrance.'

So that is how our journey together ended. For years afterwards I intended to go and visit Kirkpatrick on his farm in the Cape. I wanted to meet his father to see for myself what this hero of the Empire was really like. I never did go, and then one day it was too late: I read in the obituaries that Colonel Kirkpatrick was dead of heart failure. I still intend, one day, to stop over at the farm.

Hassani Juma was wounded with the Nigerians at the battle of Mahiwa. So much shrapnel exploded above the trenches there that the blood from the wounded and the dead dripped from the trees for two days afterwards. I suppose he never did feel that his brother had been avenged. The colonial government sent him a medal and a small pension. And he retired to a smallholding with his wife, Zainabu, and their children.

I never heard from Khan again, but I didn't hear of his death either. War had taken him on a longer journey than any of us – from Asia to Europe and then to Africa. All the way he had carried his memories of snow and dust and blood with him. I can only hope that he found his way home at last and found his Nadia in the marketplace beyond the wall of the mosque, still waiting for him.

Wallis disappeared from my life too. I heard somewhere that he ended up a rich man, but I don't really know what happened to him.

In the end, the doctors decided I was too sick to fight any more. The malaria had damaged my liver irreparably.

'I'm sorry,' one of them, a graduate, almost ten years younger than I, told me. 'But you have to understand that it will shorten your life.'

'How long do I have?' I asked him, the cold dread filling my body.

'If you look after yourself, long enough.'

Reading did come to see me one last time. I was still recovering, but was well enough to go for a short walk with him.

'We all wanted to thank you,' I told him, 'but you slipped away.'

Reading stopped and looked at me. 'My God,' he said. 'You don't understand.'

'Understand what?'

He laughed, that strange, high-pitched, strangled sound that he always made. 'They wanted to shoot you all. That was how they were going to cover things up. I didn't have anything, no papers, no journalist. It was all a bluff.'

'But Juma's papers, where did they come from?'

'I'm sure they were genuine. I'm sure Andrew Carter did write it all down. He was a good soldier and a good man. It's the kind of thing he would have done. He knew he couldn't fight the stupidity of the generals, but he would have wanted to do something to keep the record straight. You remember how the light was on in his tent until late every night, but he never gave me anything.'

Reading smiled. 'Juma was always a player, but in that tribunal the stakes were too high. They had already decided what they wanted to do with you, and no evidence would have changed their minds. They destroyed it anyway.'

He was thoughtful for a moment. 'Of course, they believed they were only doing their duty, but they were determined to go through with it. I was angry with all of you, because you'd left me no damned way to get you out of it. It was only that morning I happened to see a letter on General Smuts' desk, from Prime Minister Botha. I thought there might be some way to use it, but it was only when Juma played his hand, and failed, that I saw my opening. I gambled for your lives with the oldest cards in the book: greed and fear. They were all I had. Luckily I succeeded.'

He shook his head, and, for a moment, his face crumpled. 'I'm sick of this war,' he said. 'So damned sick of it.'

I never saw Reading again after that, but I still remember him watching me as I walked slowly out through the polished, empty hospital corridor and into the sound and colour of the garden beyond.

At last it was over. I was going home. I thought of Helen. She was still in England, but she had written to say she would be coming home soon. For now, I would have to be content with that. *Long enough*, the doctors had said – it was all anyone could ask for.

I sat down on a bench in the shade. The wind rustled the leaves in the trees; light and shadow dappled the road outside. A single staff car drove past, its windows and polished surfaces gleaming in the sun, its tyres crunching on the hot gravel.

I watched as a company of soldiers marched along the road outside the hospital gate. The sound of their boots and the shouted orders of their officers rose into the air. I listened to them go past, and then fade into silence.

I sat there alone for a long time. Above me was the wide, blue African sky, and in the distance, the gathering smell of rain.

AFTERWORD

SALAITA HILL WAS A REAL BATTLE. Shortly after 08h00 on 12 February 1916, the South African regiments were thrown forward against the slopes of the hill. The fighting continued for a large part of the day until the South African regiments retreated in panic and disorder. They were rescued by the 130th Baluchis.

There were 172 casualties on the British side, of whom 133 were South African. 33 of these men were listed as missing. Their bodies were never found and nothing is known of their fate.

A few of the minor characters who appear in this book are historical figures, but the story itself is fiction.

Some readers may be interested to know that during my research into this book, I came across the following in a letter in volume III, page 337 of *Selections From The Smuts Papers June 1910 to November 1918* (Cambridge Press), from Prime Minister Louis Botha to Jan Smuts: 'A list of killed, wounded and missing men was published here – 172 of which 133 were Union men. This, without any information, has created rather a painful situation. Smartt and I had to use all our influence to keep it out of the House. Tighe must have got a good drubbing, but in any case, now that you are there, everything feels easier.'